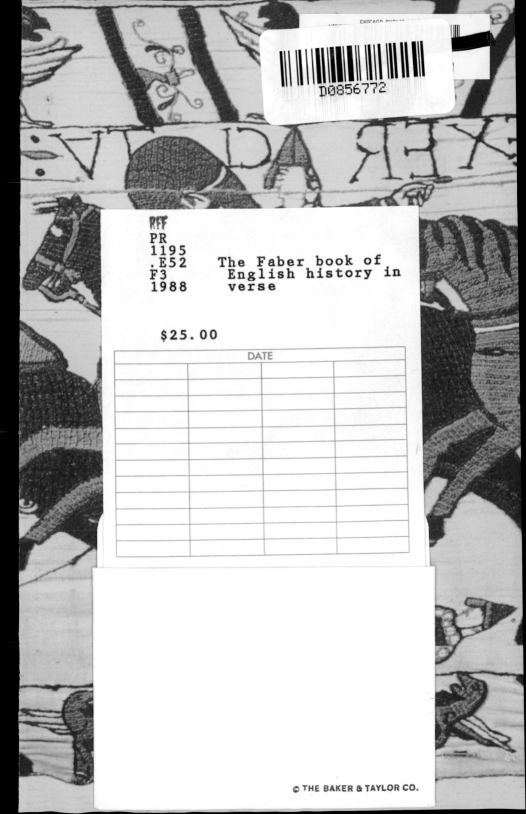

The Faber Book of English History in Verse

The Faber Book of
ENGLISH HISTORY IN VERSE

Edited by Kenneth Baker

faber and faber
LONDON · BOSTON

First published in 1988
by Faber and Faber Limited
3 Queen Square London WC1N 3AU
Reprinted 1988

Photoset by Parker Typesetting Service Leicester
Printed in Great Britain by Mackays of Chatham PLC, Kent

This collection © Kenneth Baker, 1988

British Library Cataloguing in Publication Data

The Faber book of English history in verse.
1. English poetry   2. England — History — Poetry
I. Baker, Kenneth, 1934–
821'.008'0358   PR1195.E52
ISBN 0-571-14882-4

671 8 7813

Endpapers: The author and publishers are grateful to
the Bridgeman Art Library for permission to reproduce
illustrations of William the Conqueror from the Bayeux
Tapestry and of Henry VIII by Holbein; to the Board of
Trustees of the Victoria & Albert Museum for the
Wellington Boot; and to Popperfoto for St Paul's in the
Blitz.

For all those people, including my family, who
have contributed to my education.

Contents

King Charles II (1660–85)

King James II (1685–8)

William and Mary (1688–1702)

THE HOUSE OF WINDSOR

Introduction

Anthologies grow slowly. I started to compile this history of England in verse some years ago, as I was struck by the great wealth and range of poetry which has been given over to telling the story of our country. The poems I had in mind spoke of great events and great figures, and I could see how they could be brought together in such a way as to offer a true sense of the narrative flow of our history. It is important for people living today to understand how they came to be what they are, to appreciate the forces and events that have shaped the institutions which guide and govern us, and generally to recognize how our rich and complex past has shaped what we think of as our national identity.

Each age has added something to the total picture. Roman roads, Anglo-Saxon kingship, Norman architecture, the Tudor Church of England, the rise of Parliament under the Stuarts, the thrust for empire in Hanoverian times, the satanic mills, Victorian prosperity and the wars of the twentieth century – all these have some direct bearing on how we live today. At one level the story is of kings and queens, of wars and battles, of famous victories like Trafalgar and near disasters like Dunkirk. Events of this sort are fixed in people's memories, together with a number of significant dates: 1066, 1215, 1603, 1815, 1940. A constant theme is man's mortality, and the transience of fame and fortune:

> For God's sake let us sit upon the ground,
> And tell sad stories of the death of kings –
> How some have been deposed, some slain in war,
> Some haunted by the ghosts they have deposed,
> Some poisoned by their wives, some sleeping killed;
> All murdered – for within the Hollow Crown
> That rounds the mortal temples of a king,
> Keeps Death his court . . .

Shakespeare, of course, had an incomparable understanding of history and most of his judgements stand up well to the test of modern scholarship, although he was far too harsh on Richard III. He is such a good guide that the Duke of Marlborough observed: 'Shakespeare, the only history of England I ever read.'

Running alongside the decisive events of history, and approachable, too, through the writings of poets, are the lives of the ordinary people of England. These must form part of any serious account, and so I have included an extract from *Piers Plowman* in 1370 in which William Langland pleads for the numerous poor of his time; a ballad from the Peasants' Revolt; the thoughts of a Berkshire farmer on Napoleon's invasion plans; the poem of George Loveless, the leader of the Tolpuddle Martyrs; the humour of Lancashire textile workers from Bury; the pride of an East End schoolboy wearing a red tie during the General Strike; and the sadness of a father who has lost his son in the blitz. This sea of men and women flows through our history, shaping and defining our national character. Edward Thomas's poem 'Lob' conveys something of the dogged cheerfulness of our people, and the sense of continuity their presence lends to historical events:

> The man you saw, – Lob-lie-by-the-fire, Jack Cade,
> Jack Smith, Jack Moon, poor Jack of every trade,
> Young Jack, or old Jack, or Jack What-d'ye-call,
> Jack-in-the-hedge, or Robin-run-by-the-wall,
> Robin Hood, Ragged Robin, lazy Bob,
> One of the lords of No Man's Land, good Lob, –
> Although he was seen dying at Waterloo,
> Hastings, Agincourt, and Sedgemoor too, –
> Lives yet. He never will admit he is dead
> Till millers cease to grind men's bones for bread,
> Nor till our weathercock crows once again
> And I remove my house out of the lane
> On to the road.

An appreciation of history in all its aspects, and particularly of the history of one's own country, is an essential part of life. It helps general understanding, it promotes tolerance and it gives delight. A Tudor historian, Polydor Vergil, in dedicating his book on the Welsh monk Gildas to Henry VIII, described history as 'the only unique, certain and faithful witness of times and things'. He added that it is 'not only useful and enriching, but positively essential', and that it 'displays eternally to the living those events which should be an example and those which should be a warning'. T. S. Eliot said it so well in 'Little Gidding':

> The moment of the rose and the moment of the yew-tree
> Are of equal duration. A people without history
> Is not redeemed from time, for history is a pattern
> Of timeless moments. So, while the light fails
> On a winter's afternoon, in a secluded chapel
> History is now and England.

I should make it clear that what lies in these pages is the story of England. I have not attempted to include the histories of Scotland or Wales or Northern Ireland, each of which has a great store of fine poetry and deserves an anthology of its own. I have brought them in only at those points where the history of England becomes intertwined with theirs – Edward I's invasion of Wales, for instance, and the Battle of the Boyne, and Bonnie Prince Charlie's uprising. This is essentially the history of the 'True-Born Englishman', that mongrel character whose antecedents Daniel Defoe identified so sharply:

> Thus from a mixture of all kinds began
> That heterogeneous thing, an Englishman:
> In eager rapes and furious lusts begot
> Betwixt a painted Briton and a Scot:
> Whose gend'ring offspring quickly learn'd to bow
> And yoke their heifers to the Roman plow;
> From whence a mongrel, half-bred race there came,
> With neither name nor nation, speech or fame,
> In whose hot veins new mixtures quickly ran,
> Infus'd betwixt a Saxon and a Dane;
> While their rank daughters, to their parents just,
> Receiv'd all nations with promiscuous lust.
> This nauseous brood directly did contain
> The well-extracted blood of Englishmen.

The language which the English people shaped by means of assimilation and change developed into the marvellous instrument of communication which is now used throughout the world. It is also one of the potent forces which unites us as a nation. Caxton helped to regulate the spelling of words by employing what was common practice in London in the 1480s; Shakespeare developed the usages of the Court and of the common people to extraordinary effect; the translators of the King James Bible attuned the language to the needs of worship; and Kipling found poetry in the slang of the ordinary soldier. Yet Kipling also reminds us of another trait of the English – their leaning towards taciturnity, reserve and caution:

For undemocratic reasons and for motives not of State,
They arrive at their conclusions – largely inarticulate.
Being void of self-expression they confide their views to none;
But sometimes in a smoking-room, one learns why things were done.

Yes, sometimes in a smoking-room, through clouds of 'Ers' and 'Ums,'
Obliquely and by inference, illumination comes,
On some step that they have taken, or some action they approve –
Embellished with the *argot* of the Upper Fourth Remove.

In telegraphic sentences, half nodded to their friends,
They hint a matter's inwardness – and there the matter ends.
And while the Celt is talking from Valencia to Kirkwall,
The English – ah, the English! – don't say anything at all.

Just a word on how I have put this book together: throughout the text I have provided notes of explanation which are also designed to carry the narrative forward chronologically. I cannot be blamed for the views of the poets, but those expressed in the notes are mine. I have included, along with contemporary poems, many that were written long after the events concerned, for example: Chesterton on King Alfred, Philip Larkin on the figures depicted on a medieval tombstone, Kipling on James I, Robert Graves on Nelson's funeral, Noël Coward on the death of Queen Victoria, Gavin Ewart on the 1920s, and so on. Anglo-Saxon and Latin pieces have been translated, but I have left most of the medieval verse in its original form, as with a little effort it can be understood and translation usually saps its vigour.

I decided to end this anthology at the accession of our Queen Elizabeth II. There has been a remarkable shortage of good, straight – as opposed to satirical – verse about public events in England over the past thirty years. One could name exceptions: Larkin on Britain's withdrawal from East of Suez in 1968, Adrian Mitchell on Nye Bevan's change of heart, or C. H. Sisson on the loss of the old county names through the local government reforms of 1974. It could be, too, that the immediacy of the news as it is reported on television has blunted the poetic imagination, but perhaps more public poetry will come to be written in retrospect.

I should like to take this opportunity to thank the many people who have helped and given advice to me over the years. These are principally my family, who insisted that I should let Middle English texts stand as they were; Jonathan Barker at the Poetry Library of the Arts Council; David Cook, who checked many of the historical facts; and Christopher Reid at Faber and Faber.

PRE-NORMAN

AD 61

Boadicea

When the British warrior queen,
  Bleeding from the Roman rods,
Sought, with an indignant mien,
  Counsel of her country's gods,

Sage beneath a spreading oak
  Sat the Druid, hoary chief;
Every burning word he spoke
  Full of rage, and full of grief.

'Princess! if our agèd eyes
  Weep upon thy matchless wrongs,
'Tis because resentment ties
  All the terrors of our tongues.

Rome shall perish – write that word
  In the blood that she has spilt;
Perish, hopeless and abhorred,
  Deep in ruin as in guilt.

Rome, for empire far renowned,
  Tramples on a thousand states;
Soon her pride shall kiss the ground –
  Hark! the Gaul is at her gates!

Other Romans shall arise,
  Heedless of a soldier's name;
Sounds, not arms, shall win the prize –
  Harmony the path to fame.

Then the progeny that springs
   From the forests of our land,
Armed with thunder, clad with wings,
   Shall a wider world command.

Regions Caesar never knew
   Thy posterity shall sway,
Where his eagles never flew,
   None invincible as they.'

Such the bard's prophetic words,
   Pregnant with celestial fire,
Bending, as he swept the chords
   Of his sweet but awful lyre.

She, with all a monarch's pride,
   Felt them in her bosom glow;
Rushed to battle, fought, and died;
   Dying, hurled them at the foe.

'Ruffians, pitiless as proud,
   Heaven awards the vengeance due;
Empire is on us bestowed,
   Shame and ruin wait for you.'

William Cowper

Julius Caesar came, saw and conquered in 55 BC and the Romans controlled Britain for the next 465 years. Several rebellions were crushed, including the one led by Boadicea, Queen of the Iceni, who ruled part of East Anglia. To avoid capture and the humiliation of a triumph in Rome, she took poison.

c. 300

THE ROMAN OCCUPATION

from **The Roman Centurion's Song**

Legate, I had the news last night – my Cohort ordered home
By ship to Portus Itius and thence by road to Rome.
I've marched the Companies aboard, the arms are stowed
  below:
Now let another take my sword. Command me not to go!

I've served in Britain forty years, from Vectis to the Wall.
I have none other home than this, nor any life at all.
Last night I did not understand, but, now the hour draws near
That calls me to my native land, I feel that land is here.

Here where men say my name was made, here where my work
  was done,
Here where my dearest dead are laid – my wife – my wife and
  son;
Here where time, custom, grief and toil, age, memory, service,
  love,
Have rooted me in British soil. Ah, how can I remove?
*

Let me work here for Britain's sake – at any task you will –
A marsh to drain, a road to make or native troops to drill.
Some Western camp (I know the Pict) or granite Border keep,
Mid seas of heather derelict, where our old messmates sleep.

Legate, I come to you in tears – My Cohort ordered home!
I've served in Britain forty years. What should I do in Rome?
Here is my heart, my soul, my mind – the only life I know.
I cannot leave it all behind. Command me not to go!

Rudyard Kipling

At the peak of its power, Rome kept a garrison of 50,000 soldiers in Britain, but as the Barbarians advanced from other quarters they had gradually to be withdrawn. Kipling's poem shows one soldier who wanted to stay. The Romans left behind them a network of straight roads, the ineradicable traces of their language, a capital called Londinium and many buildings. The first three of these survived, but the buildings were pillaged and razed by invaders from the North and the East and only their foundations survived the Dark Ages.

Roman wall blues

Over the heather the wet wind blows,
I've lice in my tunic and a cold in my nose.

The rain comes pattering out of the sky,
I'm a Wall soldier, I don't know why.

The mist creeps over the hard grey stone,
My girl's in Tungria; I sleep alone.

Aulus goes hanging around her place,
I don't like his manners, I don't like his face.

Piso's a Christian, he worships a fish;
There'd be no kissing if he had his wish.

She gave me a ring but I diced it away;
I want my girl and I want my pay.

When I'm a veteran with only one eye
I shall do nothing but look at the sky.

W. H. Auden

after 500

KING ARTHUR

from **Idylls of the King**

And slowly answered Arthur from the barge:
'The old order changeth, yielding place to new,
And God fulfils Himself in many ways,
Lest one good custom should corrupt the world.
Comfort thyself: what comfort is in me?
I have lived my life, and that which I have done
May He within Himself make pure! but thou,
If thou shouldst never see my face again,
Pray for my soul. More things are wrought by prayer
Than this world dreams of. Wherefore, let thy voice
Rise like a fountain for me night and day.
For what are men better than sheep or goats
That nourish a blind life within the brain,
If, knowing God, they lift not hands of prayer
Both for themselves and those who call them friend?
For so the whole round earth is every way
Bound by gold chains about the feet of God.
But now farewell. I am going a long way
With these thou seëst – if indeed I go
(For all my mind is clouded with a doubt) –
To the island-valley of Avilion;
Where falls not hail, or rain, or any snow,
Nor ever wind blows loudly; but it lies
Deep-meadowed, happy, fair with orchard-lawns
And bowery hollows crowned with summer sea,
Where I will heal me of my grievous wound.'

So said he, and the barge with oar and sail
Moved from the brink, like some full-breasted swan
That, fluting a wild carol ere her death,
Ruffles her pure cold plume, and takes the flood
With swarthy webs. Long stood Sir Bedivere
Revolving many memories, till the hull
Looked one black dot against the verge of dawn,
And on the mere the wailing died away.

Alfred, Lord Tennyson

In the fourth and fifth centuries small bands of Anglo-Saxons set sail from Denmark and North Germany to settle in Britain. The local inhabitants put up some resistance, and we have the name of at least one of their leaders, Ambrosius Aurelianus, who seems to have been a Roman 'staying on'. The one whom everybody knows, King Arthur, has achieved the status of a legend. The legend itself was written down after the Norman Conquest, and much later written up by Tennyson. One certain fact is that Arthur defeated the Anglo-Saxons at Badon, possibly on a hilltop near Bath, at some time in the early sixth century.

Tennyson drew upon the accounts of Geoffrey of Monmouth and Thomas Malory to recreate his ideal of Romantic chivalry. He wrote:

How much of history we have in the story of Arthur is doubtful. Let not my readers press too hard on details, whether for history or for allegory . . . He is meant to be a man who spent himself in the cause of honour, duty and self-sacrifice.

c. 670

Cædmon's Hymn

Nū scylun hergan   hefænrīcaes Uard,
Metudæs mæcti   end His mōdgidanc,
uerc Uuldurfadur,   suē Hē uundra gihuæs,
ēci Dryctin,   ōr āstelidæ.
Hē ǣrist scōp   ælda barnum
heben til hrōfe,   hāleg Scepen.
Thā middungeard   moncynnæs Uard,
ēci Dryctin,   æfter tīadæ
firum foldu,   Frēa allmectig.

Now we must praise the Guardian of Heaven,
the might of the Lord and His purpose of mind,
the work of the Glorious Father; for He,
God Eternal, established each wonder,
He, Holy Creator, first fashioned
heaven as a roof for the sons of men.
Then the Guardian of Mankind adorned
this middle-earth below, the world for men,
Everlasting Lord, Almighty King.

translated by Kevin Crossley-Holland

I include this as it is said to be the first poem in Old English, or more particularly in the Northumbrian dialect. It was written between 657 and 680. Bede relates that Cædmon, a tuneless old cowherd, was told in a vision to 'sing Creation', which he duly did. Hilda, the Abbess of Whitby, was so impressed that she got her monks to read Cædmon passages from the Scriptures, which he then sang into verse. Whatever the truth of the matter, the significance of it is that this is the first recorded use of heroic, pagan, Germanic-style poetry for Christian purposes. It started a tradition and introduced phrases that were to be used again and again as Christianity spread over England.

c. 880

THE VIKING INVASIONS

from **The Ballad of the White Horse**

The Northmen came about our land
  A Christless chivalry:
Who knew not of the arch or pen,
Great, beautiful half-witted men
  From the sunrise and the sea.

Misshapen ships stood on the deep
  Full of strange gold and fire,
And hairy men, as huge as sin
With hornèd heads, came wading in
  Through the long, low sea-mire.

Our towns were shaken of tall kings
  With scarlet beards like blood:
The world turned empty where they trod,
They took the kindly cross of God
  And cut it up for wood.

And there was death on the Emperor
  And night upon the Pope:
And Alfred, hiding in deep grass,
  Hardened his heart with hope.

A sea-folk blinder than the sea
  Broke all about his land,
But Alfred up against them bare
And gripped the ground and grasped the air,
  Staggered, and strove to stand.

He bent them back with spear and spade,
    With desperate dyke and wall,
With foemen leaning on his shield
And roaring on him when he reeled;
    And no help came at all.

He broke them with a broken sword
    A little towards the sea,
And for one hour of panting peace,
Ringed with a roar that would not cease,
With golden crown and girded fleece
    Made laws under a tree.

G. K. Chesterton

Alfred came to the throne in 871, at the age of twenty-three. The Vikings had conquered the rest of the country and he was driven back to a small area in Somerset, the Athelney Marshes. He decided to retaliate. He built up his army, organized a network of fortified boroughs, and had ships made which were longer and faster than those of the Norsemen. He succeeded in confining the Vikings to the so-called Danelaw, comprising Northern and Eastern England, and forced their leader Guthrum to sue for peace after his great victory at Edington in 878. He restored Christianity and even began its dissemination among the pagan Vikings, cherished the scholarship which produced the *Anglo-Saxon Chronicle*, and laid down laws enforcing loyalty to the new state. He may be said to have created the English nation and certainly deserves his title of 'Alfred the Great'.

KING ALFRED AND THE CAKES

Where lying on the hearth to bake
By chance the cake did burn:
'What! canst thou not, thou lout,' quoth she,
'Take pains the same to turn?
But serve me such another trick,
I'll thwack thee on the snout.'
Which made the patient king, good man,
Of her to stand in doubt?

Anonymous

At the time of Alfred's refuge in the Athelney Marshes, a rumour grew up which was later recorded as fact. It was said that he had to disguise himself as a peasant and live with a swineherd and his wife. One day, either preoccupied with his plans or cleaning his weapons, he let some cakes burn. The wife was angry and belaboured him, saying, 'Turn the loaves over so that they don't burn, for I see every day that you have a huge appetite.'

937

The Battle of Brunanburh

This year King Athelstan, ring-giver, lord
of earls, and Prince Eadmund his brother, earned
lasting battle-fame with blade-edge
at Brunanburh; son of Eadweard, they sundered
the shield-wall, shattered the linden shields
with smithied brands: as often in battle,
true to their lineage, they guarded treasure, land
and villages from all invaders. Enemies
fell, both Scot and seafarer sank
doomed; that field, blood-sluiced, grew slippery
from sun-rise – the famous radiance,
God's dazzling candle, soaring
over morning earth – to the setting of that fair
creation.
           There, many warriors, many a Scot
and war-worn North-man alike, lay
spear-pierced above his shield,
dead-beat. All day, West Saxon bands
ran down the foe, hacking the spines of fugitives
with swords rasped fine. No Mercian refused
the hard sword-play with hostile heroes,
Anlaf's shipment over the heaving waves,
fated to the fray. Five young kings
lay on that field, dead by the sword,
in the slump of death, with seven earls
of Anlaf, and a countless glut of Scots
and seamen. There, the North-men's leader
was put to flight, with few survivors,
driven to his prow, a quick escape
by galley across the gloomed sea. Also
Constantine, old hand at sword-play, fled
to his native North: the old
war-king drained of swagger, his kinsmen
and friends slain in the field, his own son
left dead of wounds. That grey-aged

veteran could no more vaunt of sword-clash
than could Anlaf. Neither had cause for laughter
among their army-remnants, as victors
after battle-clamour, strenuous combat
on that reddled turf with Eadweard's
sons. Then in nailed boats the North-men,
bleeding survivors of javelins, set sail
with sapped prides through slapping seas
to Dublin, Ireland. Likewise, both brothers,
king and prince battle-proud and boisterous,
returned to their own terrain,
the meadows of Mercia. They left the dark
raven behind, charcoal-coated, horny-beaked,
to jab that carrion, and the grey-coat eagle,
the white-tailed ravening war-hawk, to have
his will of the dead, and that grizzled wolf
of the wood.
      Never was wilder carnage
seen on this island, of soldiery sword-felled,
such as the tomes of clerics tell,
since Angles and Saxons came here seeking
the Britons across broad sea, when proud
warriors whelmed the Welsh-men, and brave
earls laid hold on this land.

translated from the Anglo-Saxon by Harold Massingham

King Athelstan of Wessex and his brother, Eadmund, who were grand-sons of Alfred, fought off an invasion from the North led by Olaf Guthfrithson, the Norse King of Dublin, Constantine, King of the Scots and Picts, and Owen, King of the Strathclyde Welsh. The defenders won at Brunanburh, and this great triumph was dutifully and beauti-fully recorded in the regimental magazine of the House of Alfred, the *Anglo-Saxon Chronicle*. In this 'slump of death' the raven, the eagle and the wolf had their fill, but Olaf escaped to trouble England again after Athelstan's death in 939.

954

ERIC BLOODAXE

from **Briggflatts**

Loaded with mail of linked lies,
what weapon can the king lift to fight
when chance-met enemies employ sly
sword and shoulder-piercing pike,
pressed into the mire,
trampled and hewn till a knife
– in whose hand? – severs tight
neck cords? Axe rusts. Spine
picked bare by ravens, agile
maggots devour the slack side
and inert brain, never wise.
What witnesses he had life,
ravelled and worn past splice,
yarns falling to staple? Rime
on the bent, the beck ice,
there will be nothing on Stainmore to hide
void, no sable to disguise
what he wore under the lies,
king of Orkney, king of Dublin, twice
king of York, where the tide
stopped till long flight
from who knows what smile,
scowl, disgust or delight
ended in bale on the fellside.

Basil Bunting

After a short and violent reign as King of Norway, Eric Bloodaxe fled to
Northumbria where the Norsemen welcomed him as their king. The
last adventurer of a savage society, he tried to bring together an alliance
of Dublin and York against the English. Eadred, the King of the

English, forced Eric out in 948, and again in 954 when he was betrayed
by Earl Oswulf, who was given Southern Northumbria as his prize.

c. 980–1016

Danegeld

It is always a temptation to an armed and agile nation,
　　To call upon a neighbour and to say:
'We invaded you last night – we are quite prepared to fight,
　　Unless you pay us cash to go away.'

And that is called asking for Dane-geld,
　　And the people who ask it explain
That you've only to pay 'em the Dane-geld
　　And then you'll get rid of the Dane!

It is always a temptation to a rich and lazy nation,
　　To puff and look important and to say: –
'Though we know we should defeat you, we have not the time
　　　to meet you.
　　We will therefore pay you cash to go away.'

And that is called paying the Dane-geld;
　　But we've proved it again and again,
That if once you have paid him the Dane-geld
　　You never get rid of the Dane.

It is wrong to put temptation in the path of any nation,
　　For fear they should succumb and go astray,
So when you are requested to pay up or be molested,
　　You will find it better policy to say: –

'We never pay *any* one Dane-geld,
 No matter how trifling the cost,
For the end of that game is oppression and shame,
 And the nation that plays it is lost!'

Rudyard Kipling

In 978, Ethelred the Unready succeeded to the English throne upon the murder of his brother, Edward, at Corfe Castle. Ethelred was weak and tried to buy off the invading Danes by giving them money – the famous Danegeld. Each time, the Danes asked for more, and eventually their king, Canute, became King of England in 1016. The Saxon period had come to an end and it seemed as if the country would submit to a long period of Scandinavian rule. Family rivalries, however, and the chaotic politics of the next fifty years provided an opportunity for the thrustful, well-organized and confident Normans to conquer Britain and to tie her to the French political system for nearly 400 years.

991

from The Battle of Maldon

Then the brave warrior raised his spear,
gripped his shield and stepped towards a seafarer;
thus the brave earl advanced on the churl;
each had evil designs on the other.
The Viking was the quicker – he hurled his foreign spear
wounding the lord of the warriors.
Byrhtnoth broke the shaft on the edge of his shield;
the imbedded spear-head sprang out of his wound.
Then he flung his spear in fury at the proud Viking
who dared inflict such pain. His aim was skilful.
The spear split open the warrior's neck.
Thus Byrhtnoth put paid to his enemy's life.
Then he swiftly hurled a second spear
which burst the Viking's breastplate, wounding him cruelly
in the chest; the deadly point pierced his heart.
The brave earl, Byrhtnoth, was delighted at this;
he laughed out loud and gave thanks to the Lord
that such good fortune had been granted to him.
But one of the seafarers sent a sharp javelin
speeding from his hand; it pierced the body
of earl Byrhtnoth, Ethelred's brave thane.

translated from the Anglo-Saxon by Kevin Crossley-Holland

The Old English poem from which this episode is taken records a fight
between Vikings and an army of English warriors under the leadership
of Byrhtnoth, the Ealdorman of Essex. The Vikings had demanded a
sum of money as their price for moving on and, when the English
refused to pay, a bloody battle took place at Maldon in Essex, where
Byrhtnoth was killed and the Vikings prevailed.

c. 1020

from King Canute

King Canute was weary-hearted; he had reigned for years a
    score,
Battling, struggling, pushing, fighting, killing much and
    robbing more;
And he thought upon his actions, walking by the wild sea-
    shore.

'Twixt the chancellor and bishop walked the king with steps
    sedate,
Chamberlains and grooms came after, silversticks and
    goldsticks great,
Chaplains, aides-de-camp, and pages – all the officers of state,

Sliding after like his shadow, pausing when he chose to pause:
If a frown his face contracted, straight the courtiers dropped
    their jaws;
If to laugh the king was minded, out they burst in loud hee-
    haws.

But that day a something vexed him, that was clear to old and
    young:
Thrice his grace had yawned at table, when his favourite
    gleemen sung,
Once the queen would have consoled him, but he bade her hold
    her tongue.

'Something ails my gracious master,' cried the keeper of the
    seal.
'Sure, my lord, it is the lampreys served at dinner, or the veal?'
'Pshaw!' exclaimed the angry monarch. 'Keeper, 'tis not that I feel.

''Tis the *heart*, and not the dinner, fool, that doth my rest impair:
Can a king be great as I am, prithee, and yet know no care?
Oh, I'm sick, and tired, and weary.' – Someone cried, 'The
    king's arm-chair!'

Then towards the lackeys turning, quick my lord the keeper
  nodded,
Straight the king's great chair was brought him, by two footmen
  able-bodied;
Languidly he sank into it: it was comfortably wadded.

'Leading on my fierce companions,' cried he, 'over storm and
  brine,
I have fought and I have conquered! Where was glory like to
  mine?'
Loudly all the courtiers echoed: 'Where is glory like to thine?'

*

'Might I stay the sun above us, good Sir Bishop?' Canute cried;
'Could I bid the silver moon to pause upon her heavenly ride?
If the moon obeys my orders, sure I can command the tide.

'Will the advancing waves obey me, bishop, if I make the sign?'
Said the bishop, bowing lowly, 'Land and sea, my lord, are
  thine.'
Canute turned towards the ocean – 'Back!' he said, 'thou
  foaming brine.

'From the sacred shore I stand on, I command thee to retreat;
Venture not, thou stormy rebel, to approach thy master's seat:
Ocean, be thou still! I bid thee come not nearer to my feet!'

But the sullen ocean answered with a louder, deeper roar,
And the rapid waves drew nearer, falling sounding on the
  shore;
Back the keeper and the bishop, back the king and courtiers
  bore.

And he sternly bade them never more to kneel to human clay,
But alone to praise and worship That which earth and seas obey:
And his golden crown of empire never wore he from that day.
. . . King Canute is dead and gone: parasites exist alway.

                                    William Makepeace Thackeray

Canute, whose name was also spelt Cnut, was King of Denmark and
Norway, as well as of England from 1016 to 1035. Much of his reign was
spent in holding this large empire together. Canute's rule in England
was beneficial: he encoded the law, supported the Church and maintained peace. He was a courageous and powerful figure whose reign
appears as a golden interlude shining through the Dark Ages. Powerful, though not omnipotent!

1057

Godiva

I waited for the train at Coventry;
I hung with grooms and porters on the bridge,
To watch the three tall spires; and there I shaped
The city's ancient legend into this: —

Not only we, the latest seed of Time,
New men, that in the flying of a wheel
Cry down the past, not only we, that prate
Of rights and wrongs, have loved the people well,
And loathed to see them overtax'd; but she
Did more, and underwent, and overcame,
The woman of a thousand summers back,
Godiva, wife to that grim Earl, who ruled
In Coventry: for when he laid a tax
Upon his town, and all the mothers brought
Their children, clamouring, 'If we pay, we starve.'
She sought her lord, and found him, where he strode
About the hall, among his dogs, alone,
His beard a foot before him, and his hair
A yard behind. She told him of their tears,
And pray'd him, 'If they pay this tax, they starve.'
Whereat he stared, replying, half-amazed,
'You would not let your little finger ache
For such as *these?*' – 'But I would die,' said she.
He laugh'd, and swore by Peter and by Paul:
Then fillip'd at the diamond in her ear;
'O ay, ay, ay, you talk!' – 'Alas!' she said,
'But prove me what it is I would not do.'
And from a heart as rough as Esau's hand,
He answer'd, 'Ride you naked thro' the town,
And I repeal it'; and nodding, as in scorn,
He parted, with great strides among his dogs.
So left alone, the passions of her mind,
As winds from all the compass shift and blow,
Made war upon each other for an hour,

Till pity won. She sent a herald forth,
And bade him cry, with sound of trumpet, all
The hard condition; but that she would loose
The people: therefore, as they loved her well,
From then till noon no foot should pace the street,
No eye look down, she passing; but that all
Should keep within, door shut, and window barr'd.

   Then fled she to her inmost bower, and there
Unclasp'd the wedded eagles of her belt,
The grim Earl's gift; but ever at a breath
She linger'd, looking like a summer moon
Half-dipt in cloud: anon she shook her head,
And shower'd the rippled ringlets to her knee;
Unclad herself in haste; adown the stair
Stole on; and, like a creeping sunbeam, slid
From pillar unto pillar, until she reach'd
The gateway; there she found her palfrey trapt
In purple blazon'd with armorial gold.

   Then she rode forth, clothed on with chastity:
The deep air listen'd round her as she rode,
And all the low wind hardly breathed for fear.
The little wide-mouth'd heads upon the spout
Had cunning eyes to see; the barking cur
Made her cheek flame; her palfrey's footfall shot
Light horrors thro' her pulses; the blind walls
Were full of chinks and holes; and overhead
Fantastic gables, crowding, stared: but she
Not less thro' all bore up, till, last, she saw
The white-flower'd elder-thicket from the field
Gleam thro' the Gothic archway in the wall.

   Then she rode back, clothed on with chastity:
And one low churl, compact of thankless earth,
The fatal byword of all years to come,
Boring a little auger-hole in fear,
Peep'd – but his eyes, before they had their will,
Were shrivell'd into darkness in his head,
And dropt before him. So the Powers, who wait
On noble deeds, cancell'd a sense misused;
And she, that knew not, pass'd; and all at once,

With twelve great shocks of sound, the shameless noon
Was clash'd and hammered from a hundred towers,
One after one: but even then she gain'd
Her bower; whence reissuing, robed and crown'd,
To meet her lord, she took the tax away,
And built herself an everlasting name.

Alfred, Lord Tennyson

There are so many sources for this legend that we may assume
something like it actually happened.

NORMANS AND PLANTAGENETS

The Kings and Queens of England after the Conquest

Willie, Willie, Harry, Ste,
Harry, Dick, John, Harry 3;
1, 2, 3 Neds, Richard 2,
Harries 4, 5, 6 – then who?
Edwards 4, 5, Dick the Bad,
Harries twain, and then the lad;
Mary, Bessie, James the Vain,
Charlie, Charlie, James again;
William and Mary, Anne, and *gloria!* –
4 Georges, William and Victoria,
Ned and George; repeat again;
And then Elizabeth comes to reign.

Anonymous

William the Conqueror, 1066–87

1066

THE BATTLE OF HASTINGS AND THE NORMAN CONQUEST

The Anvil

England's on the anvil – hear the hammers ring –
    Clanging from the Severn to the Tyne!
Never was a blacksmith like our Norman King –
    England's being hammered, hammered, hammered into
    line!

England's on the anvil! Heavy are the blows!
    (But the work will be a marvel when it's done)
Little bits of Kingdoms cannot stand against their foes.
    England's being hammered, hammered, hammered into
    one!

There shall be one people – it shall serve one Lord –
    (Neither Priest nor Baron shall escape!)
It shall have one speech and law, soul and strength and sword.
    England's being hammered, hammered, hammered into
    shape!

Rudyard Kipling

The one date that every schoolchild knows is 1066. In that year Edward the Confessor died without issue. Harold, Earl of Wessex, had only a distant claim to the throne, but because he was in the country at the time he quickly got himself crowned. After beating off a rival contender, Harold of Norway, at the Battle of Stamford Bridge, he marched south to fight off another, William, Duke of Normandy, who had a rather better claim, and to whom, moreover, Harold had once sworn allegiance. William had landed at Pevensey Bay, and the two armies met at Hastings, where Harold was killed probably by an arrow in the eye. His body was not given to his mother, as would have been customary, but at William's command it was buried at the top of a cliff with a stone bearing the inscription:

By the Duke's command, O Harold, you rest here a king,
That you may still be guardian of the shore and sea.

Three Norman kings ruled England until 1135. The Norman Conquest was very thorough. The Domesday survey, started by William in 1085, showed that the rental value of England was £37,000 per year and that about 250 individuals with incomes of over £100 a year in effect controlled the country. Virtually all of these were Normans. During their supremacy, only 10,000 Normans lived in England, but their grip was complete. They built castles as fortified residences for the barons. The barons exacted loyalty from their knights, and the knights from their peasants. The barons swore loyalty to the King, who in return granted them the use of his land. This feudal system of interlocking obligations was the foundation of English society for over 300 years.

At the Statue of William the Conqueror, Falaise

See him ride the roaring air
In an iron moustache and emerald hair,
Furious with flowers on a foundry cob
The bastard son of the late Lord Bob.

He writes his name with a five-flagged spear
On skies of infantry in the rear
And fixed at his feet, in chainmail stations,
Six unshaven Norman relations:

Rollo, Guillaume Longue-Épée,
Le Bon, Sans Peur, Richard Three,
Robert the Devil; and over them all
The horse's tail, like a waterfall.

Many a shell struck Talbot's Tower
From Henry the Fifth to Eisenhower,
But never a splinter scratched the heel
Of the bully in bronze at the Hôtel de Ville.

On the chocolate wall of the tall château
Tansy, pimpernel, strawberry grow;
And down by the tanyard the washing hangs wet
As it did in the dirty days of Arlette.

Hubert and Arthur and Holy Joan
Knew this staring stack of stone
Where William scowls in a Saracen cap
And sat out the fight for the famous Gap.

Gallop on, General with cider eyes,
Until the snow-coasts of Sussex rise!
Silence the tearful and smiling with thunder
As you spring from the sea, bringing history under.

Charles Causley

THE NORMANS IN ENGLAND

from **The True-Born Englishman**

He rais'd no Money, for he paid in Land.
He gave his Legions their Eternal Station,
And made them all Freeholders of the Nation.
He canton'd out the Country to his Men,
And ev'ry Soldier was a Denizen.
The Rascals thus enrich'd, he call'd them *Lords*,
To please their Upstart Pride with new-made Words:
And *Doomsday-Book* his Tyranny records.
   And here begins the Ancient Pedigree
That so exalts our Poor Nobility:
  'Tis that from some *French* Trooper they derive,
Who with the *Norman* Bastard did arrive:
The Trophies of the Families appear;
Some show the Sword, the Bow, and some the Spear,
Which their Great Ancestor, *forsooth*, did wear.
These in the Heralds Register remain,
Their Noble Mean Extraction to explain.
Yet who the Hero was, no man can tell,
Whether a Drummer or a Colonel:
The silent Record blushes to reveal
Their Undescended Dark Original.
   But grant the best, How came the Change to pass;
A *True-Born Englishman* of *Norman* Race?
A *Turkish* Horse can show more History,
To prove his Well-descended Family.
Conquest, as by the Moderns 'tis exprest,
May give a Title to the Lands possest:
But that the Longest Sword shou'd be so Civil,
To make a *Frenchman English*, that's the Devil.

Daniel Defoe

1087

DEATH OF WILLIAM THE CONQUEROR

He ordered the poor to build castles.
This was very hard work.
The king was a tough man
And he took many gold coins from his people
And many more hundreds of pounds in silver . . .
This was most unfair, and he did not really need the money . . .
He marked out a huge area for deer, and made laws about it.
Anyone who killed a hart or a hind
Was to be blinded . . .
He loved the stags as dearly
As though he had been their father . . .
The rich complained and the poor wept.
But he was too merciless to care if everyone hated him.
And they just had to obey him.
Otherwise, they lost their lives and their lands
And their goods and their king's friendship.
Alas! that any man should behave in this proud way
And declare that he is so far above all other men!
May Almighty God show mercy on his soul
And pardon him his sins.

The Peterborough Chronicler

This chronicler, who in fact wrote in prose, but of a kind that suggests the rhythms of verse, as it has been set out here, noted both the good and the bad things of William's reign. The King had a powerful physical presence, and indeed this was an essential element of medieval kingship. William of Malmesbury recorded that he had 'a fierce face', and that 'he was majestic . . . although his pot-belly rather spoiled his appearance'.

King William II, 1087–1100

1100

The Death of Rufus

To hunt rode fierce King Rufus,
   Upon a holy morn –
The Church had summon'd him to pray,
   But he held the Church in scorn.
Sir Walter Tyrrel rode with him,
   And drew his good bow-string;
He drew the string to smite a deer,
   But his arrow smote the king!

Hurl'd from his trembling charger,
   The death-struck monarch lay;
While fast, as flees the startled deer,
   Rash Tyrrel fled away:
On the spot where his strong hand had made
   So many desolate,
He died with none to pity him –
   Such was the tyrant's fate!

None mourn'd for cruel Rufus:
   With pomp they buried him;
But no heart grieved beside his bier –
   No kindly eye grew dim;
But poor men lifted up their heads,
   And clasp'd their hands, and said:
'Thank God, the ruthless Conqueror
   And his stern son are dead!'

Menella Smedley

The most memorable thing about William Rufus's reign was his mysterious death in the New Forest. While alive, he had debased the coinage, fallen out with the Church and disinherited many baronial families. His chroniclers, mainly churchmen, deplored the morals of the royal court and lamented the oppressive nature of the King's rule. Nevertheless, he was a shrewd and successful politician and, further to his credit, he started building one of the finest and most important civic edifices of medieval times, Westminster Hall. This poem, by a little-known Victorian writer, is the only one on the subject that I have been able to find.

King Stephen, 1135–54

from **King Stephen**

ACT I

Scene I. – Field of Battle.

Alarum. Enter King STEPHEN, *Knights, and Soldiers.*

STEPHEN: If shame can on a soldier's vein-swoll'n front
Spread deeper crimson than the battle's toil,
Blush in your casing helmets! for see, see!
Yonder my chivalry, my pride of war,
Wrench'd with an iron hand from firm array,
Are routed loose about the plashy meads,
Of honour forfeit. O that my known voice
Could reach your dastard ears, and fright you more!
Fly, cowards, fly! Gloucester is at your backs!
Throw your slack bridles o'er the flurried manes,
Ply well the rowel with faint trembling heels,
Scampering to death at last!
1ST KNIGHT: The enemy
Bears his flaunt standard close upon their ear.
2ND KNIGHT: Sure of a bloody prey, seeing the fens
Will swamp them girth-deep.
STEPHEN: Over head and ears,
No matter! 'Tis a gallant enemy;
How like a comet he goes streaming on.
But we must plague him in the flank, – hey, friends?
We are well-breath'd – follow!

*

Scene III. – The Field of Battle. Enter STEPHEN *unarmed.*

STEPHEN: Another sword! And what if I could seize
One from Bellona's gleaming armoury,
Or choose the fairest of her sheaved spears!
Where are my enemies? Here, close at hand,
Here come the testy brood. O, for a sword!
I'm faint – a biting sword! A noble sword!
A hedge-stake – or a ponderous stone to hurl
With brawny vengeance, like the labourer Cain.
Come on! Farewell my kingdom, and all hail
Thou superb, plumed, and helmeted renown!
All hail! I would not truck this brilliant day
To rule in Pylos with a Nestor's beard –
Come on!

John Keats

In 1819, Keats started to write a play for Edmund Kean, the great actor. Kean, alas, left for a tour of America, and so the poet abandoned it after only three scenes. But these are enough to show the heroic character of his protagonist, Stephen. Henry I's son had died in the wreck of the White Ship in 1120, leaving as heir to the throne his sister, Matilda, to whom Henry made his nobles swear allegiance. On his death, however, they lent their support to Stephen, and a civil war started, in the course of which Stephen was himself captured at the battle of Lincoln in 1141. A brave and courageous warrior, he was able to regain the kingdom, but he never fully controlled his nobles, and when his own son died he accepted Matilda's son, Henry, as his heir.

King Henry II, 1154–88

1172

THE MURDER OF THOMAS À BECKET

from **Murder in the Cathedral**

KNIGHTS: Where is Becket, the traitor to the King?
    Where is Becket, the meddling priest?
Come down Daniel to the lion's den,
    Come down Daniel for the mark of the
      beast.

Are you washed in the blood of the Lamb?
    Are you marked with the mark of the
      beast?
Come down Daniel to the lions' den,
    Come down Daniel and join in the feast.

Where is Becket the Cheapside brat?
    Where is Becket the faithless priest?
Come down Daniel to the lions' den,
    Come down Daniel and join in the feast.

THOMAS: It is the just man who
Like a bold lion, should be without fear.
I am here.
No traitor to the King. I am a priest,
A Christian, saved by the blood of Christ,
Ready to suffer with my blood.
This is the sign of the Church always,
The sign of blood. Blood for blood.
His blood given to buy my life,
My blood given to pay for His death,
My death for His death.

FIRST KNIGHT: Absolve all those you have excommunicated.

SECOND KNIGHT: Resign the powers you have arrogated.

THIRD KNIGHT: Restore to the King the money you
appropriated.

FOURTH KNIGHT: Renew the obedience you have violated.

THOMAS: For my Lord I am now ready to die,
That his Church may have peace and liberty.
Do with me as you will, to your hurt and
shame;
But none of my people, in God's name,
Whether layman or clerk, shall you touch.
This I forbid.

KNIGHTS: Traitor! traitor! traitor!

THOMAS: You, Reginald, three times traitor you:
Traitor to me as my temporal vassal,
Traitor to me as your spiritual lord,
Traitor to God in desecrating His Church.

FIRST KNIGHT: No faith do I owe to a renegade,
And what I owe shall now be paid.

T. S. Eliot

Henry II and Thomas à Becket had been close friends, but the latter,
who was made Chancellor of England as well as Archbishop of Canterbury, underwent a marked change, becoming increasingly devout and
aloof. He defended the power of the Catholic Church against the
growing secular authority of Henry's state. Becket fled to France, but
was then coaxed back and, after a short reconciliation with the King,
was murdered in Canterbury Cathedral. Within three years he was
canonized, in time becoming England's most popular saint.

King Richard I, 1189–99

THE THIRD CRUSADE

With numberless rich pennons streaming
And flags and banners of fair seeming
Then thirty thousand Turkish troops
And more, ranged in well ordered groups,
Garbed and accoutred splendidly,
Dashed on the host impetuously.
Like lightning speed their horses fleet,
And dust rose thick before their feet.
Moving ahead of the emirs
There came a band of trumpeters
And other men with drums and tabors
There were, who had no other labours
Except upon their drums to hammer
And hoot, and shriek and make great clamour.
So loud their tabors did discord
They had drowned the thunder of the Lord.

Ambroise the Chronicler

Richard the Lionheart looked upon England as a treasure house from which to fund his campaigns abroad. He spent only two years of his reign in the country, which has earned him a splendid statue outside the Houses of Parliament. In 1190 he set out at the head of the Third Crusade with the purpose of seizing Jerusalem, recapturing a piece of wood from the Holy Cross, and, more to the point, acquiring as much gold and silver as possible. He forced the Turks' leader, Saladin, to abandon the city of Acre in Palestine. This poem describes the battle of Arsuf, a triumph for Richard, though he was unable to capture Jerusalem itself. On the way back to England, he was imprisoned in

Germany and had to be ransomed. After a short spell in England in 1194, he spent the rest of his reign fighting in France. He was wounded by a bolt from a crossbow shot by a man whose shield was a frying-pan. The wound turned septic and Richard died, forgiving his assailant.

King John, 1199–1216

1215

MAGNA CHARTA

The Reeds of Runnymede

At Runnymede, at Runnymede,
  What say the reeds at Runnymede?
The lissom reeds that give and take,
That bend so far, but never break.
They keep the sleepy Thames awake
  With tales of John at Runnymede.

At Runnymede, at Runnymede,
  Oh hear the reeds at Runnymede: –
'You mustn't sell, delay, deny,
A freeman's right or liberty,
It wakes the stubborn Englishry,
  We saw 'em roused at Runnymede!

'When through our ranks the Barons came,
With little thought of praise or blame,
But resolute to play the game,
  They lumbered up to Runnymede;
And there they launched in solid line,
The first attack on Right Divine –
The curt, uncompromising "Sign!"
  That settled John at Runnymede.

'At Runnymede, at Runnymede,
  Your rights were won at Runnymede!
No freeman shall be fined or bound,
Or dispossessed of freehold ground,
Except by lawful judgment found
And passed upon him by his peers!
Forget not, after all these years,
  The Charter signed at Runnymede.'

And still when Mob or Monarch lays
Too rude a hand on English ways,
The whisper wakes, the shudder plays,
  Across the reeds at Runnymede.
And Thames, that knows the moods of kings,
And crowds and priests and suchlike things,
Rolls deep and dreadful as he brings
  Their warning down from Runnymede!

Rudyard Kipling

Unlike his brother Richard, King John lost too many battles. He was nicknamed 'Softsword' after surrendering Normandy in 1204. He tried to intimidate the over-mighty barons by keeping their sons as hostages, and he exacted high taxes from them. In 1215, on an island in the Thames at Runnymede, they replied by making him sign a list of promises which came to be known as Magna Charta. Some clauses were trivial – concerning, for instance, fish traps in the Medway – but the thirty-ninth declared: 'No free man shall be arrested, or imprisoned, or have his property taken away, or be outlawed, or exiled, or in any way ruined, except by lawful judgment . . . or by the law of the land.' Future kings of England had to swear to accept the terms of Magna Charta. Although 'King John was not a good man', one good thing he did was to proclaim that the Jews should not be persecuted.

1216

THE DEATH OF KING JOHN

from **King John**

ACT V *Scene VII*
The Orchard of Swinstead Abbey.
Enter the BASTARD

BAST: O, I am scalded with my violent motion,
And spleen of speed to see your majesty!
K. JOHN: O cousin, thou art come to set mine eye:
The tackle of my heart is crack'd and burn'd,
And all the shrouds wherewith my life should sail
Are turned to one thread, one little hair;
My heart hath one poor string to stay it by,
Which holds but till thy news be uttered;
And then all this thou seest is but a clod
And module of confounded royalty.
BAST: The Dauphin is preparing hitherward,
Where heaven He knows how we shall answer him;
For in a night the best part of my power,
As I upon advantage did remove,
Were in the Washes all unwarily
Devoured by the unexpected flood.

[*The* KING *dies.*]

*

PRINCE HENRY: At Worcester must his body be interr'd;
For so he will'd it.
BAST:　　　　　　Thither shall it then:
And happily may your sweet self put on
The lineal state and glory of the land!
To whom, with all submission, on my knee,
I do bequeath my faithful services
And true subjection everlastingly.
SALISBURY: And the like tender of our love we make,
To rest without a spot for evermore.
P. HEN: I have a kind soul that would give you thanks,
And knows not how to do it but with tears.
BAST: O, let us pay the time but needful woe
Since it hath been beforehand with our griefs.
This England never did, nor never shall,
Lie at the proud foot of a conqueror,
But when it first did help to wound itself.
Now these her princes are come home again,
Come the three corners of the world in arms,
And we shall shock them. Nought shall make us rue,
If England to itself do rest but true.　　　　[*Exeunt*]

William Shakespeare

King Henry III, 1216–72

1264

SIMON DE MONTFORT'S REBELLION

from **The Song of Lewes**

So whether it is that the King, misled
By flattering talk to giving his consent,
And truly ignorant of their designs
Unknowingly approves such wrongs as these
Whose only end can be destruction, and
The ruin of his land; or whether he,
With malice in his heart, and ill-intent,
Commits these shameful crimes by raising up
His royal state and power far beyond
The reach of all his country's laws, so that
His whim is satisfied by the abuse
Of royal privilege and strength; if thus
Or otherwise this land of ours is brought
To total rack and ruin, and at last
The kingdom is left destitute, it is
The duty of the great and noble men
To rescue it, to purge the land of all
Corruption and all false authority.

*

For in this year of grace, twelve sixty-four,
The feast of Good Saint Pancras four days past,
The English army rode the heavy storm
Of mighty war, at Lewes' Castle walls.
Then reason to blind fury did give way,
And life to the bright sword. They battle joined
The fourteenth day of May, and dreadful was
The strife in Sussex County, and the See
Of Chichester's Lord Bishop. Hundreds fell,
For mighty was the sword; virtue prevailed,
And evil men took to their heels and fled.
Against these wicked men, our great good Lord
Stood firm, and with the radiant shield of truth
Endued with righteous strength the pure of heart.
Routed their foes, by strength of arms without,
And craven fear within, on them did shine,
More to increase their valour, Heaven's smile.

Roger de Berksted

Henry III had accepted Magna Charta, but his reckless and extravagant behaviour as king led to bankruptcy and he resorted to arbitrary levies and taxes. The nobles, with the former royal favourite Simon de Montfort at their head, sought to control Henry through regular meetings of their Council, sometimes called Parliament, but he resisted and civil war broke out. In 1264 de Montfort won a victory over the royal army at Lewes, capturing both Henry and his heir, Edward. But his success was short-lived. Several of his principal supporters found him insufferably arrogant and deserted him. Within a year he was defeated and killed at Evesham by Edward, a man of sterner stuff than his father. This poem, thought to be by a Franciscan friar, and written in Latin, gives voice to the rebels' grievances and would seem to indicate the strength of feeling against the king.

King Edward I, 1272–1307

1276

THE SUBJUGATION OF WALES

from **The Bard**

'Ruin seize thee, ruthless King!
   Confusion on thy banners wait;
Tho' fann'd by Conquest's crimson wing,
   They mock the air with idle state.
Helm, nor hauberk's twisted mail,
Nor e'en thy virtues, Tyrant shall avail
   To save thy secret soul from nightly fears,
   From Cambria's curse, from Cambria's tears!'
Such were the sounds that o'er the crested pride
   Of the first Edward scatter'd wild dismay,
As down the steep of Snowdon's shaggy side,
   He wound with toilsome march his long array.
Stout Glo'ster stood aghast in speechless trance:
'To arms!' cried Mortimer, and couch'd his quiv'ring lance.

   On a rock whose haughty brow
Frowns o'er cold Conway's foaming flood,
   Robed in the sable garb of woe,
With haggard eyes the poet stood;
(Loose his beard, and hoary hair
Stream'd, like a meteor, to the troubled air;)
And with a master's hand, and prophet's fire,
Struck the deep sorrows of his lyre.

'Hark, how each giant-oak, and desert cave,
Sighs to the torrent's awful voice beneath!
O'er thee, oh King! their hundred arms they wave,
   Revenge on thee in hoarser murmurs breathe;
Vocal no more, since Cambria's fatal day,
To high-born Hoel's harp, or soft Llewellyn's lay.

'Cold is Cadwallo's tongue,
   That hush'd the stormy main:
Brave Urien sleeps upon his craggy bed:
   Mountains, ye mourn in vain
   Modred, whose magic song
Made huge Plinlimmon bow his cloud-topt head.
   On dreary Arvon's shore they lie,
Smear'd with gore, and ghastly pale:
Far, far aloof th' affrighted ravens sail;
   The famish'd eagle screams, and passes by.
Dear lost companions of my tuneful art,
   Dear as the light that visits these sad eyes,
Dear as the ruddy drops that warm my heart,
   Ye died amidst your dying country's cries –

No more I weep. They do not sleep.
   On yonder cliffs, a grisly band,
I see them sit, they linger yet,
   Avengers of their native land:
With me in dreadful harmony they join,
   And weave with bloody hands the tissue of thy line . . .'

                                              Thomas Gray

Gray was the author of a famous poem, but this is not it. Here he depicts a bard cursing the advance of Edward I's armies into Snowdonia, which had been the bastion of Welsh resistance to English rule. The cause of Llewellyn, the Welsh prince, was lost, and a string of fine castles was built to make permanent the conquest of Wales. At the most magnificent of these, Caernarvon, Edward's son was proclaimed Prince of Wales.

ROBIN HOOD

The Ballad of Robin Hood and the Bishop of Hereford

Come, gentlemen all, and listen a while;
    A story I'll to you unfold –
How Robin Hood servèd the Bishop,
    When he robb'd him of his gold.

As it befel in merry Barnsdale,
    And under the green-wood tree,
The Bishop of Hereford was to come by,
    With all his companye.

'Come, kill a ven'son,' said bold Robin Hood,
    'Come, kill me a good fat deer;
The Bishop's to dine with me to day,
    And he shall pay well for his cheer.

'We'll kill a fat ven'son,' said bold Robin Hood,
    'And dress't by the highway-side,
And narrowly watch for the Bishop,
    Lest some other way he should ride.'

He dress'd himself up in shepherd's attire,
    With six of his men also;
And the Bishop of Hereford came thereby,
    As about the fire they did go.

'What matter is this?' said the Bishop;
    'Or for whom do you make this a-do?
Or why do you kill the King's ven'son,
    When your company is so few?'

'We are shepherds,' said bold Robin Hood,
    'And we keep sheep all the year;
And we are disposed to be merry this day,
    And to kill of the King's fat deer.'

'You are brave fellowes,' said the Bishop,
 'And the King of your doings shall know;
Therefore make haste, come along with me,
 For before the King you shall go.'

'O pardon, O pardon,' says bold Robin Hood,
 'O pardon, I thee pray!
For it never becomes your lordship's coat
 To take so many lives away.'

'No pardon, no pardon!' the Bishop says;
 'No pardon I thee owe;
Therefore make haste, come along with me,
 For before the King you shall go.'

Robin set his back against a tree,
 And his foot against a thorn,
And from underneath his shepherd's coat
 He pull'd out a bugle horn.

He put the little end to his mouth,
 And a loud blast did he blow,
Till threescore and ten of bold Robin's men
 Came running all on a row;

All making obeisance to bold Robin Hood;
 – 'Twas a comely sight for to see:
'What matter, my master,' said Little John,
 'That you blow so hastilye?' –

'O here is the Bishop of Hereford,
 And no pardon we shall have.' –
'Cut off his head, master,' said Little John,
 'And throw him into his grave.' –

'O pardon, O pardon,' said the Bishop,
 'O pardon, I thee pray!
For if I had known it had been you,
 I'd have gone some other way.' –

'No pardon, no pardon!' said Robin Hood;
  'No pardon I thee owe;
Therefore make haste, come along with me,
  For to merry Barnsdale you shall go.'

Then Robin has taken the Bishop's hand
  And led him to merry Barnsdale;
He made him to stay and sup with him that night,
  And to drink wine, beer and ale.

'Call in the reckoning,' said the Bishòp,
  'For methinks it grows wondrous high.' –
'Lend me your purse, Bishop,' said Little John,
  'And I'll tell you by-and-by.'

Then Little John took the Bishop's cloak,
  And spread it upon the ground,
And out of the Bishop's portmantua
  He told three hundred pound.

'So now let him go,' said Robin Hood;
  Said Little John, 'That may not be;
For I vow and protest he shall sing us a mass
  Before that he go from me.'

Robin Hood took the Bishop by the hand,
  And bound him fast to a tree,
And made him to sing a mass, God wot,
  To him and his yeomandrye.

Then Robin Hood brought him through the wood
  And causèd the music to play,
And he made the Bishop to dance in his boots,
  And they set him on 's dapple-grey,
And they gave the tail within his hand –
  And glad he could so get away!

Anonymous

The legend of Robin Hood was spread by word of mouth in the Middle Ages. The first written reference dates from the 1370s, and scholars have argued over whether he lived in the reign of King John, Edward I, or Edward III. The only certainty is that he operated as an outlaw in Sherwood Forest, north of Nottingham. Over the centuries, his status as a highway robber was transformed into that of a social hero and freedom fighter. His enemies were the enemies of the common people: grasping landlords, corrupt sheriffs and corpulent clergy. Highway robbery was rife in the Middle Ages and in 1390 the poet Chaucer was pounced upon and relieved of £20. No wonder the pilgrims travelled to Canterbury in convoy. Posterity is unlikely to treat the muggers of the twentieth century so fondly.

King Edward II, 1307–27

1314

THE BATTLE OF BANNOCKBURN

Robert Bruce's March to Bannockburn

Scots, wha hae wi' Wallace bled,
    Scots, wham Bruce has aften led;
Welcome to your gory bed,
    Or to victorie.

Now's the day, and now's the hour;
See the front o' battle lower,
See approach proud Edward's power –
    Chains and slaverie!

Wha will be a traitor knave?
Wha can fill a coward's grave?
Wha sae base as be a slave?
    Let him turn and flee!

Wha for Scotland's King and law,
Freedom's sword will strongly draw,
Free-man stand, or free-man fa'?
    Let him follow me!

By oppression's woes and pains!
By your sons in servile chains!
We will drain our dearest veins,
    But they shall be free!

Lay the proud usurpers low!
Tyrants fall in every foe!
Liberty's in every blow!
Let us do, or die!

Robert Burns

In 1306, a year after Wallace's beheading in London, a great Scottish landowner, Robert Bruce, was crowned King of Scotland at Scone. At last a leader had emerged who could avenge his country's shameful submission to English conquest. Edward I died fighting on his way to crush Bruce's rebellion, and his son, Edward II, was decisively beaten at Bannockburn in 1314. Bruce's armies ravaged the North of England, reaching as far as York. In 1328 the English recognized Scotland's independence, but in the following year Bruce died from leprosy, leaving the kingdom to his six-year-old son, David, and his heart to an old friend, James Douglas, who took it with him on a crusade.

PIERS GAVESTON

from Vita Edwardi Secundi

Though handsome, rich and clever you may be,
Through insolence we may your ruin see.

translated from the Latin by N. Denholm-Young

On his accession in 1307 Edward II recalled his favourite, Piers Gaveston, who had been in exile, and loaded him with titles, honours and jewels. Contemporary chroniclers were quite clear that the two were lovers. In 1311 the nobles ganged up against Gaveston and took him prisoner at Scarborough, where the Earl of Warwick later had him executed as a traitor. His body lay where it had fallen until four cobblers raised it on a ladder, sewed the head back on, and took it to the only people who would receive it, the Dominicans at Oxford. It could not, however, be buried, as Gaveston had been excommunicated.

EDWARD AGAINST THE NOBLES

from **Edward the Second**

K. EDW: Now, lusty lords now, not by chance of war,
But justice of the quarrel and the cause,
Vailed is your pride; methinks you hang the heads,
But we'll advance them, traitors; now 'tis time
To be avenged on you for all your braves,
And for the murder of my dearest friend,
To whom right well you knew our soul was knit,
Good Pierce of Gaveston, my sweet favourite.
Ah, rebels! recreants! you made him away.
Accursèd wretches, was't in regard of us,
When we had sent our messenger to request
He might be spared to come to speak with us,
And Pembroke undertook for his return,
That thou, proud Warwick, watched the prisoner,
Poor Pierce, and headed him 'gainst law of arms?
For which thy head shall overlook the rest,
As much as though in rage outwent'st the rest.

Christopher Marlowe

THE FALL OF EDWARD

In winter woe befell me;
By cruel Fortune thwarted,
My life now lies a ruin.
Full oft have I experienced,
There's none so fair, so wise,
So courteous nor so highly famed,
But, if Fortune cease to favour,
Will be a fool proclaimed.

Edward II,
translated from the Norman by A. R. Myers

Edward's Queen, Isabella, deserted his side and, with the help of her lover, Mortimer, contrived to depose him in favour of the King's son. Edward wrote this poem in captivity, before being brutally murdered at Berkeley Castle by having a red-hot poker thrust into his bowels.

King Edward III, 1327–77

1348–9

THE BLACK DEATH

The Shilling in the Armpit

We see death coming into our midst like black smoke,
a plague which cuts off the young, and has no mercy for the fair
 of face.
Woe is me of the shilling in the armpit:
it is seething, terrible, wherever it may come,
a white lump that gives pain and causes a loud cry,
a burden carried under the arms, a painful angry knob.
It is of the form of an apple, like the head of an onion,
a small boil that spares no one.
Great is its seething, like a burning cinder . . .

Ieuan Gethyn

The Black Death started in Asia in the 1330s, reaching Turkey in 1347. From there it spread quickly through Italy and France, arriving in England in 1348, and Scotland in 1349. It lasted for only two years, although it reappeared on several occasions in England before the Great Plague of London in 1665. The bubonic plague was carried by fleas that lived on rats, and as soon as humans were bitten it became contagious. As described by this Welsh poet, boils, oozing pus and patchy blackening of the skin were symptoms of the disease. Death followed in a few days. According to some estimates, one third of the population of Europe died in consequence.

c. 1370

THE KNIGHTHOOD

from **The General Prologue to the Canterbury Tales**

A Knyght ther was and that a worthy man,
That fro the tyme that he first bigan
To riden out, he loved chivalrie,
Trouthe and honour, fredom and curteisie.
Ful worthy was he in his lordes werre,
And therto had he riden, no man ferre,
As wel in cristendom as in the hethenesse,
And ever honoured for his worthynesse.
At Alisaundre he was whan it was wonne;
Ful ofte tyme he hadde the bord bigonne
Aboven alle nacions in Pruce.
In Lettow had he reysed and in Ruce,
No cristen man so ofte in his degree.
In Gernade at the seege eek hadde he be
Of Algezir, and riden in Belmarye.
At Lyeys was he, and at Satalye,
Whan they were wonne; and in the Grete See
At many a noble armee hadde he be.
At mortal batailles hadde he been fiftene,
And foughten for our feith at Tramyssene
In lystes thries, and ay slayn his foo.
This ilke worthy knyght hadde been also
Somtyme with the lord of Palatye
Agayn another hethen in Turkye;
And evermoore he hadde a sovereyn prys.
And though that he were worthy, he was wys,
And of his port as meeke as is a mayde,
He never yet no vileynye ne sayde,
In al hys lyf, unto no maner wight.
He was a verray parfit, gentil knyght.

Geoffrey Chaucer

Chaucer, the Father of English Poetry, started to write in the 1360s. He had been a minor courtier, occasionally a diplomat, and for a while he was Comptroller of Customs. He lost his post in 1386 when his patron, John of Gaunt, was temporarily out of favour, and it is possible that this was when, with time on his hands, he felt he could start to put together *The Canterbury Tales*. During Edward III's reign he had been allowed a pitcher of wine every day, but this was later changed to a tun once a year, which is what our present Poet Laureate now receives. When Chaucer died in 1400, he was buried in Westminster Abbey, the first writer to be so honoured.

The General Prologue to *The Canterbury Tales* offers a most vivid picture of some of the people who made up the England of the Middle Ages. Each portrait is precise and memorable. Among those represented is the Knight, who was indeed a valiant Crusader, with fifteen 'mortal battles' to his credit. Algeciras (1344), Attalia (1352), Alexandria (1365) and Armenia (1367) are among those cited by Chaucer.

THE NOBILITY

An Arundel Tomb

Side by side, their faces blurred,
The earl and countess lie in stone,
Their proper habits vaguely shown
As jointed armour, stiffened pleat,
And that faint hint of the absurd –
The little dogs under their feet.

Such plainness of the pre-baroque
Hardly involves the eye, until
It meets his left-hand gauntlet, still
Clasped empty in the other; and
One sees, with a sharp tender shock,
His hand withdrawn, holding her hand.

They would not think to lie so long.
Such faithfulness in effigy
Was just a detail friends would see:
A sculptor's sweet commissioned grace
Thrown off in helping to prolong
The Latin names around the base.

They would not guess how early in
Their supine stationary voyage
The air would change to soundless damage,
Turn the old tenantry away;
How soon succeeding eyes begin
To look, not read. Rigidly they

Persisted, linked, through lengths and breadths
Of time. Snow fell, undated. Light
Each summer thronged the glass. A bright
Litter of birdcalls strewed the same
Bone-riddled ground. And up the paths
The endless altered people came,

Washing at their identity.
Now, helpless in the hollow of
An unarmorial age, a trough
Of smoke in slow suspended skeins
Above their scrap of history,
Only an attitude remains:

Time has transfigured them into
Untruth. The stone fidelity
They hardly meant has come to be
Their final blazon, and to prove
Our almost-instinct almost true:
What will survive of us is love.

Philip Larkin

the 1370s

THE POOR

from **Piers Plowman**

The most needy aren oure neighbores, and we nime good
    heede,
As prisones in pittes, and poure folke in cotes,
Charged with children and chef lordes rente:
That they with spinninge may spare, spenen hit in hous-hire;
Bothe in milk and in mele to make with papelotes,
To aglotie with here gurles that greden after foode.
Also hemselve suffren muche hunger,
And wo in winter-time with wakinge a nightes
To rise to the ruel to rocke the cradel,
Both to carde and to cembe, to clouten and to washe,
To ribbe and to reli, rushes to pilie,
That reuthe is to rede othere in rime shewe
The wo of these women that wonieth in cotes;
And of meny other men that muche wo suffren,
Bothe afingrede and afurst to turne the faire outwarde,
And beth abashed for to begge, and wolle nat be aknowe
What hem needeth at here neighbores at noon and at even.
This ich wot witerly, as the worlde techeth,
What other bihoveth that hath meny children,
And hath no catel bote his crafte to clothy hem and to fede,
And fele to fonge therto, and fewe pans taketh.
Ther is pain and peny-ale as for a pitaunce ytake,
Colde flesh and cold fish for veneson ybake;
Fridayes and fasting-dayes a ferthing-worth of muscles
Were a feste for suche folke, other so fele cockes.

William Langland

The great medieval poem from which these lines come was written by a
monk from the Midlands in about the 1370s. It is full of revealing details
of the social life of the time.

1376

THE DEATH OF THE BLACK PRINCE

Such as thou art, some time was I
Such as I am, such shalt thou be.
I little thought on the hour of death
So long as I enjoyed breath.

Great riches here I did possess
Whereof I made great nobleness.
I had gold, silver, wardrobes and
Great treasure, horses, houses, land

But now a caitiff poor am I,
Deep in the ground, lo here I lie.
My beauty great is all quite gone,
My flesh is wasted to the bone.

*

And if ye should see me this day
I do not think but ye would say
That I had never been a man;
So much altered now I am.

For God's sake pray to the heavenly King
That he my soul to heaven would bring.
All they that pray and make accord
For me unto my God and Lord,
God place them in his Paradise,
Wherein no wretched caitiff lies.

Richard Barber

Edward III's son, the Black Prince, led his father's armies to victory in
France and earned the reputation of being 'the flower of chivalry of all
the world'. He developed dropsy and died at the age of forty-six,
leaving as heir to the old, sick and tired King his young son, Richard of

Bordeaux. The Black Prince had laid down instructions for his funeral, including these words to be inscribed on his tomb.

1377

THE DEATH OF EDWARD III

Sum tyme an Englis schip we had,
　Nobel hit was, and heih of tour;
Thorw al Christendom hit was drad,
　And stif wold stonde in uch a stour,
　And best dorst byde a scharp schour,
And other stormes smale and grete;
　Nou is that schip, that bar the flour,
Selden sei3e and sone for3ete.

*

The rother was nouther ok ne elm,
　Hit was Edward the thridde the noble kniht;
The prince his sone bar up his helm,
　That never scoumfited was in fiht.
　The king him rod and rouwed ariht,
The prince dredde nouther stok nor streete.
　Nou of hem we lete ful liht;
That selden is sei3e is sone for3ete.

Anonymous

Edward III had been a great king and a commanding personality. He possessed a fierce temper and it was rumoured that he had once killed a servant with his own hands in a fit of rage. His armies won great victories at Crécy in 1346 and Poitiers in 1356, and in 1347 the key French port of Calais was captured for the English. But the last years of his reign went badly, so that by 1375 England held only Calais, a few ports in Brittany, and a part of Gascony – less than he had inherited on his accession to the throne. For all that, his reign was looked upon by the Tudors as a golden age.

King Richard II, 1377–99

1381

THE PEASANTS' REVOLT

from **A Prologue to the play 'Watt Tyler'**

Too seldom, if the righteous fight is won,
Rebellion boasts a Tell or Washington;
But if the champion of the People fail,
Foes only live to tell Misfortune's tale,
And meanness blots, while none to praise is nigh.
The hero's virtues, with a coward's lie.
Tonight we bring, from his insulted grave,
A man too honest to become a slave:
How few admire him! few, perhaps, bewail'd!
He was a vulgar hero – for he fail'd:
Such glorious honours soothe the patriot's shade!
Of such materials History is made!
But had his followers triumph'd, where he fell
Fame would have hymn'd her village Hampden well,
And Watt the Tyler been a William Tell.

Ebenezer Elliott

This uprising started in Kent and was led by a priest, John Ball, together with Jack Straw and Wat Tyler. The people were oppressed by taxes and alarmed by a series of military setbacks in France. They marched from Kent, pillaging manors, and as they advanced on London they killed the Treasurer and the Archbishop of Canterbury. The King issued letters of pardon and briefly rode out to meet the rebel forces at Smithfield. When Jack Straw and Wat Tyler approached the King, the Lord Mayor of London, Sir William Walworth, struck off Tyler's head. The mob was leaderless and the King rode among them saying, 'Sirs, will you shoot your own king? I will be your captain.'

This was a genuine revolt of ordinary people. Ball preached an early form of Communism, and he caught the nobles and yeomen farmers on the hop. He was hanged, drawn and quartered, and his remains were put on show around the country. His egalitarian philosophy is summed up in the little rhyme of which he was the author:

> When Adam delved and Eve span,
> Who was then the gentleman?

from The Peasants' Revolt

> Tax has tenet us alle,
> *probat hoc mors tot validorum,*
> The kyng therof hade smalle,
> *fuit in manibus cupidorum;*
> Hit hade harde honsalle,
> *dans causam fine dolorum;*
> Revrawnce nede most falle,
> *propter peccata malorum.*
>
> In Kent this kare began,
> *mox infestando potentes,*
> In rowte the rybawdus ran,
> *sua pompis arma ferentes;*
> Folus dred no mon,
> *regni regem neque gentes,*
> Churles were hor chevetan,
> *vulgo pure dominantes.*
>
> *
>
> Laddus loude thay lo₃e,
> *clamantes voce sonora,*
> The bisschop wen thay slo₃e,
> *et corpora plura decora;*
> Maners down thay drow₃e,
> *in regno non meliora;*
> Harme thay dud ino₃e,
> *habuerunt libera lora.*
>
> *

Owre kyng hadde no rest,
   alii latuere caverna,
To ride he was ful prest,
   recolendo gesta paterna;
Jak Straw down he kest
   Smythfield virtute superna.
Lord, as thou may best,
   regem defende guberna.

Anonymous

This is the only poem about the Peasants' Revolt that we know to be by a contemporary. With a little poetic licence, and omitting the Latin, I have made a modern English version of it that preserves something of the effect of the abrupt rhyming lines of the original:

Tax has hit us all;
The King's revenue is small;
It bears hard on us all;
Reverence now must fall.

In Kent this trouble began:
In riot the rebels ran,
For fools fear no man.
Churls were their chieftain.

Loud the lads did bray,
When the bishop they did slay.
Manors they burnt in a day –
Harm that won't go away.

Our King had no rest;
To ride forth he was pressed.
Jack Straw was a pest.
May his Majesty be blessed!

1399

THE STATE OF ENGLAND

from **King Richard the Second**

ACT II *Scene I.*
London. A Room in Ely House.
GAUNT *on a couch; the* DUKE OF YORK, *and others, standing by him.*

GAUNT: Methinks, I am a prophet new inspired;
And thus, expiring, do foretell of him:
His rash fierce blaze of riot cannot last;
For violent fires soon burn out themselves:
Small showers last long, but sudden storms are short;
He tires betimes, that spurs too fast betimes;
With eager feeding, food doth choke the feeder;
Light vanity, insatiate cormorant,
Consuming means, soon preys upon itself.
This royal throne of kings, this scepter'd isle,
This earth of majesty, this seat of Mars,
This other Eden, demi-paradise;
This fortress, built by nature for herself
Against infection, and the hand of war;
This happy breed of men, this little world;
This precious stone set in the silver sea,
Which serves it in the office of a wall,
Or as a moat defensive to a house,
Against the envy of less happier lands;
This blessed plot, this earth, this realm, this England,
This nurse, this teeming womb of royal kings,
Fear'd by their breed, and famous by their birth,
Renowned for their deeds as far from home,
(For Christian service, and true chivalry,)
As is the sepulchre in stubborn Jewry,
Of the world's ransom, blessed Mary's son:
This land of such dear souls, this dear dear land,
Dear for her reputation through the world,
Is now leased out, (I die pronouncing it,)
Like to a tenement, or pelting farm:

England, bound in with the triumphant sea,
Whose rocky shore beats back to the envious siege
Of watery Neptune, is now bound in with shame,
With inky blots, and rotten parchment bonds;
That England, that was wont to conquer others,
Hath made a shameful conquest of itself:
O, would the scandal vanish with my life,
How happy then were my ensuing death!

William Shakespeare

THE DEPOSITION OF RICHARD II

from **King Richard the Second**

ACT IV. *Scene I.*
Westminster Hall.
BOLINGBROKE *in Council with the Lords and Commons.*
Re-enter YORK, *with* KING RICHARD, *and* OFFICERS
bearing the crown, etc.

K. RICH: Alack, why am I sent for to a king,
Before I have shook off the regal thoughts
Wherewith I reign'd? I hardly yet have learn'd
To insinuate, flatter, bow, and bend my knee; –
Give sorrow leave a while to tutor me
To this submission. Yet I will remember
The favours of these men: Were they not mine?
Did they not sometimes cry, All hail! to me?
So Judas did to Christ: but he, in twelve,
Found truth in all but one; I, in twelve thousand none.
God save the king! – Will no man say Amen?
Am I both priest and clerk? well then, Amen.
God save the king! although I be not he;
And yet, Amen, if Heaven do think him me. –
To do what service am I sent for hither?
YORK: To do that office, of thine own good will,
Which tired majesty did make thee offer, –
The resignation of thy state and crown
To Henry Bolingbroke.
K. RICH: Give me the crown: – Here, cousin, seize the crown;
Here, on this side, my hand; on that side, thine.
Now is this golden crown like a deep well,
That owes two buckets filling one another;
The emptier ever dancing in the air,
The other down, unseen, and full of water:
The bucket down, and full of tears, am I,
Drinking my griefs, whilst you mount up on high.
BOLING: I thought you had been willing to resign.

K. RICH: My crown I am; but still my griefs are mine:
You may my glories and my state depose,
But not my griefs; still am I king of those.
BOLING: Part of your cares you give me with your crown.
K. RICH: Your cares set up, do not pluck my cares down.
My care is – loss of care, by old care done;
Your care is – gain of care, by new care won;
The cares I give, I have, though given away;
They tend the crown, yet still with me they stay.
BOLING: Are you contented to resign the crown?
K. RICH: Ay, no; – no, ay: for I must nothing be;
Therefore no no, for I resign to thee.
Now mark me how I will undo myself: –
I give this heavy weight from off my head,
And this unwieldy sceptre from my hand,
The pride of kingly sway from out my heart;
With mine own tears I wash away my balm,
With mine own hand I give away my crown,
With mine own tongue deny my sacred state,
With mine own breath release all duteous oaths:
All pomp and majesty I do forswear;
My manors, rents, and revenues, I forego;
My acts, decrees, and statutes, I deny;
God pardon all oaths, that are broke to me!
God keep all vows unbroke, are made to thee!
Make me, that nothing have, with nothing grieved;
And thou with all pleased, that hast all achieved
Long may'st thou live in Richard's seat to sit,
And soon lie Richard in an earthly pit!
God save King Henry, unking'd Richard says,
And send him many years of sunshine days! –
What more remains?

William Shakespeare

A weak king was the curse of medieval England. When Richard II succeeded his grandfather, Edward III – one of the strongest of our monarchs – he was a boy of eleven. He was by nature an aesthete who created a cultured court hospitable to writers and painters, and the beautiful hammer-beam roof in Westminster Hall dates from his reign. He failed, however, to control the great baronial families, and so resorted to a series of arbitrary and quixotic ploys in order to maintain his rule. In 1399, on the death of his uncle, John of Gaunt, he seized the lands of Gaunt's son, Henry of Lancaster, who had fled to Paris. No one, it appeared, was safe. But Henry returned to England, where the King, deserted by the rest of the nobles and loathed by the merchants for his forced loans, found himself isolated among his own subjects. Henry thereupon claimed the throne by right of descent, vindicated by conquest. The thirty-three-year-old Richard, last of the Plantagenets, was taken to Pontefract Castle where he was either starved to death or suffocated. Henry said a solemn requiem mass for him at St Paul's.

The House of Lancaster had started its reign and Shakespeare was to be its retrospective Poet Laureate.

Requiem for the Plantagenet Kings

For whom the possessed sea littered, on both shores,
Ruinous arms; being fired, and for good,
To sound the constitution of just wars,
Men, in their eloquent fashion, understood.

Relieved of soul, the dropping-back of dust,
Their usage, pride, admitted within doors;
At home, under caved chantries, set in trust,
With well-dressed alabaster and proved spurs
They lie; they lie; secure in the decay
Of blood, blood-marks, crowns hacked and coveted,
Before the scouring fires of trial-day
Alight on men; before sleeked groin, gored head,
Budge through the clay and gravel, and the sea
Across daubed rock evacuates its dead.

Geoffrey Hill

LANCASTER AND YORK

King Henry IV, 1399–1413

from An Address to the King

O worthi noble kyng, Henry the ferthe,
In whom the glade fortune is befalle
The poeple to governe uppon this erthe,
God hath the chose in comfort of ous alle:
The worschipe of this lond, which was doun falle,
Now stant upriht thurgh grace of thi goodnesse,
Which every man is holde forto blesse.

The highe god of his justice allone
The right which longeth to thi regalie
Declared hath to stonde in thi persone,
And more than god may no man justefie.
Thi title is knowe uppon thin ancestrie,
The londes folk hath ek thy riht affermed;
So stant thi regne of god and man confermed.

John Gower

This is the beginning of a long poem, most of which urges Henry to
follow a policy of peace and to avoid war. Apart from dealing with
several rebellions at home, however, Henry did embark on costly
foreign warfare at the end of his reign. Gower takes care to emphasize
Henry's claim to the throne through descent from John of Gaunt,
Edward III's third son, adding for good measure that God had chosen
him and that he had the support of the people of the land. Even so, the
new king was looked upon as a usurper. In Shakespeare's words,
'Uneasy lies the head that wears a crown.'

PRINCE HAL

from King Henry the Fourth, Part Two

ACT IV *Scene V*
KING HENRY *lying on a bed*.
PRINCE: I never thought to hear you speak again.
K. HEN.: Thy wish was father, Harry, to that thought:
I stay too long by thee, I weary thee.
Dost thou so hunger for my empty chair
That thou wilt needs invest thee with mine honours.
Before thy hour be ripe? O foolish youth!
Thou seek'st the greatness that will overwhelm thee.
Stay but a little; for my cloud of dignity
Is held from falling with so weak a wind
That it will quickly drop: my day is dim.
Thou has stol'n that which after some few hours
Were thine without offence; and at my death
Thou hast seal'd up my expectation:
Thy life did manifest thou lov'dst me not,
And thou wilt have me die assur'd of it.
Thou hid'st a thousand daggers in thy thoughts,
Which thou hast whetted on thy stony heart,
To stab at half an hour of my life.
What! canst thou not forbear me half an hour?
Then get thee gone and dig my grave thyself,
And bid the merry bells ring to thine ear
That thou art crowned, not that I am dead.
Let all the tears that should bedew my hearse
Be drops of balm to sanctify thy head:
Only compound me with forgotten dust;
Give that which gave thee life unto the worms.
Pluck down my officers, break my decrees;
For now a time is come to mock at form.
Harry the Fifth is crown'd! Up, vanity!
Down, royal state! all you sage counsellors, hence!
And to the English court assemble now,
From every region, apes of idleness!

Now, neighbour confines, purge you of your scum:
Have you a ruffian that will swear, drink, dance,
Revel the night, rob, murder, and commit
The oldest sins the newest kind of ways?
Be happy, he will trouble you no more:
England shall double gild his treble guilt,
England shall give him office, honour, might;
For the fifth Harry from curb'd licence plucks
The muzzle of restraint, and the wild dog
Shall flesh his tooth in every innocent.
O my poor kingdom! sick with civil blows.
When that my care could not withhold thy riots,
What wilt thou do when riot is thy care?
O! thou wilt be a wilderness again,
Peopled with wolves, thy old inhabitants.

William Shakespeare

In the famous scene from which this passage is taken, Prince Hal, son
and heir to Henry IV, believing his father to be dead, tries on the
crown, but the old king wakes and delivers this majestic rebuke. After
leading a riotous life with such companions as Sir John Falstaff, and the
mercenary soldiers Pistol and Bardolph, the prince acceded to the
throne as Henry V, cast off his old friends and became a national hero –
or so the genius of Shakespeare would have it.

King Henry V, 1413–22

1415

from The Battle of Agincourt

Fair stood the wind for France
When we our sails advance,
Nor now to prove our chance
    Longer will tarry;
But putting to the main,
At Caux, the mouth of Seine,
With all his martial train
    Landed King Harry.

And taking many a fort,
Furnished in warlike sort,
Marcheth towards Agincourt
    In happy hour;
Skirmishing day by day
With those that stopped his way,
Where the French general lay
    With all his power;

*

And turning to his men,
Quoth our brave Henry then,
'Though they to one be ten,
    Be not amazèd;
Yet have we well begun,
Battles so bravely won
Have ever to the sun
    By fame been raisèd.

*

'Poitiers and Cressy tell,
When most their pride did swell,
Under our swords they fell;
   No less our skill is
Than when our grandsire great,
Claiming the regal seat,
By many a warlike feat
   Lopped the French lilies.'

      *

They now to fight are gone,
Armour on armour shone,
Drum now to drum did groan,
   To hear was wonder:
That with the cries they make
The very earth did shake;
Trumpet to trumpet spake,
   Thunder to thunder.

Well it thine age became,
O noble Erpingham,
Which didst the signal aim
   To our hid forces!
When, from a meadow by,
Like a storm suddenly
The English archery
   Struck the French horses:

With Spanish yew so strong,
Arrows a cloth-yard long,
That like to serpents stung,
   Piercing the weather;
None from his fellow starts,
But, playing manly parts,
And like true English hearts,
   Stuck close together.

When down their bows they threw,
And forth their bilbos drew,
And on the French they flew,
    Not one was tardy;
Arms were from shoulders sent,
Scalps to the teeth were rent,
Down the French peasants went:
    Our men were hardy.

This while our noble King,
His broad sword brandishing,
Down the French host did ding
    As to o'erwhelm it;
And many a deep wound lent,
His arms with blood besprent,
And many a cruel dent
    Bruisèd his helmet.

*

Upon Saint Crispin's day
Fought was this noble fray,
Which fame did not delay
    To England to carry;
Oh, when shall English men
With such acts fill a pen?
Or England breed again
    Such a King Harry?

Michael Drayton

from King Henry the Fifth

ACT IV *Scene III*
The English camp.

KING HENRY: . . . This day is call'd the feast of Crispian:
He that outlives this day, and comes safe home,
Will stand a tip-toe when this day is nam'd,
And rouse him at the name of Crispian.
He that shall live this day, and see old age,
Will yearly on the vigil feast his neighbours,
And say, 'To-morrow is Saint Crispian':
Then will he strip his sleeve and show his scars,
And say, 'These wounds I had on Crispin's day.'
Old men forget: yet all shall be forgot,
But he'll remember with advantages
What feats he did that day. Then shall our names,
Familiar in his mouth as household words,
Harry the king, Bedford and Exeter,
Warwick and Talbot, Salisbury and Gloucester,
Be in their flowing cups freshly remember'd.
This story shall the good man teach his son;
And Crispin Crispian shall ne'er go by,
From this day to the ending of the world,
But we in it shall be remembered;
We few, we happy few, we band of brothers;
For he to-day that sheds his blood with me
Shall be my brother; be he ne'er so vile
This day shall gentle his condition:
And gentlemen in England, now a-bed
Shall think themselves accurs'd they were not here,
And hold their manhoods cheap whiles any speaks
That fought with us upon Saint Crispin's day.

William Shakespeare

Henry V showed himself determined to reclaim for England the old
Angevin Empire in France, and in 1415 he set sail for that purpose with

1,500 ships and 10,000 fighting men. Within a few months, however, after capturing the fortified town of Harfleur, the number of his men had been reduced to 6,000 by death in battle and dysentery. Withdrawing to the coast, this small army met a much larger French one and, through Henry's personal inspiration and skilful use of the long bow, defeated it. Thereafter England was committed to a ruinously expensive war on the Continent: in 1418 alone the army ordered one million goose feathers for its arrows. In 1420 the Treaty of Troyes established Henry as heir to the French throne through his marriage to Catherine of Valois. From England's point of view, that represented the high point of the Hundred Years War, and from then on it was downhill all the way until at last Mary Tudor lost Calais. Henry died in 1422, from dysentery caught on the campaign, and he made the unforgivable mistake, for a medieval king, of leaving an heir just one year old.

1420

DICK WHITTINGTON'S THIRD TERM AS LORD MAYOR OF LONDON

> Here must I tell the praise
>   Of worthy Whittington,
> Known to be in his age
>   Thrice Mayor of London.
> But of poor parentage
>   Born was he, as we hear,
> And in his tender age
>   Bred up in Lancashire.
>
> Poorly to London than
>   Came up this simple lad,
> Where with a merchant-man,
>   Soon he a dwelling had;
> And in a kitchen placed,
>   A scullion for to be,
> Whereas long time he past
>   In labour drudgingly.

His daily service was
   Turning spits at the fire;
And to scour pots of brass,
   For a poor scullion's hire.
Meat and drink all his pay,
   Of coin he had no store;
Therefore to run away,
   In secret thought he bore.

So from this merchant-man
   Whittington secretly
Towards his country ran,
   To purchase liberty.
But as he went along,
   In a fair summer's morn
London bells sweetly rung,
   'Whittington, back return!'

Evermore sounding so,
   'Turn again Whittington:
For thou in time shall grow
   Lord-Mayor of London.'
Whereupon back again
   Whittington came with speed.
A 'prentice to remain,
   As the Lord had decreed.

*

But see his happy chance!
   This scullion had a cat,
Which did his state advance,
   And by it wealth he gat.
His master ventured forth,
   To a land far unknown,
With merchandise of worth,
   As is in stories shown.

Whittington had no more
    But this poor cat as than,
Which to the ship he bore,
    Like a brave merchant-man,
'Venturing the same,' quoth he,
    'I may get store of gold,
And Mayor of London be;
    As the bells have me told.'

Whittington's merchandise
    Carried was to a land
Troubled with rats and mice,
    As they did understand.
The king of that country there,
    As he at dinner sat,
Daily remained in fear
    Of many a mouse and rat.

Meat that on trenchers lay,
    No way they could keep safe;
But by rats borne away,
    Fearing no wand or staff.
Whereupon soon they brought
    Whittington's nimble cat;
Which by the king was bought;
    Heaps of gold given for that.

Home again came these men
    With their ships loaden so,
Whittington's wealth began
    By this cat thus to grow.
Scullion's life he forsook
    To be a merchant good,
And soon began to look
    How well his credit stood.

After that he was chose
  Sheriff of the city here,
And then full quickly rose
  Higher, as did appear.
For to this cities praise,
  Sir Richard Whittington
Came to be in his day,
  Thrice Mayor of London.

Anonymous

The eponymous pantomime hero had his origins in verifiable history, catching the popular imagination as an archetype of the rags-to-riches story.

King Henry VI, 1422–61

1430

from To the King on his Coronation

Most noble prince of cristen princes alle,
  Flowryng in yowthe and vertuous innocence,
Whom God above list of his grace calle
  This day to estate of knyghtly excellence,
  And to be crowned with diewe reverence,
To grete gladness of al this regioun,
  Lawde and honour to thy magnificence,
And goode fortune unto thy high renoun.

Royal braunched, descended from two lynes,
  Of seynt Edward and of seynt Lowys;
Holy seyntes, translated in theyr shrynes,
  In theyr tyme manly, prudent, and wys;
  Arthur was knyghtly, and Charles of grete prys,
And of all these thy grene tender age,
  By the grace of God and by his advys,
Of manly prowesse shal taken tarage.

*

Prince excelent, be feythful, triewe, and stable;
  Drede God, do lawe, chastice extorcioun;
Be liberal of courage, unmutable;
  Cherisshe the chirche with hole affeccioun;
  Love thy lieges of eyther regioun;
Preferre the pees, eschewe werre and debate;
  And God shal sende from the heven downe
Grace and goode hure to thy royal estate.

attributed to John Lydgate

Lydgate, the monk of Bury St Edmunds, may have written this ode of welcome to the young King Henry who was crowned at seven years of age. Not only does the poet ascribe to him qualities which, sadly, Henry VI was not to possess, but he takes the opportunity to make a political point by stressing the dual inheritance and its legitimacy.

1436

from Plea for a Navy

The trewe processe of Englysh polycye,
  Of utterwarde to kepe thys regne in rest
Of oure England, that no man may denye,
  Nere saye of soth but one of the best
  Is thys, that who seith southe, northe, est, and west,
Cheryshe marchandyse, kepe thamyralté,
That we bee masteres of the narowe see.

*

Where bene oure shippes? where bene oure swerdes become?
  Owre enmyes bid for the shippe sette a shepe.
Allas! oure reule halteth, hit is benome;
  Who dare weel say that lordeshyppe shulde take kepe?
  I wolle asaye, thoughe myne herte gynne to wepe,
To do thys werke, yf we wole ever the,
Ffor verry shame, to kepe aboute the see.

Anonymous

For the next fifteen years England was under the control of a minority government led by Henry's brothers and Cardinal Beaufort. The English armies in France were pushed back, particularly after 1429. Paris fell in 1436, but few in England wished to give up revenue to the merchants who argued strongly for a subsidized navy.

King Edward IV, 1461–83

1461

THE RISE OF THE HOUSE OF YORK

Also scripture saithe, woo be to that regyon
   Where ys a kyng unwyse or innocent;
Moreovyr it ys right a gret abusion,
   A womman of a land to be a regent,
   Qwene Margrete I mene, that ever hathe ment
To governe alle Engeland with myght and poure,
   And to destroye the ryght lyne was here entent,
Wherfore sche hathe a fal, to here gret langoure.

*

Wherfore I lykken England to a gardayne,
   Whiche that hathe ben overgrowen many yere
Withe wedys, whiche must be mowen doune playne,
   And than schul the pleasant swete herbes appere.
   Wherfore alle trewe Englyshe peuple, pray yn fere
For kyng Edward of Rouen, oure comfortoure,
   That he kepe justice and make wedis clere,
Avoydyng the blak cloudys of langoure.

A gret signe it ys that God lovythe that knyght,
   For alle thoo that woold have destroyed hym utterly,
Alle they ar myschyeved and put to flyght.
   Than remembre hys fortune with chevalry
   Whiche at Northamptoun gate the victory,
And at Mortimers Crosse he had the honnour;
   On Palme Sonday he wan the palme of glorye,
And put hys enemyes to endelez langour.

Anonymous

Embedded in this piece of Yorkist propaganda is a very pleasant verse of poetry. The Wars of the Roses lasted from 1455 to 1485. The Yorkists triumphed at Northampton in 1460 when they captured Henry VI, but the Duke of York was himself killed at Wakefield in the same year. His son, Edward of March, regained the initiative and beat the Lancastrians at Mortimers Cross and Towton in 1461. These victories cleared the way for his coronation as Edward IV, the first Yorkist king of England.

1478

THE MURDER OF THE DUKE OF CLARENCE

from **King Richard the Third**

ACT I *Scene IV*
London. The Tower.

FIRST MURDERER: Who made thee then a bloody minister,
When gallant-springing, brave Plantagenet,
That princely novice, was struck dead by thee?
CLARENCE: My brother's love, the devil, and my rage.
FIRST MURD: Thy brother's love, our duty, and thy fault,
Provoke us hither now to slaughter thee.
CLAR: If you do love my brother, hate not me;
I am his brother, and I love him well.
If you be hir'd for meed, go back again,
And I will send you to my brother Gloucester,
Who shall reward you better for my life
Than Edward will for tidings of my death.
SECOND MURD: You are deceiv'd, your brother Gloucester hates
    you.
CLAR: O, no! he loves me, and he holds me dear: Go you to him
    from me.
BOTH MURD: Ay, so we will.
CLAR: Tell him, when that our princely father York
Bless'd his three sons with his victorious arm,
And charg'd us from his soul to love each other,
He little thought of this divided friendship:
Bid Gloucester think on this, and he will weep.
FIRST MURD: Ay, millstones; as he lesson'd us to weep.
CLAR: O! do not slander him, for he is kind.
FIRST MURD: Right,
As snow in harvest. Thou deceiv'st thyself:
'Tis he that sends us to destroy you here.
CLAR: It cannot be; for he bewept my fortune,
And hugg'd me in his arms, and swore, with sobs,
That he would labour my delivery.

FIRST MURD: Why, so he doth, now he delivers you
From this earth's thraldom to the joys of heaven.
SECOND MURD: Make peace with God, for you must die, my lord.
CLAR: Have you that holy feeling in thy soul,
To counsel me to make my peace with God,
And art thou yet to thy own soul so blind,
That thou wilt war with God by murdering me?
O! sirs, consider, they that set you on
To do this deed will hate you for the deed.
SECOND MURD: What shall we do?
CLAR: Relent and save your souls.
FIRST MURD: Relent! 'tis cowardly and womanish.
CLAR: Not to relent, is beastly, savage, devilish.
Which of you, if you were a prince's son,
Being pent from liberty, as I am now,
If two such murderers as yourselves came to you,
Would not entreat for life?
My friend, I spy some pity in thy looks;
O! if thine eye be not a flatterer,
Come thou on my side, and entreat for me,
As you would beg, were you in my distress:
A begging prince what beggar pities not?
SECOND MURD: Look behind you, my lord.
FIRST MURD: Take that, and that: (*Stabs him.*)
                              If all this will not do,
I'll drown you in the malmsey-butt within.

                              (*Exit, with the body.*)

                              William Shakespeare

If the Duke of Clarence had not met his end in a butt of malmsey wine,
his death would no doubt have been forgotten amid the baronial
mayhem of the fifteenth century. He was a younger brother of Edward
IV and was of an ambitious and unstable disposition. He supported
Warwick the Kingmaker during his rebellion of 1469–71, but upon
Edward's return from exile in 1471 defected back to his brother and
fought alongside him at Barnet and Tewkesbury. Although restored to
favour, he was never satisfied with his power, and in 1478 Edward had
him arrested for high treason. Tradition relates that he was executed by

drowning in his favourite wine. Shakespeare depicted Richard of Gloucester as his murderer, but there is no external evidence for this and the full responsibility must lie with Edward.

King Edward V, 1483, and King Richard III, 1483–5

THE MURDER OF THE PRINCES IN THE TOWER

from **King Richard the Third**

ACT IV *Scene III*
London. A Room of State in the Palace.
(*Enter* TYRREL)
TYR: The tyrannous and bloody act is done;
The most arch deed of piteous massacre,
That ever yet this land was guilty of,
Dighton, and Forest, whom I did suborn
To do this piece of ruthless butchery,
Albeit they were flesh'd villains, bloody dogs,
Melting with tenderness and mild compassion,
Wept like two children, in their death's sad story.
O thus, quoth Dighton, *lay the gentle babes,–*
Thus, thus, quoth Forrest, *girdling one another*
Within their alabaster innocent arms:
Their lips were four red roses on a stalk,
Which, in their summer beauty, kiss'd each other.
A book of prayers on their pillow lay;
Which once, quoth Forrest, *almost changed my mind:*
But, O, the devil – there the villain stopp'd;
When Dighton thus told on, *– we smothered*
The most replenished sweet work of nature.
That, from the prime creation e'er she framed. –
Hence both are gone with conscience and remorse,
They could not speak; and so I left them both,
To bear this tidings to the bloody king:
And here he comes.
                    (*Enter* KING RICHARD)
                    All health, my sovereign lord!
K. RICH: Kind Tyrrel! am I happy in thy news?

William Shakespeare

In April 1483 Edward IV died and was succeeded by his twelve-year-old
son, Edward V, whose coronation was planned for 22 June. Richard of
Gloucester, Edward IV's brother and the young King's uncle, was
made Protector. He realized that the Woodville family, relations of
Edward, would wait until the King came of age and then turn upon
Richard himself. So he moved quickly to place Edward and his younger
brother under guard in the Tower of London, an act which had the full
support of the Archbishop of Canterbury. With that accomplished, he
claimed the throne and was crowned in July. Tudor propaganda
accused him of suffocating the princes in the Tower; of killing Henry
VI; and of having his brother, the Duke of Clarence, murdered. So bad
was his reputation that he was obliged personally to deny that he had
done away with his wife, Anne, in order to marry his niece.

> The Cat, the Rat and Lovel our dog
> Rule all England under the Hog.

> *William Collingbourne*

This scathing couplet was found pinned to the door of St Paul's Cathedral in London. It alludes to Catesby, Ratcliffe and Lovel, ministers of
the King, who is represented here by his heraldic emblem, a white
boar. But this was no age for satire. Collingbourne was caught and, on
a new gallows specially constructed on Tower Hill, he was hanged.
According to report, he was cut down while still alive to have 'his
bowels ripped out of his belly and cast into the fire there by him', and
even so he 'lived till the butcher put his hand into the bulk of his body;
insomuch that he said in the same instant, "O Lord Jesus, yet more
trouble," and so died to the great compassion of much people'. As
another couplet has it:

> The axe was sharp, the block was hard,
> In the fourth year of King Richard.

1485

THE BATTLE OF BOSWORTH

from King Richard the Third

SCENE IV
Another part of the field.
Alarum; excursions. Enter NORFOLK *and forces fighting;*
to him CATESBY.

CATESBY: Rescue, my Lord of Norfolk, rescue, rescue!
The king enacts more wonders than a man,
Daring an opposite to every danger:
His horse is slain, and all on foot he fights,
Seeking for Richmond in the throat of death.
Rescue, fair lord, or else the day is lost!
(*Alarums. Enter* KING RICHARD)
KING RICHARD: A horse! a horse! my kingdom for a horse!
CATESBY: Withdraw, my lord; I'll help you to a horse.
KING RICHARD: Slave, I have set my life upon a cast,
And I will stand the hazard of the die.
I think there be six Richmonds in the field;
Five have I slain to-day instead of him.
A horse! a horse! my kingdom for a horse!   [*Exeunt.*]
Another part of the field.
Alarum. Enter KING RICHARD *and* RICHMOND; *they fight.* RICHARD *is*
slain. Retreat and flourish. Re-enter RICHMOND, DERBY *bearing the*
crown, with divers other Lords.

RICHMOND: God and your arms be praised, victorious
friends!
The day is ours; the bloody dog is dead.
DERBY: Courageous Richmond, well hast thou acquit thee.
Lo, here, this long usurped royalty
From the dead temples of this bloody wretch
Have I pluck'd off, to grace thy brows withal;
Wear it, enjoy it, and make much of it.

*

RICHMOND: O now, let Richmond and Elizabeth,
The true succeeders of each royal house,
By God's fair ordinance conjoin together;
And let their heirs, (God, if thy will be so,)
Enrich the time to come with smooth-faced peace,
With smiling plenty, and fair prosperous days;
Now civil wounds are stopp'd, peace lives again:
That she may long live here, God say – Amen.
                                              [*Exeunt.*]

William Shakespeare

Richard was feared and detested by many of the noble families. In August 1485 Henry Tudor, Earl of Richmond, landed at Milford Haven, and within three weeks was King. The decisive factors in Richard's defeat at Bosworth were the inertia of the Earl of Northumberland, who failed to appear, and the treachery of the Stanley family who, in spite of having been handsomely rewarded by Richard, switched their allegiance to Henry. So ended Richard III's reign. Some historians have tried to restore his good name, but it's no easy match to take on Shakespeare.

THE TUDORS

King Henry VII, 1485–1509

THE TUDOR ROSE

'I loue the rose both red & white.'
'Is that your pure perfite appetite?'
'To here talke of them is my delite!'
'Ioyed may we be,
oure prince to se,
& rosys thre!'

Anonymous

Henry Tudor, of the red rose of Lancaster, married Elizabeth, daughter of Edward IV, of the white rose of York, and thereby brought the dynastic Wars of the Roses to an end. The resulting hybrid, the Tudor rose, the third alluded to here, was personified in the figure of Arthur, Henry's heir, who, however, died young, leaving the succession to his brother, Henry VIII.

1491

THE DEATH OF CAXTON

Fiat Lux

Thy prayer was 'Light – more Light – while Time shall last!'
Thou sawest a glory growing on the night,
But not the shadows which that light would cast,
Till shadows vanish in the Light of Light.

Alfred, Lord Tennyson

William Caxton had been a merchant and a diplomat, but in 1476, after his retirement, he set up a printing press in the precincts of Westminster Abbey, the first in the country. There he printed works by Chaucer, Lydgate, Gower and Malory, and anything else he thought he could sell. By adopting the spelling that was common in London, he helped to regularize that of the whole English language. The invention of printing had a revolutionary effect on communications. Hitherto the business of scholarship had been a monopoly of the clergy, by whom it was jealously guarded as being the main source of their influence and power. Now it was to be available to anyone. Tennyson wrote this epitaph for Caxton's tomb in St Margaret's, Westminster.

King Henry VIII, 1509–47

HENRY'S WIVES

Divorced, beheaded, died,
Divorced, beheaded, survived.

Anonymous

This simple mnemonic describes the fate of each of the six wives of Henry VIII: Catherine of Aragon, Anne Boleyn, Jane Seymour, Anne of Cleves, Catherine Howard and Catherine Parr.

c. 1510

A TUDOR TEXTILE FACTORY

from **The Pleasant History of Jack of Newbury**

Within one roome, being large and long
There stood two hundred Loomes full strong.
Two hundred men, the truth is so,
Wrought in the Loomes all in a row.
By every one a pretty boy
Sate making quilts with mickle joy,
And in another place hard by
A hundred women merrily
Were carding hard with joyful cheere
Who singing sate with voyces cleere,
And in a chamber close beside
Two hundred maidens did abide,
In petticoats of Stammell red,
And milk white kerchiefs on their head.
Their smocke-sleeves like to winter snow
That on the Westerne mountaines flow,
And each sleeve with a silken band
Was featly tied at the hand.
These pretty maids did never lin
But in that place all day did spin,
And spinning so with voyces meet
Like nightingales they sang full sweet.
Then to another roome, came they
Where children were in poore aray;
And every one sate picking wool
The finest from the course to cull:
The number was sevenscore and ten
The children of poore silly men:
And these their labours to requite
Had every one a penny at night,
Beside their meat and drinke all day,
Which was to them a wondrous stay.
Within another place likewise

Full fifty proper men he spies
And these were sheremen everyone,
Whose skill and cunning there was showne:
And hard by them there did remaine
Full four-score rowers taking paine.
A Dye-house likewise had he then,
Wherein he kept full forty men:
And likewise in his Fulling Mill
Full twenty persons kept he still.

Thomas Deloney

Deloney's poem was written in 1597 and achieved great popularity. It celebrates a legendary figure of the Tudor cloth industry, John Winchcombe, who lived in the reign of Henry VIII and, among other things, led one hundred of his apprentices into battle at Flodden Field in 1513. The manufacture of cloth was the major economic activity of Tudor England. In the Middle Ages the various processes involved in the making of cloth were organized by separate guilds. In the sixteenth century, however, rich merchants began the practice of gathering the various trades under a single roof, while weavers regularly petitioned Parliament against this early manifestation of capitalism.

1515–29

CARDINAL WOLSEY'S ASCENDANCY

from **Why Come Ye not to Courte?**

To tell the truth plainly
He is so ambitious,
So shameless and so vicious,
And so superstitious
And so much oblivious
From whence that he came
That he falleth into a *caeciam*
Which, truly to express,
Is a forgetfulness,
Or wilful blindness.

*

Howbeit the primordial
Of his wretched original
And his base progeny
And his greasy genealogy
He came of the sang royall
That was cast out of a butcher's stall.

*

Such is a kinges power
To make within an hour
And work such a miracle
That shall be a spectacle
Of renown and wordly fame.
In likewise now the same
Cardinal is promoted,
Yet with lewd conditions coated
As hereafter ben noted,
Presumption and vainglory,
Envy, wrath, and lechery,
Couvetise and gluttony,
Slothful to do good,
Now frantic, now starke wood.

Set up a wretch on high
In a throne triumphantly,
Make him a great estate
And he will play checkmate
With royal majesty.

John Skelton

The son of an Ipswich butcher, Thomas Wolsey more or less ran the
country in the early years of Henry's reign. As a Cardinal, Archbishop
of York, and Lord Chancellor of England, he lived in sumptuous style,
the envy of the nobility and, eventually, of the King himself. He dined
off gold plate, had his red hat carried before him, and built Hampton
Court; but he failed, when required, to obtain for his master a divorce
from Catherine of Aragon. He fell from grace and was arrested, but
died while being taken to be tried in London.

1518

THE FRENCH FASHION OF THE ENGLISH GALLANT

He struts about
In cloaks of fashion French. His girdle, purse,
And sword are French. His hat is French.
His nether limbs are cased in French costume.
His shoes are French. In short, from top to toe
He stands the Frenchman.

*

With accent French he speaks the Latin tongue,
With accent French the tongue of Lombardy,
To Spanish words he gives an accent French,
German he speaks with his same accent French,
In truth he seems to speak with accent French,
All but the French itself. The French he speaks
With accent British.

translated from the Latin of Thomas More

Henry VIII admired French clothes and French manners, and he made
French the language of his courtiers. Thomas More, in a Latin poem,
pointed out the spuriousness of this attempted conversion, all the more
untimely when the national consciousness of England was being
formed through the break from Rome, and William Tyndale was about
to start his translation of the Bible into English.

c. 1520

TUDOR FOOTBALL

Eche time and season hath his delite and joyes,
Loke in the stretes, behold the little boyes,
Howe in fruite season for joy they sing and hop,
In Lent is each one full busy with his top
And nowe in winter for all the greevous colde
All rent and ragged a man may them beholde,
They have great pleasour supposing well to dine,
When men be busied in killing of fat swine,
They get the bladder and blowe it great and thin,
With many beanes or peason put within,
It ratleth, soundeth, and shineth clere and fayre,
While it is throwen and caste up in the ayre,
Eche one contendeth and hath a great delite
With foote and with hande the bladder for to smite,
If it fall to grounde, they lifte it up agayne,
This wise to labour they count it for no payne,
Renning and leaping they drive away the colde,
The sturdie plowmen lustie, strong and bolde
Ouercommeth the winter with driving the foote-ball,
Forgetting labour and many a grevous fall.

Alexander Barclay

THE KING'S PLEASURES

The Hunt is Up

The hunt is up, the hunt is up,
And it is well nigh day;
And Harry our King is gone hunting
To bring his deer to bay.

The east is bright with morning light,
And darkness it is fled,
The merry horn wakes up the morn
To leave his idle bed.

The horses snort to be at the sport,
The dogs are running free,
The woods rejoice at the merry noise
Of hay-taranta-tee-ree.

The sun is glad to see us clad
All in our lusty green,
And smiles in the sky as he rideth high
To see and to be seen.

Awake all men, I say again
Be merry as you may:
For Harry our king is gone hunting
To bring his deer to bay.

Anonymous

The most extrovert of English kings, Henry VIII, threw himself into vigorous physical activity of all kinds. The chronicler Edward Hall notes that, during a royal progress in 1511, the King indulged 'in shooting, singing, dancing, wrestling, casting the bar, playing at the recorders, flute and virginals, and in setting of songs and making of ballads, and did set two godly masses'. He spent many days of his life in the saddle. In 1524 he was almost killed in a joust with the Duke of Suffolk because

he had refused to put his visor down. In the next year, while out
hawking – his favourite pastime – he tried to leap over a ditch with a
pole, but fell into the mud head first and was only just saved from
drowning. In 1536, at the age of forty-four, he was unseated in a joust
and lay unconscious for two hours after his horse had rolled over him.
But the big, heavy, old body withstood all this, and even managed to
survive that most dreadful thing, Tudor medicine, until Henry's fifty-
fifth year.

1529

THE FALL OF WOLSEY

from King Henry the Eighth

ACT III *Scene II*
Antechamber to the KING's *Apartment*.
CARDINAL WOLSEY: . . . I have ventur'd,
Like little wanton boys that swim on bladders,
This many summers in a sea of glory;
But far beyond my depth: my high-blown pride
At length broke under me; and now has left me,
Weary and old with service, to the mercy
Of a rude stream, that must for ever hide me.
Vain pomp and glory of this world, I hate ye!
I feel my heart new open'd. O, how wretched
Is that poor man that hangs on princes' favours!
There is, betwixt that smile we would aspire to,
That sweet aspéct of princes, and their ruin,
More pangs and fears than wars or women have;
And when he falls, he falls like Lucifer,
Never to hope again.

*

WOLSEY: (*To* CROMWELL) . . . Serve the king;
And, – pr'ythee, lead me in:
There take an inventory of all I have;
To the last penny, 't is the king's: my robe,
And my integrity to heaven, is all
I dare now call mine own. O Cromwell, Cromwell!
Had I but serv'd my God with half the zeal
I serv'd my king, he would not in mine age
Have left me naked to mine enemies.

William Shakespeare

1533

THE RISE OF CRANMER

Cranmer

Cranmer was parson of this parish
And said Our Father beside barns
Where my grandfather worked without praying.

From the valley came the ring of metal
And the horses clopped down the track by the stream
As my mother saw them.

The Wiltshire voices floated up to him
How should they not overcome his proud Latin
With We depart answering his *Nunc Dimittis*?

One evening he came over the hillock
To the edge of the churchyard already filled with bones
And saw in the smithy his own fire burning.

C. H. Sisson

Thomas Cranmer's studies for the priesthood at Cambridge were inter-
rupted by his marriage to an innkeeper's daughter, who later died.
During the 1520s he was associated with scholars who were ques-
tioning the supremacy and infallibility of the Pope. He was used by
Henry VIII in the matter of his first divorce and in 1533 he was
appointed Archbishop of Canterbury. It was he, in effect, who founded
the Church of England, establishing the Bible in English, translating the
Prayer Book himself, and promulgating the Thirty-nine Articles. On the
death of Edward VI he foolishly supported Lady Jane Grey and was
condemned for treason. Mary wanted to punish him for heresy and he
was duly convicted, but under duress he recanted and this was seen as
a great triumph for Catholicism. Though it did not save him from the
stake, he finally regained his courage, renounced his recantation and,
approaching the flames that were to consume him, thrust in first the
hand which had signed it.

1535

THE EXECUTION OF SIR THOMAS MORE

Sir Thomas More

Holbein's More, my patron saint as a convert,
the gold chain of S's, the golden rose,
the plush cap, the brow's damp feathertips of hair,
the good eyes' stern, facetious twinkle, ready
to turn from executioner to martyr –
or saunter with the great King's bluff arm on your neck,
feeling that friend-slaying, terror-dazzled heart
balooning off into its awful dream –
a noble saying, 'How the King must love you!'
And you, 'If it were a question of my head,
or losing his meanest village in France . . .'
then by the scaffold and the headsman's axe –
'Friend, give me your hand for the first step,
as for coming down, I'll shift for myself.'

Robert Lowell

Thomas More was a true Renaissance man – a scholar, a poet, a philosopher, a Member of Parliament and a diplomat. He succeeded Wolsey as Lord Chancellor in 1529, but resigned the post in 1532. In 1534 he refused to take the oath asserting Henry VIII's supremacy over the Pope and legitimizing his divorce from Catherine of Aragon. More knew that this refusal to compromise his principles would cost him his life, and it did.

1536

THE DEATH OF ANNE BOLEYN

As for them all I do not thus lament,
But as of right my reason doth me bind;
But as the most doth all their deaths repent,
Even so do I by force of mourning mind.
Some say, 'Rochford, haddest thou been not so proud,
For thy great wit each man would thee bemoan,
Since as it is so, many cry aloud
It is great loss that thou art dead and gone.'

Ah! Norris, Norris, my tears begin to run
To think what hap did thee so lead or guide
Whereby thou hast both thee and thine undone
That is bewailed in court of every side;
In place also where thou hast never been
Both man and child doth piteously thee moan.
They say, 'Alas, thou art far overseen
By thine offences to be thus dead and gone.'

Ah! Weston, Weston, that pleasant was and young,
In active things who might with thee compare?
All words accept that thou diddest speak with tongue,
So well esteemed with each where thou diddest fare.

And we that now in court doth lead our life
Most part in mind doth thee lament and moan;
But that thy faults we daily hear so rife,
All we should weep that thou are dead and gone.

*

Ah! Mark, what moan should I for thee make more,
Since that thy death thou hast deserved best,
Save only that mine eye is forced sore
With piteous plaint to moan thee with the rest?
A time thou haddest above thy poor degree,
The fall whereof thy friends may well bemoan:
A rotten twig upon so high a tree
Hath slipped thy hold, and thou art dead and gone.

And thus farewell each one in hearty wise!
The axe is home, your heads be in the street;
The trickling tears doth fall so from my eyes
I scarce may write, my paper is so wet.
But what can hope when death hath played his part,
Though nature's course will thus lament and moan?
Leave sobs therefore, and every Christian heart
Pray for the souls of those be dead and gone.

attributed to Thomas Wyatt

A FINAL WORD FROM HER OWN BOOK OF HOURS

Remember me when you do pray,
That hope doth lead from day to day.

Anne Boleyn

In 1525 Henry became infatuated with one of the Ladies of the Court, Anne Boleyn. She was beautiful, ambitious and resolute. In 1529 she played an important role in the downfall of Wolsey. Henry showered her with gifts and she went out riding and hunting with him. Around 1531 they started to sleep together and in 1532 she found herself pregnant. Henry, in the mean time, had proclaimed himself the head of the Church in England, and arranged for his divorce from Catherine. He married Anne secretly in January, 1533; her coronation took place in June; and in September she gave birth to a daughter, Elizabeth, who was to prove the most notable Queen in English history.

Henry, however, wanted a son to secure the stability of his succession. Anne suffered a miscarriage in 1534, and again in 1536. But already the King's eye had alighted on another Lady of the Court, Jane Seymour. Anne's position grew increasingly isolated. Henry's chief minister, Thomas Cromwell, divined his master's wish that she must go, either by divorce or by some other means. At Easter in 1536 Henry and Anne quarrelled in public and Cromwell decided to act. Within four weeks Anne was arrested, tried, executed and buried in the Tower. The charges brought against her included incest with her brother Rochford, and adultery with the various courtiers named in the poem which is attributed to Thomas Wyatt. Wyatt himself was arrested on the grounds that he had been Anne's lover before her marriage, but he was later released.

Cromwell manufactured whatever evidence he needed, and rigged the juries. Anne may have been flirtatious, but it is unlikely that she was so rash as to have actively deceived Henry. The coup against her worked because she had so many enemies – the friends of Mary Tudor, of the late Thomas More, and of the up-and-coming Seymours. But her greatest enemy was no doubt the King himself, who had grown bored with her and was able to exploit the services of Cromwell, one of the most efficient civil servants of the Tudor period. Anne did not have a chance.

She was executed on 19 May. On the next day Henry was betrothed to Jane Seymour, and on 30 May they were married.

1537

THE DEATH OF QUEEN JANE

Queen Jane was in travail
For six weeks or more,
Till the women grew tired,
And fain would give o'er.
'O women! O women!
Good wives if ye be,
Go, send for King Henrie,
And bring him to me.'

King Henrie was sent for,
He came with all speed,
In a gownd of green velvet
From heel to the head.
'King Henrie! King Henrie!
If kind Henrie you be,
Send for a surgeon,
And bring him to me.'

The surgeon was sent for,
He came with all speed,
In a gownd of black velvet
From heel to the head.
He gave her rich caudle,
But the death-sleep slept she.
Then her right side was opened,
And the babe was set free.

The babe it was christened,
And put out and nursed,
While the royal Queen Jane
She lay cold in the dust.

*

So black was the mourning,
And white were the wands,
Yellow, yellow the torches,
They bore in their hands.
The bells they were muffled,
And mournful did play,
While the royal Queen Jane
She lay cold in the clay.

Six knights and six lords
Bore her corpse through the grounds;
Six dukes followed after,
In black mourning gownds.
The flower of Old England
Was laid in cold clay,
Whilst the royal King Henrie
Came weeping away.

Anonymous

Historically speaking, this poem is quite inaccurate. In October of the
year in question, Henry and Jane were separated by the outbreak of
plague and Jane was without the King's company when her son
Edward was born by Caesarean section. Nor did she die in childbirth.
She lived for a further twelve days, and Cromwell blamed her death on
the Queen's attendants who, he said, 'had suffered her to take great
cold and to eat things her fantasy called for'. At last Henry had a
legitimate son. Jane had done her duty and could be laid to rest. He
paid her the compliment of remaining single for two years, but he soon
tired of the role of widower.

1539

THE DISSOLUTION OF THE MONASTERIES

Little Jack Horner
Sat in the corner,
Eating a Christmas pie;
He put in his thumb,
And pulled out a plum,
And said, What a good boy am I!

Anonymous

According to one interpretation of this otherwise puzzling nursery
rhyme, Jack Horner was steward to the last Abbot of Glastonbury.
Hoping to appease Henry VIII's insatiable greed for Church property,
at a time when the King was presiding over the wholesale dissolution
of old monastic institutions, the Abbot sent Jack to London with a pie in
which the title deeds of twelve manors were concealed. On the way,
Jack opened the pie and extracted the title deed to the manor of Mells.
The Horner family did in fact acquire the manor of Mells at the time of
the Dissolution, but always claimed that the title was fairly bought.

THE ACHIEVEMENTS OF HENRY VIII

As I walked alone
and mused on things,
That have in my time
been done by great kings,
I bethought me of abbeys
that sometime I saw,
Which are now suppressed
all by a law.
O Lord, (thought I then)
what occasion was here
To provide for learning
and make poverty clear.
The lands and the jewels
that hereby were had
Would have found godly preachers
which might well have led
The people aright
that now go astray
And have fed the poor
that famish every day.

Robert Crowley

Opinions on Henry VIII are sharply divided. His defenders argue that he created the Church of England, built up the power of Parliament as the agent of his Protestant Reformation, made England a force to be reckoned with in European politics, established a strong monarchy, and encouraged the arts. His detractors point out that he pillaged the monasteries to pay off the nobility and his own supporters, and that he was vain, greedy, cruel, lecherous, self-pitying, and treacherous to his friends and ministers. The more one reads about him, indeed, the less attractive does he appear. Dickens was unequivocal: 'The plain truth is, that he was a most intolerable ruffian, a disgrace to human nature, and a blot of blood and grease upon the History of England.'

King Edward VI, 1547–53

EDWARD VI'S SHILLING

About my circle, I a Posie have
The title God unto the King first gave.
The circle that encompasseth my face
Declares my Soveraigne's title, by God's grace.

*

You see my face is beardless, smoothe and plaine.
Because my soveraigne was a child 'tis knowne
When as he did put on the English Crowne.
But had my stamp been bearded, as with haire,
Long before this it had beene worne and bare.
For why? With me the unthrifts every day,
With my face downwards do at shove-board play . . .

John Taylor

The shillings of Henry VIII had become clipped and debased. Edward VI issued new ones, which proved very popular until they too became debased. Pistol in *The Merry Wives of Windsor* confirms what we are told by the seventeenth-century poet John Taylor, that they were widely used in the game of shove halfpenny.

1549

Kett's Rebellion

On Mousehold Heath they gathered
Kett's ragtail army, 30,000 peasants.
Below them the city of Norwich
trembled, a mirage in the summer heat.
Mayor Codd and his burgesses
flapping like chickens overcircled by a hawk
sent deputies bowing up the hillside
to bargain for time with bread and meat,
meanwhile sunk their valuables in wells
and out of a secret gate
sped messengers to London squawking for help
against Kett 'that Captain of Mischief'
and his 'parcel of vagabonds . . . brute beasts.'

For six weeks up on Mousehold Heath they sat
high on heather, sky and hope.
"Twas a merry world when we were yonder
eating of mutton' one would look back.
The sun poured down like honey

and there was work for work-shaped hands, –
stakes to be sharpened, trenches to be dug,
a New Jerusalem of turf thrown up.
Hacking down the hated fences
and rounding up gentry was for sport.
Meanwhile the Dreamer under the Oak
wrote these words with the tip of his tongue:
'We desire that Bondmen may be free
as Christ made all free, His precious blood shedding.'
The sentries lay back on cupped palms.
Crickets in the dry grass wound their watch.
City-men crawled like ants.
Clouds coasted round the edge . . .

'The country gnoffs, Hob, Dick, and Hick
With clubs and clouted shoon
Shall fill the Vale of Dussindale
With slaughtered bodies soon.'

August 27th, 1549.
A long black cloud against the blood-red sunrise
Warwick and his mounted Landsknechts showed up.
One puff of their cannon
took the skull of Mousehold Heath clean off.
Then down the hill they tumbled
with their pitchforks, their birdslings, their billhooks.
They had no chance, – less
than rabbits making a run for it
when the combine rips into the last patch
and the Guns stand by, about to make laconic remarks.
So they laid themselves down, ripe for sacrifice,
till the brook got tired of undertaking
and Dussindale was bloodily fulfilled.
Kett, found shivering in a barn,
was dragged through the city in ankle-chains
then hung upside down from the castle wall, –
they made fun of Death in those days.

Then Mayor Codd called for a Thanksgiving Mass
followed by feasting in the streets.
While many a poor cottage-woman
waiting for her menfolk to come back
heard tapping on the shutters that night
but it was handfuls of rain.

Keith Chandler

During Edward VI's troubled reign there were risings in the West Country against the Reformation, and in Norfolk against the enclosing of land by capitalist farmers. Kett was a well-off East Anglian tanner; but he put himself at the head of what was in effect a peasants' revolt that posed a major threat to local shire governors. His ragged army captured Norwich. This was the only act of rebellion in the whole of the Tudor period to have social aims – the lowering of rents and the abolition of bond men, game laws and enclosures. The regency government saw it as a serious challenge to the stability of the realm and it was suppressed mercilessly, German mercenaries being used to kill 3,000 of those involved. A further 300 were hanged, for Tudor justice was not tempered by leniency.

Mary Tudor, 1553–8

from **Lady Jane Grey**

An apartment in the Castle of Framlingham.
(*enter* QUEEN MARY, *with a prayer-book in her hand, like a nun.*)
MARY: Thus like a nun, not like a princess born,
Descended from the royal Henry's loins,
Live I environ'd in a house of stone.
My brother Edward lives in pomp and state;
I in a mansion here all ruinate.
Their rich attire, delicious banqueting,
Their several pleasures, all their pride and honour,
I have forsaken for a rich prayer-book.
The golden mines of wealthy India
Are all as dross comparèd to thy sweetness:
Thou art the joy and comfort of the poor;
The everlasting bliss in thee we find.
This little volume enclosèd in this hand,
Is richer than the empire of this land.

John Webster

When Edward VI died, the Duke of Northumberland tried to place his daughter-in-law, Lady Jane Grey, upon the throne, but the country rallied to Mary Tudor, Henry VIII's elder daughter and, according to his will, the rightful heir. Mary married Philip II of Spain, eleven years her junior, and their child was expected to inherit England, Burgundy and the Netherlands.

MARY AND PHILIP

Still amorous, and fond, and billing,
Like Philip and Mary on a shilling.

Samuel Butler

from The Alchemist

FACE: Have you provided for her grace's servants?
DAPPER: Yes, here are six score Edward shillings.
FACE: Good!
DAPPER: And an old Harry's sovereign.
FACE: Very good!
DAPPER: And three James shillings, and an Elizabeth groat. Just twenty nobles.
FACE: O, you are too just. I would you had had the other noble in Maries.
DAPPER: I have some Philip and Maries.
FACE: Ay, those same are best of all: where are they?

Ben Jonson

After Mary's marriage to Philip, coins were struck showing husband and wife facing each other. The inscription around the rim declared that Philip was not only King of England, but also King of Naples and Prince of Spain. On the reverse, the arms of England were matched by those of the House of Habsburg. But this so alarmed people that new coins were quickly struck, simply recording that Philip was the King of England – a country he visited only twice.

1554

ELIZABETH'S IMPRISONMENT

Oh, Fortune! how thy restlesse wavering state
Hath fraught with cares my troubled witt!
Witnes this present prisonn, wither fate
   Could beare me, and the joys I quit.
Thus causedst the guiltie to be losed
From bandes, wherein are innocents inclosed:
   Causing the guiltíes to be straite reserved.
   And freeing those that death hath well deserved.
But by her envie can be nothing wroughte,
So God send to my foes all they have thoughte.

Elizabeth I

In 1554 Mary's sister, Elizabeth, was imprisoned after the discovery of a plot to overthrow the Queen, who would also have liked to debar her from succession to the throne. Living throughout Mary's reign under the shadow of the scaffold, Elizabeth devoted herself to her studies and was to become one of the most learned of England's monarchs, able to address universities in Latin and ambassadors in their own tongues.

THE PROTESTANT MARTYRS

The Martyrdom of Bishop Farrar

Burned by Bloody Mary's men at Caermarthen. 'If I flinch from the pain of the burning, believe not the doctrine that I have preached.' (His words on being chained to the stake.)

Bloody Mary's venomous flames can curl;
They can shrivel sinew and char bone
Of foot, ankle, knee, and thigh, and boil
Bowels, and drop his heart a cinder down;
And her soldiers can cry, as they hurl
Logs in the red rush: 'This is her sermon.'

The sullen-jowled watching Welsh townspeople
Hear him crack in the fire's mouth; they see what
Black oozing twist of stuff bubbles the smell
That tars and retches their lungs: no pulpit
Of his ever held their eyes so still,
Never, as now his agony, his wit.

An ignorant means to establish ownership
Of his flock! Thus their shepherd she seized
And knotted him into this blazing shape
In their eyes, as if such could have cauterized
The trust they turned towards him, and branded on
Its stump her claim, to outlaw question.

So it might have been: seeing their exemplar
And teacher burned for his lessons to black bits,
Their silence might have disowned him to her,
And hung up what he had taught with their Welsh hats:
Who sees his blasphemous father struck by fire
From heaven, might well be heard to speak no oaths.

But the fire that struck here, come from Hell even,
Kindled little heavens in his words
As he fed his body to the flame alive.
Words which, before they will be dumbly spared,
Will burn their body and be tongued with fire
Make paltry folly of flesh and this world's air.

When they saw what annuities of hours
And comfortable blood he burned to get
His words a bare honouring in their ears,
The shrewd townsfolk pocketed them hot:
Stamp was not current but they rang and shone
As good gold as any queen's crown.

Gave all he had, and yet the bargain struck
To a merest farthing his whole agony,
His body's cold-kept miserdom of shrieks
He gave uncounted, while out of his eyes,
Out of his mouth, fire like a glory broke,
And smoke burned his sermons into the skies.

Ted Hughes

from The Register of the Martyrs

1555
February
    When raging reign of tyrants stout,
Causeless, did cruelly conspire
To rend and root the simple out,
With furious force of sword and fire;
When man and wife were put to death:
    We wished for our Queen ELIZABETH.

February
4   When ROGERS ruefully was brent;
8   When SAUNDERS did the like sustain;
     When faithful FARRAR forth was sent
     His life to lose, with grievous pain;
22   When constant HOOPER died the death:
      We wished for our ELIZABETH.

*

October
     When learned RIDLEY, and LATIMER,
16   Without regard, were swiftly slain;
     When furious foes could not confer
     But with revenge and mortal pain.
     When these two Fathers were put to death:
      We wished for our ELIZABETH.

*

1556
February
     When two women in Ipswich town,
19   Joyfully did the fire embrace;
     When they sang out with cheerful sound,
     Their fixed foes for to deface;
     When NORWICH NO-BODY put them to death,
      We wished for our ELIZABETH.

March
12   When constant CRANMER lost his life
     And held his hand into the fire;
     When streams of tears for him were rife
     And yet did miss their just desire:
     When Popish power put him to death,
      We wished for our ELIZABETH.

*

1557
July
2   When GEORGE EGLES, at Chelmsford town,
     Was hanged, drawn, and quarterèd;
     His quarters carried up and down,
     And on a pole they set his head.
     When wrestèd law put him to death,
      We wished for our ELIZABETH.

*

1558
November

5 When JOHN DAVY, and eke his brother,
5 With PHILIP HUMFREY kissed the cross;
When they did comfort one another
Against all fear, and worldly loss;
When these, at Bury, were put to death,
 We wished for our ELIZABETH.

November

When, last of all (to take their leave!),
At Canterbury, they did some consume,
Who constantly to CHRIST did cleave;
Therefore were fried with fiery fume:
But, six days after these were put to death,
 GOD sent us our ELIZABETH!

Our wished wealth hath brought us peace.
Our joy is full; our hope obtained;
The blazing brands of fire do cease,
The slaying sword also restrained.
The simple sheep, preserved from death
 By our good Queen, ELIZABETH.

Thomas Bright

Mary was determined to restore England to the Catholic faith, and she got Parliament to revive the medieval heresy laws which would enable Protestants to be rooted out and saved from eternal perdition by being burned in this world rather than the next. In 1555 seventy condemned heretics were burned at the stake, and by the end of Mary's reign the total had exceeded 300. The victims included the bishops Ridley and Latimer, who died in the town ditch at Oxford, and Thomas Cranmer. Such a programme of persecution was politically disastrous, and from it sprang one of the great works of Protestant literature, Foxe's *Book of Martyrs*. When, in 1558, France waged war on Spain, the last British possession on the Continent, Calais, was lost. Mary died with the name 'Calais' supposedly engraved on her heart, and her subjects celebrated her passing with bonfires in the streets of London.

1558

THE DEATH OF MARY TUDOR

Cruel Behold my Heavy Ending

Goodnight is Queen Mary's death:
a lute that bore her heavy end
through city-prisoning towers
and martyrs' candles.

Without her father's desperate gaiety
she clung to confessors
and watched the ghost of a dog
flung through her window at night
ear-clipped
howling the hanging of priests.

Then the lute resolved
the tragic cadence unfulfilled
and the Queen merciful
in all matters but religion
heard the flame of Latimer's cry
and died.

Peter Jones

Queen Elizabeth I, 1558–1603

LORD BURGHLEY

To Mistress Anne Cecil, upon Making Her a New Year's Gift

As years do grow, so cares increase;
 And time will move to look to thrift!
Though years in me work nothing less;
 Yet, for your years, and New Year's gift,
 This housewife's toy is now my shift!
  To set you on work, some thrift to feel;
  I send you now a Spinning Wheel!

But one thing first, I wish and pray,
 Lest thirst of thrift might soon you tire,
Only to spin one pound a day;
 And play the rest, as time require!
 Sweat not! (O, fie!) fling rock in fire!
  God send, who sendeth all thrift and wealth,
  You, long years; and your father health!

William Cecil, Lord Burghley

William Cecil was Elizabeth's intimately trusted chief minister and he provided the solid core of government for most of her long reign. His successor in this role was his son, Robert, who served both Elizabeth and James I. As this poem indicates, he could also, in common with many other public figures of the time, turn his hand to versification.

1569

THE NORTHERN REBELLION

The Daughter of Debate

The doubt of future foes exiles my present joy,
And Wit me warns to shun such snares as threaten my annoy,
For falsehood now doth flow, and subjects' faith doth ebb
Which would not be if Reason ruled, or Wisdom move the web,
But clouds of toys untried to cloak aspiring minds,
Which turn to rain of late repent by course of changed winds.
The top of hope supposed, the root of ruth will be,
And fruitless all their grafted guiles, as ye shall shortly see.
Those dazzled eyes with pride, which great ambition blinds,
Shall be unsealed by worthy wights, whose foresight falsehood
    blinds.
The daughter of debate, that eke discord doth sow,
Shall reap no gain where former rule hath taught still peace to
    grow.
No foreign banish'd wight shall anchor in this port;
Our realm it brooks no stranger's force, let them elsewhere
    resort;
Our rusty sword, with rest, shall first his edge employ,
To poll their tops that seek such change, and gape for joy.

Elizabeth I

In 1569 the Northern Earls, Westmorland and Northumberland, tried to raise the North in the Catholic cause. Their figurehead was Mary Stuart, Queen of Scots, whom they planned to marry to Elizabeth's cousin, the Duke of Norfolk. They took the city of Durham and said Mass there, but in the cold winter months that followed, the spirit of revolt petered out and the rebels fled to Scotland. The vast estates which they left behind were divided among those who had remained loyal to Elizabeth. She had survived the most dangerous threat to her sovereignty and she celebrated by writing this poem.

1583

Sir Humphrey Gilbert

Southward with fleet of ice
  Sailed the corsair Death;
Wild and fast blew the blast,
  And the east-wind was his breath.

His lordly ships of ice
  Glisten in the sun;
On each side, like pennons wide,
  Flashing crystal streamlets run.

His sails of white sea-mist
  Dripped with silver rain;
But where he passed there were cast
  Leaden shadows o'er the main.

Eastward from Campobello
  Sir Humphrey Gilbert sailed;
Three days or more seaward he bore,
  Then, alas! the land-wind failed.

Alas! the land-wind failed,
  And ice-cold grew the night;
And never more, on sea or shore,
  Should Sir Humphrey see the light.

He sat upon the deck,
  The Book was in his hand:
'Do not fear! Heaven is as near,'
  He said, 'by water as by land!'

In the first watch of the night,
  Without a signal's sound,
Out of the sea, mysteriously,
  The fleet of Death rose all around.

The moon and the evening star
  Were hanging in the shrouds;
Every mast, as it passed,
  Seemed to rake the passing clouds.

They grappled with their prize,
  At midnight black and cold!
As of a rock was the shock;
  Heavily the ground-swell rolled.

Southward through day and dark
  They drift in close embrace,
With mist and rain o'er the open main;
  Yet there seems no change of place.

Southward, for ever southward,
  They drift through dark and day;
And like a dream, in the Gulf-Stream
  Sinking, vanish all away.

Henry Wadsworth Longfellow

Humphrey Gilbert was Sir Walter Ralegh's half-brother, and they journeyed together on voyages of discovery. In 1583 Gilbert established the first British colony in North America at Newfoundland. He published a treatise urging the discovery of the so-called North West Passage to the Indies and he perished looking for it.

1587

THE EXECUTION OF MARY, QUEEN OF SCOTS

Elizabeth Reflects on Hearing of Mary's Execution

She was my heir. Her severed head they say
    Was old and grey, and wigged: That Queen of France
And Scotland, who long dreamed to reign today
    On England's throne. Courage she had. Her dance

Led men to die: her death may lead still more.
    What was arranged is done. Our sorrow shows
Itself. Queens should not lightly die. The store
    And show of our distress may keep the throws

Of anguish fresh before all governments.
    What moves upon this news will Europe make?
Too many troops may strike their cantonments.
    And for ourselves? At least we must ask Drake

To fleece (with our support obscure) and bleed
Those ships by Spanish shore. Oh this land we lead!

John Loveridge

Alas! Poor Queen

She was skilled in music and the dance
And the old arts of love
At the court of the poisoned rose
And the perfumed glove,
And gave her beautiful hand
To the pale Dauphin
A triple crown to win –
And she loved little dogs
   And parrots
    And red-legged partridges
And the golden fishes of the Duc de Guise
And a pigeon with a blue ruff
She had from Monsieur d'Elbœuf.

Master John Knox was no friend to her;
She spoke him soft and kind,
Her honeyed words were Satan's lure
The unwary soul to bind.
'Good sir, doth a lissome shape
And a comely face
Offend your God His Grace
Whose Wisdom maketh these
Golden fishes of the Duc de Guise?'

She rode through Liddesdale with a song;
'Ye streams sae wondrous strang,
Oh, mak' me a wrack as I come back
But spare me as I gang.'
While a hill-bird cried and cried
Like a spirit lost
By the grey storm-wind tost.

Consider the way she had to go,
Think of the hungry snare,
The net she herself had woven,
Aware or unaware,
Of the dancing feet grown still,
The blinded eyes –
Queens should be cold and wise,
And she loved little things,
       Parrots
       And red-legged partridges
And the golden fishes of the Duc de Guise
And the pigeon with the blue ruff
She had from Monsieur d'Elbœuf.

Marion Angus

Mary Stuart was in fact Elizabeth's heir, but she was excluded from succession to the throne by the Act of Supremacy, passed in 1534. Elizabeth saw her as a constant threat none the less. Although kept in virtual imprisonment in England for almost the last twenty years of her life, she continued to inspire plots against the English Queen, and at last, on 1 February 1587, Elizabeth signed her death warrant. Mary was executed on 8 February and her son, James VI of Scotland, who had been brought up by Calvinists, in turn became Elizabeth's heir.

Mary, Mary, quite contrary,
How does your garden grow?
With silver bells and cockle shells,
And pretty maids all in a row.

Anonymous

The old nursery rhyme is supposed to be about Mary Stuart, the 'silver bells' alluding to those used in the Mass, the 'cockle shells' to the badge of St James of Compostela, worn by pilgrims, and the 'pretty maids' to the famous four Marys who attended the Queen of Scots.

THE PUBLIC EXECUTIONER

Portraits of Tudor Statesmen

Surviving is keeping your eyes open,
Controlling the twitchy apparatus
Of iris, white, cornea, lash and lid.

So the literal painter set it down –
The sharp raptorial look; strained eyeball;
And mail, ruff, bands, beard, anything, to hide
The violently vulnerable neck.

U. A. Fanthorpe

The Public Executioner was one of the busiest public servants in Tudor England. Three Queens were beheaded – Anne Boleyn, Catherine Howard and Mary, Queen of Scots – and one who aspired to be queen, Lady Jane Grey. Other victims were prominent statesmen such as Thomas More and Thomas Cromwell; bishops such as Cranmer, Latimer and Ridley; courtiers such as Surrey and Essex; and many thousands besides.

THE ELIZABETHAN ARMY

An Old Soldier of the Queen's

Of an old Soldier of the Queen's,
With an old motley coat, and a Malmsey nose,
And an old jerkin that's out at the elbows,
And an old pair of boots, drawn on without hose
Stuft with rags instead of toes;
    And an old Soldier of the Queen's,
    And the Queen's old Soldier.

With an old rusty sword that's hackt with blows,
And an old dagger to scare away the crows,
And an old horse that reels as he goes,
And an old saddle that no man knows,
 And an old Soldier of the Queen's,
 And the Queen's old Soldier.

With his old wounds in Eighty Eight,
Which he recover'd, at Tilbury fight;
With an old Passport that never was read,
That in his old travels stood him in great stead;
 And an old Soldier of the Queen's,
 And the Queen's old Soldier.

With his old gun, and his bandeliers,
And an old head-piece to keep warm his ears,
With an old shirt is grown to wrack,
With a huge louse, with a great list on his back,
Is able to carry a pedlar and his pack;
 And an old Soldier of the Queen's,
 And the Queen's old Soldier.

Anonymous

While Philip II of Spain did his best to stir up trouble in Scotland and among the English Catholics, Elizabeth had her eye on the Netherlands, which formed a crucial part of the Habsburg Empire. Her ingenious diplomacy was directed towards maintaining peace for England, at the same time as keeping France and Spain at loggerheads. She was able to play a significant part in European politics because her credit was good: she borrowed at between 8 and 9 per cent, while Philip was obliged to pay interest at 12 or even 18 per cent. In 1586, however, meaning to lend active support to the Protestants, she sent a military expedition to the Netherlands which ended in miserable failure. Her soldiers appear to have been as feeble as her sailors were brilliant.

SIR FRANCIS DRAKE

Drake's Drum

Drake he's in his hammock an' a thousand mile away,
    (Capten, art tha sleepin' there below?),
Slung atween the round shot in Nombre Dios Bay,
    An' dreamin' arl the time o' Plymouth Hoe.
Yarnder lumes the Island, yarnder lie the ships,
    Wi' sailor lads a dancin' heel-an'-toe,
An' the shore-lights flashin', an' the night-tide dashin',
    He sees et arl so plainly as he saw et long ago.

Drake he was a Devon man, an' rüled the Devon seas,
    (Capten, art tha sleepin' there below?),
Rovin' tho' his death fell, he went wi' heart at ease,
    An' dreamin' arl the time o' Plymouth Hoe.
'Take my drum to England, hang et by the shore,
    Strike et when your powder's runnin' low;
If the Dons sight Devon, I'll quit the port o' Heaven,
    An' drum them up the Channel as we drummed them long
        ago.'

Drake he's in his hammock till the great Armadas come,
    (Capten, art tha sleepin' there below?),
Slung atween the round shot, listenin' for the drum,
    An' dreamin' arl the time o' Plymouth Hoe.

Call him on the deep sea, call him up the Sound,
    Call him when ye sail to meet the foe;
Where the old trade's plyin' an' the old flag flyin'
    They shall find him ware an' wakin', as they found him long
        ago!

Henry Newbolt

Elizabethan seamen carried the English flag across the world. Ralegh settled Virginia as a colony of the Crown, Gilbert claimed Newfoundland, John Hawkins shipped slaves from Portuguese West Africa to the Caribbean, and English merchants searching for the North-East Passage to the Indies reached Moscow. In 1572 Francis Drake delivered a severe blow to England's major rival in foreign trade and colonial expansion, Spain, when at Nombre de Dios on the Panama isthmus he intercepted the Spanish mule convoy bearing silver from Peru. From 1577 to 1580 he sailed his ship, *The Golden Hind*, around the world and was knighted by the Queen on his return, Elizabeth being not only proud of her merchant adventurers, but also a shareholder in several of their expeditions. In 1587 Drake made a daring pre-emptive strike against the Spanish fleet where it lay in the harbour of Cadiz, and in 1588 he helped destroy the Armada as it sailed to invade England.

1588

THE SPANISH ARMADA

Our gracious Queen
    doth greet you everyone
And saith 'She will among you be
    in every bitter storm.
Desiring you
    true English hearts to bear
To God, to her, and to the land
    Wherein you nursèd were.'

Thomas Deloney

The Spanish Armada of 197 ships sailed up the English Channel with the intention of uniting with the Spanish army in the Netherlands and forming the great force that would invade England. The English army was drawn up at Tilbury to protect London. Elizabeth, putting on a metal breastplate, joined her troops there and delivered one of the most heroic speeches in English history, including the famous sentence: 'I know I have the body of a weak and feeble woman, but I have the heart and stomach of a King, and a King of England too.' The English admiral, Lord Howard, ordered fireships to be launched against the Spanish fleet, creating chaos, and by the end of the affair only thirty-four Spanish ships remained in commission.

The Armada

Attend, all ye who list to hear our noble England's praise;
I tell of the thrice famous deeds she wrought in ancient days,
When that great fleet invincible against her bore in vain
The richest spoils of Mexico, the stoutest hearts of Spain.

It was about the lovely close of a warm summer day,
There came a gallant merchant-ship full sail to Plymouth Bay;
Her crew hath seen Castile's black fleet, beyond Aurigny's isle,
At earliest twilight, on the waves lie heaving many a mile.
At sunrise she escaped their van, by God's especial grace;
And the tall Pinta, till the noon, had held her close in chase.
Forthwith a guard at every gun was placed along the wall;
The beacon blazed upon the roof of Edgecumbe's lofty hall;
Many a light fishing-bark put out to pry along the coast,
And with loose rein and bloody spur rode inland many a post.
With his white hair unbonneted, the stout old sheriff comes;
Behind him march the halberdiers; before him sound the drums;
His yeomen round the market cross make clear an ample space;
For there behoves him to set up the standard of Her Grace.
And haughtily the trumpets peal, and gaily dance the bells,
As slow upon the labouring wind the royal blazon swells.
Look how the Lion of the sea lifts up his ancient crown,
And underneath his deadly paw treads the gay lilies down.
So stalked he when he turned to flight, on that famed Picard field,
Bohemia's plume, and Genoa's bow, and Cæsar's eagle shield.
So glared he when at Agincourt in wrath he turned to bay,
And crushed and torn beneath his claws the princely hunters lay.
Ho! strike the flagstaff deep, sir Knight: ho! scatter flowers, fair
    maids:
Ho! gunners, fire a loud salute: ho! gallants, draw your blades:
Thou sun, shine on her joyously; ye breezes, waft her wide;

Our glorious SEMPER EADEM, the banner of our pride.

The freshening breeze of eve unfurled that banner's massy fold;
The parting gleam of sunshine kissed that haughty scroll of gold;
Night sank upon the dusky beach, and on the purple sea,
Such night in England ne'er had been, nor e'er again shall be.
From Eddystone to Berwick bounds, from Lynn to Milford Bay,
That time of slumber was as bright and busy as the day;
For swift to east and swift to west the ghastly war-flame spread,
High on St Michael's Mount it shone: it shone on Beachy Head.
Far on the deep the Spaniard saw, along each southern shire,
Cape beyond cape, in endless range, those twinkling points of fire.
The fisher left his skiff to rock on Tamar's glittering waves:
The rugged miners poured to war from Mendip's sunless caves:
O'er Longleat's towers, o'er Cranbourne's oaks, the fiery herald
    flew:
He roused the shepherds of Stonehenge, the rangers of Beaulieu.
Right sharp and quick the bells all night rang out from Bristol town,
And ere the day three hundred horse had met on Clifton down;
The sentinel on Whitehall gate looked forth into the night,
And saw o'erhanging Richmond Hill the streak of blood-red light.
Then bugle's note and cannon's roar the deathlike silence broke,
And with one start, and with one cry, the royal city woke.
At once on all her stately gates arose the answering fires;
At once the wild alarum clashed from all her reeling spires;
From all the batteries of the Tower pealed loud the voice of fear;
And all the thousand masts of Thames sent back a louder cheer:
And from the furthest wards was heard the rush of hurrying feet,
And the broad streams of pikes and flags rushed down each
    roaring street;
And broader still became the blaze, and louder still the din,
As fast from every village round the horse came spurring in:
And eastward straight from wild Blackheath the warlike errand
    went,
And roused in many an ancient hall the gallant squires of Kent.
Southward from Surrey's pleasant hills flew those bright couriers
    forth;
High on bleak Hampstead's swarthy moor they started for the
    north;
And on, and on, without a pause, untired they bounded still:

All night from tower to tower they sprang; they sprang from hill
  to hill:
Till the proud peak unfurled the flag o'er Darwin's rocky dales,
Till like volcanoes flared to heaven the stormy hills of Wales,
Till twelve fair counties saw the blaze on Malvern's lonely height,
Till streamed in crimson on the wind the Wrekin's crest of light.
Till broad and fierce the star came forth on Ely's stately fane,
And tower and hamlet rose in arms o'er all the boundless plain;
Till Belvoir's lordly terraces the sign to Lincoln sent,
And Lincoln sped the message on o'er the wide vale of Trent;
Till Skiddaw saw the fire that burned on Gaunt's embattled pile,
And the red glare on Skiddaw roused the burghers of Carlisle.

Thomas Babington, Lord Macaulay

THE EARL OF LEICESTER

Here lieth the worthy warrior
  Who never bloodied sword;
Here lieth the noble counsellor,
  Who never held his word.

Here lieth his Excellency,
  Who ruled all the state;
Here lieth the Earl of Leicester,
  Whom all the world did hate.

Anonymous

Robert Dudley, Earl of Leicester, was a handsome, proud and
ambitious man. He had witnessed his father's execution after the
attempt to place Lady Jane Grey on the throne and had only just been
reprieved from the same fate. Rumour accused him of having killed
his first wife, Amy Robsart, who in 1560 was found dead, with her neck
broken, at the bottom of a staircase in an empty house, Kenilworth.
Another rumour suggested that he had killed the husband of his
mistress and it was pointed out that the husband of his second wife had
died in mysterious circumstances. According to yet another rumour, he

used crushed pearls and amber as an aphrodisiac. What is certainly true is that he enraptured the Queen and, as her favourite, was forgiven almost all his mistakes. Not, however, his disastrous leadership of the Netherlands campaign in 1586. After his death in 1588, the Queen locked herself in her room for seven days until eventually the door had to be forced. When she died, a little ring-box covered with pearls was found beside her bed, and in it a letter from Leicester on which the Queen had written, 'His last letter'.

The Looking-Glass

(A Country Dance)

Queen Bess was Harry's daughter. Stand forward partners all!
  In ruff and stomacher and gown
She danced King Philip down-a-down,
And left her shoe to show 'twas true –
  (The very tune I'm playing you)
In Norgem at Brickwall!

The Queen was in her chamber, and she was middling old.
Her petticoat was satin, and her stomacher was gold.
Backwards and forwards and sideways did she pass,
Making up her mind to face the cruel looking-glass.
The cruel looking-glass that will never show a lass
As comely or as kindly or as young as what she was!

Queen Bess was Harry's daughter. Now hand your partners all!

The Queen was in her chamber, a-combing of her hair.
There came Queen Mary's spirit and It stood behind her chair,
Singing 'Backwards and forwards and sideways may you pass,
But I will stand behind you till you face the looking-glass.
The cruel looking-glass that will never show a lass
As lovely or unlucky or as lonely as I was!'

Queen Bess was Harry's daughter. Now turn your partners all!

The Queen was in her chamber, a-weeping very sore,
There came Lord Leicester's spirit and It scratched upon the
  door,
Singing 'Backwards and forwards and sideways may you pass,
But I will walk beside you till you face the looking-glass.
The cruel looking-glass that will never show a lass,
As hard and unforgiving or as wicked as you was!'

Queen Bess was Harry's daughter. Now kiss your partners all!

The Queen was in her chamber, her sins were on her head.
She looked the spirits up and down and statelily she said: –
'Backwards and forwards and sideways though I've been,
Yet I am Harry's daughter and I am England's Queen!'
And she faced the looking-glass (and whatever else there was)
And she saw her day was over and she saw her beauty pass
In the cruel looking-glass, that can always hurt a lass
More hard than any ghost there is or any man there was!

Rudyard Kipling

1591

THE DEATH OF SIR RICHARD GRENVILLE

The Revenge

A Ballad of the Fleet

At Flores in the Azores Sir Richard Grenville lay,
And a pinnace, like a fluttered bird, came flying from far away:
'Spanish ships of war at sea! we have sighted fifty-three!'
Then sware Lord Thomas Howard: "Fore God I am no coward;
But I cannot meet them here, for my ships are out of gear,
And the half my men are sick. I must fly, but follow quick.
We are six ships of the line; can we fight with fifty-three?'

Then spake Sir Richard Grenville: 'I know you are no coward;
You fly them for a moment to fight with them again.
But I've ninety men and more that are lying sick ashore.
I should count myself the coward if I left them, my Lord
    Howard,
To these Inquisition dogs and the devildoms of Spain.'

So Lord Howard passed away with five ships of war that day,
Till he melted like a cloud in the silent summer heaven;
But Sir Richard bore in hand all his sick men from the land
Very carefully and slow,
Men of Bideford in Devon,
And we laid them on the ballast down below;
For we brought them all aboard,
And they blest him in their pain, that they were not left to
    Spain,
To the thumbscrew and the stake for the glory of the Lord.

He had only a hundred seamen to work the ship and to fight,
And he sailed away from Flores till the Spaniard came in sight,
With his huge sea-castles heaving upon the weather bow.
'Shall we fight or shall we fly?
Good Sir Richard, tell us now,
For to fight is but to die!
There'll be little of us left by the time this sun be set.'
And Sir Richard said again: 'We be all good English men.
Let us bang those dogs of Seville, the children of the devil,
For I never turned my back upon Don or devil yet.'

Sir Richard spoke and he laughed, and we roared a hurrah, and
    so
The little Revenge ran on sheer into the heart of the foe,
With her hundred fighters on deck, and her ninety sick below;
For half their fleet to the right and half to the left were seen,
And the little Revenge ran on through the long sea-lane
    between.

Thousands of their soldiers looked down from their decks and
    laughed,
Thousands of their seamen made mock at the mad little craft
Running on and on, till delayed
By their mountain-like San Philip that, of fifteen hundred tons,
And up-shadowing high above us with her yawning tiers of
    guns,
Took the breath from our sails, and we stayed.

And while now the great San Philip hung above us like a cloud
Whence the thunderbolt will fall
Long and loud,
Four galleons drew away
From the Spanish fleet that day,
And two upon the larboard and two upon the starboard lay,
And the battle thunder broke from them all.

But anon the great San Philip, she bethought herself and went,
Having that within her womb that had left her ill content;
And the rest they came aboard us, and they fought us hand to
    hand,
For a dozen times they came with their pikes and musqueteers,
And a dozen times we shook 'em off as a dog that shakes his
    ears
When he leaps from the water to the land.

And the sun went down, and the stars came out far over the
    summer sea,
But never a moment ceased the fight of the one and the fifty-
    three.
Ship after ship, the whole night long, their high-built galleons
    came,
Ship after ship, the whole night long, with her battle-thunder
    and flame;
Ship after ship, the whole night long, drew back with her dead
    and her shame.
For some were sunk and many were shattered, and so could
    fight us no more –
God of battles, was ever a battle like this in the world before?

For he said, 'Fight on! fight on!'
Though his vessel was all but a wreck;
And it chanced that, when half of the short summer night was
    gone,
With a grisly wound to be drest he had left the deck,
But a bullet struck him that was dressing it suddenly dead,
And himself he was wounded again in the side and the head,
And he said, 'Fight on! fight on!'

And the night went down and the sun smiled out far over the
    summer sea,
And the Spanish fleet with broken sides lay round us all in a
    ring;
But they dared not touch us again, for they feared that we still
    could sting.
So they watched what the end would be.
And we had not fought them in vain,
But in perilous plight were we,
Seeing forty of our poor hundred were slain,
And half of the rest of us maimed for life
In the crash of the cannonades and the desperate strife;
And the sick men down in the hold were most of them stark and
    cold,
And the pikes were all broken or bent, and the powder was all
    of it spent;
And the masts and the rigging were lying over the side;
But Sir Richard cried in his English pride:
'We have fought such a fight for a day and a night
As may never be fought again!
We have one great glory, my men!
And a day less or more
At sea or ashore,
We die – does it matter when?
Sink me the ship, Master Gunner – sink her, split her in twain!
Fall into the hands of God, not into the hands of Spain!'

And the gunner said, 'Ay, ay,' but the seamen made reply:
'We have children, we have wives,
And the Lord hath spared our lives.
We will make the Spaniard promise, if we yield, to let us go;
We shall live to fight again and to strike another blow.'
And the lion there lay dying, and they yielded to the foe.

And the stately Spanish men to their flagship bore him then,
Where they laid him by the mast, old Sir Richard caught at last,
And they praised him to his face with their courtly foreign grace;
But he rose upon their decks, and he cried:
'I have fought for Queen and Faith like a valiant man and true;
I have only done my duty as a man is bound to do:
With a joyful spirit I Sir Richard Grenville die!'
And he fell upon their decks and he died.

And they stared at the dead that had been so valiant and true,
And had holden the power and glory of Spain so cheap
That he dared her with one little ship and his English few;
Was he devil or man? He was devil for aught they knew,
But they sank his body with honour down into the deep,
And they manned the Revenge with a swarthier alien crew,
And away she sailed with her loss and longed for her own;
When a wind from the lands they had ruined awoke from sleep,
And the water began to heave and the weather to moan,
And or ever that evening ended a great gale blew,
And a wave like the wave that is raised by an earthquake grew,
Till it smote on their hulls and their sails and their masts and
   their flags,
And the whole sea plunged and fell on the shot-shattered navy
   of Spain,
And the little Revenge herself went down by the island crags
   to be lost evermore in the main.

Alfred, Lord Tennyson

All the great sailors of Elizabethan England were engaged in the lucrative business of pillaging the Spanish treasure-fleets. Such exploits earned the approval and financial backing of the Queen and the city of London. To meet the threat, the Spanish arranged to sail in convoys protected by large galleons. It was a fleet of this kind that fell upon the much smaller English one, of which all ships, except the *Revenge*, escaped. Its master, Grenville, died heroically.

ELIZABETHAN LETTERS

from Master Francis Beaumont to Ben Jonson

What things have we seen
Done at the Mermaid! heard words that have been
So nimble, and so full of subtle flame,
As if that every one from whence they came
Had meant to put his whole wit in a jest,
And had resolved to live a fool the rest
Of his dull life.

Francis Beaumont

from Lines on the Mermaid Tavern

Souls of Poets dead and gone,
What Elysium have ye known,
Happy field or mossy cavern,
Choicer than the Mermaid Tavern?

John Keats

The Mermaid Tavern in Bread Street was a favourite meeting-place for the poets and playwrights of Elizabethan London. Ralegh, Shakespeare, Donne and Jonson were among its habitués. This was a time of extraordinary literary achievement. The English theatre, in particular, was one of the great glories of Elizabeth's reign. Such dramatists as Kyd, Marlowe and Greene came to it from the academic world, but

Shakespeare was an actor-manager who turned to writing plays. Noblemen financed their own groups of players and the public flocked into the 'wooden O' to be shocked, thrilled, amused and stirred to pride by what was often fairly undisguised political propaganda. Francis Beaumont, of the Beaumont and Fletcher team of playwrights, witnessed this creative abundance at first hand, while Keats looks back on it wistfully.

1601

THE FALL OF ESSEX

from Polyhymnia

Then proudly shocks amid the martial throng
Of lusty lanciers, all in sable sad,
Drawn on with coal-black steeds of dusky hue,
In stately chariot full of deep device,
Where gloomy Time sat whipping on the team,
Just back to back with this great champion. –
Young Essex, that thrice-honourable Earl:
Y-clad in mighty arms of mourner's dye,
And plume as black as is a raven's wing,
That from his armour borrow'd such a light
As boughs of yew receive from shady stream:
His staves were such, or of such hue at least,
As are those banner-staves that mourners beat;
And all his company in funeral black;
As if he mourn'd to think of him he miss'd,
Sweet Sidney, fairest shepherd of our green,
Well-letter'd warrior, whose successor he
In love and arms, had ever vow'd to be:
In love and arms, O, may he so succeed
As his deserts, as his desires would speed!

Robert Peele

Robert Devereux, second Earl of Essex, was a protégé of the courtier
and poet Sir Philip Sidney. Sidney died from a gangrenous wound after
the battle of Zutphen in 1586, the occasion on which he is reported to
have yielded a drink to a more grievously wounded soldier with the
immortal words: 'Thy need is yet greater than mine.' The court went
into mourning for him, and soon afterwards the Earl of Essex was able
to attend a tournament in an outfit of the most fetching deep black with
which he caught the eye of the Queen, later going on to become her last
favourite. In 1599 he was appointed to quell the uprising of the Earl of
Tyrone in Ireland, but he failed disastrously. On his return to England,
he was rebuffed after bursting into the Queen's own apartments while
she was in the middle of dressing. He planned to take over the government from Cecil, but his attempted coup was a botched affair and the
loyal people of London refused to support him. He was tried and found
guilty, and on Shrove Tuesday, after attending the performance of a
play, Elizabeth signed the death warrant of one of the two men for
whom she had deeply cared. The following verse from a street ballad
shows that Essex had at least a measure of popular support:

> Count him not like Campion,
>   (those traitrous men), or Babington;
> Not like the Earl of Westmorland
>   By whom a number were undone.
> He never yet hurt mother's son –
>   His quarrell still maintained the right;
> For which the tears my cheeks down run
>   When I think on his last Goodnight.

1603

THE DEATH OF ELIZABETH I

Gloriana Dying

None shall gainsay me. I will lie on the floor.
Hitherto from horseback, throne, balcony,
I have looked down upon your looking up.
Those sands are run. Now I reverse the glass
And bid henceforth your homage downward, falling
Obedient and unheeded as leaves in autumn
To quilt the wakeful study I must make
Examining my kingdom from below.
How tall my people are! Like a race of trees
They sway, sigh, nod heads, rustle above me,
And their attentive eyes are distant as starshine.
I have still cherished the handsome and well-made:
No queen has better masts within her forests
Growing, nor prouder and more restive minds
Scabbarded in the loyalty of subjects;
No virgin has had better worship than I.
No, no! Leave me alone, woman! I will not
Be put into a bed. Do you suppose
That I who've ridden through all weathers, danced
Under a treasury's weight of jewels, sat
Myself to stone through sermons and addresses,
Shall come to harm by sleeping on a floor?
Not that I sleep. A bed were good enough
If that were in my mind. But I am here
For a deep study and contemplation,
And as Persephone, and the red vixen,
Go underground to sharpen their wits,
I have left my dais to learn a new policy
Through watching of your feet, and as the Indian
Lays all his listening body along the earth
I lie in wait for the reverberation
Of things to come and dangers threatening.
Is that the Bishop praying? Let him pray on.

If his knees tire his faith can cushion them.
How the poor man grieves Heaven with news of me!
Deposuit superbos. But no hand
Other than my own has put me down –
Not feebleness enforced on brain or limb,
Not fear, misgiving, fantasy, age, palsy,
Has felled me. I lie here by my own will,
And by the curiosity of a queen.
I dare say there is not in all England
One who lies closer to the ground than I.
Not the traitor in the condemned hold
Whose few straws edge away from under his weight
Of ironed fatality; not the shepherd
Huddled for cold under the hawthorn bush,
Nor the long dreaming country lad who lies
Scorching his book before the dying brand.

Sylvia Townsend Warner

You poets all, brave Shakespeare, Jonson, Green,
Bestow your time to write for England's Queen. . . .
Return your songs and sonnets and your says,
To set forth sweet Elizabetha's praise.

Anonymous

Nor doth the silver-tonguèd Melicert
Drop from his honeyed muse one sable tear,
To mourn her death that gracèd his desert
And to his lays opened her royal ear.
   Shepherd, remember our Elizabeth,
   And sing her Rape, done by that Tarquin, Death.

Henry Chettle

Elizabeth died at Richmond Palace on 24 March 1603. She had attained the great age of seventy. A horseman waiting below her room was thrown one of the rings she had been wearing, and with this proof of her death galloped off to Scotland where James VI was expecting it. In the library at Chequers there is a ring in the shape of a skull which is said to be that ring. The anonymous popular ballad quoted above urges the great poets of the time to sing her praises, but, as Henry Chettle noted, the greatest of them all remained silent. This is not entirely surprising, as only two years earlier Shakespeare's patron, the Earl of Southampton, had been sentenced to death for his part in the Essex affair, and reprieved only at the last minute.

THE STUARTS

King James I, 1603–25

James I

The child of Mary Queen of Scots,
   A shifty mother's shiftless son,
Bred up among intrigues and plots,
   Learnèd in all things, wise in none.
Ungainly, babbling, wasteful, weak,
   Shrewd, clever, cowardly, pedantic,
The sight of steel would blanch his cheek,
   The smell of baccy drive him frantic,
He was the author of his line –
   He wrote that witches should be burnt;
He wrote that monarchs were divine,
   And left a son who – proved they weren't!

Rudyard Kipling

James VI of Scotland was crowned James I of England. The two most enduring achievements of his reign were literary: the publication in 1611 of the King James Version of the English Bible, on which a committee had been working since 1604, and in 1623 of the First Folio of Shakespeare's plays. Both served to enlarge, enrich and enshrine the great glory of the English language. Early settlers in Jamestown, Virginia, and in New England had as their resource what was to become the mother tongue of a mighty continent.

James himself was strong in opinions, but weak in action; and he was much taken up with two favourites, Robert Carr, Earl of Somerset, and George Villiers, Duke of Buckingham. Kipling's contempt for James had been preceded by that of Dickens, who wrote: 'A creature like his Sowship on the throne is like the Plague, and everybody receives infection from him.' And to other writers his name had been a by-word for pedantry.

from **The Dunciad**

Oh (cry'd the Goddess) for some pedant Reign!
Some gentle JAMES, to bless the land again;
To stick the Doctor's Chair into the Throne,
Give law to Words, or war with Words alone,
Senates and Courts with Greek and Latin rule,
And turn the council to a Grammar School!
For sure, if Dulness sees a grateful Day,
'Tis in the shade of Arbitrary Sway.
O! if my sons may learn one earthly thing,
Teach but that one, sufficient for a King;
That which my Priests, and mine alone, maintain,
Which as it dies, or lives, we fall, or reign:
May you, may Cam, and Isis preach it long!
'The RIGHT DIVINE of Kings to govern wrong.'

Alexander Pope

1605

Gunpowder Plot Day

Please to remember
The Fifth of November,
Gunpowder, treason and plot;
I see no reason
Why gunpowder treason
Should ever be forgot.

Anonymous

The Gunpowder Plotters were driven to action by disappointment that James, whose wife had secretly turned Catholic, had not relaxed the laws against Catholics in general. They prepared plans to do away with King and Parliament together, but these were betrayed by Francis Tresham, who could not bear the thought of his own kinsmen being blown to eternity by the barrels of gunpowder which Guido Fawkes was to ignite. After the plot had been discovered, Catholics were debarred from all public office and forbidden to venture more than five miles from their homes.

1605

ENGLISH SETTLEMENTS IN AMERICA

from To the Virginian Voyage

You brave heroic minds,
Worthy your country's name,
That honour still pursue,
Go and subdue;
Whilst loitering hinds
Lurk here at home with shame.

Britons, you stay too long;
Quickly aboard bestow you,
And with a merry gale
Swell your stretched sail,
With vows as strong,
As the winds that blow you.

Your course securely steer;
West and by South forth keep:
Rocks, lee shores, nor shoals,
When Eolus scolds,
You need not fear,
So absolute the deep.

And cheerfully at sea
Success you still entice
    To get the pearl and gold;
    And ours to hold
Virginia,
Earth's only paradise.

Where nature has in store
Fowl, venison and fish;
    And the fruitfullest soil,
    Without your toil,
Three harvests more,
All greater than your wish.
                    *
And in regions far
Such heroes bring you forth,
    As those from whom we came;
    And plant our name
Under the star
Not known unto our North.

Michael Drayton

In 1603 England had no colonies, but by 1660 she had the beginnings of
an empire. The Elizabethan settlements had all failed. In James's reign
the flag was raised in India, the East Indies, Virginia and Massachusetts. Colonies were founded by private-enterprise companies set
up to develop the wealth of the new lands. In 1601 a company was
formed to finance an expedition to Virginia. The pioneers landed at
Chesapeake Bay, sailed up what was to be called the James River and
landed at the site of Jamestown. Their early years proved a struggle and
their numbers were soon reduced from 143 to 38; but in 1617 they sent
back to England what was to be the source of their subsequent wealth –
a cargo of Virginian tobacco.

The first colonists were people who sought adventure, land, wealth
and religious freedom. In 1620 a band of Puritans, the 'Pilgrim Fathers',
sailed from Plymouth in the *Mayflower* to found a new plantation
which, after twenty years, amounted to some 600 souls. James I did
little to help this colonial expansion, his only gesture being to order the

exportation of criminals to Virginia. Charles I did scarcely better. It was left to Oliver Cromwell to be the first real imperialist, when he recognized the necessity for an efficient organization of sea power that would enable England to defend its colonies and attack the colonies of others.

1607

THE SCOTTISH INVASION OF ENGLAND UNDER JAMES I

from The True-Born Englishman

The Offspring of this Miscellaneous Crowd,
Had not their new Plantations long enjoy'd,
But they grew *Englishmen*, and rais'd their Votes
At Foreign Shoals of *Interloping Scots*.
The Royal Branch from *Pict-land* did succeed,
With Troops of *Scots* and Scabs from *North-by-Tweed*.
The Seven first Years of his Pacifick Reign,
Made him and half his Nation *Englishmen*.
Scots from the *Northern* Frozen Banks of *Tay*,
With Packs and Plods came *Whigging* all away:
Thick as the Locusts which in *Egypt* swarm'd,
With Pride and hungry Hopes compleatly arm'd:
With Native Truth, Diseases, and No Money,
Plunder'd our *Canaan* of the Milk and Honey.
Here they grew quickly Lords and Gentlemen,
And all their Race are *True-Born Englishmen*.

Daniel Defoe

In 1607 James tried to unite England and Scotland as one country. Debates in the House of Commons brought out the worst of English bigotry. It was variously alleged that the Scots were sly and beggarly, but it was the London merchants who prevailed when they shrewdly argued that, once the Scots were let in, they would take over the best English companies. Plans for the Union were shelved for a further hundred years.

1609

THE DIVINE ORDER

from **Troilus and Cressida**

ACT I *Scene III*
The Grecian.camp.

ULYSSES: . . . The heavens themselves, the planets, and this centre
Observe degree, priority and place,
Insisture, course, proportion, season, form,
Office and custom, all in line of order;
And therefore is the glorious planet Sol
In noble eminence enthron'd and spher'd
Amidst the other, whose med'cinable eye
Corrects the ill aspects of planets evil,
And posts like the commandment of a king,
Sans check, to good and bad. But when the planets
In evil mixture to disorder wander;
What plagues and what portents, what mutiny,
What raging of the sea, shaking of earth,
Commotion in the winds! Frights, changes, horrors,
Divert and crack, rend and deracinate,
The unity and married calm of states
Quite from their fixture! O, when degree is shak'd,
Which is the ladder of all high designs,
The enterprise is sick! How could communities,
Degrees in schools, and brotherhoods in cities,
Peaceful commerce from dividable shores,
The primogeniture and due of birth,
Prerogative of age, crowns, sceptres, laurels,
But by degree away, untune that string,
And hark, what discord follows! Each thing melts

In mere oppugnancy: the bounded waters
Should lift their bosoms higher than the shores,
And make a sop of all this solid globe;
Strength should be lord of imbecility,
And the rude son should strike his father dead;
Force should be right; or, rather, right and wrong –
Between whose endless jar justice resides –
Should lose their names, and so should justice too.

William Shakespeare

In the famous speech which he gives to the character of Ulysses in *Troilus and Cressida* (1609), Shakespeare emphasizes to his Jacobean audience the importance of an authority which is divinely ordained and which is maintained by the hierarchical nature of society. It is not quite a text for the Divine Right of Kings, but it does offer a clear warning of what would happen should the state of things be undermined.

1611

THE AUTHORIZED VERSION OF THE ENGLISH BIBLE

Ecclesiasticus XLIV, 1–14

Let us now praise famous men, and our fathers that begate us.

The Lorde hath wrought great glory by them through his great power from the beginning.

Such as did beare rule in the kingdomes, men renowned for their power, giving counsell by their understanding, and declaring prophecies:

Leaders of the people by their counsels, and by their knowledge of learning meet for the people, wise and eloquent in their instructions.

Such as found out musical tunes and recited verses in writing.

Rich men furnished with ability, living peaceably in their habitations.

All these were honoured in their generations, and were the glory of their times.

There be of them, that have left a name behind them, that their praises might be reported.

And some there be, which have no memorial, who are perished as though they had never bene, and are become as though they had never bene borne, and their children after them.

But these were mercifull men, whose righteousness hath not beene forgotten.

With their seede shall continually remaine a good inheritance, and their children are within the covenant.

Their seed stands fast, and their children for their sakes.

Their seed shall remaine for ever, and their glory shall not be blotted out.

Their bodies are buried in peace, but their name liveth for evermore.

From 1604 scholars had been working at Oxford, Cambridge and Westminster to make an authoritative translation of the Bible into English, in an attempt to bridge the gap between Protestant and Puritan factions of the Church. The leading scholar was John Bois of Cambridge, whose particular job it was to translate the Apocrypha, where the book of Ecclesiasticus is to be found. The first English translation of the Bible had been made by John Wyclif in the 1380s and it had been condemned as heretical. Tyndale published his in 1525, and in the next forty years another five versions appeared. The King James committee, however, produced a work of outstanding beauty. The scholars used a relatively small vocabulary of some 8,000 words, which may account for the directness of its appeal. Shakespeare used a much wider vocabulary of some 30,000 words, a number of which he invented himself. The plays of Shakespeare and the King James Bible established the English language as the greatest glory of Western civilization.

1615

THE FALL OF SOMERSET

Upon the Sudden Restraint of the Earl of Somerset

Dazzled thus with height of place,
Whilst our hopes our wits beguile,
No man marks the narrow space
'Twixt a prison and a smile.

Then, since Fortune's favours fade,
You that in her arms do sleep;
Learn to swim, and not to wade,
For the hearts of Kings are deep.

But, if Greatness be so blind
As to trust in towers of air,
Let it be with Goodness lined,
That at least the fall be fair.

Then, though darkened, you shall say,
When friends fail, and Princes frown,
Virtue is the roughest way,
But proves at night a bed of down.

Henry Wotton

Robert Carr, a blond and handsome page, became James's favourite, was made the Earl of Somerset, and in 1613 was one of the King's principal advisers. Another courtier, Sir Thomas Overbury, expressed his resentment at Somerset's infatuation with Frances Howard, the Countess of Essex, who was reputed to be a witch and whom Somerset wanted to marry. Overbury was thrown in the Tower, where he was poisoned by the Countess. She then secured a divorce and married Somerset, but the scandal leaked abroad and not even James could save the couple from public disgrace. This led the way for the Duke of Buckingham to become the new favourite.

1616

THE DEATH OF SHAKESPEARE

To the Memory of my Beloved Mr William Shakespeare

I, therefore, will begin. Soul of the Age!
  The applause, delight, the wonder of our Stage!
My Shakespeare, rise; I will not lodge thee by
  Chaucer, or Spenser, or bid Beaumont lie
A little further, to make thee a room:
  Thou art a monument, without a tomb,
And art alive still, while thy book doth live,
  And we have wits to read and praise to give.
That I not mix thee so, my brain excuses;
  I mean with great, but disproportioned Muses:
For, if I thought my judgement were of years,
  I should commit thee surely with thy peers,
And tell how far thou didst our Lyly out-shine,
  Or sporting Kyd, or Marlowe's mighty line.
And though thou hadst small Latin and less Greek,
  From thence to honour thee, I would not seek
For names; but call forth thundering Æschylus,
  Euripides, and Sophocles to us,
Paccuvius, Accius, him of Cordova dead,
  To life again, to hear thy buskin tread,
And shake a stage; or, when thy socks were on,
  Leave thee alone, for the comparison
Of all that insolent Greece or haughty Rome
  Sent forth, or since did from their ashes come.
Triumph, my Britain, thou hast one to show
  To whom all scenes of Europe homage owe.
He was not of an age but for all time!
  And all the Muses still were in their prime
When, like Apollo, he came forth to warm
  Our ears, or, like a Mercury, to charm!

Ben Jonson

1618

THE EXECUTION OF SIR WALTER RALEGH

His Epitaph

Which He Writ the Night Before His Execution

Even such is time, that takes in trust
   Our youth, our joys, our all we have,
And pays us but with age and dust;
   Who in the dark and silent grave,
When we have wandered all our ways,
Shuts up the story of our days!
But from this earth, this grave, this dust,
The Lord shall raise me up, I trust!

Walter Ralegh

Ralegh had been condemned to death in 1603 on trumped-up charges.
Reprieved, he lived in the Tower of London until 1616, when he was
released and put in charge of a disastrous expedition to find Eldorado.
Spiteful and petty as ever, James I took it upon himself to strike down
the last of the Elizabethans, who by then was nearly seventy years old.
When, at the second stroke of the axe, Ralegh's head fell from his body,
a voice from the crowd in the New Palace Yard cried out, 'We have not
such another head to be cut off.'

King Charles I, 1625–49

Ten years the world upon him falsely smiled,
Sheathing in fawning looks the deadly knife . . .

Richard Fanshawe

James I had expounded the theory of the Divine Right of Kings, and his son Charles tried to implement it in the 1630s. The question was whether the King could rule without Parliament. The Members of Parliament themselves, moneyed and landed men, asserted their representative rights against royal absolutism. The principles for which they stood were a far cry from democracy and general suffrage, but those ideals have their beginnings in this conflict and the Civil War to which it eventually led probably prevented revolution at a later date. Colonel Thomas Rainborough, MP for Droitwich, pointed the way forward when he said: 'I think the meanest He that is in England hath a life as well as the greatest He; and therefore, truly sir, I think that every man that is to live under a government ought, first, by his own consent to put himself under that government.'

THE THREAT TO THE KING

from **The Secret People**

The face of the King's servants grew greater than the King.
He tricked them and they trapped him and drew round him in a
  ring;
The new grave lords closed round him that had eaten the
  abbey's fruits,
And the men of the new religion with their Bibles in their boots,
We saw their shoulders moving to menace and discuss.
And some were pure and some were vile, but none took heed of
  us;
We saw the King when they killed him, and his face was proud
  and pale,
And a few men talked of freedom while England talked of ale.

G. K. Chesterton

the 1630s

THE PURITANS

Here lies the corpse of William Prynne,
A bencher late of Lincoln's Inn,
Who restless ran through thick and thin.

This grand scripturient paper-spiller,
This endless, needless margin-filler,
Was strangely tost from post to pillar.

His brain's career was never stopping,
But pen with rheum of gall still dropping,
Till hand o'er head brought ears to cropping.

Nor would he yet surcease such themes,
But prostitute new virgin reams
To types of his fanatic dreams.

But whilst he this hot humour hugs,
And for more length of tedder tugs,
Death fang'd the remnant of his lugs.

Samuel Butler

William Prynne was a fully paid-up member of God's awkward squad. He was a thorough-going Puritan who, in 1632, wrote a 1,000-page attack on the theatre. The Puritans had a special dislike of theatres. In 1642 they ordained that all such places of entertainment should be closed, and in 1647 that actors should be pursued as rogues. When these measures failed, they proposed that playgoers should be liable to a fine of five shillings.

In 1634 Prynne was sentenced to life imprisonment and his ears to be cut off in the pillory. This did not, however, stop the flow of pamphlets, and in 1637 he was sentenced to have the stumps of his ears shorn and to be branded. Released by the Long Parliament, he led the prosecution of Archbishop Laud and urged the execution of Charles, but he managed to fall out with Cromwell, who put him back in prison. Prynne died in 1669.

1641

THE EXECUTION OF STRAFFORD

Epitaph on the Earl of Strafford

Here lies wise and valiant dust,
Huddled up 'twixt fit and just,
Strafford, who was hurried hence
'Twixt treason and convenience.
He spent his time here in a mist,
A Papist, yet a Calvinist;
His Prince's nearest joy and grief,
He had, yet wanted, all relief;
The prop and ruin of the State,
The people's violent love and hate;
One in extremes loved and abhorred.
Riddles lie here, or in a word,
Here lies blood, and let it lie
Speechless still, and never cry.

John Cleveland

As a Member of Parliament, the Earl of Strafford had prepared the
Petition of Right against Charles in 1628, but in the next year he went
over to the Royalist side and served as the King's most able and
devoted minister. In the 1630s he governed Ireland, returning in 1639 to
help his master in the struggle to retain his personal authority. But it
was too late. The royal army was defeated in an encounter with Scottish
rebels and the King had to recall Parliament, which had been in abey-
ance throughout the decade. Parliament used Strafford as the King's
scapegoat and took revenge on his earlier defection by passing an Act
of Attainder which Charles was forced to sign, thereby in effect signing
Strafford's death warrant. In a letter to Charles before the signing,
Strafford did not plead for mercy, but instead offered himself as a
sacrifice to appease Parliament's wrath. This is one of the most heroic
documents of British history. Strafford wrote:

I do most humbly beseech your Majesty . . . to pass this Bill, and by
this means remove, I cannot say this accursed, but I confess this

unfortunate, thing forth of the way towards that blessed agreement which God, I trust, shall ever establish between you and your subjects.

Archbishop Laud, who was also to be executed, wrote of Strafford: 'He served a mild and gracious Prince, who knew not how to be or to be made great.'

1642

RAISING MONEY FOR THE CIVIL WAR

from Hudibras

Did Saints, for this, bring in their Plate,
And crowd as if they came too late.
For when they thought the Cause had need on't,
Happy was he that could be rid on't,
Did they coin Piss-Pots, Bowls, and Flaggons,
Int' officers of horse and dragoons;
And into pikes and musquetteers,
Stamp beakers, cups, and porringers?
A thimble, bodkin, and a spoon,
Did start up living men, as soon
As in the furnace they were thrown,
Just like the dragon's teeth being sown.
Then was the Cause of Gold and Plate,
The brethren's offerings, consecrate,
Like th' Hebrew Calf, and down before it
The Saints fell prostrate, to adore it,
So say the wicked.

Samuel Butler

Both the King and Parliament needed metal to mint the coins that would fund their armies during the inevitable conflict. Londoners were urged by Parliament to bring their gold and silver to the Guildhall, and so great was the suc ess of the appeal that the Royalists called the Roundheads 'the Thimble and Bodkin Army'. Charles established his mint at Oxford and required the Colleges to lend him their plate, promising to repay them 'as soon as God shall enable Us'.

1642

THE BATTLE OF EDGEHILL

After Edgehill, 1642

1 Villagers Report 'The Late Apparitions'

A December Saturday, star-clear
at Kineton. Three months since the battle,
the village collects itself – Christmas
perhaps a demarcation, a control
in the blood-letting. Yet on the ridge
of Edge Hill, the night resounds,
armies grinding one against the other
re-enacting the action, re-dying the deaths.

Shepherds hear trumpets, drums –
expect a visitation of holy kings with retinues.
Instead, the spectral soldiers strike,
icy night skies crack with cries,
steel clashing and the sput of muskets.
A knot of Kineton men watch, witness;
Samuel Marshall, the Minister, says
the Devil's apparitions seize the dead.

2 A Ghost Speaks

I am unplanted, my world this waste –
the heath where bone was split, undressed of flesh,
where arteries unleashed their flood, the colour
of death. What is the colour of honour? The blue
in which we dissolve into air? the white of ashes?
Can I be woven into the braids of her hair, my lady,
or exist in the quick of my son's fingernails?
I, who carried the Standard, once drove the plough,
turning up earth, the harvest of worms. Now I envy
the seeds in the furrow, their dark cradle.

My blood is this Midlands field, this hacked hedgerow
where I lie, hearing the drumbeat of the dead,
corpses strewn rotting, graveless.
I glide up and down these rows of human manure,
the faces of soldiers like fallen cameos.
Here is Sir Edmund Verney, Thomas Transome –
they look skywards, lolling near my own wistful face.
Sir Edmund is grimacing slightly as he did in life,
Thomas Transome's skull a broken eggshell.

The brittle linnet flies from me. Dry leaves relinquish
their hold on twigs. A hair sits motionless, watching,
listening to last groans forever in the wind.

I see a troop of Horse on the skyline – Parliament's.
They charge our pikemen; now they vanish
like moving cloud-shadows across the field.
I cannot follow the clouds; I am chained to my carcass
hovering, as others are, above their unburied selves.

3 A Dragoon Observes Colonel Cromwell

Like a falcon from the gauntlet, he throws off these deaths.
He tells us 'Smile out to God in Praise', for his is the sword
of the Lord. I see his horse, piebald with blood.

Gladys Mary Coles

In August 1642 Charles raised his standard at Nottingham and the first battle of the Civil War took place at Edgehill on 23 October. Charles's German cousin, Prince Rupert, led one of his famous cavalry charges, which swept everything before it, but ran out of control. The foot-soldiers of the Parliamentary army held on doggedly. The Royalist Sir Edmund Verney was killed clutching the standard so firmly that his right hand had to be cut off. William Harvey, the scientist, who also fought, pulled a dead body over himself as he lay wounded, to protect himself against the freezing cold. Oliver Cromwell did not take part in this battle, for it seems that he arrived too late, but he took notice of what had happened and resolved to reorganize his army accordingly. Strange rumours soon began to circulate about Edgehill: shepherds claimed to have heard unaccountable sounds of battle – shots, trumpets and drums – while ghostly soldiers were seen riding and fighting. Charles sent agents to investigate these reports and pamphlets were written by both sides alleging that divine messages could be read in them.

1643

To Lucasta, Going to the Wars

Tell me not, Sweet, I am unkind,
   That from the nunnery
Of thy chaste breast and quiet mind
   To war and arms I fly.

True, a new mistress now I chase,
   The first foe in the field;
And with a stronger faith embrace
   A sword, a horse, a shield.

Yet this inconstancy is such
   As thou too shalt adore;
I could not love thee, Dear, so much,
   Loved I not Honour more.

Richard Lovelace

WOMEN TO THE DEFENCE OF LONDON

from Hudibras

What have they done or what left undone,
That might advance the Cause at London?
March'd rank and file with Drum and Ensign,
T'entrench the City for defence in;
Rais'd Rampiers with their own soft hands,
To put the enemy to stands;
From Ladies down to Oyster-wenches
Labour'd like Pioneers in Trenches,
Fell to their Pick-axes and Tools,
And help'd the men to dig like Moles?

Samuel Butler

The Cavalier poet Lovelace expresses the romance of service to the Royalist cause, while Butler describes the equal determination of the women of London to resist the King's advance.

1645

The Battle of Naseby

Oh! wherefore come ye forth, in triumph from the North,
  With your hands, and your feet, and your raiment all red?
And wherefore doth your rout sent forth a joyous shout?
  And whence be the grapes of the wine-press which ye tread?

Oh evil was the root, and bitter was the fruit,
  And crimson was the juice of the vintage that we trod;
For we trampled on the throng of the haughty and the strong,
  Who sate in the high places, and slew the saints of God.

It was about the noon of a glorious day in June,
  That we saw their banners dance, and their cuirasses shine,
And the Man of Blood was there, with his long essenced hair,
  And Astley, and Sir Marmaduke, and Rupert of the Rhine.

Like a servant of the Lord, with his Bible and his sword,
  The General rode along us to form us to the fight,
When a murmuring sound broke out, and swell'd into a shout,
  Among the godless horsemen upon the tyrant's right.

And hark! like the roar of the billows on the shore,
  The cry of battle rises along their charging line!
For God! for the Cause! for the Church, for the Laws!
  For Charles King of England, and Rupert of the Rhine!

The furious German comes, with his clarions and his drums,
  His bravoes of Alsatia, and pages of Whitehall;
They are bursting on our flanks. Grasp your pikes, close your
    ranks;
  For Rupert never comes but to conquer or to fall.

They are here! They rush on! We are broken! We are gone!
  Our left is borne before them like stubble on the blast.
O Lord, put forth thy might! O Lord, defend the right!
  Stand back to back, in God's name, and fight it to the last.

Stout Skippon hath a wound; the centre hath given ground:
  Hark! hark! – What means the trampling of horsemen on our
    rear?
Whose banner do I see, boys? 'Tis he, thank God! 'tis he, boys,
  Bear up another minute: brave Oliver is here.

Their heads all stooping low, their points all in a row,
  Like a whirlwind on the trees, like a deluge on the dikes,
Our cuirassiers have burst on the ranks of the accurst,
  And at a shock have scattered the forest of his pikes.

Fast, fast, the gallants ride, in some safe nook to hide
  Their coward heads, predestined to rot on Temple Bar:
And he – he turns, he flies: – shame on those cruel eyes
  That bore to look on torture, and dare not look on war.

Ho! comrades, scour the plain; and, ere ye strip the slain,
  First give another stab to make your search secure,
Then shake from sleeves and pockets their broadpieces and
    lockets,
  The tokens of the wanton, the plunder of the poor.

Fools, your doublets shone with gold, and your hearts were gay
    and bold,
  When you kissed your lily hands to your lemans today;
And tomorrow shall the fox, from her chambers in the rocks,
  Lead forth her tawny cubs to howl above the prey.

Where be your tongues that late mocked at heaven and hell and
    fate,
  And the fingers that once were so busy with your blades,
Your perfumed satin clothes, your catches and your oaths,
  Your stage-plays and your sonnets, your diamonds and your
    spades?

Down, down, for ever down with the mitre and the crown,
  With the Belial of the Court, and the Mammon of the Pope;
There is woe in Oxford Halls; there is wail in Durham's Stalls:
  The Jesuit smites his bosom; the Bishop rends his cope.

And She of the seven hills shall mourn her children's ills,
  And tremble when she thinks of the edge of England's sword;
And the Kings of earth in fear shall shudder when they hear.
  What the hand of God hath wrought for the Houses and the
  Word.

Thomas Babington, Lord Macaulay

This splendid poem describes the decisive battle of the Civil War. The Royalist troops were heavily outnumbered by Roundheads, largely because the forces led by Lord Goring, who was jealous of Prince Rupert, failed to turn up. A brilliant charge by Rupert nearly won the day, but Cromwell's cavalry stood firm. Macaulay, in his enthusiasm for the Protestant and Parliamentary cause, overlooked the fact that Cromwell's men brutally murdered as many of the Royalist women camp-followers as they could lay their hands on. As usual, Cromwell had no doubts about the reason for his victory: 'Sir, there is none other than the hand of God.'

1646

THE LONG PARLIAMENT

On the New Forcers of Conscience under the Long Parliament

Because you have thrown off your Prelate Lord,
   And with stiff vows renounced his Liturgy,
   To seize the widow'd whore Plurality
   From them whose sin ye envied, not abhorr'd;
Dare ye for this adjure the civil sword
   To force our consciences that Christ set free,
   And ride us with a classic hierarchy
   Taught ye by mere A. S. and Rutherford?
Men whose life, learning, faith and pure intent
   Would have been held in high esteem with Paul
   Must now be named and printed heretics
By shallow Edwards and Scotch What-d'ye-call.
   But we do hope to find out all your tricks,
   Your plots and packings, worse than those of Trent,
      That so the Parliament
   May with their wholesome and preventive shears
   Clip your phylacteries, though baulk your ears,
      And succour our just fears,
   When they shall read this clearly in your charge:
   New Presbyter is but old Priest writ large.

John Milton

In the 1640s, the Long Parliament allowed the Presbyterians to dismantle the Church of England. They proved to be quite as intolerant as the Catholics and attacked all who would not conform, including Milton, who had become an Independent. The Presbyterians mentioned in this poem had denounced Milton's tracts on divorce. In 1649 Rutherford advocated the death penalty for heresy, proving the truth of Milton's famous last line.

1648

FAIRFAX

On the Lord General Fairfax, at the Siege of Colchester'

Fairfax, whose name in arms through Europe rings
   Filling each mouth with envy or with praise,
   And all her jealous monarchs with amaze
   And rumours loud, that daunt remotest kings;
Thy firm unshaken virtue ever brings
   Victory home, though new rebellions raise
   Their Hydra heads, and the false North displays
   Her broken league, to imp their serpent wings.
O yet a nobler task awaits thy hand;
   For what can war but endless war still breed,
   Till truth and right from violence be freed,
And public faith clear'd from the shameful brand
   Of public fraud? In vain doth Valour bleed,
   While Avarice and Rapine share the land.

John Milton

Fairfax was the great general who with Cromwell had created the New Model Army, victorious at the battles of Marston Moor and Naseby. In the second part of the Civil War he fought the Royalists in the Southeast and starved Colchester to surrender. After Charles's execution, he withdrew from public life and lived peacefully for twenty years.

1649

THE EXECUTION OF CHARLES I

from **An Horatian Ode upon Cromwell's Return from Ireland**

What field of all the civil wars
Where his were not the deepest scars?
    And Hampton shows what part
    He had of wiser art;

Where, twining subtle fears with hope,
He wove a net of such a scope
    That Charles himself might chase
    To Car'sbrook's narrow case;

That thence the Royal Actor borne
The tragic scaffold might adorn:
    While round the armèd bands
    Did clap their bloody hands.

He nothing common did or mean
Upon that memorable scene,
    But with his keener eye
    The axe's edge did try;

Nor called the Gods, with vulgar spite,
To vindicate his helpless right;
    But bowed his comely head
    Down, as upon a bed.

This was that memorable hour
Which first assured the forcèd power:
    So when they did design
    The Capitol's first line,

A bleeding head, where they begun,
Did fright the architects to run;
    And yet in that the State
    Foresaw its happy fate!

Andrew Marvell

This is an extract from a poem written to celebrate Cromwell's triumphant return from Ireland in 1650. Marvell recognizes Charles's courage
and serenity, but has no doubts about the justice of the Parlia-
mentarian cause.

Oh let that day from time be blotted quite,
And let belief of't in next age be waived.
In deepest silence th'act concealed might,
So that the Kingdom's credit might be saved.
          *
But if the Power Divine permitted this,
His Will's the law and ours must acquiesce.

Lord General Fairfax

Fairfax was at the Banqueting Hall in Whitehall on the morning of
Charles's execution and spoke with the King a few hours before the
event. On the night preceding it, he had been approached by several
people, including two Dutch ambassadors, who had urged him to save
the King. But the entire area had been filled with troops by Cromwell
and, although Fairfax had no wish to be responsible for the King's
death, he did nothing to prevent it. In a great fit of hand-wringing and
guilt-assuaging he composed these verses, and even managed to pass
the buck to God.

Samuel Pepys, who was present at the King's death, was also in 1660 a
witness at the execution of one of the leading Parliamentarians. In his
diary he wrote:

> I went out to Charing cross to see Maj.-Gen. Harrison hanged,
> drawn, and quartered – which was done there – he looking as
> cheerfully as any man could do in that condition. He was presently
> cut down and his head and his heart shown to the people, at which
> there was great shouts of joy . . . Thus it was my chance to see the
> King beheaded at Whitehall and to see the first blood shed in revenge
> for the blood of the King at Charing cross. From thence to my Lord's
> and took Capt. Cuttance and Mr. Sheply to the Sun taverne and did
> give them some oysters.

By the Statue of King Charles I at Charing Cross

Sombre and rich, the skies;
Great glooms, and starry plains.
Gently the night wind sighs;
Else a vast silence reigns.

The splendid silence clings
Around me; and around
The saddest of all kings
Crowned, and again discrowned.

Comely and calm, he rides
Hard by his own Whitehall:
Only the night wind glides:
No crowds, nor rebels, brawl . . .

Which are more full of fate:
The stars; or those sad eyes?
Which are more still and great:
Those brows; or the dark skies?

Although his whole heart yearns
In passionate tragedy:
Never was face so stern
With sweet austerity.

Vanquished in life, his death
By beauty made amends:
The passing of his breath
Won his defeated ends.

Brief life, and hapless? Nay:
Through death, life grew sublime.
Speak after sentence? Yea:
And to the end of time . . .

Lionel Johnson

This famous equestrian statue was commissioned from the sculptor Le Sueur in 1630 and erected in 1648. After Charles's execution, Parliament sold it to a brass merchant, John Rivet of Holborn, with orders that it should be destroyed. Rivet buried it and then sold spoons and knife-handles allegedly made from its metal. After the Restoration, Rivet presented it intact to Charles II who had it erected at the top of Whitehall, where his father had been executed. On 30 January each year devout Royalists and Catholics place flowers at the base of the monument. Lionel Johnson wrote his poem towards the end of the nineteenth century.

The Commonwealth, 1649–60

OLIVER CROMWELL

Rupert of the Rhine
Thought Cromwell was a swine.
He felt quite sure
After Marston Moor

E. C. Bentley

To the Lord General Cromwell

Cromwell, our chief of men, who through a cloud
  Not of war only, but detractions rude,
  Guided by faith and matchless fortitude,
  To peace and truth thy glorious way hast ploughed,
And on the neck of crownèd Fortune proud
  Hast reared God's trophies, and his work pursued;
  While Darwen stream, with blood of Scots imbrued,
  And Dunbar field resounds thy praises loud,
And Worcester's laureate wreath: yet much remains
  To conquer still; Peace hath her victories
  No less renowned than War: new foes arise,
Threatening to bind our souls with secular chains.
  Help us to save free conscience from the paw
  Of hireling wolves, whose Gospel is their maw.

John Milton

Cromwell, a wealthy East Anglian farmer, became an MP in the Long Parliament, but emerged after the Roundhead victories in 1644 and 1645 as the leader of the Protestant revolution. He routed the Royalists in the second civil war of 1648, and then came to accept that Charles must be executed. He ruthlessly crushed the uprisings that took place after Charles's death: in Ireland in 1650; among the Scots in the same year; and in England in 1651 – this last ending with his victory at Worcester. In 1653 he became Lord Protector and, even more quickly than Charles, fell out with Parliament, crying: 'Take away that fool's bauble, the mace!' Thereafter he ruled England, not with MPs, but with Major-Generals. His devotion to the cause of parliamentary democracy is recognized by the statue of him erected outside the public entrance to the House of Commons.

1649

from **The Diggers' Song**

'You noble Diggers all, stand up now, stand up now,
   You noble Diggers all, stand up now,
The waste land to maintain, seeing Cavaliers by name
Your digging do disdain and persons all defame.
      Stand up now, stand up now.

Your houses they pull down, stand up now, stand up now,
   Your houses they pull down, stand up now;
Your houses they pull down to fright poor men in town,
But the Gentry must come down, and the poor shall wear the
      crown.
      Stand up now, Diggers all!

*

The Lawyers they conjoin, stand up now, stand up now,
   The Lawyers they conjoin, stand up now!
To arrest you they advise, such fury they devise,
The devil in them lies, and hath blinded both their eyes.
      Stand up now, stand up now.

The Clergy they come in, stand up now, stand up now,
　　The Clergy they come in, stand up now;
The Clergy they come in, and say it is a sin
That we should now begin our freedom for to win.
　　　Stand up now, Diggers all!

*

The Cavaliers are foes, stand up now, stand up now,
　　The Cavaliers are foes, stand up now;
The Cavaliers are foes, themselves they do disclose
By verses, not in prose, to please the singing boys.
　　　Stand up now, Diggers all!

To conquer them by love, come in now, come in now,
　　To conquer them by love, come in now;
To conquer them by love, as it does you behove,
For He is King above, no Power is like to Love.
　　　Glory here, Diggers all!'

Gerrard Winstanley

A ferment of revolutionary ideas was released during the 1640s. The
Levellers, led by John Lilburne, advocated egalitarianism, but a weaver
from Wigan, Gerrard Winstanley, went further. He demanded the
communal ownership of all property. In 1649, with a band of twenty
followers, he occupied some common land on St George's Hill in
Surrey, his stated purpose being 'to sow corn for the succour of men'.
Cromwell would not have any of this, and the Diggers were moved on
and dispersed a year later. In the same year he crushed the Levellers at
Burford, and after that the Ranters, who had carried their libertarian
views to the extent of sharing their wives.

The Leveller's Rant

To the hall, to the hall,
For justice we call,
On the king and his pow'rful adherents and friends,
Who still have endeavour'd, but we work their ends.
'Tis we will pull down whate'er is above us,
And make them to fear us, that never did love us,
　We'll level the proud, and make very degree,
　To our royalty bow the knee,
　　　　'Tis no less than treason,
　　　　'Gainst freedom and reason
for our brethren to be higher than we.

First the thing, call'd a king,
To judgment we bring,
And the spawn of the court, that were prouder than he,
And next the two Houses united shall be:
It does to the Roman religion inveigle,
For the state to be two-headed like the spread-eagle;
　We'll purge the superfluous members away,
　They are too many kings to sway,
　　　　And as we all teach,
　　　　'Tis our liberty's breach,
For the free-born saints to obey.

Not a claw, in the law,
Shall keep us in awe;
We'll have no cushion-cuffers to tell us of Hell,
For we are all gifted to do it as well:
'Tis freedom that we do hold forth to the nation
To enjoy our fellow-creatures as at the creation;
　The carnal men's wives are for men of the spirit,
　Their wealth is our own by merit,
　　　　For we that have right,
　　　　By the law called might,
Are the saints that must judge and inherit.

Alexander Brome

This is a spirited response by a Cavalier poet to the Levellers and
Ranters.

1653

A Prophecy

The land shall be free of all taxation
And men in their minds shall be freed of all vexation . . .
Sorrow and care shall torment us no more,
Some men shall grow rich and some shall grow poor . . .
Men shall next year be kind to their wives
That women shall live most excellent lives . . .
If a traveller chance to be weary, he may
Call at the first ale-house he find in his way
And there for his money he welcome may be,
All this next year you are certain to see.

Will Lilly

Lilly, a pedlar of almanacs, wrote this while in prison.

from On the Victory obtained by *Blake* over the *Spaniards*,
   in the Bay of *Sanctacruze*, in the Island of *Teneriff*. 1657

Now does *Spains* Fleet her spatious wings unfold,
Leaves the new World and hastens for the old:
But though the wind was fair, they slowly swoome
Frayted with acted Guilt, and Guilt to come:
For this rich load, of which so proud they are,
Was rais'd by Tyranny, and rais'd for War;
Every capatious Gallions womb was fill'd,
With what the Womb of wealthy Kingdomes yield,
The new Worlds wounded Intrails they had tore,
For wealth wherewith to wound the old once more.
                         *
They dreaded to behold, Least the Sun's light,
With *English* Streamers, should salute their sight:
In thickest darkness they would choose to steer,
So that such darkness might suppress their fear;
At length theirs vanishes, and fortune smiles;
For they behold the sweet Canary Isles.
                         *
For *Sanctacruze* the glad Fleet takes her way,
And safely there casts Anchor in the Bay.
Never so many with one joyful cry,
That place saluted, where they all must dye.
Deluded men! Fate with you did but sport,
You scap't the Sea, to perish in your Port.
                         *
   With hast they therefore all their Gallions moar,
And flank with Cannon from the Neighbouring shore.
Forts, Lines, and Sconces all the Bay along,
They build and act all that can make them strong.
                         *

Those forts, which there, so high and strong appear,
Do not so much suppress, as shew their fear.
Of Speedy Victory let no man doubt,
Our worst works past, now we have found them out.
Behold their Navy does at Anchor lye,
And they are ours, for now they cannot fly.

*

The Thund'ring Cannon now begins the Fight,
And though it be at Noon, creates a Night.
The Air was soon after the fight begun,
Far more enflam'd by it, then by the Sun.
Never so burning was that Climate known,
War turn'd the temperate, to the Torrid Zone.
Fate these two Fleets, between both Worlds had brought.
Who fight, as if for both those Worlds they fought.
Thousands of wayes, Thousands of men there dye,
Some Ships are sunk, some blown up in the skie.
Nature ne'r made Cedars so high aspire,
As Oakes did then, Urg'd by the active fire.
Which by quick powders force, so high was sent,
That it return'd to its own Element.
Torn Limbs some leagues into the Island fly,
Whilst others lower, in the Sea do lye.
Scarce souls from bodies sever'd are so far,
By death, as bodies there were by the War.
Th' all-seeing Sun, neer gaz'd on such a sight,
Two dreadful Navies there at Anchor Fight.

*

Our Cannon now tears every Ship and Sconce,
And o're two Elements Triumphs at once.
Their Gallions sunk, their wealth the Sea does fill,
The only place where it can cause no Ill.
    Ah would those Treasures which both Indies have,
Were buryed in as large, and deep a grave,
Wars chief support with them would buried be,
And the Land owe her peace unto the Sea.
Ages to come, your conquering Arms will bless,
There they destroy, what had destroy'd their Peace.
And in one War the present age may boast,
The certain seeds of many Wars are lost.
    All the Foes Ships destroy'd, by Sea or fire,
Victorious *Blake*, does from the Bay retire,
His Seige of *Spain* he then again pursues,
And there first brings of his success the news;
The saddest news that ere to *Spain* was brought,
Their rich Fleet sunk, and ours with Lawrel fraught.
Whilst fame in every place, her Trumpet blowes,
And tell the World, how much to you it owes.

Andrew Marvell

Cromwell studiously built up the navy, and Robert Blake was the great admiral who reasserted England's supremacy at sea by defeating the Dutch fleet under its veteran commander, van Tromp, in 1653. In the next year Jamaica was captured from Spain. As Elizabeth I had done, Cromwell set about harassing the great Spanish treasure-fleets. One was captured off Cadiz and another was sunk by Blake in harbour at the Canaries, as Marvell relates. Spain's power was crippled, but as the English fleet headed back to Plymouth Blake died on board.

1658

THE DEATH OF CROMWELL

from A Poem upon the Death of His late Highnesse the Lord Protector

I saw him dead, a leaden slumber lyes
And mortall sleep over those wakefull eys:
Those gentle Rayes under the lidds were fled
Which through his lookes that piercing sweetnesse shed:
That port which so Majestique was and strong,
Loose and depriv'd of vigour stretch'd along:
All wither'd, all discolour'd, pale and wan,
How much another thing, no more that man?
Oh human glory vaine, Oh death, Oh wings,
Oh worthless world, Oh transitory things!

*

Thee many ages hence in martiall verse
Shall th'English souldier ere he charge rehearse:
Singing of thee inflame themselvs to fight
And with the name of Cromwell armyes fright.
As long as rivers to the seas shall runne,
As long as Cynthia shall relieve the sunne,
While staggs shall fly unto the forests thick,
While sheep delight the grassy downs to pick,
As long as future time succeeds the past,
Always thy honour, praise and name shall last.

Andrew Marvell

Cromwell suffered from malaria, called marsh-fever in his day. During the 1630s the wife of a Spanish envoy in Lima, who had been cured of malaria by the use of quinine, popularized it in Europe. Quinine is a powder made from the bark of a tree, the Cinchona, named after her. It also came to be known as 'Jesuit's Bark'. Cromwell could have taken it and been cured, but he died, as he had lived, a Protestant bigot, calling quinine 'the powder of the Devil'.

King Charles II, 1660–85

In 1660 the Puritan Revolution had exhausted all public enthusiasm for it and in effect it petered out. So another experiment was tried – the restoration of the monarchy. Charles I's son returned from exile and became Charles II. Cromwell's body was exhumed and those who had signed the death warrant of the previous King were mercilessly pursued. The Book of Common Prayer was reintroduced, and the Test Acts were passed to keep Dissenters and Catholics alike out of office.

Parliament struggled to reassert its power and denied the supply of money to the King. Charles circumvented this by taking large bribes from Louis XIV of France. England fought Holland and allied herself with France, though many people would have preferred the opposite. The political situation was dominated by Charles's inability to produce an heir, although this was not for want of trying. It appeared more and more likely that his brother, a declared Catholic sympathizer, would succeed him.

Whig historians have praised the Puritan Revolution, while condemning the profligacy, deceitfulness and self-indulgence of the court of Charles II. Yet this was also an age which produced England's greatest scientist, Newton, its greatest architect, Wren, and its greatest political poet, Dryden.

1660

THE RESTORATION

from **Iter Boreale**

Now sing the triumphs of the men of war,
The glorious rays of the bright Northern Star,
Created for the nonce by Heav'n to bring
The wise men of three nations to their King.
Monck! the great Monck! that syllable outshines
Plantagenet's bright name or Constantine's.
'Twas at his rising that our day begun;
Be he the morning star to Charles our sun.
He took rebellion rampant by the throat,
And made the canting Quaker change his note.
His hand it was that wrote (we saw no more)
Exit tyrannus over Lambert's door.
Like to some subtle lightning, so his words
Dissolved in their scabbards rebels' swords.
He with success the sov'reign skill hath found
To dress the weapon and so heal the wound.
George and his boys, as spirits do, they say,
Only by walking scare our foes away.

Robert Wild

Wild's poem celebrates Charles II's return to London in May 1660.
George Monck, one of Cromwell's generals, played the key role in
Charles's restoration. After Cromwell's death, his son, Richard, briefly
took over, but those who wanted the Republic to continue decided to
recall the Rump Parliament, which Cromwell had dissolved. The army
under General Lambert suppressed some Royalist uprisings in 1659.
Returning with his army from Scotland to London, Monck played his
cards so close to his chest throughout the subsequent negotiations that
few knew whether he favoured Parliament or Charles. In 1660, however, he resolved the issue and went to Breda in Holland to bring the
King back to England.

THE CHARACTER OF THE KING

Epitaph on Charles II

In the Isle of Great *Britain* long since famous known,
For breeding the best C[ully] in *Christendom*;
There reigns, and long may he reign and thrive,
The easiest prince and best bred man alive:
Him no ambition moves to seek renown,
Like the *French* fool to wander up and down,
Starving his subjects, hazarding his crown.
Nor are his high desires above his strength,
His scepter and his p . . . are of a length,
And she that plays with one may sway the other,
And make him little wiser than his brother.
I hate all monarchs and the thrones they sit on,
From the Hector of *France* to the Cully of *Britain*.
Poor Prince, thy p . . . like the buffoons at court,
It governs thee, because it makes thee sport;
Tho' safety, law, religion, life lay on't,
'Twill break through all to its way to c . . .
Restless he rolls about from whore to whore,
A merry Monarch, scandalous and poor.
To *Carewell* the most dear of all thy dears.
The sure relief of thy declining years;
Oft he bewails his fortune and her fate,
To love so well, and to be lov'd so late;
For when in her he settles well his t . . .
Yet his dull graceless buttocks hang an Arse.
This you'd believe, had I but time to tell you,
The pain it costs to poor laborious *Nelly*,
While she employs hands, fingers, lips and thighs,
E'er she can raise the member she enjoys.

John Wilmot, Earl of Rochester

1665

THE GREAT PLAGUE

Ring-a-ring o' roses,
A pocket full of posies,
A-tishoo! A-tishoo!
We all fall down

Anonymous

Pindarique Ode Made in the Time of the Great Sickness

I thought on every pensive thing,
That might my passion strongly move,
That might the sweetness sadness bring;
Oft did I think on death, and oft on Love,
The triumphs of the *little God*, and that same *ghastly King*.
The *ghastly King*, what has he done?
How his pale Territories spread!
Strait scantlings now of consecrated ground
His swelling Empire cannot bound,
But every day new *Colonies* of dead
Enhance his Conquests, and advance his Throne.
The mighty *City* sav'd from storms of war,
Exempted from the Crimson floud,
When all the Land o'reflow'd with blood,
Stoops yet once more to a new Conqueror:
The *City* which so many Rivals bred,
Sackcloth is on her loyns, and ashes on her head.

When will the frowning heav'n begin to smile;
　Those pitchy clouds be overblown,
　That hide the mighty Town,
　That I may see the mighty pyle?
When will the angry Angel cease to slay;
　And turn his brandisht sword away
From that illustrous *Golgotha* . . .?

Thomas Flatman

The nursery rhyme is said to date from the time of the Great Plague itself. The give-away symptom was a rash of red spots, and people tried to fend off the infection by carrying nosegays of herbs. As the sickness developed, breathing became more difficult before the inevitability of death.

1666

THE GREAT FIRE OF LONDON

from Annus Mirabilis

The fire, mean time, walks in a broader gross,
　To either hand his wings he opens wide:
He wades the streets, and straight he reaches cross,
　And plays his longing flames on th' other side.

At first they warm, then scorch, and then they take:
　Now with long necks from side to side they feed:
At length, grown strong, their Mother fire forsake,
　And a new Collony of flames succeed.

To every nobler portion of the Town,
　The curling billows roul their restless Tyde:
In parties now they straggle up and down,
　As Armies, unoppos'd, for prey divide.

One mighty Squadron, with a side wind sped,
    Through narrow lanes his cumber'd fire does haste:
By pow'rful charms of gold and silver led,
    The *Lombard* Banquers and the *Change* to waste.

Another backward to the *Tow'r* would go,
    And slowly eats his way against the wind:
But the main body of the marching foe
    Against th' Imperial Palace is design'd.

Now day appears, and with the day the King,
    Whose early care had robb'd him of his rest:
Far off the cracks of falling houses ring,
    And shrieks of subjects pierce his tender breast.

Near as he draws, thick harbingers of smoke,
    With gloomy pillars, cover all the place:
Whose little intervals of night are broke
    By sparks that drive against his Sacred Face.

*

Nor with an idle care did he behold:
    (Subjects may grieve, but Monarchs must redress.)
He chears the fearful, and commends the bold,
    And makes despairers hope for good success.

Himself directs what first is to be done,
    And orders all the succours which they bring.
The helpful and the good about him run,
    And form an Army worthy such a King.

He sees the dire contagion spread so fast,
    That where it seizes, all relief is vain:
And therefore must unwillingly lay waste
    That Country which would, else, the foe maintain.

The powder blows up all before the fire:
    Th' amazed flames stand gather'd on a heap;
And from the precipices brinck retire,
    Afraid to venture on so large a leap.

Thus fighting fires a while themselves consume,
  But straight, like *Turks*, forc'd on to win or die,
They first lay tender bridges of their fume,
  And o'r the breach in unctuous vapours flie.

Part stays for passage till a gust of wind
  Ships o'r their forces in a shining sheet:
Part, creeping under ground, their journey blind,
  And, climbing from below, their fellows meet.

Thus, to some desart plain, or old wood side,
  Dire night-hags come from far to dance their round:
And o'r brode Rivers on their fiends they ride,
  Or sweep in clowds above the blasted ground.

No help avails: for, *Hydra*-like, the fire,
  Lifts up his hundred heads to aim his way.
And scarce the wealthy can one half retire,
  Before he rushes in to share the prey.

John Dryden

LONDON AFTER THE GREAT FIRE

from **Annus Mirabilis**

Me-thinks already, from this Chymick flame,
  I see a City of more precious mold:
Rich as the Town which gives the *Indies* name,
  With Silver pav'd, and all divine with Gold.

Already, Labouring with a mighty fate,
  She shakes the rubbish from her mounting brow,
And seems to have renew'd her Charters date,
  Which Heav'n will to the death of time allow.

More great then humane, now, and more *August*,
   New deifi'd she from her fires does rise:
Her widening streets on new foundations trust,
   And, opening, into larger parts she flies.

Before, she like some Shepherdess did show,
   Who sate to bathe her by a River's side:
Not answering to her fame, but rude and low,
   Nor taught the beauteous Arts of Modern pride.

Now, like a Maiden Queen, she will behold,
   From her high Turrets, hourly Sutors come:
The East with Incense, and the West with Gold,
   Will stand, like Suppliants, to receive her doom.

John Dryden

The Great Plague had carried off as many as 68,000 Londoners and in the following year the Great Fire destroyed the heart of the city. Yet this provided the opportunity for the architects of the time, most notably Sir Christopher Wren, to redesign London in a more planned way and to erect some of the most beautiful buildings since the medieval cathedrals. Wren's epitaph, composed by his son, is inscribed over the north door inside St Paul's Cathedral and reads: 'Si monumentum requiris, circumspice' ('If you seek his monument, look around').

1667

THE DUTCH IN THE MEDWAY

from **The Last Instructions to a Painter**

Ruyter the while, that had our ocean curb'd,
Sail'd now among our rivers undisturb'd,
Survey'd their crystal streams and banks so green
And beauties ere this never naked seen.
Through the vain sedge the bashful nymphs he ey'd:
Bosoms and all which from themselves they hide.
The sun much brighter, and the skies more clear,
He finds the air and all things sweeter here.
The sudden change and such a tempting sight
Swells his old veins with fresh blood, fresh delight.
Like am'rous victors he begins to shave,
And his new face looks in the English wave.
His sporting navy all about him swim
And witness their complacence in their trim.
Their streaming silks play through the weather fair
And with inveigling colors court the air,
While the red flags breathe on their top-masts high
Terror and war but want an enemy.
Among the shrouds the seamen sit and sing,
And wanton boys on every rope do cling.

Andrew Marvell

England and Holland went to war over the control of trade routes. At first England showed the upper hand. She defeated the Dutch at the battle of Lowestoft in 1665, but the Lord High Admiral, Charles II's brother James, Duke of York, failed to follow up the advantage and let the Dutch fleet escape. This did not stop Parliament voting him a payment of £120,000. In 1666 there was further, inconclusive fighting, but in 1667 England suffered its most humiliating naval defeat when the ageing Dutch Admiral De Ruyter broke through the chain defences at Chatham and sailed up the Medway. There was enormous incompetence on the English side, but the admiral concerned, Monck, now the Duke of Albemarle, may have been incapacitated by a singularly painful wound received the year before. As Marvell delicately put it:

> Most with story of his hand or thumb
> Conceal (as Honor would) his Grace's bum,
> When the rude bullet a large collop tore
> Out of that buttock never turn'd before.
> Fortune, it seem'd, would give him by that lash
> Gentle correction for his fight so rash,
> But should the Rump perceiv't, they'd say that Mars
> Had now reveng'd them upon Aumarle's arse.

1671

THE ATTEMPT ON THE CROWN JEWELS

On Blood's Stealing the Crown

> When daring Blood, his rents to have regain'd
> Upon the English diadem distrain'd,
> He chose the cassock, surcingle, and gown
> (No mask so fit for one that robs a crown),
> But his lay-pity underneath prevail'd,
> And while he spar'd the Keeper's life, he fail'd.
> With the priest's vestments had he but put on
> A bishop's cruelty, the crown was gone.

Andrew Marvell

Colonel Blood, an adventurer, seeking redress over a land dispute, made an ingenious plan to steal the Crown Jewels. Under the disguise of a priest, he ingratiated himself with the Keeper of the Jewel House, Talbot Edwards, and was granted a special viewing, whereupon he and his companions turned upon Edwards and bound and gagged him. One stuffed the Orb down his breeches, another tried to saw the Sceptre in half, and Blood popped the Crown under his priest's cloak. Unfortunately for them, at that very moment Edwards's son returned on

leave from Flanders and they were captured. Charles II pardoned
Blood, possibly because he had proven himself too valuable as a spy.

1672

RELATIONS WITH FRANCE

Lines Written in a Lincoln's Inn Boghouse

From peace with the French and war with the Dutch,
From a new mouth which will cost us as much,
And from councils of wits which advise us to such,
                              Libera nos, Domine.

From Pope and from priests which lead men astray,
From fools that by cheats will be so led away,
From saints that 'Go to the Devil' will pray,
                              Libera nos, Domine.

From Parliament-sellers elected for ale,
Who sell the weal public to get themselves bail,
And if e'er it be dissolv'd will die in a jail,
                              Libera nos, Domine.

Anonymous

From 1670 Charles II followed a policy of being friendly to France, of
encouraging Catholicism, and of having as little as possible to do with
Parliament. None of this was popular, and his relations with the French
king, Louis XIV, whose territorial ambitions many Englishmen thought
should be checked, caused particular suspicion.

THE KING'S WHORES

Barbara Palmer, Duchess of Cleveland

Let Ancients boast no more
Their lewd Imperial Whore
Whose everlasting Lust
Surviv'd her Body's latest thrust,
And when that Transitory dust
Had no more vigour left in Store
Was still as fresh and active as before.

*

When shee had jaded quite
Her allmost boundless Appetite,
Cloy'd with the choicest Banquetts of delight,
She'l still drudge on in Tastless vice
As if shee sinn'd for Exercise
Disabling stoutest Stallions ev'ry hour,
And when they can perform no more
She'l rail at 'em and kick 'em out of door.

Monmouth and *Candish* droop
As first did *Henningham* and *Scroop*
Nay Scabby *Ned* looks thinn and pale
And sturdy *Frank* himself begins to fail
But Woe betide him if he does
She'l sett her *Jocky* on his Toes
And he shall end the Quarell without Blows . . .

attributed to John Wilmot, Earl of Rochester

Nell Gwynne

Hard by Pall Mall lives a wench call'd Nell.
  King Charles the Second he kept her.
She hath got a trick to handle his p—,
  But never lays hands on his sceptre.
All matters of state from her soul she does hate,
  And leave to the politic bitches.
The whore's in the right, for 'tis her delight
  To be scratching just where it itches.

Anonymous

Nell Gwynne, the orange-seller from Covent Garden, became the King's mistress in 1669. Her rags-to-riches story made her popular with the crowds. As distinct from the King's other whores, she was not a Catholic. She once escaped from a mob in Oxford, after being mistaken for the Duchess of Portsmouth, by saying: 'Pray, good people, be civil – I am the Protestant whore.'

1673–80

THE POPISH PLOT

from **Absalom and Achitophel**

From hence began that Plot, the nation's curse,
Bad in itself, but represented worse.
Rais'd in extremes, and in extremes decri'd;
With oaths affirm'd, with dying vows deni'd.
Not weigh'd or winnow'd by the multitude;
But swallow'd in the mass, unchew'd and crude.
Some truth there was, but dash'd and brew'd with lies,
To please the fools, and puzzle all the wise.
Succeeding times did equal folly call
Believing nothing, or believing all.

John Dryden

TITUS OATES

from **Absalom and Achitophel**

Sunk were his eyes, his voice was harsh and loud,
Sure signs he neither choleric was nor proud.
His long chin prov'd his wit; his saintlike grace
A church vermilion, and a Moses' face.
His memory, miraculously great,
Could plots exceeding man's belief repeat;
Which therefore cannot be accounted lies,
For human wit could never such devise.
Some future truths are mingl'd in his book;
But, where the witness fail'd, the prophet spoke.
Some things like visionary flights appear;
The spirit caught him up, the Lord knows where,
And gave him his Rabbinical degree
Unknown to foreign university.
His judgement yet his mem'ry did excel;
Which piec'd his wondrous evidence so well,
And suited to the temper of the times,
Then groaning under Jebusitic crimes.

John Dryden

In October 1678 Titus Oates, a charlatan, made accusations before a magistrate, Sir Edmund Berry Godfrey, that a plot had been hatched by Papists to kill the King and put his brother James on the throne. Three weeks later the body of Godfrey was found on Primrose Hill, impaled on his own sword. A cursory medical examination indicated that he could have been strangled as well. The murder hunt was on. A Catholic suspect under torture confessed, declaring that Godfrey had been strangled in front of three Catholic priests. Those found guilty were executed. Some years later Oates admitted that all his evidence had been fabricated and he was sentenced to be whipped from Newgate to Tyburn. The affair created a wave of mass hysteria which was exploited by the politicians of the time, most notably the Earl of Shaftesbury.

1681

THE EARL OF SHAFTESBURY

from Absalom and Achitophel

Of these the false Achitophel was first,
A name to all succeeding ages curst.
For close designs and crooked counsels fit;
Sagacious, bold, and turbulent of wit.
Restless, unfix'd in principles and place;
In pow'r unpleas'd, impatient of disgrace.
A fiery soul which, working out its way,
Fretted the pigmy body to decay,
And o'er-inform'd the tenement of clay.
A daring pilot in extremity;
Pleas'd with the danger, when the waves went high
He sought the storms; but, for a calm unfit,
Would steer too nigh the sands to boast his wit.
Great wits are sure to madness near alli'd,
And thin partitions do their bounds divide;
Else why should he, with wealth and honor blest,
Refuse his age the needful hours of rest?
Punish a body which he could not please;
Bankrupt of life, yet prodigal of ease?
And all to leave what with his toil he won
To that unfeather'd, two-legg'd thing, a son,
Got while his soul did huddl'd notions try,
And born a shapeless lump, like anarchy.
In friendship false, implacable in hate;
Resolv'd to ruin or to rule the state;
To compass this the triple bond he broke,
The pillars of the public safety shook,
And fitted Israel for a foreign yoke.
Then, seiz'd with fear, yet still affecting fame,
Usurp'd a Patriot's all-atoning name.
So easy still it proves in factious times
With public zeal to cancel private crimes.
How safe is treason, and how sacred ill,

Where none can sin against the people's will;
Where crowds can wink, and no offense be known,
Since in another's guilt they find their own!

John Dryden

'Absalom and Achitophel' is perhaps the finest political poem in the English language. Asked to write it by the King, Dryden applied his majestic Augustan couplets to satirizing the Whigs, and particularly, in the figure of Achitophel, Anthony Ashley Cooper, the Earl of Shaftesbury, who had been arrested for high treason in July 1681. Shaftesbury had led the Whig opposition to the King, openly supporting the Duke of Monmouth as Protestant heir to the throne; masterminding the campaign to exclude the King's brother, James; exploiting the public feeling stirred up by the Popish Plot; and striving to ensure that Parliament was not suspended. He had, in effect, created the post of Leader of the Opposition. It was he who first made use of the slogan that 'Popery and slavery, like two sisters, go hand in hand.'

WHIGS AND TORIES

My Opinion

After thinking this fortnight of Whig and of Tory,
This to me is the long and the short of the story:
They are all fools or knaves, and they keep up this pother
On both sides, designing to cheat one another.

Poor Rowley (whose maxims of state are a riddle)
Has plac'd himself much like the pin in the middle;
Let which corner soever be tumbl'd down first,
'Tis ten thousand to one but he comes by the worst.

'Twixt brother and bastard (those Dukes of renown)
He'll make a wise shift to get rid of his crown;
Had he half common sense (were it ne'er so uncivil)
He'd have had 'em long since tipp'd down to the Devil.

The first is a Prince well-fashion'd, well-featur'd,
No bigot to speak of, not false, nor ill-natur'd;
The other for government can't be unfit,
He's so little a fop, and so plaguy a wit.

Had I this soft son, and this dangerous brother,
I'd hang up the one, then I'd piss upon t'other;
I'd make this the long and the short of the story:
The fools might be Whigs, none but knaves should be Tories.

Charles Sackville, Earl of Dorset

The last ten years of Charles's reign were a period of bitter political conflict and they saw the birth of two dominant parties – Whigs and Tories. When in 1679 Parliament failed to renew the Licensing Act, bitterness was increased as virulent lampoons and satires flooded from the presses. The country party, or Whigs, supported Monmouth as Protestant heir, while the Court party, or Tories, backed James. Charles, in the middle, cunningly exploited the royal prerogative and ruled without Parliament for the last four years of his reign.

CHARLES II

We have a pritty witty king
    And whose word no man relys on:
He never said a foolish thing,
    And never did a wise one.

John Wilmot, Earl of Rochester

King James II, 1685–8

from The Statue in Stocks-Market

But with all his faults restore us our King,
If ever you hope in December for Spring;
For though all the world cannot show such another,
Yet we'd rather have him than his bigoted brother.

Andrew Marvell

1685

The Humble Address of the Loyal Professors of Divinity and Law that Want Preferment and Practice

Great sir, our poor hearts were ready to burst
For the loss of your brother when we heard it at first.
But when we were told that you were to reign
We all fell a roaring out huzzas again.
With hearts full of joy, as our glasses of wine,
In this loyal address both professions do join.

May Jeffreys swagger on the bench
And James upon the throne,
Till we become slaves to the French
And Rome's dominion own;

May no man sit in Parliament
But by a false return,
Till Lords and Commons by consent
Their Magna Charta burn.
Though Smithfield now neglected lie,
Oh, may it once more shine
With Whigs in flaming heaps that fry
Of books they call divine;
From whence may such a blaze proceed,
So glorious and so bright,
That the next parish priest may read
His mass by Bible light.
Then holy water pots shall cheer
Our hearts like aqua vitae
Whilst singing monks in triumph bear
Their little God Almighty.
More blessings we could yet foretell
In this most happy reign,
But hark, the King's own chapel bell
Calls us to prayers again.
May trade and industry decay,
But may the plague increase,
Till it hath swept those Whigs away
That sign not this address.

Anonymous

James II set out to restore Catholicism to England at breakneck speed.
Within ten days of his accession, he attended a Mass in public, which
occasioned the ironical 'Humble Address'. The Test Acts, excluding all
Dissenters from state office, were his main stumbling-block, and so he
revived the power to dispense with inconvenient laws, just as his
father, Charles I, had tried to do. He suspended Parliament and
strengthened the standing army. When seven Protestant bishops

refused to read one of his declarations from the pulpit, he had them arrested and put on trial. Although they were acquitted, this gesture did more than anything to turn opinion against the King. But the last straw was the birth of a son as Prince of Wales in June 1688, which in effect barred James's two Protestant daughters – Mary, married to William of Orange, and Anne, married to Prince George of Denmark – from the throne. William, however, had been making his own preparations, egged on by Protestant exiles, and in 1688 the people of England appealed to him to release them from 'Popery and slavery'.

1685

MONMOUTH'S REBELLION

Monmouth Degraded

(Or, James Scott, the Little King in Lyme)

Come beat alarm, sound a charge
As well without as in the verge,
Let every sword and soul be large
  To make our monarch shine, boys.
Let's leave off whores and drunken souls
And windy words o'er brimming bowls,
Let English hearts exceed the Poles'
  'Gainst Perkin, King in Lyme, boys.

Such a fop-king was ne'er before
Is landed on our western shore,
Which our black saints do all adore,
  Inspir'd by Tub-Divine, boys.
Let us assume the souls of Mars
And march in order, foot and horse,
Pull down the standard at the cross
  Of Perkin, King in Lyme, boys.

Pretended son unto a King,
Subject of delights in sin,
The most ungrateful wretch of men;
    Dishonour to the shrine, boys.
Of Charles, and James the undoubted right
Of England's crown and honours bright:
While he can find us work, let's fight
    'Gainst Perkin, King in Lyme, boys.

The Sainted Sisters now look blue,
Their cant's all false if God be true;
Their teaching stallions dare not do
    No more but squeeze and whine, boys;
Exhorting all the clowns to fight
Against their God, King, Church, and Right,
Takes care, for all their wives at night,
    For Perkin, King in Lyme, boys.

'Poor Perkin' now he is no more,
But James Scott as he was before;
No honour left but soul to soar
    Till quite expir'd with time, boys.
But first he'll call his parliament
By Ferguson and Grey's consent,
Trenchard and all the boors in's tent,
    Fit for the King in Lyme, boys.

'Gainst these mock kings, each draw his sword;
In blood we'll print them on record,
'Traitors against their sovereign lord';
    Let's always fight and join, boys.
Now they're block'd up by sea and land,
By treason they must fall or stand,
We only wait the King's command
    To burn the rogues in Lyme, boys.

But now we hear they're salli'd forth,
Front and flank 'em, south and north,
Nobles of brave England's worth,
   Let your bright honours shine, boys.
Let guns and cannons roar and ring
The music of a warlike King,
And all the gods just conquest bring
   Against the rogues in Lyme, boys.

Anonymous

The handsome bastard son of Charles II, the Duke of Monmouth left
his mistress in Holland after she had sold her jewels to support his
cause, and set sail with just three ships and a few hundred men to seize
the throne of England. On 11 June 1685, he landed at Lyme in Dorset,
raised his blue banner, and was proclaimed King at Taunton. On 6 July
James II's regular army met Monmouth's straggling forces at Sedgemoor and crushed them. On 15 July, after a grovelling plea to his uncle,
Monmouth died bravely on Tower Hill, telling the executioner that his
blade was not sharp enough – which proved to be right, as it took seven
strokes to kill him.

JUDGE JEFFREYS

A True Englishman

Let a lewd judge come reeking from a wench
To vent a wilder lust upon the bench;
Bawl out the venom of his rotten heart,
Swell'd up with envy, over-act his part;
Condemn the innocent by laws ne'er fram'd
And study to be more than doubly damn'd.

Anonymous

Jeffreys was made Lord Chief Justice in 1683 after presiding over the trial of Titus Oates. James II made him Lord Chancellor, and in the aftermath of Sedgemoor he conducted what came to be known as the Bloody Assizes in the West Country.

THE MORALS OF THE TIMES

from A Faithful Catalogue of Our Most Eminent Ninnies

Curs'd be those dull, unpointed, dogg'rel rhymes,
Whose harmless rage has lash'd our impious times.
Rise thou, my muse, and with the sharpest thorn,
Instead of peaceful bays, my brows adorn;
Inspir'd with just disdain and mortal hate,
Who long have been my plague, shall feel thy weight.
I scorn a giddy and unsafe applause,
But this, ye gods, is fighting in your cause;
Let Sodom speak, and let Gomorrah tell,
If their curs'd walls deserv'd their flames so well.
Go on, my muse, and with bold voice proclaim
The vicious lives and long detested fame
Of scoundrel lords, and their lewd wives' amours,
Pimp-statesmen, bugg'ring priests, court bawds, and whores.

*

Oh, sacred James! may thy dread noddle be
As free from danger as from wit 'tis free!
But if that good and gracious Monarch's charms
Could ne'er confine one woman to his arms,
What strange, mysterious spell, what strong defense,
Can guard that front which has not half his sense?
Poor Sedley's fall e'en her own sex deplore,
Who with so small temptation turn'd thy whore.
But Grafton bravely does revenge her fate
And says, thou court'st her thirty years too late;
She scorns such dwindles, her capacious arse
Is fitter for thy scepter, than thy tarse.

Charles Sackville, Earl of Dorset

Dorset was a noted libertine, but this did not prevent him from writing a scurrilous attack on his contemporaries, including James II. On his accession, James promised his demure wife that he would put aside his mistress, Catherine Sedley, whom he had ennobled as the Countess of Dorchester. It was James's luck to have a succession of singularly unattractive mistresses, which led his brother Charles to quip: 'James had his mistresses given him by his priests for penance.'

1688

THE TRIAL OF THE SEVEN BISHOPS

A New Catch in Praise of the Reverend Bishops

True Englishmen, drink a good health to the miter;
Let our church ever flourish, though her enemies spite her.
May their cunning and forces no longer prevail;
And their malice, as well as their arguments, fail.
Then remember the Seven, which supported our cause,
As stout as our martyrs and as just as our laws!

Anonymous

The Song of the Western Men

A good sword and a trusty hand!
  A merry heart and true!
King James's men shall understand
  What Cornish lads can do.

And have they fixed the where and when?
  And shall Trelawny die?
Here's twenty thousand Cornish men
  Will know the reason why!

Out spake their captain brave and bold,
    A merry wight was he:
'If London Tower were Michael's hold,
    We'll set Trelawny free!

We'll cross the Tamar, land to land,
    The Severn is no stay,
With "one and all", and hand in hand,
    And who shall bid us nay?

And when we come to London Wall,
    A pleasant sight to view,
Come forth! come forth, ye cowards all,
    Here's men as good as you!

Trelawny he's in keep and hold,
    Trelawny he may die;
But twenty thousand Cornish bold
    Will know the reason why.'

R. S. Hawker

Trelawny was the Bishop of Bristol, and one of the seven bishops to defy James and be imprisoned in the Tower. On the evening of their acquittal, seven English magnates signed an invitation to William of Orange to become their King and establish 'free Parliaments and the Protestant religion' in the land. Hawker was a nineteenth-century vicar of Morwenstow. Each of the chimneys on the house he built there was of a different medieval design.

William and Mary, 1688–1702

On 5 November 1688, William, Prince of Orange, landed at Torbay in Devon, not far from where Monmouth had landed three years earlier. James II's army outnumbered his by two to one, but at Salisbury the King was incapacitated by severe nose-bleeding and decided not to march against William at Exeter. This delay was a great mistake. His military commander, John Churchill, defected, and James fled back to London where he threw the Great Seal of England into the Thames. He never put up a fight.

Lilli Burlero

Ho, brother Teague, dost hear de decree,
   Lilli burlero, bullen a-la;
Dat we shall have a new debittie,
   Lilli burlero bullen a-la,
     Lero lero, lero lero, lilli burlero, bullen a-la;
     Lero lero, lero lero, lilli burlero, bullen a-la.

Ho, by my shoul, it is a Talbot,
And he will cut de Englishman's troat.

Though, by my shoul, de English do prat,
De law's on dare side, and Chreist knows what.

But if dispense do come from de Pope,
Weel hang Magno Cart and demselves on a rope.

And the good Talbot is made a lord,
And he with brave lads is coming aboard.

Who'll all in France have taken a swear,
Dat day will have no Protestant heir.

Oh, but why does he stay behind,
Ho, by my shoul, 'tis a Protestant wind.

Now Tyrconnel is come a-shore,
And we shall have commissions gillore.

And he dat will not go to mass,
Shall turn out and look like an ass.

Now, now, de heretics all go down,
By Chreist and St Patrick, the nation's our own!

attributed to Thomas Wharton

The words of 'Lilli Burlero', possibly by Thomas Wharton, were written
in 1687 as an attack on the new Governor of Ireland, Tyrconnel, and an
arrangement of the tune was published by Henry Purcell. But the song
instantly transcended its topical purpose and became extraordinarily
popular everywhere, especially among soldiers. It has been said that it
'sang a deluded Prince out of three Kingdoms'.

1689

A CATHOLIC VIEW OF THE CORONATION

A Dainty Fine King Indeed

The eleventh of April has come about,
To Westminster went a rabble rout,
In order to crown a bundle of clouts;
      A dainty fine king indeed.

He's half a knave and half a fool,
The Protestant joyner's crooked tool,
Oh! its splutters, and nails shall such an one rule;
      A dainty fine king indeed.

He has gotten part of the shape of a man,
But more of a monkey, deny it who can;
He has the head of a goose, but the legs of a cran;
    A dainty fine king indeed.

In Hide Park he rides like a hog in armour,
In Whitehall he creeps like a country farmer,
Old England may boast of a godly reformer;
    A dainty fine king indeed.

Anonymous

THE PROTESTANT VIEW OF WILLIAM III

A New Song of an Orange

Good People come buy
  The Fruit that I cry,
That now is in Season, tho' Winter is nigh;
  'Twill do you all good
  And sweeten your Blood,
I'm sure it will please when you've once understood
                  'tis an *Orange.*

It's Cordial Juice,
  Does much Vigour produce,
I may well recommend it to every Mans use,
  Tho' some it quite chills,
  And with fear almost kills,
Yet certain each Healthy Man benefit feels
                  by an *Orange.*

To make Claret go down,
Sometimes there is found
A jolly good Health, to pass pleasantly round;
But yet, I'll protest,
Without any Jest,
No Flavour is better then that of the taste
                                    of an *Orange*.

                                    Anonymous

WILLIAM III'S VIEW OF HIMSELF

As I walk'd by my self
And talk'd to my self,
My self said unto me,
Look to thy self,
Take care of thy self,
For nobody cares for Thee.

I answer'd my self,
And said to my self,
In the self-same Repartee,
Look to thy self
Or not look to thy self,
The self-same thing will be.

                                    William III

1689

Bonnie Dundee

To the Lords of Convention 'twas Claver'se who spoke,
'Ere the King's crown shall fall there are crowns to be broke;
Then each cavalier who loves honour and me,
Let him follow the bonnet of Bonnie Dundee.
   'Come fill up my cup, come fill up my can,
   Come saddle your horses, and call up your men;
   Come open the West Port, and let me gang free,
And it's room for the bonnets of Bonnie Dundee!'

Dundee he is mounted, he rides up the street,
The bells are rung backward, the drums they are beat;
But the Provost, douce man, said, 'Just e'en let him be,
The Gude Town is weel quit o' that De'il of Dundee.'
   'Come fill up my cup,' etc.

'There are hills beyond Pentland, and lands beyond Forth.
If there's lords in the Lowlands, there's chiefs in the north;
There are wild Duniewassals, three thousand times three,
Will cry "hoigh!" for the bonnet of Bonnie Dundee.
   'Come fill up my cup,' etc.

'Away to the hills, to the caves, to the rocks –
Ere I own an usurper. I'll couch with the fox;
And tremble, false Whigs, in the midst of your glee.
You have not seen the last of my bonnet and me.
   'Come fill up my cup,' etc.

Walter Scott

The Convention was the Parliamentary assembly which formalized the
abdication of James II. There the Presbyterians of the Scottish Lowlands, who had been persecuted under James, were glad to proclaim
William as the new King. The leader of the Catholics, Claverhouse,

Viscount Dundee, rode out of the West Port of Edinburgh to raise the
Highlands in the Stuart cause. The King's troops marched north to
capture Blair Atholl Castle, but were met in the narrow pass of Killie-
crankie by the Highlanders, who charged down upon the Redcoats
only half an hour before sunset. Their heavy claymores cut through the
Royalist army, which withdrew to Stirling. At the moment of victory,
however, Bonny Dundee was shot and killed, as some said, by a silver
bullet.

1690

THE BATTLE OF THE BOYNE

from **The Boyne Water**

July the First, of a morning clear, one thousand six hundred and
    ninety,
King William did his men prepare, of thousands he had thirty;
To fight King James and all his foes, encamped near the Boyne
    Water,
He little fear'd though two to one, their multitudes to scatter.

King William call'd his officers, saying: 'Gentlemen, mind your
    station,
And let your valour here be shown before this Irish nation;
My brazen walls let no man break, and your subtle foes you'll
    scatter,
Be sure you show them good English play as you go over the
    water.'

*

Within four yards of our fore-front, before a shot was fired,
A sudden snuff they got that day, which little they desired;
For horse and man fell to the ground, and some hung in their
   saddle;
Others turn'd up their forked ends, which we call 'coup de
   ladle'.

Prince Eugene's regiment was the next, on our right hand
   advanced,
Into a field of standing wheat, where Irish horses pranced –
But the brandy ran so in their heads, their senses all did scatter,
They little thought to leave their bones that day at the Boyne
   Water.

Both men and horse lay on the ground, and many there lay
   bleeding;
I saw no sickles there that day – but, sure, there was sharp
   shearing.

*

So praise God, all true Protestants, and I will say no further,
But had the Papists gain'd the day there would have been open
   murder.
Although King James and many more were ne'er that way
   inclined,
It was not in their power to stop what the rabble they designed.

Anonymous

Three months after William had landed in England, James left France to
lead an uprising of his supporters in Ireland. He laid siege to
Londonderry, which bravely held out for fifteen weeks, and then had
to withdraw to Dublin where he was reinforced by 6,000 French troops.
William landed in the north and marched on Dublin, but found his path
blocked by James's army where it was drawn up by the River Boyne, in
a strong defensive position. However, William's 36,000 soldiers crossed
the river and defeated James's 25,000. It proved a decisive victory, for it
established the ascendancy of the Protestant minority all over Ireland,
until the forces unleashed by the French Revolution led to an
independent Catholic Ireland.

1698

New Year's Day Song

Chorus
What then should happy Britain do?
Blest with the gift and giver too.

On warlike enterprizes bent
To foreign fields the hero went;
    The dreadful part he there perform'd
    Of battles fought, and cities storm'd:
But now the drum and trumpet cease,
    And wish'd success his sword has sheath'd,
    To us returns, with olive wreath'd,
To practice here the milder arts of peace.

Grand chorus
Happy, happy, past expressing,
Britain, if thou know'st thy blessing;
Home-bred discord ne'er alarm thee,
Other mischief cannot harm thee.
Happy, if thou know'st thy blessing
Happy, happy, past expressing.

Nahum Tate

William was almost constantly engaged in protecting his Seven Provinces against the predatory ambitions of Louis XIV. He undertook campaigns in 1691, 1692, 1693 and 1694, and negotiated an advantageous peace in 1697. This lasted until 1702, when the fight against Louis was resumed in the War of the Spanish Succession, and after Louis had proclaimed his support for James II's son, the 'Old Pretender', as heir to the English throne. William was essentially a military commander, but it says much for his political acumen, too, that he managed to maintain a large standing army in spite of Parliament's suspicions and fears. It was this army which John Churchill, the Duke of Marlborough, was to lead so brilliantly.

1701

THE EXECUTION OF CAPTAIN KIDD

Great Black-backed Gulls

Said Cap'n Morgan to Cap'n Kidd:
'Remember the grand times, Cap'n, when
The Jolly Roger flapped on the tropic breeze,
And we were the terrors of the Spanish Main?'
And Cap'n Kidd replied: 'Aye when our restless souls
Were steeped in human flesh and bone;
But now we range the seven seas, and fight
For galley scraps that men throw overboard.'

Two black-backed gulls, that perched
On a half-sunken spar –
Their eyes were gleaming-cold and through
The morning fog that crept upon the grey-green waves
Their wicked laughter sounded.

John Heath-Stubbs

Sir Henry Morgan and William Kidd were the two most notorious
pirates of the Spanish Main. They plundered the merchant ships
engaged in the circular trade of slaves from Africa and sugar to Europe.
Morgan died as Lieutenant-Governor of Jamaica, but Kidd was hanged
at Execution Dock on the Thames in 1701.

1702

THE DEATH OF WILLIAM III

But *William* had not Govern'd Fourteen Year,
To be an unconcern'd Spectator here:
His Works like Providence were all Compleat,
And made a Harmony we Wonder'd at.
The Legislative Power he set Free,
And led them step by step to Liberty,
'Twas not his Fault if they cou'd not Agree.
Impartial Justice He protected so,
The Laws did in their Native Channels flow,
From whence our sure Establishment begun,
And *William* laid the first Foundation Stone:
On which the stately Fabrick soon appear'd,
How cou'd they sink when such a Pilot steer'd?
He taught them due defences to prepare,
And make their future Peace their present care:
By him directed, Wisely they Decreed,
What Lines shou'd be expell'd, and what succeed;
That now he's Dead, there's nothing to be done,
But to take up the Scepter he laid down.

Daniel Defoe

William served England well, but by the winter of 1701 he was worn out and did not expect to see another summer. In February 1702 his horse, Sorrel, stumbled, it is said, on a molehill, and threw the King off, breaking his collar-bone. Within three weeks he was dead. He had never been a popular figure: people did not like his asthmatic cough, his hooked nose, his solitariness, or the fact that he was foreign. An elegy on his horse appeared promptly, but Defoe tried to set the record straight.

Queen Anne, 1702–14

from **An Ode Humbly Inscrib'd to the Queen**

But, Greatest *Anna*! while Thy Arms pursue
Paths of Renown, and climb Ascents of Fame
Which nor *Augustus* nor *Eliza* knew;
What *Poet* shall be found to sing Thy Name?
What Numbers shall Record? What Tongue shall say
Thy Wars on Land, Thy Triumphs on the Main?
Oh Fairest Model of Imperial Sway!
What Equal Pen shall write Thy wond'rous Reign?
Who shall Attempts and Victories rehearse
By Story yet untold, unparallell'd by Verse?

Matthew Prior

Anne ruled for twelve years and, for eleven of those, British armies were busy fighting Louis XIV and winning great victories. The politics of Anne's reign were Byzantine, but they saw the consolidation of identifiable groupings of Whigs and Tories. It was a glittering period in terms of military and literary achievement, but the Queen herself remains a shadowy figure. As much as most people are able to say about her is that 'Queen Anne is dead'. In 1712 her statue was erected outside St Paul's and there it stands to this day. As an anonymous squib-writer put it:

Brandy Nan, Brandy Nan,
You're left in the lurch
With your face to the gin shop
And your back to the Church.

1704

THE BATTLE OF BLENHEIM

from **The Campaign**

But O, my muse, what numbers wilt thou find
To sing the furious troops in battle joined?
Methinks I hear the drum's tumultuous sound
The victor's shouts and dying groans confound,
The dreadful burst of cannon rend the skies,
And all the thunder of the battle rise.
'Twas then great Marlborough's mighty soul was proved,
That, in the shock of changing hosts unmoved,
Amidst confusion, horror and despair,
Examined all the dreadful scenes of war;
In peaceful thought the field of death surveyed,
To fainting squadrons sent the timely aid,
Inspired repulsed battalions to engage,
And taught the doubtful battle where to rage.
So when an angel by divine command
With rising tempests shakes a guilty land,
Such as of late o'er pale Britannia past,
Calm and serene he drives the furious blast;
And, pleased th' Almighty's orders to perform,
Rides in the whirlwind, and directs the storm.

Joseph Addison

The Duke of Marlborough led a huge army of English and European
troops on the long march from Cologne to Austria, where one of Louis
XIV's armies was threatening to capture the Habsburg capital, Vienna.
A battle was fought over a three-mile front and through the village of
Blenheim, between armies of much the same size – about 60,000 men
each. It was indeed a bloody contest, for about half of the French force
was killed. After seventeen hours in the saddle, Marlborough was able
to scribble a note on the back of a tavern bill: 'Let the Queen know, her
Army has had a Glorious Victory.' The power of Louis XIV, the Sun

King, had suffered a serious set-back for the first time in forty years. In 1705 the Queen, with the consent of Parliament, granted her Captain-General the royal manor of Woodstock – 16,000 acres on which Marlborough asked Sir John Vanbrugh, the playwright and architect, to build him a palace.

On Sir John Vanbrugh

Under this stone, reader, survey
Dead Sir John Vanbrugh's house of clay.
Lie heavy on him, earth! for he
Laid many heavy loads on thee.

Abel Evans

from After Blenheim

'Twas a summer evening,
  Old Kaspar's work was done,
And he before his cottage door
  Was sitting in the sun,
And by him sported on the green
His little grandchild, Wilhelmine.

She saw her brother Peterkin
  Roll something large and round,
Which he beside the rivulet
  In playing there had found;
He came to ask what he had found
That was so large, and smooth, and round.

Old Kaspar took it from the boy
   Who stood expectant by;
And then the old man shook his hand.
   And with a natural sigh –
   ''Tis some poor fellow's skull,' said he,
'Who fell in that great victory.'

'I find them in the garden,
For there's many here about;
And often when I go to plough
   The ploughshare turns them out.
For many thousand men,' said he,
'Were slain in that great victory.'

'Now tell us what 'twas all about,'
   Young Peterkin, he cries;
And little Wilhelmine looks up
   With wonder-waiting eyes;
'Now tell us all about the war,
And what they fought each other for.'

'It was the English,' Kaspar cried,
   'Who put the French to rout;
But what they fought each other for
   I could not well make out;
But everybody said,' quoth he,
'That 'twas a famous victory.

*

'And everybody praised the Duke
   Who this great fight did win.'
'But what good came of it at last?'
   Quoth little Peterkin.
'Why, that I cannot tell,' said he,
'But 'twas a famous victory.'

Robert Southey

1707

THE UNION

Just such a happy Change, our Nation finds:
If we Unite, our once Contented Minds,
With our rich Neighbour: then, doth dawn the day,
Which drives all Feuds and enmities away.
Let base Revenge and Damn'd Envy be gone,
And all our Int'rests be conjoyn'd in one.
No *Mastiff Devil* can our good withstand,
If as true Friends, we do join hand to hand,
That so no more of jealousies be known;
And in our Isle, no more Dissention sown,
And each now, more than Self, his Country mind,
So henceforth, we that Blessedness shall find,
Which, n'ere before, we luckily cou'd reach,
No *Wonder*. Since so damnable a breach,
Did two brave *Neighbours* fatally divide;
What cou'd but war and Poverty betide?
Yet there's no State, in the vast *Universe*,
Might more enjoy of bless or happiness,
Than we, the *Natives* of this admir'd Isle:
If we would banish prejudice and guile,
And let no more, our foolish ears be stunn'd,
With lies, mistakes, and fears, that have no ground.
'Tis true, oft *England* hath us roughly us'd,
And has our ruine and destruction chus'd;
Stop, *Envy*, stop, *Scotland* is guilty too;
How oft did she her Warlike hands imbrue
In *English* Blood? We can't Excuse pretend.
But let's no more 'bout former Strifes contend:
For if we Search, our Histories can tell,
Both have resisted one another *Well*.

Daniel Defoe

Various rulers had tried to unite England and Scotland: Edward I by conquest, James I by parliamentary agreement, Cromwell by force, William III by hope. It was left to Anne to see it achieved. She offered the Scots a guarantee of the Protestant Succession, and the Whig Lords secured guarantees against the Jacobites. Defoe himself was sent to Scotland as a spy by the Tory leader, Robert Harley, his mission being to penetrate Jacobite groups and send reports on their activities back to London. This he did with no thanks or subsequent recognition from Harley.

On the Union

The Queen has lately lost a Part
Of her entirely-*English* Heart,
For want of which by way of Botch,
She piec'd it up again with *Scotch*.
Blest Revolution, which creates
Divided Hearts, united States.
See how the double Nation lies;
Like a rich Coat with Skirts of Frize:
As if a Man in making Posies
Should bundle Thistles up with Roses.
Whoever yet a Union saw
Of Kingdoms, without Faith or Law.
Henceforward let no Statesman dare,
A Kingdom to a Ship compare;
Lest he should call our Commonweal,
A Vessel with a double Keel:
Which just like ours, new rigg'd and man'd,
And got about a League from Land,
By Change of Wind to Leeward Side
The Pilot knew not how to guide.
So tossing Faction will o'erwhelm
One crazy double-bottom'd Realm.

Jonathan Swift

Swift could not abide the Union, as is clear from this poem, which, however, was not published until after his death in 1745. The double keel to which he refers was invented by Sir William Petty, the founder of the Royal Society. Petty had settled in Ireland, where he designed and built boats with this peculiarity. The last of these was launched in Dublin in 1684. It was hopelessly unseaworthy and never got beyond the bar of Dublin harbour.

THE WHIG JUNTO

An Acrostick on Wharton

Whig's the first Letter of his odious Name;
Hypocrisy's the second of the same;
Anarchy's his Darling; and his Aim
Rebellion, Discord, Mutiny, and Faction;
Tom, Captain of the Mob in Soul and Action;
O'ergrown in Sin, cornuted, old, in Debt,
Noll's Soul and Ireton's live within him yet.

Anonymous

Thomas Wharton was a leading Whig politician and one of the five members of the party's so-called Junto, or inner circle. He is thought to have written the words of 'Lilli Burlero' and had been a drinking companion of William III. A shrewd and successful organizer of elections, he liked to be called 'Honest Tom', but the Tories dubbed him 'King Tom'. He gambled, fornicated, hunted and raced on an extravagant scale, and his morals were such that Macaulay later commented that 'to the end of his long life the wives and daughters of his nearest friends were not safe from his lecherous plots'. On the day after he became Lord Lieutenant of Ireland, the bailiffs moved into his London house to seize his furniture in payment of debts. He thought like a Roundhead, but lived like a Cavalier.

HAMPTON COURT

from The Rape of the Lock

Close by those meads, for ever crowned with flowers,
Where Thames with pride surveys his rising towers,
There stands a structure of majestic frame,
Which from the neighb'ring Hampton takes its name.
Here Britain's statesmen oft the fall foredoom
Of foreign tyrants and of nymphs at home;
Here thou, great Anna! whom three realms obey,
Dost sometimes counsel take – and sometimes tea.
Hither the heroes and the nymphs resort,
To taste awhile the pleasures of a court;
In various talk the instructive hours they passed,
Who gave the ball, or paid the visit last;
One speaks the glory of the British Queen,
And one describes a charming Indian screen;
A third interprets motions, looks, and eyes;
At every word a reputation dies.
Snuff, or the fan, supply each pause of chat,
With singing, laughing, ogling, and all that.
Meanwhile, declining from the noon of day,
The sun obliquely shoots his burning ray;
The hungry judges soon the sentence sign,
And wretches hang that jury-men may dine;
The merchant from the Exchange returns in peace,
And the long labours of the toilet cease.

Alexander Pope

Christopher Wren had designed a great and elegant extension to the
Tudor palace of Hampton Court. It was this which nearly burnt down
on Easter Monday 1986, when a fire was accidentally started by a
candle. William III and Queen Anne both spent a lot of time there, and
their courtiers indulged in the comparatively new fashion of taking tea.
Tea, coffee and cocoa were introduced to England in the middle of the
seventeenth century. The East India Company had been given the

monopoly of trade to the Far East and by Queen Anne's reign it had pushed the Dutch into second place in that field. Thousands of tons of tea were imported each year, with porcelain as a makeweight, and at its height tea accounted for 5 per cent of British imports. Britain was well on its way to becoming a nation of tea-drinkers. The tea which Queen Anne drank came from China, for Indian tea reached these shores only as late as 1840, and she would have drunk it from a Chinese bowl without handles – these were not added until 1750.

THE HANOVERIAN HEIR

The crown's far too weighty
For shoulders of eighty;
She could not sustain such a trophy;
Her hand, too, already
Has grown so unsteady
She can't hold a sceptre;
So Providence kept her
Away. – Poor old Dowager Sophy.

Thomas D'Urfey

Anne was childless and her successor was the ageing Sophia Dorothea, Electress and Dowager Duchess of Hanover. Anne did not care for this distant relative, and D'Urfey got fifty guineas as a reward for singing her the song from which this snatch is taken. As it happened, Sophia died before Anne, and so her son, George, succeeded.

1714

QUEEN ANNE DIES

A Farewell to the Year

Farewell old year, for Thou canst ne're return,
No more than the great Queen for whom we mourn;
Farewell old year, with thee the Stuart race
Its Exit made, which long our Isle did grace;
Farewell old year, the Church hath lost in Thee
The best Defender it will ever see;
Farewell old year, for Thou to us did bring
Strange changes in our State, a stranger King;
Farewell old year, for thou with Broomstick hard
Hast drove poor Tory from St James's Yard;
Farewell old year, old Monarch, and old Tory,
Farewell old England, Thou hast lost thy glory.

Anonymous

THE HOUSE OF HANOVER

King George I, 1714–27

George I – Star of Brunswick

He preferr'd Hanover to England,
He preferr'd two hideous mistresses
To a beautiful and innocent wife.
He hated arts and despised literature;
But he liked train-oil in his salads,
And gave an enlighten'd patronage to bad oysters.
And he had Walpole as a minister;
Consistent in his preference for every kind of corruption.

H. J. Daniel

At the age of fifty-four, George, the Elector of Hanover, came to the throne of a country he had never visited, whose language he never spoke and whose people he never loved. He had two mistresses – one thin and tall, known as 'the Maypole', and one short and fat, known as 'the Elephant'.

England came under the sway of three great statesmen: Stanhope and Walpole until 1742, and then the elder Pitt. Walpole presided over a period of peace, prosperity and stability; Pitt had a vision of a great and powerful empire spreading over the world and he set about achieving it. During this time the power of the House of Commons was established firmly, and the royal veto was never used after 1714. It became the task of the Duke of Newcastle to provide through his enormous wealth and patronage a majority for the government of the day, a service he undertook for over forty years.

The Wee, Wee German Lairdie

Wha the deil hae we gotten for a king,
   But a wee, wee German lairdie?
And, when we gaed to bring him hame,
   He was delving in his yardie;
Sheughing kail and laying leeks,
   But the hose and but the breeks;
And up his beggar duds he cleeks –
   This wee, wee German lairdie.

And he's clapt doun in our guidman's chair,
   The wee, wee German lairdie;
And he's brought fouth o' foreign trash
   And dibbled them in his yardie.
He's pu'd the rose o' English loons,
   And broken the harp o' Irish clowns;
But our thistle taps will jag his thumbs –
   This wee, wee German lairdie.

Come up amang our Highland hills,
   Thou wee, wee German lairdie,
And see how the Stuarts' lang-kail thrive
   They dibbled in our yardie;
And if a stock ye dare to pu',
   Or haud the yoking o' a plough,
We'll break your sceptre ower your mou',
   Thou wee bit German lairdie.

Our hills are steep, our glens are deep,
   Nae fitting for a yardie;
And our Norland thistles winna pu',
   Thou wee bit German lairdie;
And we've the trenching blades o' weir,
   Was prune ye o' your German gear –
We'll pass ye 'neath the claymore's shear,
   Thou feckless German lairdie!

Auld Scotland, thou'rt ower cauld a hole
   For nursin' siccan vermin;
But the very dogs o' England's court
   They bark and howl in German.
Then keep thy dibble in thy ain hand,
   Thy spade but and thy hardie;
For wha the deil now claims your land,
   But a wee, wee German lairdie?

Anonymous

1715

THE FIRST JACOBITE UPRISING

A Jacobite's Epitaph

To my true king I offered free from stain
Courage and faith; vain faith, and courage vain.
For him I threw lands, honours, wealth, away,
And one dear hope, that was more prized then they.
For him I languished in a foreign clime,
Grey-haired with sorrow in my manhood's prime;
Heard on Lavernia Scargill's whispering trees,
And pined by Arno for my lovelier Tees;
Beheld each night my home in fevered sleep,
Each morning started from the dream to weep;
Till God, who saw me tried too sorely, gave
The resting-place I asked, an early grave.
O thou, whom chance leads to this nameless stone,
From that proud country which was once mine own,
By those white cliffs I never more must see,
By that dear language which I spake like thee,
Forget all feuds, and shed one English tear.
O'er English dust. A broken heart lies here.

Thomas Babington, Lord Maucaulay

The Stuart cause was kept alive by the son of James II. Known as the Old Pretender and kept in Paris by the favour of Louis XIV, he became the hope of all malcontents in England. And he failed them all. Nine months after the accession of George I, he encouraged the Earl of Mar to raise a rebellion in the Highlands. It was a botched and bungled affair and, although some rebels reached Preston, they were trounced and fled northwards again. James himself eventually arrived in Perth, just in time to retreat to Dundee, and within four weeks he was back in France, before finally settling in Italy.

1720

THE SOUTH SEA BUBBLE

from **The Bubble**

Ye wise philosophers, explain
   What magic makes our money rise,
When dropt into the Southern main;
   Or do these jugglers cheat our eyes?

Put in your money fairly told;
   Presto! be gone – 'Tis here again:
Ladies and gentlemen, behold,
   Here's every piece as big as ten.

Thus in a basin drop a shilling,
   Then fill the vessel to the brim,
You shall observe, as you are filling,
   The pond'rous metal seems to swim.

It rises both in bulk and height,
   Behold it mounting to the top;
The liquid medium cheats your sight:
   Behold it swelling like a sop.

In stock three hundred thousand pounds,
    I have in view a Lord's estate;
My manors all contiguous round,
    A coach and six, and served in plate!

Thus the deluded bankrupt raves,
    Puts all upon a desperate bet,
Then plunges in the Southern waves,
    Dipt over head and ears – in debt.

                    *

The sea is richer than the land,
    I heard it from my Grannam's mouth,
Which now I clearly understand,
    For by the sea she meant the South.

Thus by Directors we are told,
    Pray, Gentlemen, believe your eyes:
Our ocean's covered o'er with gold;
    Look round about how thick it lies.

We, Gentlemen, are your assisters,
    We'll come and hold you by the chin;
Alas! all is not gold that glisters:
    Ten thousand sunk by leaping in.

                    *

May he, whom Nature's laws obey,
    Who lifts the poor, and sinks the proud,
Quiet the raging of the sea,
    And still the madness of the crowd!

But never shall our isle have rest,
    Till those devouring swine run down,
(The devils leaving the possest)
    And headlong in the waters drown.

> The nation then too late will find,
>   Computing all their cost and trouble,
> Directors' promises but wind,
>   South Sea at best a mighty bubble.

Jonathan Swift

In 1719 the South Sea Company, which in 1711 had been assigned the monopoly of England's trade with Spanish America, proposed a scheme to convert part of the National Debt into its shares. The Commons approved it and in 1720 stocks were issued to, among others, the King's mistresses, the Chancellor of the Exchequer, and various ministers. The directors of the Company had to keep the price of the stock high and a wild boom started, with the price rising from £130 to £1,050 between February and June. Bubble companies sprang up and, when Parliament banned them, the market slumped, so that by November the price was down to £135. The Chancellor of the Exchequer was sent to the Tower, but the crash made Sir Robert Walpole First Lord of the Treasury, and our first Prime Minister.

1722

THE DEATH OF MARLBOROUGH

A Satirical Elegy on the Death of a Late Famous General

> His Grace! impossible! what dead!
> Of old age too, and in his bed!
> And could that Mighty Warrior fall?
> And so inglorious after all!

Well, since he's gone, no matter how,
The last loud trump must wake him now:
And, trust me, as the noise grows stronger,
He'd wish to sleep a little longer.
And could he be indeed so old
As by the news-papers we're told:
Threescore, I think, is pretty high;
'Twas time in conscience he should die.
This world he cumber'd long enough;
He burnt his candle to the snuff;
And that's the reason, some folks think,
He left behind *so great a s—k.*
Behold his funeral appears,
Nor widow's sighs, nor orphan's tears,
Wont at such times each heart to pierce,
Attend the progress of his herse.
But what of that, his friends may say,
He had those honours in his day.
True to his profit and his pride,
He made them weep before he dy'd.

Come hither, all ye empty things,
Ye bubbles rais'd by breath of Kings;
Who float upon the tide of state,
Come hither, and behold your fate.
Let pride be taught by this rebuke,
How very mean a thing's a Duke;
From all his ill-got honours flung,
Turn'd to that dirt from whence he sprung.

Jonathan Swift

After Blenheim, Marlborough went on to win three more celebrated victories – at Ramallies (1706), Oudenarde (1708) and Malplaquet (1709). Swift loathed Marlborough, who had started penniless and died the richest man in England. In the winter of 1711 Swift joined with the Tories Harley and Bolingbroke in a move to overthrow the great Duke, and they succeeded. This was the only time in his life that Swift was really at the centre of political affairs. He expected a good reward, especially for the brilliant pamphlet he had written under the title 'The Conduct of the Allies', but no bishopric came his way, only the deanery of St Patrick's in Dublin. How lucky for the world, as it was there, in virtual exile, that he wrote *Gulliver's Travels*. When Marlborough died in 1721, Swift could not resist another burst of spleen against his old enemy.

1727

THE DEATH OF SIR ISAAC NEWTON

from **To the Memory of Sir Isaac Newton**

Even *Light itself*, which every thing displays,
Shone undiscover'd, till his brighter mind
Untwisted all the shining robe of day;
And, from the whitening undistinguish'd blaze,
Collecting every ray into his kind,
To the charm'd eye educ'd the gorgeous train
Of *Parent-Colours*. First the flaming *Red*
Sprung vivid forth; the tawny *Orange* next;
And next delicious *Yellow*; by whose side
Fell the kind beams of all-refreshing *Green*.
Then the pure *Blue*, that swells autumnal skies,
Ethereal play'd; and then, of sadder hue,
Emerg'd the deepen'd *Indico*, as when
The heavy-skirted evening droops with frost.
While the last gleamings of refracted light
Dy'd in the fainting *Violet* away.
These, when the clouds distil the rosy shower,
Shine out distinct adown the watry bow;
While o'er our heads the dewy vision bends
Delightful, melting on the fields beneath.
Myriads of mingling dies from these result,
And myriads still remain – Infinite source
Of beauty, ever-flushing, ever-new!
   Did ever poet image ought so fair,
Dreaming in whispering groves, by the hoarse brook!
Or prophet, to whose rapture heaven descends!
Even now the setting sun and shifting clouds,
Seen, *Greenwich*, from thy lovely heights, declare
How just, how beauteous the *refractive Law*.

James Thomson

Newton was a genius in mathematics, physics, astronomy and philosophy. His great works were *Philosophiae naturalis principia mathematica* (1687) and *Opticks* (1704). He formulated the Law of Gravity and the three Laws of Motion, established that white light consists of a mixture of all colours, and developed calculus. Voltaire, who was at Newton's funeral, commended the English for honouring a scientist of heretical religious views with burial in Westminster Abbey. Einstein's view of Newton was that he 'determined the course of Western thought, research and practice to an extent that nobody before or since can touch'.

Epitaph Intended for Sir Isaac Newton, in Westminster Abbey

Nature, and Nature's laws lay hid in night:
God said, *Let Newton be!* and all was light.

Alexander Pope

It did not last: the Devil howling 'Ho!
Let Einstein be!' restored the status quo.

J. C. Squire

King George II, 1727–60

In most things I did as my father had done,
I was false to my wife and I hated my son:
My spending was small, and my avarice much,
My kingdom was English, my heart was High-Dutch:
At Dettingen fight I was not known to blench,
I butcher'd the Scotch, and I bearded the French:
I neither had morals, nor manners, nor wit;
I wasn't much miss'd when I died in a fit.
Here set up my statue, and make it complete,
With Pitt on his knees at my dirty old feet.

H. J. Daniels

George II had been bullied by his father, and in turn he tried to bully his son. He was lucky to have a loving and clever wife, Caroline. Walpole used the Queen to persuade the King to support his policies, or, as he put it in his earthy Norfolk way, he 'took the right sow by the ear'. George II was the last monarch to lead a British army to victory, which he did at Dettingen in Bavaria. He liked all things military and was able to recall in detail the uniforms of European regiments. His great love, however, was for music, and he made it possible for Handel to live in England. In his will he asked that his coffin be laid alongside that of his wife, with the two near sides open so that their dusts might mingle.

SIR ROBERT WALPOLE

Two Character Studies

1

With favour and fortune fastidiously blest,
He's loud in his laugh and he's coarse in his jest;
Of favour and fortune unmerited vain,
A sharper in trifles, a dupe in the main.
Achieving of nothing, still promising wonders,
By dint of experience improving in blunders;
Oppressing true merit, exalting the base,
And selling his country to purchase his peace.
A jobber of stocks by retailing false news,
A prater at court in the style of the stews,
Of virtue and worth by profession a giber,
Of juries and senates the bully and briber:
Though I name not the wretch you know who I mean –
'Tis the cur dog of Britain and spaniel of Spain.

2

And first: to make my observation right,
I place a statesman full before my sight,
A bloated minister in all his geer,
With shameless visage, and perfidious leer;
Two rows of teeth arm each devouring jaw;
And, ostrich-like, his all-digesting maw,
My fancy drags this monster to my view
To shew the world his chief reverse in you.
Of loud unmeaning sounds a rapid flood
Rolls from his mouth in plenteous streams of mud;
With these the court and senate-house he plies,
Made up of noise, and impudence, and lies.

Jonathan Swift

Walpole was Prime Minister from 1721 to 1742, which is a record yet to be surpassed. His policy was, proverbially, to let sleeping dogs lie – to avoid war, encourage trade and reduce taxation. He exercised enormous patronage, finding so many jobs for his sons, brothers, cousins and friends that his administration came to be known as the 'Robinocracy'. He was also the last PM to make a huge personal fortune while in office: government surpluses passed though his own account and enabled him to speculate on a grand scale. He amassed some superb paintings, which one of his descendants sold to Catherine the Great of Russia and which now form the heart of the Hermitage Museum in Leningrad. For all this, he gave England peace for eighteen years; he reinforced the power of the House of Commons; he consolidated the achievements of the Whig revolution; and he eliminated from politics the savagery and vindictiveness which in previous generations could lead those who had fallen on misfortune to the gallows or into exile. Swift saw Walpole as the barrier to his preferment in England, and loathed him for it.

1739

THE LAST DAYS OF DICK TURPIN

My Poor Black Bess

When fortune, blind goddess, she fled my abode,
Old friends proved ungrateful, I took to the road;
To plunder the wealthy to aid my distress,
I bought thee to aid me, my poor Black Bess.

When dark sable night its mantle had thrown
O'er the bright face of nature, how oft we have gone
To famed Hounslow Heath, though an unwelcome guest
To the minions of fortune, my poor Black Bess.

How silent thou stood when a carriage I've stopped,
And their gold and their jewels its inmates I've dropped;
No poor man I plundered or e'er did oppress
The widow or orphan, my poor Black Bess.

When Argus-eyed justice did me hotly pursue,
From London to York like lightning we flew;
No toll-bar could stop thee, thou the river didst breast,
And in twelve hours reached it, my poor Black Bess.

Anonymous

Tradition has transformed Dick Turpin into romantic figure, but in real life he was no more than a poacher, thief, highwayman and murderer. He did not even make the famous twelve-hour ride to York which has been attributed to him: that was the feat of another highwayman in 1676. For a while, Turpin lived in York under the name of Palmer, but he was discovered after a quarrel with an innkeeper over a gamecock. He was executed in 1739, having paid five people to mourn for him.

1740

THE GROWTH OF THE BRITISH EMPIRE

from The Masque of Alfred

When Britain first at Heaven's command
    Arose from out the azure main,
This was the charter of the land,
    And guardian angels sang this strain,.
        'Rule, Britannia, rule the waves,
        Britons never will be slaves.

'The nations not so blest as thee
    Must in their turn to tyrants fall,
While thou shalt flourish great and free,
    The dread and envy of them all.

'Still more majestic shalt thou rise,
  More dreadful from each foreign stroke;
As the loud blast that tears the skies
  Serves but to root thy native oak.

'Thee haughty tyrants ne'er shall tame;
  All their attempts to bend thee down
Will but arouse thy generous flame,
  But work their woe and thy renown.

'To thee belongs the rural reign,
  Thy cities shall with commerce shine;
All thine shall be the subject main,
  And every shore it circles thine.

'The muses, still with freedom found,
  Shall to thy happy coast repair;
Blest Isle! with matchless beauty crowned,
  And manly hearts to guard the fair!
    'Rule, Britannia, rule the waves,
    Britons never will be slaves.'

James Thomson

George II's reign saw the steady expansion and consolidation of the British Empire, although only one new colony was founded, namely Georgia, which was initially settled by debtors from the Fleet Prison. In the 1750s British armies won sweeping victories in Europe, as well as in India under Clive and in Canada under Wolfe.

1745

THE SECOND JACOBITE UPRISING

Charlie is my Darling

Charlie is my darling, my darling, my darling,
Charlie is my darling, the young Chevalier.

'Twas on a Monday morning,
  Right early in the year,
When Charlie came to our toun,
  The young Chevalier.

As he came marching up the street,
  The pipes played loud and clear,
And a' the folk came running out
  To meet the Chevalier.

We' Hieland bonnets on their heads,
  And claymores bright and clear,
They came to fight for Scotland's right,
  And the young Chevalier.

They've left their bonnie Hieland hills,
  Their wives and bairnies dear,
To draw the sword for Scotland's lord,
  The young Chevalier.

Oh, there were mony beating hearts,
  And mony a hope and fear:
And mony were the pray'rs put up
  For the young Chevalier.

Lady Nairne

In July 1745 Prince Charles Edward Stuart, the Young Pretender, landed in Scotland with the intention of recapturing the three kingdoms lost by his grandfather, James II. He had no troops with him, no money, and only seven friends. The Highland clans, led by the Macdonalds, rallied to him, and by September he had entered Edinburgh and won the skirmish of Prestonpans. Then he made the mistake of marching into England, passing through Preston and Manchester, and finally reaching Derby where his men refused to go further. England failed to rally to him and he retreated north, pursued by the Duke of Cumberland.

In 1746 the opposing armies met at Culloden, where Cumberland's 9,000 men ran down and slaughtered Charles's 5,000. For five months the Prince wandered through the Highlands, sheltered by poor crofters and rescued at one point by the now famous Flora Macdonald, but at last he returned to the Continent. The whole rash escapade had been poorly planned, poorly financed and poorly conducted. It was sustained by a romantic myth, but it led to the deaths of many thousands of Scots at the hands of 'Butcher' Cumberland. The flower known in England as Sweet William is called Stinking Billy in Scotland, in memory of his savage reprisals.

1746

THE BATTLE OF CULLODEN

Lament for Culloden

The lovely lass o' Inverness,
Nae joy nor pleasure can she see;
For e'en and morn she cries, Alas!
And aye the saut tear blins her ee:
Drumossie moor – Drumossie day –
A waefu' day it was to me!
For there I lost my father dear,
My father dear, and brethren three.

Their winding-sheet the bluidy clay,
Their graves are growing green to see:
And by them lies the dearest lad
That ever blest a woman's ee!
Now wae to thee, thou cruel lord,
A bluidy man I trow thou be,
For mony a heart thou hast made sair
That ne'er did wrang to thine or thee.

Robert Burns

Bonnie Charlie's Now Awa

Bonnie Charlie's now awa,
Safely owre the friendly main;
Mony a heart will break in twa,
Should he ne'er come back again.
   Will ye no come back again?
   Will ye no come back again?
   Better lo'ed ye canna be,
   Will ye no come back again?

Lady Nairne

1759

THE BRITISH CONQUEST OF CANADA

Bold General Wolfe to his men did say,
Come, come, my lads and follow me,
To yonder mountains that are so high
All for the honour, all for the honour,
Of your king and country.

The French they are on the mountains high,
While we poor lads in the vallies laid,
I see them falling like moths in the sun,
Thro' smoke and fire, thro' smoke and fire
All from our British guns.

The very first volley they gave to us,
Wounded our General in his left breast,
Yonder he sits for he cannot stand,
Fight on so boldly, fight on so boldly,
For whilst I've life I'll have command.

Here is my treasure lies all in gold,
Take it and part it, for my blood runs cold,
Take it and part it, General Wolfe did say,
You lads of honour, you lads of honour,
Who made such gallant play.

Anonymous

Wolfe landed in Canada in 1759 to overthrow the French. He surprised them by scaling the Heights of Abraham and defeated their general, Montcalme. Quebec surrendered and Canada, with its rich trade in fish and fur, became British. Wolfe died in the battle, and his murmured last words were, 'Now God be praised, I will die in peace.' Pitt, Prime Minister of the time, trusted daring and unconventional soldiers like Wolfe. George II was once told that Wolfe was a mad dog, to which he replied that he should bite some of his other generals.

from Stanzas on the Taking of Quebec

Alive, the foe thy dreadful vigour fled,
    And saw thee fall with joy-pronouncing eyes;
Yet they shall know thou conquerest, though dead!
    Since from thy tomb a thousand heroes rise.

Oliver Goldsmith

1759

QUIBERON BAY

Hawke

In seventeen hundred and fifty nine,
  When Hawke came swooping from the West,
The French King's Admiral with twenty of the line,
  Was sailing forth, to sack us, out of Brest.
The ports of France were crowded, the quays of France a-hum
With thirty thousand soldiers marching to the drum,
For bragging time was over and fighting time was come
  When Hawke came swooping from the West.

'Twas long past noon of a wild November day
  When Hawke came swooping from the West;
He heard the breakers thundering in Quiberon Bay
  But he flew the flag for battle, line abreast.
Down upon the quicksands roaring out of sight
Fiercely beat the storm-wind, darkly fell the night,
But they took the foe for pilot and the cannon's glare for light
  When Hawke came swooping from the West.

The Frenchmen turned like a covey down the wind
  When Hawke came swooping from the West;
One he sank with all hands, one he caught and pinned,
  And the shallows and the storm took the rest.
The guns that should have conquered us they rusted on the
    shore,
The men that would have mastered us they drummed and
    marched no more,
For England was England, and a mighty brood she bore
  When Hawke came swooping from the West.

Henry Newbolt

In 1759 France planned what was to be her last attempt of the Seven Years War to invade Britain. Admiral Sir Edward Hawke blockaded one of the French fleets at Brest for over six months, but then because of bad weather he relaxed his hold and the French admiral Conflans steered his ships out of port on 14 November. Hawke gave chase, forcing the French to head south, and six days later he caught up with them at Belle-Ile, where he pushed Conflans into Quiberon Bay. By the dawn of 21 November the French fleet had scattered, its flagship having run aground, three other vessels being sunk and one captured. Hawke wrote: 'Had we but two hours' more daylight, the whole had been totally destroyed or taken.' He had broken common navy practice by keeping a blockade up well into winter; he had turned French tactics on their head by joining battle in a storm along the most dangerous coast in France; and he had crushed all hopes France had of invading Britain.

SEA POWER

Hearts of Oak

Come cheer up my lads, 'tis to glory we steer,
To add something new to this wonderful year;
To honour we call you, not press you like slaves,
For who are so free as the sons of the waves?

Hearts of Oak are our ships, Hearts of Oak are our men,
We always are ready,
Steady, boys, steady,
We'll fight and we'll conquer again and again.

We ne'er meet our foes but we wish them to stay,
They ne'er meet us but they wish us away;
If they run, then we follow, and drive them ashore,
For if they won't fight us, we cannot do more.
Hearts of Oak, &c.

*

They talk to invade us, these terrible foes,
They frighten our women, our children, and beaux;
But, if their flat bottoms in darkness come o'er,
Sure Britons they'll find to receive them on shore.
Hearts of Oak, &c.

We'll make them to run, and we'll make them to sweat,
In spite of the Devil and Russel's Gazette;
Then cheer up my lads, with one heart let us sing,
Our soldiers, our sailors, our statesmen, our king.
                    Hearts of Oak, &c.

David Garrick

The great actor-manager David Garrick wrote this song for his panto-mime, *Harlequin's Invasion*, to celebrate British victories over the French at Lagos, Quiberon Bay and Quebec.

WRECKING

Song of the Cornish Wreckers

Not that they shall, but if they must –
Be just, Lord, wreck them off St Just.

Scythes beneath the water, Brisons,
Reap us a good crop in all seasons.

We would be meek, but meat we lack.
Pile wrecks on Castle Kenidjack.

Our children's mouths gape like a zawn.
Fog, hide the sharp fangs of Pendeen.

You put Your own Son first, Jehovah,
And so do we. Send bread to Morvah.

Crowbar of oceans, stove the wood
Treasure-troves on Gurnard's Head.

Mermaids, Mary-Anne, Morwenna,
Sing them to the crags of Zennor.

Food, Lord, food! Our starving flock
Looks for manna but finds a rock.

Hard land you give us. Mist and stones.
Not enough trees to bury our bones.

To save the drowning we'll risk our lives.
But hurl their ships upon St Ives.

Guide us, when through death we sail,
Past the burning cliffs of Hell.

Soul nor sailor mean we harm.
But our blue sky is their black storm.

D. M. Thomas

SMUGGLING

A Smuggler's Song

If you wake at midnight, and hear a horse's feet,
Don't go drawing back the blind, or looking in the street
Them that ask no questions isn't told a lie.
Watch the wall, my darling, while the Gentlemen go by!
   Five and twenty ponies,
   Trotting through the dark –
   Brandy for the Parson,
   'Baccy for the Clerk;
   Laces for a lady, letters for a spy,
And watch the wall, my darling, while the Gentlemen go by!

Running round the woodlump if you chance to find
Little barrels, roped and tarred, all full of brandy-wine,
Don't you shout to come and look, nor use 'em for your play.
Put the brushwood back again – and they'll be gone next day!

If you see the stable-door setting open wide;
If you see a tired horse lying down inside;
If your mother mends a coat cut about and tore;
If the lining's wet and warm – don't you ask no more!

If you meet King George's men, dressed in blue and red,
You be careful what you say, and mindful what is said.
If they call you 'pretty maid,' and chuck you 'neath the chin,
Don't you tell where no one is, nor yet where no one's been!

Knocks and footsteps round the house – whistles after dark –
You've no call for running out till the house-dogs bark.
Trusty's here, and *Pincher's* here, and see how dumb they lie –
They don't fret to follow when the Gentlemen go by!

If you do as you've been told, 'likely there's a chance,
You'll be given a dainty doll, all the way from France,
With a cap of Valenciennes, and a velvet hood –
A present from the Gentlemen, along o' being good!
         Five and twenty ponies,
         Trotting through the dark –
         Brandy for the Parson,
         'Baccy for the Clerk.
Them that asks no questions isn't told a lie –
Watch the wall, my darling, while the Gentlemen go by!

Rudyard Kipling

In the eighteenth century British sailors ruled the seas, dominating trade, extending empire and beating off all comers in the competition for naval supremacy. These two poems show the darker side of things – the business of wrecking and smuggling. The places mentioned in Thomas's poem are on the north-west coast of Cornwall, near to Land's End. There was a medieval law which stated that the goods salvaged from a wreck belonged to those who got possession of them. Some ships were lured on to the rocks by false beacons, and when in trouble were followed along the cliff-tops by entire village communities, ready to pounce on what floated ashore. Sailors escaping a wreck knew that they would also have to flee the locals, who would be quite prepared to push them under as they grabbed what was going.

King George III, 1760–1820

George III's long reign was one of the most momentous in English history. Britannia really did rule the waves, though not well enough to hold the American colonies. Britain was the only major European country which was not overrun by Napoleon. The Napoleonic Wars called forth Britain's most famous sailor, Nelson, who died at the moment of victory at Trafalgar in 1805, bequeathing his mistress, Lady Hamilton, to the nation; and its most famous soldier, Wellington, who survived his victory at Waterloo in 1815 to become Prime Minister and godfather to the future King Edward VII.

George III himself was a conscientious but inadequate monarch. He had fifteen children, more than any other British king, but was sadly let down by them, for they proved a gaggle of spendthrifts, drunkards and adulterers. He suffered from bouts of madness and was permanently insane for the last eleven years of his reign. He had what has now been diagnosed as Porphyria, which can be treated, but he was forced to endure seclusion and strait-jackets, although his doctors did also advise him to bathe in the sea for therapeutic purposes, which incidentally started the fashion of the seaside holiday.

> George the Third
> Ought never to have occurred.
> One can only wonder
> At so grotesque a blunder.
>
> *E. C. Bentley*

A PORTRAIT OF THE KING

from Mr Whitbread's Brewhouse

> Now Majesty into a pump so deep
> Did with an opera-glass so curious peep,
> Examining with care each won'drous matter
> That brought up water!

Thus have I seen a magpie in the street,
A chatt'ring bird we often meet,
A bird for curiosity well known,
      With head awry,
      And cunning eye,
Peep knowingly into a marrow-bone.

And now his curious Majesty did stoop
To count the nails on ev'ry hoop;
And lo! no single one came in his way,
That, full of deep research, he did not say,
'What's this? hae, hae? what's that? what's this? what's that?'
So quick the words too, when he deign'd to speak,
As if each syllable would break its neck.

               *

To Whitbread now deign's Majesty to say,
'Whitbread, are all your horses fond of hay?'
'Yes, please your Majesty,' in humble notes,
The Brewer answer'd – 'also, Sir, of oats:
Another thing my horses too maintains,
And that, an't please your Majesty, are grains.'

'Grains, grains,' said Majesty, 'to fill their crops?
Grains, grains? – that comes from hops – yes, hops, hops,
  hops?'

Here was the King, like hounds sometimes, at fault –
'Sire,' cry'd the humble Brewer, 'give me leave
Your sacred Majesty to undeceive:
Grains, Sire, are never made from hops, but malt.'

'True,' said the cautious Monarch, with a smile;
From malt, malt, malt – I meant malt all the while.'
'Yes,' with the sweetest now, rejoin'd the Brewer,
'An't please your Majesty, you did, I'm sure.'
'Yes,' answer'd Majesty, with quick reply,
'I did, I did, I did, I, I, I, I.'

                        Peter Pindar

Writing under the pseudonym of Peter Pindar, John Wolcot, a
Devonshire clergyman, launched frequent satirical attacks on the slow-
wittedness of the King, here depicted on a tour of Whitbread's Brewery
in Islington.

1770

AGRICULTURAL DECLINE

from The Deserted Village

Sweet smiling village, loveliest of the lawn,
Thy sports are fled, and all thy charms withdrawn;
Amidst thy bowers the tyrant's hand is seen,
And desolation saddens all thy green:
One only master grasps the whole domain,
And half a tillage stints thy smiling plain:
No more thy glassy brook reflects the day,
But chok'd with sedges, works its weedy way.
Along thy glades, a solitary guest,
The hollow-sounding bittern guards its nest;
Amidst thy desert walks the lapwing flies,
And tires their echoes with unvaried cries.
Sunk are thy bowers, in shapeless ruin all,
And the long grass o'ertops the mouldering wall;
And, trembling, shrinking from the spoiler's hand,
Far, far away, thy children leave the land.

Ill fares the land, to hastening ills a prey,
Where wealth accumulates, and men decay:
Princes and lords may flourish, or may fade;
A breath can make them, as a breath has made;
But a bold peasantry, their country's pride,
When once destroy'd, can never be supplied.

A time there was, ere England's griefs began,
When every rood of ground maintain'd its man;
For him light labour spread her wholesome store,
Just gave what life requir'd, but gave no more:
His best companions, innocence and health;
And his best riches, ignorance of wealth.

But times are alter'd; trade's unfeeling train
Usurp the land and dispossess the swain;
Along the lawn, where scatter'd hamlets rose,
Unwieldy wealth, and cumbrous pomp repose;
And every want to opulence allied,
And every pang that folly pays to pride.

Oliver Goldsmith

The Lincolnshire Poacher

When I was bound apprentice in famous Lincolnshire,
Full well I served my Master for more than seven year,
Till I took up with poaching, as you shall quickly hear:
Oh! 'tis my delight on a shiny night in the season of the year!

As me and my comrades were setting of a snare,
'Twas then we seed the gamekeeper – for him we did not care,
For we can wrestle and fight, my boys, and jump o'er
   anywhere,
Oh! 'tis my delight, *etc.*

As me and my comrades were setting four or five,
And taking on him up again, we caught the hare alive;
We caught the hare alive, my boys, and through the woods did
   steer:
Oh! 'tis my delight, *etc.*

I threw him on my shoulder, and then we trudged home,
We took him to a neighbour's house and sold him for a crown;
We sold him for a crown, my boys, but I did not tell you
   where,
Oh! 'tis my delight, *etc.*

Bad luck to every magistrate that lives in Lincolnshire,
Success to every poacher that wants to sell a hare;
Bad luck to every gamekeeper that will not sell his deer:
Oh! 'tis my delight, *etc.*

Anonymous

During George III's reign, poaching was such a menace that more
than fifty statutes were passed in the effort to suppress it. Yet as more
and more common land was enclosed, the rural poor had increasing
need to practise it. Heavy sentences were passed, and even the death
penalty was applied, but with the discovery of Australia a new possi-
bility arose, and English magistrates started to populate the colony
with poachers. This folk song became a favourite of George IV, probably because he enjoyed neither shooting nor hunting.

1775

THE AMERICAN WAR OF INDEPENDENCE

Concord Hymn

By the rude bridge that arched the flood,
   Their flag to April's breeze unfurled,
Here once the embattled farmers stood,
   And fired the shot heard round the world.

The foe long since in silence slept;
   Alike the conqueror silent sleeps;
And Time the ruined bridge has swept
   Down the dark stream which seaward creeps.

On this green bank, by this soft stream,
  We set to-day a votive stone;
That memory may their deed redeem,
  When, like our sires, our sons are gone.

Spirit, that made those heroes dare
  To die, or leave their children free,
Bid Time and Nature gently spare
  The shaft we raise to them and thee.

Ralph Waldo Emerson

In the 1770s Lord North's government, in an attempt to reassert the sovereignty of the English crown over the American colonies, which had shown an increasingly independent spirit, took various unpopular measures, including the levying of duty on tea. In London, Lord Chatham pleaded for moderation and the withdrawal of troops, and Burke in a famous speech declared: 'Magnanimity in politics is not seldom the truest wisdom, and a great Empire and little minds go ill together.' But by 1775 open conflict was inevitable. Massachusetts had armed its militia against the troops of the English general, Gage, who set out to seize its armoury at Concord. On the way there a skirmish took place at Lexington, and the first shots of the war were fired. Sixty Americans and 273 British soldiers were killed. In July George Washington was recognized as Commander-in-Chief of the rebels and a year later the Declaration of Independence was signed. In 1777 a British army under 'Gentleman Johnny' Burgoyne surrendered at Saratoga Springs, and in 1781 another, under Lord Cornwallis, surrendered at Yorktown.

The British government's policy of imposing taxes without consent had been foolish, and its agents, from North to Gage, Burgoyne and Cornwallis, were inadequate to the task of seeing it through. Cornwallis went on to become Governor-General of India, where his heavy hand all but provoked rebellion in Bengal.

1781

A Prophecy, *from* America

The Guardian Prince of Albion burns in his nightly tent,
Sullen fires across the Atlantic glow to America's shore,
Piercing the souls of warlike men who rise in silent night.
Washington, Franklin, Paine & Warren, Gates, Hancock &
   Green
Meet on the coast glowing with blood from Albion's fiery
   Prince.

Washington spoke: 'Friends of America, look over the Atlantic
   sea!
A bended bow is lifted in heaven, & a heavy iron chain
Descends link by link from Albion's cliffs across the sea to bind
Brothers & sons of America, till our faces pale and yellow,
Heads deprest, voices weak, eyes downcast, hands work-
   bruis'd,
Feet bleeding on the sultry sands, and the furrows of the whip
Descend to generations that in future times forget.'

The strong voice ceas'd, for a terrible blast swept over the
   heaving sea:
The eastern cloud rent: on his cliffs stood Albion's wrathful
   Prince,
A dragon form, clashing his scales; at midnight he arose,
And flam'd red meteors round the land of Albion beneath:
His voice, his locks, his awful shoulders and his glowing eyes
Appear to the Americans upon the cloudy night.

Solemn heave the Atlantic waves between the gloomy nations,
Swelling, belching from its deeps red clouds & raging fires.
Albion is sick! America faints! enrag'd the Zenith grew.
As human blood shooting its veins all round the orbèd heaven,
Red rose the clouds from the Atlantic in vast wheels of blood,
And in the red clouds rose a Wonder o'er the Atlantic sea,
Intense, naked, a Human fire, fierce glowing as the wedge
Of iron heated in the furnace; his terrible limbs were fire,
With myriads of cloudy terrors, banners dark & towers
Surrounded; heat but not light went thro' the murky
    atmosphere.

The King of England, looking westward, trembles at the vision.

William Blake

In this prophetic statement, written some years after the War of
Independence, Blake interprets the spirit of rebellion as a far more
radical force than Washington himself is likely to have considered it.

1782

EIGHTEENTH-CENTURY CONSCRIPTION

The Press-gang

Oh, where will you hurry my dearest?
    Say, say, to what clime or what shore?
You tear him from me, the sincerest
    That ever lov'd mortal before.

Ah! cruel, hard-hearted to press him
    And force the dear youth from my arms!
Restore him, that I may caress him,
    And shield him from future alarms.

In vain you insult and deride me
  And make but a scoff of my woes;
You ne'er from my dear shall divide me –
  I'll follow wherever he goes.

Think not of the merciless ocean –
  My soul any terror can brave,
For soon as the ship makes its motion,
  So soon shall the sea be my grave.

Charles Dibdin

Service in the British navy was so unpopular that men had to be pressed into it. Recruiting parties toured the ports, seizing the gullible and the unemployed, drunk or sober. Through the invocation of an Elizabethan Vagrancy Act, the prisons were emptied to man the fleet. Merchant ships were stopped on the high seas and crew forcibly transferred. Such treatment was one of the major sources of discontent among the American colonies. It was remarkable that there were so few mutinies, although one that took place at the Nore in 1797 almost brought the war effort to an end. Impressment ceased in practice in 1815, and in law in 1853, with the introduction of the service system.

1783

The Condemned Cell at Newgate

All you that in the condemned hole do lie,
Prepare you for tomorrow you shall die.
Watch all and pray; the hour is drawing near
That you before the Almighty must appear.
Examine well yourselves, in time repent,
That you may not to eternal flames be sent,
And when St Sepulchre's bell in the morning tolls
The Lord have mercy on your souls.

Anonymous

The night before an execution, a gaoler at Newgate Prison would pronounce these cheering words outside the cell of the condemned. At least until 1783, those to be hanged were taken by cart on the long journey to the Tyburn gallows at Marble Arch. The cart would be stopped outside St Sepulchre's, where the great bell was rung – one of the bells of Old Bailey. Only Jack Shepherd ever escaped from Newgate. Other distinguished residents had been Ben Jonson, Christopher Marlowe and Daniel Defoe.

1784

PITT THE YOUNGER

But mark what he did
   For to get to his station:
He told a damned lie
   In the ear of the king.
Then a shite on his name,
   For I'm all for the nation,
So don't bother me
   With the name of the thing.
His taxes now prove
   His great love for the people,
So wisely they're managed
   To starve the poor souls.
Sure the praise of the man
   Should be rung in each steeple
That would rob them of daylight,
   Of candles and coals. . .

Charles Morris

The National Saviour

When Faction threaten'd Britain's land,
Thy new-made friends – a desperate band,
  Like Ahab – stood reprov'd:
Pitt's powerful tongue their rage could check;
His counsel sav'd, 'midst general wreck,
  The Israel that he loved.

Anonymous

After a period of squabbling among the Whigs, a general election took place in 1784 and William Pitt the Younger became Prime Minister at the age of twenty-five. He held this office until 1801, seeing the country through the period of the French Revolution and the beginning of the Napoleonic Wars. He died during an additional term of office in 1806, his last words being, 'My country! Oh, my country!' His great political rival was Charles James Fox, who got one of his cronies, Charles Morris, to write the piece above, so as to remind the electorate that Pitt had promised not to raise taxes on windows or candles, but had done just that within months of his victory at the polls. Fox himself barely held office, but by opposing Pitt on almost every single issue with eloquent attacks in the House of Commons, he may be said to have defined for later ages the role of leader of His Majesty's Opposition.

1790

THE KING'S MADNESS

from **For the King's Birthday, 1790**

And lo, amid the watery roar
In Thetis' car she skims the shore,
   Where Portland's brows, embattled high
   With rocks, in rugged majesty
Frown o'er the billows, and the storm restrain,
   She beckons Britain's scepter'd pair
   Her treasures of the deep to share!
Hail then, on this glad morn, the mighty main!
Which leads the boon divine of lengthen'd days
To those who wear the noblest regal bays:
That mighty main, which on its conscious tide
Their boundless commerce pours on every clime,
   Their dauntless banner bears sublime;
And wafts their pomp of war, and spreads their thunder wide!

Thomas Warton

This Poet Laureate faced something of a problem, for in 1788 the King had gone mad. In 1789 he and Queen Charlotte visited Weymouth in the hope that sea bathing would cure him, as his doctors had recommended. The diarist Fanny Burney, who had seen one of the new-fangled bathing machines, recorded that it 'follows the Royal one into the sea, filled with fiddlers, who play God Save the King as his Majesty takes the plunge'.

1791

THE RIGHTS OF MAN

from **God Save Great Thomas Paine**

God save great Thomas Paine,
His 'Rights of Man' explain
        To every soul.
He makes the blind to see
What dupes and slaves they be,
And points out liberty,
        From pole to pole.

Thousands cry 'Church and King'
That well deserve to swing,
        All must allow:
Birmingham blush for shame,
Manchester do the same,
Infamous is your name,
        Patriots vow.

Pull proud oppressors down,
Knock off each tyrant's crown,
        And break his sword;
Down aristocracy,
Set up democracy,
And from hypocrisy
        Save us good Lord.
      *

Despots may howl and yell,
Though they're in league with hell
        They'll not reign long;
Satan may lead the van,
And do the worst he can,
Paine and his 'Rights of Man'
        Shall be my song.

Joseph Mather

In 1791 the radical Thomas Paine published the first part of *The Rights of Man* in reply to Edmund Burke's *Reflections on the Revolution in France*. To avoid persecution for it, Paine fled to France, but soon fell out with the revolutionaries there and narrowly escaped the guillotine. He died in New York, but not before he had fallen out with the colonial rebels whose cause he had earlier espoused.

1792

THE DEATH OF SIR JOSHUA REYNOLDS

from Retaliation

Here Reynolds is laid and, to tell you my mind,
He has not left a better or wiser behind:
His pencil was striking, resistless and grand;
His manners were gentle, complying and bland;
Still born to improve us in every part,
His pencil our faces, his manners our heart;
To coxcombs averse, yet most civilly steering,
When they judged without skill he was still hard of hearing;
When they talked of their Raphaels, Correggios and stuff,
He shifted his trumpet and only took snuff.

Oliver Goldsmith

When Goldsmith died in 1774, it was found that he had written a series of sketches of his closest friends in the form of epitaphs. This is what he wrote about the great painter Reynolds. Reynolds had settled in London in 1753 and had come to dominate British painting. In 1768 he enhanced the status of his profession by establishing the Royal Academy, of which he was the first President. He was very deaf and much preferred the company of literary men like Johnson, Goldsmith and Burke to that of painters. When Goldsmith's death was announced, Burke burst into tears and Reynolds threw down his palette and stopped painting for the day.

1793

THE SLAVE TRADE

The Negro's Complaint

Forc'd from home, and all its pleasures,
   Afric's coast I left forlorn;
To increase a stranger's treasures,
   O'er the raging billows borne,
Men from England bought and sold me.
   Paid my price in paltry gold;
But though theirs they have enroll'd me,
   Minds are never to be sold.

Still in thought as free as ever,
   What are England's rights, I ask,
Me from my delights to sever,
   Me to torture, me to task?
Fleecy locks, and black complexion
   Cannot forfeit nature's claim;
Skins may differ, but affection
   Dwells in white and black the same.

Why did all-creating Nature
   Make the plant for which we toil?
Sighs must fan it, tears must water,
   Sweat of ours must dress the soil.
Think, ye masters, iron-hearted,
   Lolling at your jovial boards;
Think how many backs have smarted
   For the sweets your cane affords.

Is there, as ye sometimes tell us,
   Is there one who reigns on high?
Has he bid you buy and sell us,
   Speaking from his throne the sky?
Ask him, if your knotted scourges,
   Matches, blood-extorting screws,
Are the means which duty urges
   Agents of his will to use!

Hark! he answers – Wild tornadoes,
   Strewing yonder sea with wrecks;
Wasting towns, plantations, meadows,
   Are the voice with which he speaks.
He, forseeing what vexations
   Afric's sons should undergo,
Fix'd their tyrants' habitations
   Where his whirlwinds answer – No.

By our blood in Afric wasted,
   Ere our necks receiv'd the chain;
By the mis'ries we have tasted,
   Crossing in your barks the main;
By our suff'rings since ye brought us
   To the man-degrading mart;
All sustain'd by patience, taught us
   Only by a broken heart:

Deem our nation brutes no longer
   Till some reason ye shall find
Worthier of regard and stronger
   Than the colour of our kind.
Slaves of gold, whose sordid dealings
   Tarnish all your boasted pow'rs,
Prove that you have human feelings,
   Ere you proudly question ours!

William Cowper

In the triangular trade-system of the eighteenth century, ships from Europe took cloth, salt and guns to West Africa, then slaves from Africa to the Caribbean, and lastly sugar from the Caribbean back to Europe. This trade was based upon Europe's addiction to sugar and it was that addiction which required and sustained the appalling institution of slavery. More than twenty million slaves crossed the Atlantic and an even greater number died on the journey. One slave produced about a ton of sugar in the course of his lifetime. The Quakers were among the first to condemn slavery, and Dr Johnson proposed a toast at Oxford to 'success to the next revolt of the Negroes in the West Indies'.

In 1772, the great Chief Justice Lord Mansfield had given his judgment against slavery: 'The Black must go free.' Adam Smith condemned the traffic and William Wilberforce, Pitt's close friend, moved bill after bill to ban it. In 1807 the Ministry of All Talents passed an act banning the trade and British ships were deputed to see that this was observed. Yet the traffic continued, and it was not until 1833 that an act was passed to outlaw slavery in all British possessions. Even then a young MP, W. E. Gladstone, whose family had Caribbean interests, predicted evil consequences for the West Indies and for the slaves themselves.

1797

THE DEATH OF EDMUND BURKE

from Retaliation

Here lies our good Edmund, whose genius was such,
We scarcely can praise it or blame it too much;
Who, born for the universe, narrowed his mind,
And to party gave up what was meant for mankind;
Though fraught with all learning, yet straining his throat
To persuade Tommy Townshend to lend him a vote;
Who, too deep for his hearers, still went on refining,
And thought of convincing, while they thought of dining;
Though equal to all things, for all things unfit;
Too nice for a statesman, too proud for a wit;
For a patriot, too cool; for a drudge, disobedient;
And too fond of the *right* to pursue the *expedient*;
In short, 'twas his fate, unemployed or in place, sir,
To eat mutton cold and cut blocks with a razor.

Oliver Goldsmith

Edmund Burke was more important as a political philosopher than as a politician. He held office for only a short time, during the extraordinary coalition between Fox and North in 1783. Burke's writings, however, have had a profound influence. He set out the classic definition of an MP, as being a representative rather than a delegate. As he said in his address to the electors of Bristol in 1774: 'You choose a member indeed, but when you have chosen him, he is not a member of Bristol, but he is a member of Parliament.' He opposed the power of the Crown and asserted the need for political parties: 'Parties must ever exist in a free country.' In his famous *Reflections on the Revolution in France* (1790), he warned that revolutions would inevitably lead to despotism and he reaffirmed the value of tradition, moderation and slow harmonious change. When Disraeli was ennobled, he chose for his title the name of Burke's village, Beaconsfield.

1799

THE INCOME TAX

Oh what wonders, what novels in this age there be,
And the man that lives longest the most he will see;
For fifty years back pray what man would have thought,
That a tax upon income would be brought.
    Sing, tantara rara new tax.

We're engag'd in a war who can say but 'tis just,
That some thousands of Britons as laid in the dust,
And the nation of millions it's made shift to drain,
Yet to go on with vigour each nerve we will strain.
    Sing, tantara rara will strain.

From the peer so down to the mechanical man,
They must all come beneath our minister's plan,
And curtail their expences to pay their share,
To preserve their great rights & their liberties dear.
    Sing tantara rara how dear.

If you've not 60 l. you'll have nothing to pay,
That's an income too small to take any away,
But from that to a hundred does gradually rise,
All above, nothing less than the tenth will suffice,
    Sing tantara rara one tenth.

This tax had produc'd what most wish to conceal,
The true state of their income few love to reveal,
What long faces it's caus'd, and of oaths not a few
Whilst papers they sign'd for to pay in their due.
    Sing tantara rara long face.

Anonymous

Pitt introduced Income Tax in 1799. It was intended as a temporary measure to help pay for the French wars, but although it was waived for a short while between 1802 and 1803, and later from 1816 to 1842, it was brought back then and is still with us today.

1803

THE NAPOLEONIC WARS

The Berkshire Farmer's Thoughts on Invasion

So! Bonaparte's coming, as folks seem to say,
(But I hope to have time to get in my hay).
And while he's caballing, and making a parley,
Perhaps I shall house all my wheat and my barley.
                              Fal la de ral, &c.

Then I shall have time to attend to my duty,
And keep the starved dogs from making a booty
Of what I've been toiling for, both late and early,
To support my old woman, whom I love so dearly.
                              Fal la de ral, &c.

Then, there are my children, and some of them feeble,
I wish, from my soul, that they were more able
To assist their old father, in drubbing the knaves,
For we ne'er will submit to become their tame slaves.
                              Fal la de ral, &c.

But then, there's son Dick, who is both strong and lusty,
And towards the French he is damnable crusty;
If you give him a pitchfork or any such thing,
He will fight till he's dead, in defence of his King.
                              Fal la de ral, &c.

And I'll answer for Ned, too, he'll never give out;
He should eat no more bacon, if I had a doubt.
And wish every one, who's not staunch in the cause,
May ne'er get a bit more to put in their jaws.

                         Fal la de ral, &c.

So you see, Bonaparte, how you are mistaken,
In your *big little* notions of stealing our bacon.
And your *straight way to London*, I this will you tell,
Your straight way to London is your short way to Hell.

                         Fal la de ral, &c.

                             Anonymous

From 1793 to 1815 Britain was almost continually at war with France. Napoleon rapidly came to dominate the whole of Europe. It was the British navy under Horatio Nelson which checked the French advance on different fronts at the Battle of the Nile in 1798, and again at Copenhagen in 1801. In 1803 Napoleon was ready to invade England and, with a huge army of 160,000 men gathered in Northern Europe, he practised embarking and landing. Pitt, out of office since 1801, was recalled and the country prepared to meet the invasion. Nelson saved the day. In 1805 he commanded the force which destroyed the French and Spanish fleets off Cape Trafalgar. With his twenty-seven ships he out-manoeuvred, out-gunned and out-fought the considerably greater numbers against him, but died from a sniper's wound at the hour of victory.

1805

At Viscount Nelson's lavish funeral,
    While the mob milled and yelled about the Abbey,
A General chatted with an Admiral:

'One of your Colleagues, Sir, remarked today
    That Nelson's *exit*, though to be lamented,
Falls not inopportunely, in its way.'

'He was a thorn in our flesh,' came the reply –
  'The most bird-witted, unaccountable,
Odd little runt that ever I did spy.

'One arm, one peeper, vain as Pretty Poll,
  A meddler, too, in foreign politics
And gave his heart in pawn to a plain moll.

'He would dare lecture us Sea Lords, and then
  Would treat his ratings as though men of honour
And play at leap-frog with his midshipmen!

'We tried to box him down, but up he popped,
  And when he'd banged Napoleon at the Nile
Became too much the hero to be dropped.

'You've heard that Copenhagen "blind eye" story?
  We'd tied him to Nurse Parker's apron-strings –
By G–d, he snipped them through and snatched the glory!'

'Yet,' cried the General, 'six-and-twenty sail
  Captured or sunk by him off Trafalgar –
That writes a handsome *finis* to the tale.'

'Handsome enough. The seas are England's now.
  That fellow's foibles need no longer plague us.
He died most creditably, I'll allow.'

'And, Sir, the secret of his victories?'
  'By his unServicelike, familiar ways, Sir,
He made the whole Fleet love him, damn his eyes!'

                                        Robert Graves

1809

THE BATTLE OF CORUNNA

The Burial of Sir John Moore after Corunna

Not a drum was heard, not a funeral note,
    As his corpse to the rampart we hurried;
Not a soldier discharged his farewell shot
    O'er the grave where our hero we buried.

We buried him darkly at dead of night,
    The sods with our bayonets turning,
By the struggling moonbeam's misty light
    And the lanthorn dimly burning.

No useless coffin enclosed his breast,
    Not in sheet or in shroud we wound him;
But he lay like a warrior taking his rest
    With his martial cloak around him.

Few and short were the prayers we said,
    And we spoke not a word of sorrow;
But we steadfastly gazed on the face that was dead,
    And we bitterly thought of the morrow.

We thought, as we hollowed his narrow bed
    And smoothed down his lonely pillow,
That the foe and the stranger would tread o'er his head,
    And we far away on the billow!

Lightly they'll talk of the spirit that's gone,
    And o'er his cold ashes upbraid him –
But little he'll reck, if they let him sleep on
    In the grave where a Briton has laid him.

But half of our heavy task was done
    When the clock struck the hour for retiring;
And we heard the distant and random gun
    That the foe was sullenly firing.

Slowly and sadly we laid him down,
    From the field of his fame fresh and gory;
We carved not a line, and we raised not a stone,
    But we left him alone with his glory.

Charles Wolfe

In 1803 Napoleon annexed Spain and installed one of his brothers as King. In reply, the Duke of Wellington led a British army from Portugal to victory at Vimiera, but Napoleon then burst into Spain with 200,000 veterans, captured Madrid and forced the British, now under the command of Sir John Moore, to retreat. They marched 250 miles in nineteen days. Moore fought a rearguard action at Corunna while what was left of his army embarked. It was the Dunkirk of the Peninsular Wars, which Wellington eventually won in 1813.

1812

THE ASSASSINATION OF THE PRIME MINISTER

Lines on the Death of Mr P–R–C–V–L

In the dirge we sung o'er him no censure was heard,
    Unembittered and free did the tear-drop descend;
We forgot in that hour how the statesman had erred,
    And wept, for the husband, the father and friend.

Oh! proud was the meed his integrity won,
    And generous indeed were the tears that we shed,
When in grief we forgot all the ill he had done,
    And though wronged by him living, bewailed him when
      dead.

Even now, if one harsher emotion intrude,
  'Tis to wish he had chosen some lowlier state –
Had known what he was, and, content to be good,
  Had ne'er for our ruin aspired to be great.

So, left through their own little orbit to move,
  His years might have rolled inoffensive away;
His children might still have been blessed with his love,
  And England would ne'er have been cursed with his sway.

Thomas Moore

If Spencer Percival had not been assassinated as he entered the House of Commons on 11 May 1812, he would probably have joined the ranks of the now forgotten Prime Ministers. He had been PM for two years and was a politician of strong reactionary views. He was shot by a madman, John Bellingham, who was tried and publicly executed within a week. The House of Commons voted Percival's widow a capital sum of £50,000, but the country as a whole took the matter rather differently. In Bolton the mob ran wild with joy; in Nottingham a crowd paraded with drums beating and colours flying; while in the Potteries a man ran down the streets, shouting: 'Percival is shot. Hurrah!'

THE LUDDITES

from **General Ludd's Triumph**

Chant no more your old rhymes about bold Robin Hood,
His feats I but little admire,
I will sing the Achievements of General Ludd,
Now the Hero of Nottinghamshire.

*

Now by force unsubdued, and by threats undismay'd
Death itself can't his ardour repress
The presence of Armies can't make him afraid
Nor impede his career of success
Whilst the news of his conquests is spread far and near
How his Enemies take the alarm
His courage, his fortitude, strikes them with fear
For they dread his Omnipotent Arm . . .
And when in the work of destruction employed
He himself to no method confines,
By fire and by water he gets them destroyed
For the Elements aid his designs.
Whether guarded by Soldiers along the Highway
Or closely secured in the room,
He shivers them up both by night and by day,
And nothing can soften their doom.

Anonymous

Enoch Made Them – Enoch Shall Break Them

And night by night when all is still,
And the moon is hid behind the hill,
We forward march to do our will
　　With hatchet, pike and gun!
Oh, the cropper lads for me,
The gallant lads for me,
Who with lusty stroke
The shear frames broke,
The cropper lads for me!

Great Enoch still shall lead the van
Stop him who dare! stop him who can!
Press forward every gallant man
　　With hatchet, pike, and gun!
Oh, the cropper lads for me . . .

Anonymous

In 1811 the textile and hosiery trades were depressed for three reasons: the trade embargo imposed as a punishment upon America for supporting Napoleon had slashed exports; men's fashions were changing and the old fabrics were no longer in such heavy demand; and new machinery threatened the jobs of skilled craftsmen. Well-organized gangs went from village to village in Lancashire, Yorkshire and Nottinghamshire, breaking up machines. Many of the hammers they used for this task had been made by Enoch Taylor of Marsden, a blacksmith, who also manufactured the new frames, which gave rise to the slogan quoted above. The Government, rattled by the recent assassination of the Prime Minister, declared frame-breaking a capital offence and sent 12,000 troops to police the North – more than Wellington had commanded in Spain four years earlier. George Mellor, who led a famous, if futile, attack on Rawfold's Mill in the Spen Valley, was captured and, with sixteen other men, was hanged at York in January 1813.

Song for the Luddites

As the Liberty lads o'er the sea
Bought their freedom, and cheaply, with blood,
        So we, boys, we
        Will die fighting, or live free,
And down with all kings but King Ludd!

When the web that we weave is complete,
And the shuttle exchanged for the sword,
        We will fling the winding sheet
        O'er the despot at our feet,
And dye it deep in the gore he has pour'd.

Though black as his heart its hue,
Since his veins are corrupted to mud,
        Yet this is the dew
        Which the tree shall renew
Of Liberty, planted by Ludd!

George Gordon, Lord Byron

Luddism remained fitfully alive for a few years, ending in an outburst in 1816. But it achieved little. As the war ended, trade picked up, wages rose and more machines were needed to meet higher demand. In 1817, in Yorkshire, there were at least sixty more gig mills, and 1,300 more mechanical shears, than there had been before the troubles. There was, of course, no such figure as General Ludd in reality. The Nottinghamshire men had adopted the name of a legendary apprentice, said to have broken his stocking frame after he had been unfairly punished by his father.

1813

A DIVERSION OF THE TIMES

Song in Praise of Gowfing

O rural diversions, too long has the chace,
All the honours usurp'd, and assum'd the chief place;
But truth bids the Muse from henceforward proclaim,
That Gowf, first of sports, shall stand foremost in fame.

At Gowf we contend, without rancour or spleen,
And bloodless the laurels we reap on the green;
From vig'rous exertion our pleasures arise,
And to crown our delights no poor fugitive dies.

O'er the heath see our heroes in uniform clad,
In parties well match'd, how they gracefully spread;
While with long strokes and short strokes they tend to the goal,
And with put well-directed plump into the hole.

From exercise strong, from strength active and bold,
We'll traverse the green, and forget to grow old.
Blue devils, diseases, dull sorrow and care,
Knock'd down by our balls as they whizz thro' the air.

Health, happiness, harmony, friendship, and fame,
Are the fruits and rewards of our favourite game;
A sport so distinguish'd, the fair must approve,
Then to Gowf give the day, and the evening to love.

Andrew Duncan

Duncan wrote this for the Blackheath Club, near London. James I had
played golf on Blackheath Common in 1608 and the club now established there claims to be the oldest in the world, although the one
founded at St Andrews in 1754 is more famous. It is curious to note
that the game was flourishing during the Napoleonic Wars.

1815

THE BATTLE OF WATERLOO

from **Childe Harold's Pilgrimage**

There was a sound of revelry by night,
    And Belgium's Capital had gathered then
    Her Beauty and her Chivalry, and bright
    The lamps shone o'er fair women and brave men;
    A thousand hearts beat happily; and when
    Music arose with its voluptuous swell,
    Soft eyes looked love to eyes which spake again,
And all went merry as a marriage bell;
But hush! hark! a deep sound strikes like a rising knell!

Did ye not hear it? – No; 'twas but the wind,
  Or the car rattling o'er the stony street;
  On with the dance! let joy be unconfined;
  No sleep till morn, when Youth and Pleasure meet
  To chase the glowing Hours with flying feet –
  But hark – that heavy sound breaks in once more,
  As if the clouds its echo would repeat;
  And nearer, clearer, deadlier than before!
Arm! Arm! it is – it is – the cannon's opening roar!

*

And there was mounting in hot haste: the steed,
  The mustering squadron, and the clattering car,
  Went pouring forward with impetuous speed,
  And swiftly forming in the ranks of war;
  And the deep thunder peal on peal afar;
  And near, the beat of the alarming drum
  Roused up the soldier ere the morning star;
  While thronged the citizens with terror dumb,
Or whispering, with white lips – The foe! They come! they
  come!'

*

Last noon beheld them full of lusty life,
  Last eve in Beauty's circle proudly gay,
  The midnight brought the signal-sound of strife,
  The morn the marshalling in arms, – the day
  Battle's magnificently-stern array!
  The thunder-clouds close o'er it, which when rent
  The earth is covered thick with other clay
  Which her own clay shall cover, heaped and pent,
Rider and horse, – friend, foe, – in one red burial blent!

George Gordon, Lord Byron

After the failure of his Russian campaign in 1812, Napoleon had abdicated and gone into exile on the island of Elba. But in 1815 he contrived a brilliant return and his old soldiers flocked to rejoin him.

The nations of Europe rallied in opposition and the two armies met at Waterloo in Belgium. It was a hard-fought battle, which the allied army under Wellington came close to losing on two occasions, but as the sun set at 8.15 the Duke gave the order for a general advance and won the day. Interestingly, although Waterloo tends to be acclaimed as a British victory, in an allied army of 67,000 men only 21,000 were in fact British.

THE 'CHORUS OF THE YEARS' SURVEYS THE FIELD OF WATERLOO BEFORE THE BATTLE

from The Dynasts

Yea, the coneys are scared by the thud of hoofs,
And their white scuts flash at their vanishing heels,
And swallows abandon the hamlet-roofs.

The mole's tunnelled chambers are crushed by wheels,
The lark's eggs scattered, their owners fled;
And the hedgehog's household the sapper unseals.

The snail draws in at the terrible tread,
But in vain; he is crushed by the felloe-rim;
The worm asks what can be overhead,

And wriggles deep from a scene so grim,
And guesses him safe; for he does not know
What a foul red flood will be soaking him!

Beaten about by the heel and toe
Are butterflies, sick of the day's long rheum,
To die of a worse than the weather-foe.

Trodden and bruised to a miry tomb
Are ears that have greened but will never be gold,
And flowers in the bud that will never bloom.

Thomas Hardy

NAPOLEON'S CAREER

Boney was a warrior,
      Way-aye-yah!
A warrior, a terrier,
      Johnny Franswor!

Boney beat the Prussians,
The Osstrians and the Rooshians.

He beat the Prussians squarely,
He whacked the English nearly.

We licked him in Trafalgar's bay,
Carried his main topm'st away,

'Twas on the plains of Waterloo,
He met the boy who put him through.

He met the Duke of Wellington,
That day his downfall had begun.

Boney went a-cruisin',
Aboard the Billy Ruffian.

Boney went to Saint Helen',
An' he never came back agen.

They sent him into exile,
He died on Saint Helena's isle.

Boney broke his heart an' died,
In Corsica he wisht he styed.

He wuz a rorty general,
A rorty, snorty general.

Anonymous

Lines Written during the Time of the Spy System

I saw great Satan like a Sexton stand,
With his intolerable spade in hand,
Digging three graves. Of coffin shape they were
For those who coffinless must enter there,
With unblest rites. The shrouds were of that cloth
Which Clotho weaveth in her blackest wrath.
The pillows to these baleful beds were toads,
Large, living, livid, melancholy loads,
Whose softness shocked. Worms of all monstrous size
Crawled round; and one, upcoiled, that never coils.
A dismal bell, inculcating despair,
Was always ringing in the heavy air:
And all about the detestable pit
Strange headless ghosts, and quarter'd forms did flit;
Rivers of blood from dripping traitors spilt,
By treachery stung from poverty to guilt.
I asked the Fiend, for whom those rites were meant?
'These graves,' quoth he, 'when life's short oil is spent, –
When the dark night comes, and they're sinking bedwards –
I mean for Castles, Oliver and Edwards.'

Charles Lamb

From 1792 to 1820 the Government used spies extensively to get information about revolutionary groups. Of the spies named here by Lamb, Castles was busy in London and betrayed the leaders of the Spa Fields Riots in 1816, as Edwards did for the Cato Street Conspirators, while Oliver, the most infamous, reported directly to the Home Secretary on details of the Pentridge rising in Nottingham in 1817. Juries in London refused to convict men on the evidence of such informers, but this was not so at Nottingham, where those found guilty were hanged. The years immediately following Waterloo saw economic distress and political turmoil, as tens of thousands of soldiers and sailors joined the ranks of the workless. In 1817 habeas corpus was suspended; the embryonic trade unions were banned; and England only just escaped revolution.

1819

THE PETERLOO MASSACRE

With Henry Hunt We'll Go

With Henry Hunt we'll go, my boys,
With Henry Hunt we'll go;
We'll mount the cap of liberty
In spite of Nadin Joe.

'Twas on the sixteenth day of August,
Eighteen hundred and nineteen,
A meeting held in Peter Street
Was glorious to be seen;
Joe Nadin and his big bull-dogs,
Which you might plainly see,
And on the other side
Stood the bloody cavalry.

Anonymous

Orator Hunt was a radical reformer who advocated annual Parliaments
and universal suffrage. He was billed to speak to a mass meeting at St
Peter's Fields, Manchester, on 16 August 1819. Alarmed at the possi-
bility of a general uprising, the authorities ordered the Manchester
Yeomanry, which consisted largely of merchants, farmers and small
tradesmen, to charge the mob that had gathered. In this famous
engagement, known as the Peterloo Massacre, eleven people were
killed. Hunt was arrested and imprisoned for two and a half years. This
is the only surviving fragment of a popular song commemorating the
event. Joe Nadin was the Deputy Constable of Manchester.

ANARCHY

from **The Mask of Anarchy**

As I lay asleep in Italy
There came a voice from over the Sea,
And with great power it forth led me
To walk in the visions of Poesy.

I met Murder on the way –
He had a mask like Castlereagh –
Very smooth he looked, yet grim;
Seven blood-hounds followed him:

All were fat; and well they might
Be in admirable plight,
For one by one, and two by two,
He tossed them human hearts to chew
Which from his wide cloak he drew.

Next came Fraud, and he had on,
Like Eldon, an ermined gown;
His big tears, for he wept well,
Turned to mill-stones as they fell.

And the little children, who
Round his feet played to and fro,
Thinking every tear a gem,
Had their brains knocked out by them.

Clothed with the Bible, as with light,
And the shadows of the night,
Like Sidmouth, next Hypocrisy
On a crocodile rode by.

And many more Destructions played
In this ghastly masquerade,
All disguised, even to the eyes,
Like Bishops, lawyers, peers, or spies.

Last came Anarchy: he rode
On a white horse, splashed with blood;
He was pale even to the lips,
Like Death in the Apocalypse.

And he wore a kingly crown;
And in his grasp a sceptre shone;
On his brow this mark I saw –
'I AM GOD, AND KING, AND LAW!'

With a pace stately and fast,
Over English land he passed,
Trampling to a mire of blood
The adoring multitude.

And a mighty troop around,
With their trampling shook the ground,
Waving each a bloody sword,
For the service of their Lord.

And with glorious triumph, they
Rode through England proud and gay,
Drunk as with intoxication
Of the wine of desolation.

O'er fields and towns, from sea to sea,
Passed the Pageant swift and free,
Tearing up, and trampling down;
Till they came to London town.

And each dweller, panic-stricken,
Felt his heart with terror sicken
Hearing the tempestuous cry
Of the triumph of Anarchy.

Percy Bysshe Shelley

Written 'on the occasion of the massacre at Manchester', the poem from which these first stanzas are taken serves as a passionate incitement to revolution and expresses the dismay shared by many of the more advanced thinkers of the time.

England in 1819

An old, mad, blind, despised, and dying king, –
Princes, the dregs of their dull race, who flow
Through public scorn, – mud from a muddy spring, –
Rulers who neither see, nor feel, nor know,
But leech-like to their fainting country cling,
Till they drop, blind in blood, without a blow, –
A people starved and stabbed in the untilled field, –
An army, which liberticide and prey
Makes as a two-edged sword to all who wield, –
Golden and sanguine laws which tempt and slay;
Religion Christless, Godless – a book sealed;
A Senate, – Time's worst statute unrepealed, –
Are graves, from which a glorious Phantom may
Burst, to illumine our tempestuous day.

Percy Bysshe Shelley

King George IV, 1820–30

1820

THE PRINCE REGENT

from The Political House that Jack Built

This is THE MAN – all shaven and shorn,
All cover'd with Orders – and all forlorn;
THE DANDY OF SIXTY, who bows with a grace,
And has *taste* in wigs, collars, cuirasses and lace;
Who, to tricksters, and fools, leaves the State and its treasure,
And, when Britain's in tears, sails about at his pleasure;
Who spurn'd from his presence the Friends of his youth,
And now has not one who will tell him the truth;
Who took to his counsels, in evil hour,
The Friends to the Reasons of lawless Power;
That back the Public Informer, who
Would put down the *Thing*, that, in spite of new Acts,
And attempts to restrain it, by Soldiers of Tax,
Will *poison* the Vermin,
That plunder the Wealth,
That lay in the House,
That Jack built.

William Hone

William Hone started out as a bookseller, but went on to become a radical publisher. He published William Hazlitt's *Political Essays* and was made to stand trial on three occasions. In 1820 he issued what was to be the most popular satirical pamphlet of the nineteenth century, 'The Political House that Jack Built', illustrated by George Cruikshank, who later achieved fame with his illustrations for *Oliver Twist*. Hone's pamphlet satirized many famous people, and within a year it had run into fifty-two editions.

QUEEN CAROLINE

The Bath

'. . . The wide sea
Hath drops too few to wash her clean'

William Shakespeare

The weather's hot – the cabin's free!
    And she's as free and hot as either!
And Berghy is as hot as she!
    In short, they all are hot together!
Bring then a large capacious tub,
    And pour great pails of water in,
In which the frowzy nymph may rub
    The itchings of her royal skin.

Let none but Berghy's hand untie
    The garter, or unlace the boddice;
Let none but Berghy's faithful eye
    Survey the beauties of the goddess.

While *she* receives the copious shower
    He gets a step in honour's path,
And grows from this auspicious hour
    A K-night Companion of the Bath.

William Hone

George had married Caroline in 1795 and, after the birth of a daughter, Charlotte, they separated. When he became Regent in 1811, Caroline went to live on the Continent, accompanied by her major-domo, Bartolomeo Bergami, who served, it was said, all her needs. In 1820, on George's accession, she returned, and the luckless Prime Minister, Lord Liverpool, had to move a Bill dissolving the marriage and depriving her of the title of Queen. Her case was taken up by the Whigs and she became as popular as her husband was unpopular. The Bill was dropped, but she was refused entry to Westminster Abbey at the

Coronation and died a year later. Max Beerbohm said of Caroline that she had been cast for a tragic role, but played it in tights.

On the Queen

Most Gracious Queen, we thee implore
To go away and sin no more,
But if that effort be too great,
To go away at any rate.

Anonymous

ENCLOSURES

from The Fallen Elm

Thus came enclosure – ruin was its guide
But freedoms clapping hands enjoyed the sight
Though comforts cottage soon was thrust aside
& workhouse prisons raised upon the scite
Een natures dwellings far away from men
The common heath became the spoilers prey
The rabbit had not where to make his den
& labours only cow was drove away
No matter – wrong was right & right was wrong
& freedoms bawl was sanction to the song
– Such was thy ruin music making elm
The rights of freedom was to injure thine
As thou wert served so would they overwhelm
In freedoms name the little that is mine
& there are knaves that brawl for better laws
& cant of tyranny in stronger powers
Who glue their vile unsatiated maws
& freedoms birthright from the weak devours

John Clare

Clare was a poet of the Northamptonshire countryside and no one wrote more movingly about the rural poor, or the struggles of the small farmer and agricultural labourer. The eighteenth century had seen a revolution in farming. Turnips were introduced to allow for crop rotation, and clover was planted to fatten livestock. Drainage became popular, but it required capital and larger holdings. Parliamentary acts promoted the enclosure of land. Clare was an eloquent defender of the old farming methods and the society which they created. Arthur Young, on his travels through England, acted as spokesman for the reformers and for big farming, and he vigorously disparaged the 'Goths and Vandals' of the open-field system.

1825

THE FOUNDATION OF LONDON UNIVERSITY

from The London University

Ye Dons and ye doctors, ye Provosts and Proctors,
    Who're paid to monopolize knowledge,
Come make opposition by voice and petition
    To the radical infidel College;
Come put forth your powers in aid of the towers
    Which boast of their Bishops and Martyrs,
And arm all the terrors of privileged errors
    Which live by the wax of their Charters.

Let Mackintosh battle with Canning and Vattel,
    Let Brougham be a friend to the 'niggers,'
Burdett cure the nation's misrepresentations,
    And Hume cut a figure in figures;
But let them not babble of Greek to the rabble,
    Nor teach the mechanics their letters;
The labouring classes were born to be asses,
    And not to be aping their betters.

'Tis a terrible crisis for Cam and for Isis!
  Fat butchers are learning dissection;
And looking-glass makers become Sabbath-breakers
  To study the rules of reflection;
'Sin: ϕ' and 'sin: θ' what sins can be sweeter?
  Are taught to the poor of both sexes,
And weavers and sinners jump up from their dinners
  To flirt with their Y's and their X's.

Chuckfarthing advances the doctrine of chances
  In spite of the staff of the beadle;
And menders of breeches between the long stitches
  Write books on the laws of the needle;
And chandlers all chatter of luminous matter,
  Who communicate none to their tallows,
And rogues get a notion of the pendulum's motion
  Which is only of use at the gallows.

Winthrop Mackworth Praed

Until 1825 there had been four universities in Scotland, but only two in England, Oxford and Cambridge; and these had excluded Jews, Catholics and Dissenters. The Scottish poet Thomas Campbell and Henry Brougham, a prickly politician – who was later to retire to France and make Cannes a fashionable resort – decided to establish a new university in London, with no clergy on its governing body. They sold shares in it, and representatives of the great liberal families subscribed – J. S. Mill, Macaulay and Goldsmid among them. They founded University College in Gower Street. There, towards the end of the century, J. A. Fleming invented the thermionic valve, without which one could not have had the wireless, television or the computer.

A RETROSPECT

George the First was always reckoned
Vile, but viler George the Second;
And what mortal ever heard
Any good of George the Third?
When from earth the Fourth descended
(God be praised!) the Georges ended.

Walter Savage Landor

King William IV, 1830–7

1832

THE REFORM BILL

from Pledges, by a Ten-pound Householder

When a gentleman comes
With his trumpet and drums,
And hangs out a flag at the Dragon,
Some pledges, no doubt,
We must get him to spout
To the shopkeepers, out of a wagon.

For although an MP
May be wiser than we
Till the House is dissolved, in December,
Thenceforth, we're assured,
Since Reform is secured,
We'll be wiser by far than our member.

A pledge must be had
That, since times are so bad
He'll prepare a long speech, to improve them;
And since taxes, at best,
Are a very poor jest,
He'll take infinite pains to remove them.

*

He must solemnly say
That he'll vote no more pay
To the troops, in their ugly red jackets;
And that none may complain
On the banks of the Seine,
He'll dismast all our ships, but the packets.

That the labourer's arm,
May be stout on the farm,
That our commerce may wake from stagnation,
That our trades may revive,
And our looms look alive,
He'll be pledged to all free importation.

*

We must bind him, poor man,
To obey their divan,
However their worships may task him,
To swallow their lies
Without any surprise,
And to vote black is white, when they ask him.

These hints I shall lay,
In a forcible way,
Before an intelligent quorum,
Who meet to debate
Upon matters of State,
Tonight, at the National Forum

Winthrop Mackworth Praed

In 1830 the Tory Government under Wellington was defeated at the polls and a coalition of Whigs, Liberals and Independents, led by the seventy-year-old Earl Grey, took office. Several future PMs – Lord John Russell, Melbourne and Palmerston – were in the Cabinet, and they were determined to bring in a Reform Bill that would abolish the rotten boroughs and widen the franchise to the extent of giving the vote to any male who occupied a house with a rental value of ten pounds or more. There was initial resistance in the Lords, but the Tories were badly led by Wellington and eventually the Bill was forced through. The measure itself had limited scope, being mainly a reform instituted by the middle classes on behalf of the middle classes, but the electorate was increased from 435,000 to 685,000. Revolution was avoided by a classic compromise, and England was set upon a path which was to lead to universal suffrage.

1834

THE TOLPUDDLE MARTYRS

God is our guide! from field, from wave,
From plough, from anvil, and from loom;
We come, our country's rights to save,
And speak a tyrant faction's doom:
We raise the watchword liberty;
We will, we will, we will be free!

God is our guide! no swords we draw,
We kindle not war's battle fires;
By reason, union, justice, law,
We claim the birthright of our sires:
We raise the watchword liberty;
We will, we will, we will be free!!!

George Loveless

George Loveless was the leader of a group of Dorsetshire labourers who had 'combined together' to protect their jobs and their pay. This was an illegal act and the offenders were sentenced to seven years' deportation. After two years of protest, however, they were reprieved and Loveless returned to join the Chartists. He scribbled this poem on a piece of paper as his sentence was passed. He wrote: 'While we were being guarded back to prison, our hands being locked together, I tossed the above lines to some people that we passed; the guard, however, seizing hold of them, they were instantly carried back to the judge; and by some this was considered a crime of no less magnitude than high treason.' Tolpuddle has become the shrine of the Trade Union movement.

1835–41

MELBOURNE'S PREMIERSHIP

To promise, pause, prepare, postpone
And end by letting things alone:
In short, to earn the people's pay
By doing nothing every day.

Winthrop Mackworth Praed

Lord Melbourne told his secretary that being Prime Minister was 'a damned bore'. But he held the office for almost seven years and left it reluctantly in 1841. His behaviour was certainly laid-back, but the march of progress went on: local government was established, the Poor Law was introduced and the first factory acts were passed. From 1837 Melbourne relished the role of guide and mentor to the young Queen Victoria, who was convinced as a result that Whigs were good and Tories bad.

THE VICTORIAN AGE

Queen Victoria, 1837–1901

Welcome now, VICTORIA!
Welcome to the throne!
May all the trades begin to stir,
   Now you are Queen of England;
For your most gracious Majesty,
May see what wretched poverty,
Is to be found on England's ground,
   Now you are Queen of England.

While o'er the country you preside,
Providence will be your guide,
The people then will never chide
   Victoria, Queen of England.
She doth declare it her intent
To extend reform in Parliament,
On doing good she's firmly bent,
   While she is Queen of England.

Says she, I'll try my utmost skill,
That the poor may have their fill;
Forsake them! – no, I never will,
   When I am Queen of England.
For oft my mother said to me,
Let this your study always be,
To see the people blest and free,
   Should you be Queen of England.

Anonymous

Victoria was eighteen years old when she succeeded her uncle, William IV, and during her long reign Britain was to enjoy unparalleled prosperity and power, ruling a vast empire and serving as the workshop of the world. The Queen was a small woman, being less than five feet tall, but she had the strength to bear nine children. In 1840 she married one of her cousins, Albert of Saxe-Coburg, and for the first time in two hundred years the English monarchy enjoyed domestic bliss. Victoria imposed respectability upon the nation: satire dried up and parlour songs became the order of the day.

PRINCE ALBERT

I am a German just arrived,
  With you for to be mingling,
My passage it was paid,
  From Germany to England;
To wed your blooming Queen.
  For better or worse I take her,
My father is a duke,
  And I'm a sausage maker.

    Here I am in rags and jags,
      Come from the land of all dirt,
    I married England's Queen.
      My name it is young Albert.

I am a cousin to the Queen,
  And our mothers they are cronies,
My father lives at home,
— And deals in nice polonies:
Lots of sour crout and broom,
  For money he'll be giving,
And by working very hard,
  He gets a tidy living.

                  Here I am, &c.

She says now we are wed.
   I must not dare to tease her,
But strive both day and night,
   All e'er I can to please her,
I told her I would do
   For her all I was able,
And when she had a son
   I would sit and rock the cradle.

           Here I am, &c.

           Anonymous

1838

THE CHARTER

When thrones shall crumble and moulder to dust,
    And sceptres shall fall from the hands of the great,
And all the rich baubles a Monarch might boast,
    Shall vanish before the good sense of a state;
When Lords, (produced by the mandate of Kings),
    So proud and dominant, rampant with power.
Shall be spoken of only as by-gone things
    That shall blast this part of creation no more,
Based firm upon truth, the Charter shall stand
The land-mark of ages – sublimely grand!

When class-distinctions shall wither and die,
    And conscious merit shall modestly bear
The garlands wrought by its own industry,
    The proper rewards of labour and care;
When man shall rise to his station as man,
    To passion or vice no longer a slave;
When the *march of mind* already begun,
    Shall gathering roll like a vast mountain wave,
The Charter shall stand the text of the free,
Of a Nation's rights the sure guarantee.

Anonymous

The Charter was published in 1838 and it called for six reforms, including annual parliaments, the payment of MPs, secret ballots and universal male suffrage. The Chartist cause peaked in 1839, briefly flaring up again in 1848. It failed through the inability of its leaders to suppress their differences, although its spirit survives. Karl Marx, who was living in London at the time, expressed the opinion that England was too placid to encourage a proletarian uprising.

Protest against the Ballot

Forth rushed from Envy sprung and Self-conceit,
A Power misnamed the SPIRIT of REFORM,
And through the astonished Island swept in storm,
Threatening to lay all Orders at her feet
That crossed her way. Now stoops she to entreat
Licence to hide at intervals her head
Where she may work, safe, undisquieted,
In a close Box, covert for Justice meet.
St George of England! keep a watchful eye
Fixed on the Suitor; frustrate her request –
Stifle her hope; for, if the State comply,
From such Pandorian gift may come a Pest
Worse than the Dragon that bowed low his crest,
Pierced by thy spear in glorious victory.

William Wordsworth

1838

Grace Darling

After you had steered your coble out of the storm
And left the smaller islands to break the surface,
Like draughts shaking that colossal backcloth there came
Fifty pounds from the Queen, proposals of marriage.

The daughter of a lighthouse-keeper and the saints
Who once lived there on birds' eggs, rainwater, barley
And built to keep all pilgrims at a safe distance
Circular houses with views only of the sky,

Who set timber burning on the top of a tower
Before each was launched at last in his stone coffin –
You would turn your back on mainland and suitor
To marry, then bereave the waves from Lindisfarne,

A moth against the lamp that shines still and reveals
Many small boats at sea, lifeboats, named after girls.

Michael Longley

When the steamer *Forfarshire* ran aground off the Farne rocks in September 1838, Grace Darling, the twenty-three-year-old daughter of the lighthouse keeper, rowed out with her father in a great storm and helped him save five people from the wreck. She became an instant heroine: souvenir mugs were produced and admirers offered £5 for a lock of her hair. She continued to live with her father until her death from tuberculosis just four years later. There is a marble effigy of her in Bamburgh churchyard, complete with an oar in her right hand and seaweed carved on the canopy.

1841

THE BIRTH OF EDWARD, PRINCE OF WALES

There's a pretty fuss and bother both in country and in town,
Since we have got a present, and an heir unto the Crown,
A little Prince of Wales so charming and so sly,
And the ladies shout with wonder, What a pretty little boy!

He must have a little musket, a trumpet and a kite,
A little penny rattle, and silver sword so bright,
A little cap and feather with scarlet coat so smart,
And a pretty little hobby horse to ride about the park.

He must have a dandy suit to strut about the town,
John Bull must rake together six or seven thousand pound,
You'd laugh to see his daddy, at night he homewards runs,
With some peppermint or lollipops, sweet cakes and sugar
    plums.

Now to get these little niceties the taxes must be rose,
For the little Prince of Wales wants so many suits of clothes,
So they must tax the frying pan, the windows and the doors,
The bedsteads and the tables, kitchen pokers, and the floors.

John Harkness

The Prince had to wait sixty years before ascending the throne as
Edward VII, but seems never to have lost his taste for idle and expensive pleasures.

1844

PEEL AND DISRAELI

Young England's Lament

(Young England sitting dolorously before his parlour-fire:
he grievously waileth as follows: –)

I really can't imagine why,
    With my confess'd ability –
From the ungrateful Tories, I
    Get nothing – but civility.

The 'independent' dodge I've tried,
    I've also tried servility; –
It's all the same, – they *won't* provide, –
    I only get – civility.

I've flattered PEEL; he smiles back thanks
    With Belial's own tranquillity;
But still he keeps me in 'the ranks',
    And pays me – with civility.

If not the birth, at least I've now
    The *manners* of nobility;
But yet SIR ROBERT scorns to bow
    With more than mere civility.

Well, I've been pretty mild as yet,
    But now I'll try scurrility;
It's very hard if *that* don't get
    Me more than mere civility.

Anonymous

Robert Peel was the son of a Lancashire cotton-spinner and never lost his Lancastrian accent. He was a typical member of the new, thriving and thrusting middle classes, but he led the Tory party, which was principally the party of the old landed interests. He served as Prime Minister from 1841 to 1846 – a remarkable administration, with five future Prime Ministers in the Cabinet. Gladstone said that Peel was the greatest man he had ever known. He was proud and shy, with a propensity to be stiff and stubborn. Disraeli attacked Peel bitterly and once remarked that his smile was like the plate on a coffin. In 1834 he published the first party programme, the Tamworth Manifesto, which set good government and consensus above adherence to party dogma. In 1844 Benjamin Disraeli, who in spite of asking had not been offered any post by Peel, published his novel, *Coningsby*. This argued for a new 'Young England' to arise from the old traditions and customs of the country. Still Disraeli failed to get a job, and he had to wait nearly thirty years before he himself became Prime Minister. By then the romantic dream of a Young England had faded, although Disraeli's eloquent concern for a country which he saw as split into 'Two Nations', rich and poor, was undiminished.

1846

THE REPEAL OF THE CORN LAWS

from Corn Law Rhymes

Child, is thy father dead?
  Father is gone!
Why did they tax his bread?
  God's will be done!
Mother has sold her bed;
Better to die than wed!
Where shall she lay her head?
  Home we have none!

Father clamm'd thrice a week
  God's will be done!
Long for work did he seek,
  Work he found none.
Tears on his hollow cheek
Told what no tongue could speak:
Why did his master break?
  God's will be done!

Doctor said air was best –
  Food we had none;
Father, with panting breast,
  Groan'd to be gone:
Now he is with the blest –
Mother says death is best!
We have no place of rest –
  Yes, ye have one!

Ebenezer Elliott

The big issue in the 1840s had become whether the Corn Laws, which
protected British farmers, should be repealed to allow for cheaper

foreign imports. The Anti Corn Law League, which was formed in 1839 and led by John Bright and Richard Cobden, campaigned vigorously across the country. Peel had become a convert to free trade, but what drove him to action was learning of the failure of the Irish potato crop and of the prospect of famine. In 1846 he repealed the Corn Laws, lost office and split the Tory party. Two hundred and thirty-one Tory MPs voted against him. The old party of Pitt, Canning, Liverpool and Wellington broke up. The issue – free trade as against protection – was the same that divided the Tories in 1906, and in both instances disunity was to lead to long periods of government by the opposition.

1848

THE RAILWAYS

'Mr Dombey', *from* Victorian Trains

The whistle blows. The train moves.
Thank God I am pulling away from the conversation
I had on the platform through the hissing of steam
With that man who dares to wear crape for the death of my son.
But I forget. He is coming with us.
He is always ahead of us stocking the engine.
I depend on him to convey me
With my food and my drink and my wraps and my reading
     material
To my first holiday since grief mastered me.
He is the one with the view in front of him
The ash in his whiskers, the speed in his hair.

He is richer now. He refused my tip.
Death and money roll round and round
In my head with the wheels.
I know what a skeleton looks like.
I never think of my dead son
In this connection. I think of wealth.

The railway is like a skeleton,
Alive in a prosperous body,
Reaching up to grasp Yorkshire and Lancashire
Kicking Devon and Kent
Squatting on London.
A diagram of growth
A midwinter leaf.

I am a merchant
With fantasies like all merchants.
Gold, carpets, handsome women come to me
Out of the sea, along these tracks.
I am as rich as England,
As solid as a town hall.

Patricia Beer

The first railway line, running between Stockton and Darlington, was opened in 1825, and the 1830s saw a modest expansion, until by 1838 there were more than 500 miles of track, with London and Birmingham included in the service. The railway boom, whose driving force was George Hudson, the 'Railway King', took off in the 1840s, but burst in 1847, by which time more than 5,000 miles of track had been laid and English industry and society had been transformed. Dickens published *Dombey and Son* in 1848, and the railways play an important part in the book. To Mr Dombey, the cold, proud and stubborn merchant, they represent progress. His sickly son, Paul, has a foster-mother, Polly Toodle, whose husband is a stoker and engine-driver. But Paul is removed from their care and submitted to a wretched and loveless education. Towards the end of the book the villainous Carker dies under an express train. Dickens's description of the railway excavations in North London as an event of seismic consequences is perfectly apt.

1851

THE GREAT EXHIBITION

Fountains, gushing silver light,
   Sculptures, soft and warm and fair,
Gems, that blind the dazzled sight,
   Silken trophies rich and rare,
Wondrous works of cunning skill,
   Precious miracles of art, –
How your crowding memories fill
   Mournfully my musing heart!

Fairy Giant choicest birth
   Of the Beautiful Sublime,
Seeming like the Toy of earth
   Given to the dotard Time, –
Glacier-diamond, Alp of glass,
   Sindbad's cave, Aladdin's hall, –
Must it then be crush'd, alas;
   Must the Crystal Palace fall?

Anonymous

Prince Albert organized the Great Exhibition to celebrate Britain's industrial and commercial leadership of the world. It was housed in an enormous structure of glass and steel, the Crystal Palace, which was erected in Hyde Park and later moved to South London. Disraeli, never at a loss for hyperbole, hailed it as 'an enchanted pile, which the sagacious taste and prescient philanthropy of an accomplished and enlightened Prince have raised for the glory of England and the instruction of two hemispheres'.

It made a profit and on the strength of this, land was bought in South Kensington for Imperial College and the museums that now stand there. The Crystal Palace itself was moved to Sydenham, where it proved a costly embarrassment until it was burnt down in the next century.

The Site of the Crystal Palace

A weed-mobbed terrace; plinths
deserted; an imperial symmetry
partitioned, gone to various bidders.
Down the clogged ghost-promenades

he sees like yesterday, only clearer . . .
Girders wincing, staggering in white glare,
the factory-forged dream, that ordered
brillance, stove in and shrivelling

to mere recorded fact. More real,
his mother's apron, dabbing smoke-
sting back; her grimed ordinary face,
tired then, lost thirty years now,

but flare-lit that night, immutable.

Philip Gross

1852

THE DEATH OF WELLINGTON

from **Ode on the Death of the Duke of Wellington**

Bury the Great Duke
  With an empire's lamentation,
Let us bury the Great Duke
  To the noise of the mourning of a mighty nation,
Mourning when their leaders fall,
Warriors carry the warrior's pall,
And sorrow darkens hamlet and hall.

*

Lead out the pageant: sad and slow,
As fits an universal woe,
Let the long long procession go,
And let the sorrowing crowd about it grow,
And let the mournful martial music blow;
The last great Englishman is low . . .

Alfred, Lord Tennyson

from Don Juan

You are 'the best of cut-throats:' – do not start;
    The phrase is Shakespeare's, and not misapplied: –
War's a brain-spattering, windpipe-slitting art,
    Unless her cause by right be sanctified.
If you have acted *once* a generous part,
    The world, not the world's masters, will decide,
And I shall be delighted to learn who,
Save you and yours, have gain'd by Waterloo?

I am no flatterer – you've supp'd full of flattery:
    They say you like it too – 't is no great wonder.
He whose whole life has been assault and battery,
    At last may get a little tired of thunder;
And swallowing eulogy much more than satire, he
    May like being praised for every lucky blunder,
Call'd 'Saviour of the Nations' – not yet saved,
And 'Europe's Liberator' – still enslaved.

George Gordon, Lord Byron

When he died, Wellington was given a splendid state funeral, as befitted a national hero. Writing forty years earlier, Byron evidently did not share the general adulation, but it is unlikely that Wellington, who once replied to a blackmailing courtesan with the words, 'Publish and be damned!' lost much sleep over this.

THE WEAVING INDUSTRY

from **The Hand-loom Weavers' Lament**

You gentlemen and tradesmen, that ride about at will,
Look down on these poor people; it's enough to make you crill;
Look down on these poor people, as you ride up and down,
I think there is a God above will bring your pride quite down.
    You tyrants of England, your race may soon be run,
    You may be brought unto account for what you've sorely
      done.

You pull down our wages, shamefully to tell;
You go into the markets, and say you cannot sell;
And when that we do ask you when these bad times will mend,
You quickly give an answer, 'When the wars are at an end.'
    You tyrants of England, &c.

Anonymous

Bury New Loom

As I walked between Bolton and Bury.
    'twas on a moonshiny night,
I met with a buxom young weaver whose
    company gave me delight.
She says: Young fellow, come tell me if your
    level and rule are in tune.
Come give me an answer correct, can you
    get up and square my new loom?

I said: My dear lassie, believe me, I am a
    good joiner by trade,
And many a good loom and shuttle before
    me in my time I have made.

Your short lams and jacks and long lams I
    quickly can put in tune.
My rule is in good order to get up and
    square a new loom.

She took me and showed me her loom, the
    down on her warp did appear.
The lams, jacks and healds put in motion, I
    levelled her loom to a hair.
My shuttle run well in her lathe, my treadle
    it worked up and down,
My level stood close to her breast-bone, the
    time I was reiving her loom.

The cords of my lams, jacks and treadles at
    length they began to give way.
The bobbin I had in my shuttle, the weft in
    it no longer would stay.
Her lathe it went bang to and fro, my main
    treadle still kept in tune,
My pickers went nicketty-nack all the time
    I was squaring her loom.

My shuttle it still kept in motion, her lams
    she worked well up and down.
The weights in her rods they did tremble;
    she said she would weave a new gown.
My strength now began for to fail me. I
    said: It's now right to a hair.
She turned up her eyes and said: Tommy,
    my loom you have got pretty square.

Anonymous

There were many popular songs of the early nineteenth century that
took as their theme the new industrial machinery. Some were in the
form of angry denunciations, but as 'Bury New Loom', one of the most
famous, indicates, it was also hard to resist an opportunity for humor-
ous sexual innuendo.

1853

A PUBLIC HANGING

A London Fête

All night fell hammers, shock on shock;
With echoes Newgate's granite clanged:
The scaffold built, at eight o'clock
They brought the man out to be hanged.
Then came from all the people there
A single cry, that shook the air;
Mothers held up their babes to see,
Who spread their hands, and crowed for glee;
Here a girl from her vesture tore
A rag to wave with, and joined the roar;
There a man, with yelling tired,
Stopped, and the culprit's crime inquired;
A sot, below the doomed man dumb,
Bawled his health in the world to come;
These blasphemed and fought for places;
Those half-crushed, cast frantic faces,
To windows, where, in freedom sweet,
Others enjoyed the wicked treat.
At last, the show's black crisis pended;
Struggles for better standings ended;
The rabble's lips no longer cursed,
But stood agape with horrid thirst;
Thousands of breasts beat horrid hope;
Thousands of eyeballs, lit with hell,
Burnt one way all, to see the rope
Unslacken as the platform fell.
The rope flew tight; and then the roar
Burst forth afresh; less loud, but more
Confused and affrighting than before.
A few harsh tongues for ever led
The common din, the chaos of noises,
But ear could not catch what they said.
As when the realm of the damned rejoices

At winning a soul to its will,
That clatter and clangour of hateful voices
Sickened and stunned the air, until
The dangling corpse hung straight and still.
The show complete, the pleasure past,
The solid masses loosened fast:
A thief slunk off, with ample spoil,
To ply elsewhere his daily toil;
A baby strung its doll to a stick;
A mother praised the pretty trick;
Two children caught and hanged a cat;
Two friends walked on, in lively chat;
And two, who had disputed places,
Went forth to fight, with murderous faces.

Coventry Patmore

Public executions were not stopped in England until 1868. Thackeray in 1840, and Dickens in a famous letter to *The Times* in 1849, had both tried to bring them to an end. Coventry Patmore denied in later years that he had attacked the imposition of the death penalty, but the last couplet of this poem effectively demolishes the deterrent argument.

1854

The Charge of the Light Brigade

Half a league, half a league,
    Half a league onward,
All in the valley of Death
    Rode the six hundred.
'Forward, the Light Brigade!
Charge for the guns!' he said:
Into the valley of Death
    Rode the six hundred.

'Forward, the Light Brigade!'
Was there a man dismayed?
Not though the soldier knew
   Someone had blundered:
Their's not to make reply,
Their's not to reason why,
Their's but to do and die:
Into the valley of Death
   Rode the six hundred.

Cannon to right of them,
Cannon to left of them,
Cannon in front of them
   Volleyed and thundered;
Stormed at with shot and shell,
Boldly they rode and well,
Into the jaws of Death,
Into the mouth of Hell
   Rode the six hundred.

Flashed all their sabres bare,
Flashed as they turned in air
Sabring the gunners there,
Charging an army, while
   All the world wondered:

Plunged in the battery-smoke
Right through the line they broke;
Cossack and Russian
Reeled from the sabre-stroke
   Shattered and sundered.
Then they rode back, but not
   Not the six hundred.

Cannon to right of them,
Cannon to left of them,
Cannon behind them
    Volleyed and thundered;
Stormed at with shot and shell,
While horse and hero fell,
They that had fought so well
Came through the jaws of Death,
Back from the mouth of Hell,
All that was left of them,
    Left of six hundred.

When can their glory fade?
O the wild charge they made!
    All the world wondered.
Honour the charge they made!
Honour the Light Brigade,
    Noble six hundred!

Alfred, Lord Tennyson

The Crimean War had started in 1854 to prevent Russia from annexing parts of the crumbling Turkish Empire. War fever swept the country, but the British army itself was in a ramshackle state. The soldier's pay of a shilling a day came down, after deductions, to no more than three pence; commissions were for sale; and the organization of supplies and medical care were both scandalously bad. Lord Raglan, the Commander-in-Chief, had not seen service for twenty-five years, and Lord Cardigan, who led the Light Brigade, was a buffoon. Between them they brought about one of the most memorable failures in the history of the British army. The war ended in 1856, and Russia's ambitions had been contained at the cost of 25,000 British dead.

Florence Nightingale

Through your pocket glass you have let disease expand
To remote continents of pain where you go far
With rustling cuff and starched apron, a soft hand:
Beneath the bandage maggots are stitching the scar.

For many of the men who lie there it is late
And you allow them at the edge of consciousness
The halo of your lamp, a brothel's fanlight
Or a nightlight carried in by nanny and nurse.

You know that even with officers and clergy
Moustachioed lips will purse into fundaments
And under sedation all the bad words emerge
To be rinsed in your head like the smell of wounds,

Death's vegetable sweetness at both rind and core –
Name a weed and you find it growing everywhere.

Michael Longley

In 1854 Florence Nightingale was thirty-five years old, a trained nurse,
and a friend of the War Minister, Sydney Herbert. Incensed by reports
in *The Times* of the way in which soldiers wounded in the Crimean War
were being treated, she took it upon herself to lead a small group of
volunteer nurses to Scutari, the British military hospital base in Constantinople. The conditions she found there, just ten days after the
battle of Balaclava, were appalling. Rats, maggots and lice overran the
wards; twenty chamber-pots were shared between 2,000 men; and
amid all that filth and indifference typhus, cholera, dysentery, delirium
and death flourished. With tremendous vitality and drive she set about
cleaning the place up. As she went round the wards with her lamp,
wounded soldiers would kiss her passing shadow. Her conduct
brought her enemies, principally among the doctors, and when the
chief medical officer was awarded the KCB she suggested that it stood
for 'Knight of the Crimea Burial-ground.'
   On returning to England, she was warmly supported by the Queen
and over the next fifty years she became the second most famous
woman in the country. By establishing the Nightingale School for

Nurses at St Thomas, she laid the foundations of modern nursing. She lived on until 1907 – a one-woman powerhouse, a relentless reformer and a legend. Characteristically, she once wrote: 'From committees, charity and schism – from the Church of England and all other deadly sins – from philanthropy and all the deceits of the devil – Good Lord deliver us.'

VICTORIANA

Mr Gradgrind's Country

There was a dining-room, there was a drawing-room,
There was a billiard-room, there was a morning-room,
There were bedrooms for guests and bedrooms for sons and
　　daughters,
In attic and basement there were ample servants' quarters,
There was a modern bathroom, a strong-room, and a
　　conservatory.
In the days of England's glory.

There were Turkish carpets, there were Axminster carpets,
There were oil paintings of Vesuvius and family portraits,
There were mirrors, ottomans, wash-hand-stands and
　　tantaluses,
There were port, sherry, claret, liqueur, and champagne
　　glasses,
There was a solid brass gong, a grand piano, antlers, decanters,
　　and a gentlemen's lavatory,
In the days of England's glory.

There was marqueterie and there was mahogany,
There was a cast of the Dying Gladiator in his agony,
There was the 'Encyclopaedia Britannica' in a revolving
    bookcase,
There were finger-bowls, asparagus-tongs, and inlets of real
    lace:
They stood in their own grounds and were called Chatsworth,
    Elgin, or Tobermory,
In the days of England's glory.

But now these substantial gentlemen's establishments
Are like a perspective of disused elephants,
And the current Rajahs of industry flash past their wide
    frontages
Far far away to the latest things in labour-saving cottages,
Where with Russell lupins, jade ash-trays, some Sealyham
    terriers, and a migratory
Cook they continue the story.

Sylvia Townsend Warner

Dickens's *Hard Times* appeared in 1854. Mr Gradgrind is one of its
characters: a tyrannical patriarch whose views on education are limited
to a belief in stuffing children's heads with facts.

THE ENGLISH PUBLIC SCHOOL

from **Rugby Chapel**

Coldly, sadly, descends
The autumn evening. The field
Strewn with its dark yellow drifts
Of withered leaves, and the elms,
Fade into dimness apace,
Silent; hardly a shout
From a few boys late at their play!
The lights come out in the street,
In the schoolroom windows; but cold,
Solemn, unlighted, austere,
Through the gathering darkness, arise
The chapel-walls, in whose bound
Thou, my father! art laid.

There thou dost lie, in the gloom
Of the autumn evening. But ah!
That word, *gloom*, to my mind
Brings thee back, in the light
Of thy radiant vigour, again;
In the gloom of November we passed
Days not dark at thy side;
Seasons impaired not the ray
Of thy buoyant cheerfulness clear.
Such thou wast! and I stand
In the autumn evening, and think
Of bygone autumns with thee.

*

If, in the paths of the world,
Stones might have wounded thy feet,
Toil or dejection have tried,
Thy spirit, of that we saw
Nothing – to us thou wast still
Cheerful, and helpful, and firm!

Therefore to thee it was given
Many to save with thyself;
And, at the end of thy day,
O faithful shepherd! to come,
Bringing thy sheep in thy hand.

And through thee I believe
In the noble and great who are gone;
Pure souls honoured and blest
By former ages, who else –
Such, so soulless, so poor,
Is the race of men whom I see –
Seemed but a dream of the heart,
Seemed but a cry of desire.
Yes! I believe that there lived
Others like thee in the past,
Not like the men of the crowd
Who all round me today
Bluster or cringe, and make life
Hideous, and arid, and vile;
But souls tempered with fire,
Fervent, heroic, and good,
Helpers and friends of mankind.

Servants of God! – or sons
Shall I not call you? because
Not as servants ye knew
Your Father's innermost mind,
His, who unwillingly sees
One of his little ones lost –
Yours is the praise, if mankind
Hath not as yet in its march
Fainted, and fallen, and died!

Matthew Arnold

Matthew Arnold's father, to whose shade this poem is addressed, was the great Dr Thomas Arnold, founder of Rugby School. In that institution, Dr Arnold created the prototype of the English Public School – called 'English', because boys went there to learn Latin and Greek; 'Public', because it was private; and 'School', because so much time was spent playing games. The public schools set out to produce men who would serve God and their country, practitioners of muscular Christianity. Dr Arnold was one of the four 'Eminent Victorians' so vengefully debunked by Lytton Strachey in the next century.

FACTORY CONDITIONS

from **The Cry of the Children**

Do ye hear the children weeping, O my brothers,
    Ere the sorrow comes with years?
They are leaning their young heads against their mothers, –
    And *that* cannot stop their tears.
The young lambs are bleating in the meadows;
   The young birds are chirping in the nest;
The young fawns are playing with the shadows;
   The young flowers are blowing toward the west –
But the young, young children, O my brothers,
    They are weeping bitterly –
They are weeping in the playtime of the others,
    In the country of the free.

*

'For oh,' say the children, 'we are weary,
    And we cannot run or leap –
If we cared for any meadows, it were merely
    To drop down in them and sleep.
Our knees tremble sorely in the stooping –
   We fall upon our faces, trying to go;
And, underneath our heavy eyelids drooping,
   The reddest flower would look as pale as snow.
For, all day, we drag our burden tiring,
    Through the coal-dark, underground –
Or, all day, we drive the wheels of iron.
    In the factories, round and round.

'For, all day, the wheels are droning, turning, –
    Their wind comes in our faces, –
Till our hearts turn, – our head, with pulses burning,
    And the walls turn in their places –
Turns the sky in the high window blank and reeling –
    Turns the long light that droppeth down the wall –
Turn the black flies that crawl along the ceiling –
    All are turning, all the day, and we with all –
And all day, the iron wheels are droning;
    And sometimes we could pray,
"O ye wheels," (breaking out in a mad moaning)
    "Stop! be silent for today!"'

        *

They look up, with their pale and sunken faces,
    And their look is dread to see,
For they mind you of their angels in their places,
    With eyes meant for Deity; –
'How long,' they say, 'how long, O cruel nation,
    Will you stand, to move the world, on a child's heart, –
Stifle down with a mail'd heel its palpitation,
    And tread onward to your throne amid the mart?
Our blood splashes upward, O our tyrants,
    And your purple shows your path;
But the child's sob curseth deeper in the silence
    Than the strong man in his wrath!'

Elizabeth Barrett Browning

In most factories of this time conditions were appalling. In 1830 a Tory churchman, Richard Oastler, had started a crusade in Yorkshire against child slavery. In 1834 a law was passed forbidding children under the age of nine to be put to work, while those under thirteen were restricted to a nine-hour day, and those between fourteen and eighteen to a twelve-hour day. Dickens tells of the misery he endured as a young boy employed in a blacking factory. Young girls worked in pits, drawing the wagons. Later, Lord Shaftesbury took up the cause of reform, and in 1850 a maximum ten-and-a-half-hour working day was agreed upon, with seven and a half hours on Saturdays. In 1876 Disraeli fixed a fifty-six-hour week and the Trade Unions were released from criminal liability. Shaftesbury is commemorated by the statue of Eros in Piccadilly Circus – a strange tribute in a strange place for such a good man.

1861

VICTORIA WITHOUT ALBERT

The Widow at Windsor

'Ave you 'eard o' the Widow at Windsor
   With a hairy gold crown on 'er 'ead?
She 'as ships on the foam – she 'as millions at 'ome,
   An' she pays us poor beggars in red.
     (Ow, poor beggars in red!)
There's 'er nick on the cavalry 'orses,
   There's 'er mark on the medical stores –
An' 'er troopers you'll find with a fair wind be'ind
   That takes us to various wars.
     (Poor beggars – barbarious wars!)
       Then 'ere 's to the Widow at Windsor,
         An' 'ere 's to the stores an' the guns,
       The men an' the 'orses what makes up the forces
         O' Missis Victorier's sons.
       (Poor beggars! Victorier's sons!)

Walk wide o' the Widow at Windsor,
   For 'alf o' Creation she owns:
We 'ave bought 'er the same with the sword an' the flame,
   An' we've salted it down with our bones.
     (Poor beggars – it's blue with our bones!)
Hands off o' the Sons o' the Widow,
   Hands off o' the goods in 'er shop,
For the Kings must come down an' the Emperors frown
   When the Widow at Windsor says 'Stop!'
     (Poor beggars – we're sent to say 'Stop!')
       Then 'ere 's to the Lodge o' the Widow,
         From the Pole to the Tropics it runs –
         To the Lodge that we tile with the rank an' the file,
           An' open in form with the guns.
         (Poor beggars! – it's always they guns!)

We 'ave 'eard o' the Widow at Windsor,
   It's safest to leave 'er alone:
For 'er sentries we stand by the sea an' the land
   Wherever the bugles are blown.
     (Poor beggars! – an' don't we get blown!)
Take 'old o' the Wings o' the Mornin',
   An' flop round the earth till you're dead;
But you won't get away from the tune that they play .
   To the bloomin' old rag over'ead.
     (Poor beggars – it 's 'ot over'ead!)
       Then 'ere 's to the Sons of the Widow,
         Wherever, 'owever they roam.
        'Ere 's all they desire, an' if they require
          A speedy return to their 'ome.
       (Poor beggars – they'll never see 'ome!)

Rudyard Kipling

After the death of Albert in 1861 from dysentery caused by the bad drains at Windsor Castle, Victoria entered a prolonged period of mourning. This withdrawal made her a remote and rather unpopular figure. Disraeli, however, coaxed her out of retirement and she continued to reign until 1901. This poem is supposed to have cost Kipling any sign of royal favour during the Queen's lifetime. She was not amused.

1878

TURKEY AND JINGOISM

We don't want to fight, but, by Jingo, if we do,
We've got the ships, we've got the men, we've got the money
    too.
We've fought the Bear before, and, while Britons shall be true,
    The Russians shall not have Constantinople.

G. W. Hunt

In 1877 Russia declared war on Turkey with a view to seizing as much of Turkey's Balkan Empire as it could. Popular feeling in Britain was for the Turks, in spite of the savage massacre they had inflicted upon the Bulgarians in 1876, and a wave of militarism swept the country. The topical music-hall song from which the refrain above is taken led to the coining of a new word, 'jingoism'. Disraeli ordered the fleet to sail to Constantinople, the reserves were called up and Indian troops were moved to the Mediterranean. The last thing Disraeli wanted was a war, but Russia's ambitions had to be checked, especially as its lands bordered on India. Heads of state gathered at the Congress of Berlin, and there, through his diplomacy, Disraeli secured 'peace with honour'. He should have called a general election at that point, but instead he waited until 1880, when he was defeated by Gladstone.

THE ARMY

Tommy

I went into a public-'ouse to get a pint o' beer,
The publican 'e up an' sez, 'We serve no red-coats here.'
The girls be'ind the bar they laughed an' giggled fit to die,
I outs into the street again an' to myself sez I:
    O it's Tommy this, an' Tommy that, an' 'Tommy, go away';
    But it's 'Thank you, Mister Atkins,' when the band begins
       to play –
    The band begins to play, my boys, the band begins to play,
    O it's 'Thank you, Mister Atkins,' when the band begins to
       play.

I went into a theatre as sober as could be,
They gave a drunk civilian room, but 'adn't none for me;
They sent me to the gallery or round the music-'alls,
But when it comes to fightin', Lord! they'll shove me in the stalls!
    For it's Tommy this, an' Tommy that, an' 'Tommy, wait
       outside';
    But it's 'Special train for Atkins' when the trooper's on the
       tide –
    The troopship's on the tide, my boys, the troopship's on the
       tide,
    O it's 'Special train for Atkins' when the trooper's on the
       tide.

Yes, makin' mock o' uniforms that guard you while you sleep
Is cheaper than them uniforms, an' they're starvation cheap;
An' hustlin' drunken soldiers when they're goin' large a bit
Is five times better business than paradin' in full kit.
    Then it's Tommy this, an' Tommy that, an' 'Tommy, 'ow's
       yer soul?'
    But it's 'Thin red line of 'eroes' when the drums begin to
       roll –
    The drums begin to roll, my boys, the drums begin to roll,
    O it's 'Thin red line of 'eroes' when the drums begin to roll.

We aren't no thin red 'eroes, nor we aren't no blackguards too,
But single men in barracks, most remarkable like you;
An' if sometimes our conduck isn't all your fancy paints,
Why, single men in barracks don't grow into plaster saints;
     While it's Tommy this, an' Tommy that, an' 'Tommy, fall
          be'ind,'
     But it's 'Please to walk in front, sir,' when there's trouble in
          the wind –
     There's trouble in the wind, my boys, there's trouble in the
          wind,
     O it's 'Please to walk in front, sir,' when there's trouble in the
          wind.

You talk o' better food for us, an' schools, an' fires, an' all:
We'll wait for extry rations if you treat us rational.
Don't mess about the cook-room slops, but prove it to our face
The Widow's Uniform is not the soldier-man's disgrace.
     For it's Tommy this, an' Tommy that, an' 'Chuck him out,
          the brute!'
     But it's 'Saviour of 'is country' when the guns begin to shoot;
     An' it's Tommy this, an' Tommy that, an' anything you
          please;
     An' Tommy ain't a bloomin' fool – you bet that Tommy sees!

                                        Rudyard Kipling

The army was one of the great institutions of Victorian England. Wellington had the profoundest contempt for most of his soldiers, and the campaign in the Crimea showed what a mess the War Office could make of things. From 1868 Gladstone's minister, Cardwell, brought in the reforms by which county regiments were set up, floggings abolished and modern equipment introduced. The colourful full-dress uniforms of

most of today's regiments were the creations of Victorian England. In
Patience, W. S. Gilbert satirized the Heavy Dragoon:

> When I first put this uniform on,
> I said, as I looked in the glass,
>   'It's one to a million
>   That any civilian
> My figure and form will surpass . . .'

But the great national heroes were soldiers – Wolseley, Bobs, Kitchener
– and you would be hard pushed to name a Victorian admiral. The
highest award for valour was instituted at this time and was called the
Victoria Cross. The Queen had only one big war, the Crimean, but
there were any number of little ones in China, India, Afghanistan,
Zululand, the Sudan, Egypt and West Africa, among other places. The
British 'Tommy' held the Empire together: of the 100,000 enlisted men,
three quarters served overseas. Kipling became unofficial Poet Laureate
to the ordinary soldier, upon whom British pride and power depended,
but who otherwise got little thanks. In spite of its honourable record,
however, the British army was ill prepared for 1914.

Vitaï Lampada

There's a breathless hush in the Close tonight –
    Ten to make and the match to win –
A bumping pitch and a blinding light,
    An hour to play and the last man in.
And it's not for the sake of a ribboned coat,
    Or the selfish hope of a season's fame,
But his Captain's hand on his shoulder smote –
    'Play up! play up! and play the game!'

The sand of the desert is sodden red, –
    Red with the wreck of a square that broke; –
The Gatling's jammed and the Colonel dead,
    And the regiment blind with dust and smoke.
The river of death has brimmed his banks,
    And England's far, and Honour a name,
But the voice of a schoolboy rallies the ranks:
    'Play up! play up! and play the game!'

This is the word that year by year,
   While in her place the School is set,
Every one of her sons must hear,
   And none that hears it dare forget.
This they all with a joyful mind
   Bear through life like a torch in flame,
And falling fling to the host behind –
   'Play up! play up! and play the game!'

Henry Newbolt

1885

THE DEATH OF GENERAL GORDON

from **The Hero of Khartoum**

Alas! now o'er the civilized world there hangs a gloom
For brave General Gordon, that was killed in Khartoum;
He was a Christian hero, and a soldier of the Cross,
And to England his death will be a very great loss.

He was very cool in temper, generous and brave,
The friend of the poor, the sick, and the slave;
And many a poor boy he did educate,
And laboured hard to do so early and late.

*

He always took the Bible for his guide,
And he liked little boys to walk by his side;
He preferred their company more so than men,
Because he knew there was less guile in them.

And in his conversation he was modest and plain,
Denouncing all pleasures he considered sinful and vain,
And in battle he carried no weapon but a small cane,
Whilst the bullets fell around him like a shower of rain.

*

In military life his equal couldn't be found,
No! if you were to search the wide world around,
And 'tis pitiful to think he has met with such a doom
By a base *traitor knave* while in Khartoum.

Yes, the black-hearted traitor opened the gates of Khartoum,
And through that the Christian hero has met his doom,
For when the gates were opened the Arabs rushed madly in,
And foully murdered him while they laughingly did grin.

William McGonagall

In 1882, at the instigation of the Prime Minister, William Ewart Gladstone, Britain annexed Egypt with the intention of securing the Suez Canal as the gateway to her Indian Empire. Three years later, a Muslim leader, the Mahdi, raised a revolt in the Sudan, inflicting severe losses on British troops. General Charles Gordon was sent by Gladstone – the Grand Old Man, as he was called – to restore order, but found himself besieged at Khartoum. The Government in London was slow to respond, and when a relief force was sent, it arrived to find that Gordon had been killed two days earlier. The country and the Queen were outraged. Victoria sent an open telegram in which she deplored the 'frightful' delay and spoke of 'the stain left upon England'. Gladstone was called the Murderer of Gordon, and a topical poem went:

> The G.O.M., when his life ebbs out,
> Will ride in a fiery chariot,
>   And sit in state
>   On a red-hot plate
> Between Pilate and Judas Iscariot.

The Queen never forgave Gladstone, and it was left to Lytton Strachey in *Eminent Victorians* to challenge the idolatry of Gordon.

EARLY HOPES REVISED

from **Locksley Hall**

Not in vain the distance beacons. Forward, forward let us range,
Let the great world spin for ever down the ringing grooves of
    change.
Thro' the shadow of the globe we sweep into the younger day:
Better fifty years of Europe than a cycle of Cathay . . .

Alfred, Lord Tennyson

from **Locksley Hall Sixty Years After**

Chaos, Cosmos! Cosmos, Chaos! who can tell how all will end?
Read the wide world's annals, you, and take their wisdom for
your friend.

Hope the best, but hold the Present fatal daughter of the Past,
Shape your heart to front the hour, but dream not that the hour
    will last.

Ay, if dynamite and revolver leave you courage to be wise:
When was age so cramm'd with menace? madness? written,
    spoken lies?

Envy wears the mask of Love, and, laughing sober fact to scorn,
Cries to Weakest as to Strongest, 'Ye are equals, equal-born.'

Equal-born? O yes, if yonder hill be level with the flat.
Charm us, Orator, till the Lion look no larger than the Cat,

Till the Cat thro' that mirage of overheated language loom
Larger than the Lion, – Demos end in working its own doom.

Russia bursts our Indian barrier, shall we fight her? shall we
    yield?
Pause! before you sound the trumpet, hear the voices from the
    field.

Those three hundred millions under one Imperial sceptre now,
Shall we hold them? shall we loose them? take the suffrage of
   the plow.

Nay, but these would feel and follow Truth if only you and you,
Rivals of realm-running party, when you speak were wholly
   true . . .

Alfred, Lord Tennyson

In the poem published in 1842, Tennyson voices the supreme con-
fidence of early Victorian England. But by 1886 doubts had become
apparent: democracy was on the march and party politics threatened to
bring down the country and mankind. Later, Chesterton was to charac-
terize the difference between the two times when he wrote that he
preferred the fighting of Cobbett to the feasting of Pater.

ASPECTS OF LATE VICTORIAN ENGLAND

The Countryside

from **Why England is Conservative**

Let hound and horn in wintry woods and dells
Make jocund music though the boughs be bare,
And whistling yokel guide his teaming share
Hard by the homes where gentle lordship dwells.
Therefore sit high enthroned on every hill,
Authority! and loved in every vale;
Nor, old Tradition, falter in the tale
Of lowly valour led by lofty will;
And though the throats of envy rage and rail,
Be fair proud England, proud fair England still.

Alfred Austin

The Northern Town

from Satan Absolved: a Victorian Mystery

The smoke of their foul dens
Broodeth on Thy Earth as a black pestilence,
Hiding the kind day's eye. No flower, no grass there groweth,
Only their engines' dung which the fierce furnace throweth.
Their presence poisoneth all and maketh all unclean.
Thy streams they have made sewers for their dyes analine.
No fish therein may swim, no frog, no worm, may crawl,
No snail for grime may build her house within their wall.

Wilfrid Scawen Blunt

The Suburbs

from Thirty Bob a Week

For like a mole I journey in the dark,
    A-travelling along the underground
From my Pillar'd Halls and broad Suburban Park,
    To come the daily dull official round;
And home again at night with my pipe all alight,
    A-scheming how to count ten bob a pound.

And it's often very cold and very wet,
    And my missus stitches towels for a hunks;
And the Pillar'd Halls is half of it to let –
    Three rooms about the size of travelling trunks.
And we cough, my wife and I, to dislocate a sigh,
    When the noisy little kids are in their bunks.

But you never hear her do a growl or whine,
  For she's made of flint and roses, very odd;
And I've got to cut my meaning rather fine,
  Or I'd blubber, for I'm made of greens and sod:
So p'r'aps we are in Hell for all that I can tell,
  And lost and damn'd and serv'd up hot to God.

John Davidson

1888

JACK THE RIPPER

Eight little whores, with no hope of Heaven,
Gladstone may save one, then there'll be seven.
Seven little whores begging for a shilling,
One stays in Heneage Court, then there's a killing.

Six little whores, glad to be alive,
One sidles up to Jack, then there are five.
Four and whore rhyme aright, so do three and me.
I'll set the town alight, ere there are two.

Two little whores, shivering with fright,
Seek a cosy doorway, in the middle of the night.
Jack's knife flashes, then there's but one.
And the last one's ripest for Jack's idea of fun.

Anonymous

I'm not a butcher,
I'm not a Yid,
Nor yet a foreign skipper,
But I'm your own light-hearted friend,
Yours truly, Jack the Ripper.

Anonymous

Between August and November 1888, a number of prostitutes in Whitechapel were killed in a particularly gruesome way, being ripped open and dismembered. The popular press soon invented the name Jack the Ripper for their unknown assailant – not one of Strachey's 'Eminent Victorians'. Many anonymous letters, and even poems, were sent to the police, purporting to own up. No arrest was made, but over the years an extraordinary variety of candidates has been proposed: a Harley Street surgeon whose son had contracted syphilis from one of the victims; a midwife; a Russian planted by the Tsar's police; a Jewish ritual slaughterman; and a Blackheath schoolteacher – among others. The children of the East End had their own little rhyme about it:

> Jack the Ripper's dead,
> And lying in his bed.
> He cut his throat
> With Sunlight Soap.
> Jack the Ripper's dead.

1895

FIN DE SIÈCLE

The Arrest of Oscar Wilde at the Cadogan Hotel

He sipped at a weak hock and seltzer
    As he gazed at the London skies
Through the Nottingham lace of the curtains
    Or was it his bees-winged eyes?

To the right and before him Pont Street
    Did tower in her new built red,
As hard as the morning gaslight
    That shone on his unmade bed,

'I want some more hock in my seltzer,
    And Robbie, please give me your hand –
Is this the end or beginning?
    How can I understand?

'So you've brought me the latest *Yellow Book*:
  And Buchan has got in it now:
Approval of what is approved of
  Is as false as a well-kept vow.

'More hock, Robbie – where is the seltzer?
  Dear boy, pull again at the bell!
They are all little better than *cretins*,
  Though this *is* the Cadogan Hotel.

'One astrakhan coat is at Willis's –
  Another one's at the Savoy:
Do fetch my morocco portmanteau,
  And bring them on later, dear boy.'

A thump, and a murmur of voices –
  'Oh why must they make such a din?'
As the door of the bedroom swung open
  And TWO PLAIN CLOTHES POLICEMEN came in:

'Mr Woilde, we 'ave come for tew take yew
  Where felons and criminals dwell:
We must ask yew tew leave with us quoietly
  For this *is* the Cadogan Hotel.'

He rose, and he put down *The Yellow Book*.
  He staggered – and, terrible-eyed,
He brushed past the palms on the staircase
  And was helped to a hansom outside.

John Betjeman

In 1895 Oscar Wilde was the lion of London Society, the arbiter of taste
and most celebrated of wits. His plays *The Ideal Husband* and *The
Importance of Being Earnest* were being performed to packed houses. So
brash and confident was he, that he openly flaunted his passionate
affair with Lord Alfred Douglas, son of the Marquis of Queensberry.
Incensed, the Marquis left a visiting card at Wilde's club addressed to

'Oscar Wilde posing as a Somdomite' – which was to prove a notorious misspelling. Wilde foolishly started a libel action and, in the course of a two-day cross-examination by Edward Carson, was disastrously compelled to admit that he had engaged in a number of casual homosexual affairs. He was advised to fly to France, but he went instead to the Cadogan Hotel in Sloane Street where he got slightly drunk with Douglas and his friend Robert Ross. Tried for practising 'the love that dare not speak its name', he was found guilty and sentenced to two years' hard labour. It was an appalling humiliation and Victorian society rejoiced in its revenge. From his time in prison, Wilde wrote his finest poem, 'The Ballad of Reading Gaol'. He died in poverty in France in 1900.

On reading Betjeman's poem, Lord Alfred Douglas complained that it was not very accurate.

1895

THE JAMESON RAID

Jameson's Ride

Wrong! Is it wrong? Well, may be:
    But I'm going, boys, all the same.
Do they think me a Burgher's baby,
    To be scared by a scolding name?
They may argue, and prate, and order;
    Go, tell them to save their breath:
Then, over the Transvaal border,
    And gallop for life or death!

Let lawyers and statesmen addle
    Their pates over points of law;
If sound be our sword, and saddle,
    And gun-gear, who cares one straw?
When men of our own blood pray us
    To ride to their kinsfolk's aid,
Not Heaven itself shall stay us
    From the rescue they call a raid.

There are girls in the gold-reef city,
    There are mothers and children too!
And they cry, 'Hurry up! for pity!'
    So what can a brave man do?
If even we win, they'll blame us:
    If we fail, they will howl and hiss.
But there's many a man lives famous
    For daring a wrong like this!

So we forded and galloped forward,
    As hard as our beasts could pelt,
First eastward, then trending northward,
    Right over the rolling veldt;
Till we came on the Burghers lying
    In a hollow with hills behind,
And their bullets came hissing, flying,
    Like hail on an Arctic wind!

Right sweet is the marksman's rattle,
    And sweeter the cannon's roar,
But 'tis bitterly bad to battle,
    Beleaguered, and one to four.
I can tell you it wasn't a trifle
    To swarm over Krugersdorp glen,
As they plied us with round and rifle,
    And ploughed us, again – and again.

Then we made for the gold-reef city,
    Retreating, but not in rout.
They had called to us, 'Quick! for pity!'
    And He said, 'They will sally out,
They will hear us and come. Who doubts it?'
    But how if they don't, what then?
'Well, worry no more about it,
    But fight to the death, like men.'

Not a soul had supped or slumbered
  Since the Borderland stream was cleft,
But we fought, ever more outnumbered,
  Till we had not a cartridge left.
We're not very soft or tender,
  Or given to weep for woe,
But it breaks one to have to render
  One's sword to the strongest foe.

I suppose we were wrong, were madmen,
  Still I think at the Judgment Day,
When God sifts the good from the bad men,
  There'll be something more to say.
We were wrong, but we aren't half sorry,
  And, as one of the baffled band,
I would rather have had that foray,
  Than the crushings of all the Rand.

Alfred Austin

The great wealth of the Transvaal was controlled by the Dutch-descended Boers, whose political leader was Paul Kruger. He stood in the way of Cecil Rhodes's dream of a united South Africa, stretching from the Cape to the Great Lakes and under British sway. The English-speaking inhabitants of the Transvaal had grievances and Rhodes was ready to exploit them if he could thereby overthrow the Boers. On 29 December 1895, Leander Starr Jameson, a close friend of Rhodes's, led a troop of men into Boer territory. They had one field-gun and five Maxims at their disposal, and were supposed to be riding into Johannesburg to help the English population who should have risen. As they rode, messengers from the British Government ordered them to return. Everything went wrong: the guides lost their way; the horses tired and the troopers went hungry; the Boers learned of their coming; and on 2 January they surrendered ignominiously. Jameson was tried in London and sentenced to fifteen months' imprisonment.

The Colonial Secretary, Joseph Chamberlain, was accused of approving the raid. Winston Churchill, then at the beginning of his political career, said of this last, foolish fling in the scramble for Africa: 'I date the beginning of these violent times from the Jameson Raid.' Alfred Austin, however, who had just been appointed Poet Laureate,

heedlessly sent this poem off to *The Times*. He never fully recovered
from the avalanche of criticism which greeted it, and even Queen
Victoria complained about it to the Prime Minister, Lord Salisbury.

1899–1902

The Boer War

The whip-crack of a Union Jack
In a stiff breeze (the ship will roll),
Deft abracadabra drums
Enchant the patriotic soul –

A grandsire in St James's Street
Sat at the window of his club,
His second son, shot through the throat,
Slid backwards down a slope of scrub,

Gargled his last breaths, one by one by one,
In too much blood, too young to spill,
Died difficultly, drop by drop by drop –
'By your son's courage, sir, we took the hill.'

They took the hill (Whose hill? What for?)
But what a climb they left to do!
Out of that bungled, unwise war
An alp of unforgiveness grew.

William Plomer

In 1886, gold had been discovered in the Witwatersrand and the competition for South Africa started. The Jameson Raid killed whatever
hope may have existed that there would be co-operation between Boer
settlers and British imperialists. In 1899 the Government in London
reluctantly decided to intervene to secure basic rights for the British. At
first British troops met with a succession of humiliating defeats, but

gradually, under the command of Lord Roberts, Kitchener and Baden-Powell, they won control. The cost, however, was enormous – 20,000 dead – and the greatest imperial power of the day had had to use 200,000 men to fight a mere 60,000 farmers. The Union of South Africa was the immediate result, but the end of the Empire had also moved a step closer.

Following British Failures Exposed by the Boer War

And ye vaunted your fathomless powers, and ye flaunted your
   iron pride,
Ere – ye fawned on the Younger Nations for the men who could
   shoot and ride!
Then ye returned to your trinkets; then ye contented your souls
With the flannelled fools at the wicket or the muddied oafs at
   the goals.

Rudyard Kipling

1901

THE DEATH OF QUEEN VICTORIA

from **1901**

When Queen Victoria died
The whole of England mourned
Not for a so recently breathing old woman
A wife and a mother and a widow,
Not for a staunch upholder of Christendom,
A stickler for etiquette
A vigilant of moral values
But for a symbol.
A symbol of security and prosperity
Of 'My Country Right or Wrong'
Of 'God is good and Bad is bad'
And 'What was good enough for your father
Ought to be good enough for you'
And 'If you don't eat your tapioca pudding
You will be locked in your bedroom
And given nothing but bread and water
Over and over again until you come to your senses
And are weak and pale and famished and say
Breathlessly, hopelessly and with hate in your heart
"Please Papa I would now like some tapioca pudding very much
   indeed"'
A symbol too of proper elegance
Not the flaunting, bejewelled kind
That became so popular
But a truly proper elegance,
An elegance of the spirit,
Of withdrawal from unpleasant subjects
Such as Sex and Poverty and Pit Ponies
And Little Children working in the Mines
And Rude Words and Divorce and Socialism
And numberless other inadmissible horrors.

When Queen Victoria died
They brought her little body from the Isle of Wight
Closed up in a black coffin, finished and done for,
With no longer any feelings and regrets and Memories of Albert
And no more blood pumping through the feeble veins
And no more heart beating away
As it had beaten for so many tiring years.
The coffin was placed upon a gun-carriage
And drawn along sadly and slowly by English sailors.

Noël Coward

Victoria had become a symbol in her own lifetime and the term 'Victorian', as well as denoting a period of history, came to stand for styles in furniture, architecture, painting, music and morality. Although Victoria was a constitutional monarch, her longevity and experience enhanced her personal power – she had, after all, survived sixteen different Prime Ministers.

THE HOUSE OF WINDSOR

King Edward VII, 1901–10

There will be bridge and booze 'till after three,
And, after that, a lot of them will grope
Along the corridors in *robes de nuit*,
Pyjamas, or some other kind of dope.

A sturdy matron will be sent to cope
With Lord —, who isn't 'quite the thing',
And give his wife the leisure to elope,
And Mrs James will entertain the King!

Hilaire Belloc

The new King had a lively appreciation of the sensual delights of the world. He smoked twelve large cigars and twenty cigarettes a day. Dinner for him could run to as many as twelve courses. He enjoyed grilled oysters and pheasant stuffed with snipe, all washed down with his favourite champagne. He had several mistresses and lady friends who looked after him during those weekend parties for which Edwardian high society was especially noted. Belloc's poem was never published and owes its survival to the memory of Vita Sackville-West. It dwells on the post-prandial pleasures of a weekend spent with Mrs Willie James at West Dean in Sussex; but Mrs Ronald Greville at Polesden Lacey could just as well have provided the pretext.

TWO PRIME MINISTERS

Balfour, 1902–5

The foundations of Philosophic Doubt
Are based on this single premiss:
'Shall we be able to get out
To Wimbledon in time for tennis?

Rudyard Kipling

Arthur James Balfour was renowned for his indecision, and the title of his first book, *A Defence of Philosophic Doubt*, expresses his whole attitude to life. He was also a keen tennis-player, which led someone to remark: 'His sliced forehand from the base line evoked in him gleams of pale happiness.' Kipling was far harder on him in his prose, describing him as 'avid, aloof, incurious, unthinking, unthanking, gelt'.

Asquith, 1908–16

Mr Asquith says in a manner sweet and calm:
Another little drink wouldn't do us any harm.

George Robey

Lord Oxford and Asquith, a Prime Minister in the Augustan style, was renowned for his drinking and earned the nickname 'Squiffy'. I remember my history master telling us that he had met Asquith at a dinner in Oxford in the 1920s. Brandy was brought round in glasses on a tray. In the time that it would have taken a student to pick a glass off the tray, Asquith snatched up one and drank it, then a second, which he poured into his coffee, and finally a third, to put beside his coffee.

EDWARDIAN IDYLLS

Henley Regatta, 1902

Underneath a light straw boater
In his pink Leander tie
Ev'ry ripple in the water caught the Captain in the eye.
   O'er the plenitude of houseboats
   Plop of punt-poles, creak of rowlocks,
Many a man of some distinction scanned the reach to Temple
   Island
   As a south wind fluttered by,
Till it shifted, westward drifting, strings of pennants house-boat
   high,
Where unevenly the outline of the brick-warm town of Henley
Dominated by her church tower and the sheds of Brakspear's
   Brewery
   Lay beneath a summer sky.
   Plash of sculls! And pink of ices!
And the inn-yards full of ostlers, and the barrels running dry,
   And the baskets of geraniums
   Swinging over river-gardens
Led us to the flowering heart of England's willow-cooled July.

John Betjeman

After the long, hard slog to imperial greatness under Victoria, social life
under Edward VII appears to have been relaxed, happy and indulgent,
with great sporting festivals, idyllic country weekends, groaning tables
and a general style of plush opulence. But this is only part of the
picture. Elsewhere, we must take note of the industrial unrest that was
leading to the growth of the Labour Party; of suffragette militancy; of
bitter debate as the power of the House of Lords was broken; and of the
increasing threat of civil war in Ireland. Yet the sense of a sunny glow
over Edwardian England cannot be entirely effaced, and as late as
January 1914 Lloyd George could be quoted by the *Daily Chronicle* as
saying: 'Never has the sky been more perfectly blue.'

1905

from Haymaking

In the field sloping down,
Park-like, to where the willows showed the brook,
Haymakers rested. The tosser lay forsook
Out in the sun; and the long waggon stood
Without its team: it seemed it never would
Move from the shadow of that single yew.
The team, as still, until their task was due,
Beside the labourers enjoyed the shade
That three squat oaks mid-field together made
Upon a circle of grass and weed uncut,
And on the hollow, once a chalk-pit, but
Now brimmed with nut and elder-flower so clean.
The men leaned on their rakes, about to begin,
But still. And all were silent. All was old,
This morning time, with a great age untold,
Older than Clare and Cobbett, Morland and Crome,
Than, at the field's far edge, the farmer's home
A white house crouched at the foot of a great tree.

Edward Thomas

1910

THE DEATH OF EDWARD VII

from **The Dead King (Edward VII), 1910**

And since he was Master and Servant in all that we asked him,
We leaned hard on his wisdom in all things, knowing not how
    we tasked him,
For on him each new day laid command, every tyrannous hour,
To confront, or confirm, or make smooth some dread issue of
    power;
To deliver true judgement aright at the instant, unaided,
In the strict, level, ultimate phrase that allowed or dissuaded;
To foresee, to allay, to avert from us perils unnumbered,
To stand guard on our gates when he guessed that the
    watchmen had slumbered;
To win time, to turn hate, to woo folly to service and, mightily
    schooling
His strength to the use of his Nations, to rule as not ruling.

Rudyard Kipling

King George V, 1910–36

THE SUFFRAGETTES

In the Same Boat

Here's to the baby of five or fifteen,
    Here's to the widow of fifty,
Here's to the flaunting extravagant queen,
    And here's to the hussy that's thrifty –
Please to take note, they are in the same boat:
They have not a chance of recording the vote.

Here's to the lunatic, helpless and lost,
    Of wits – well, he simply has none, Sir –
Here's to the woman who lives by her brains
    And is treated as though she were one, Sir –
Please to take note, &c.

Here's to the criminal, lodged in the gaol,
    Voteless for what he has done, Sir –
Here's to the man with a dozen of votes,
    If a woman, he would not have one, Sir –
Please to take note, &c.

Here's to the lot of them, murderer, thief,
    Forger and lunatic too, Sir –
Infants, and those who get parish relief,
    And women, it's perfectly true, Sir –
Please to take note, &c.

H. Crawford

In 1903 Emmeline Pankhurst had formed the Woman's Social and Political Union to promote the cause of Votes for Women. The campaign was led and conducted by well-educated, well-dressed, middle-class women – which disconcerted police and politicians alike. Under their purple, white and green colours, they rallied and marched, storming Parliament and Downing Street, smashing shop windows, chaining themselves to railings, mobbing Asquith, attempting to dog-whip Churchill, and interrupting the meetings of Lloyd George who, on one such occasion, said: 'I see some rats have got in; let them squeal, it doesn't matter.' Many protesters were sent to prison, where they resorted to hunger strikes and were forcibly fed. One brave martyr, Emily Davison, threw herself in front of George V's horse at the Derby in 1913.

The Liberal Government wanted to find a positive solution, but was not willing to give in to militancy, which had begun to turn the country against female suffrage. Yet it was this movement that, together with the growing number of industrial strikes and the intractable problem of Ireland, helped to bring to an end the long Indian summer of Edwardian England. In December 1917 an Electoral Reform Bill was passed in the House of Commons by a large majority and this gave women over thirty the right to vote. In 1928 the age was lowered to twenty-one. It has become a commonplace to suggest that the role which women played in the First World War won them the vote, but Mrs Pankhurst and her two formidable daughters paved the way.

from The Female of the Species

When the Himalayan peasant meets the he-bear in his pride,
He shouts to scare the monster, who will often turn aside.
But the she-bear thus accosted rends the peasant tooth and nail.
For the female of the species is more deadly than the male.

*

Man, a bear in most relations – worm and savage otherwise, –
Man propounds negotiations, Man accepts the compromise.
Very rarely will he squarely push the logic of a fact
To its ultimate conclusion in unmitigated act.

Fear, or foolishness, impels him, ere he lay the wicked low,
To concede some form of trial even to his fiercest foe.
Mirth obscene diverts his anger – Doubt and Pity oft perplex
Him in dealing with an issue – to the scandal of The Sex!

But the Woman that God gave him, every fibre of her frame
Proves her launched for one sole issue, armed and engined for
    the same;
And to serve that single issue, lest the generation fail,
The female of the species must be deadlier than the male.

*

So it comes that Man, the coward, when he gathers to confer
With his fellow-braves in council, dare not leave a place for her
Where, at war with Life and Conscience, he uplifts his erring
    hands
To some God of Abstract Justice – which no woman
    understands.

And Man knows it! Knows, moreover, that the Woman that
    God gave him
Must command but may not govern – shall enthral but not
    enslave him.
And *She* knows, because She warns him, and Her instincts
    never fail,
That the Female of Her Species is more deadly than the Male.

Rudyard Kipling

Kipling had little sympathy with the Suffragettes and, when this poem
was printed in the *Morning Post*, he fell out with his daughter over it.
He should have known better, but perhaps the blustering, saloon-bar
style of its argument springs from Kipling's own awkward awareness
of the influence two women in particular – his mother and his wife –
exerted over him.

1912

THE SINKING OF THE 'TITANIC'

The Convergence of the Twain

In a solitude of the sea
Deep from human vanity,
And the Pride of Life that planned her, stilly couches she.

Steel chambers, late the pyres
Of her salamandrine fires,
Cold currents thrid, and turn to rhythmic tidal lyres.

Over the mirrors meant
To glass the opulent
The sea-worm crawls – grotesque, slimed, dumb, indifferent.

Jewels in joy designed
To ravish the sensuous mind
Lie lightless, all their sparkles bleared and black and blind.

Dim moon-eyed fishes near
Gaze at the gilded gear
And query: 'What does this vaingloriousness down here?' . . .

Well: while was fashioning
This creature of cleaving wing,
The Immanent Will that stirs and urges everything

Prepared a sinister mate
For her – so gaily great –
A Shape of Ice, for the time far and dissociate.

And as the smart ship grew
In stature, grace, and hue,
In shadowy silent distance grew the Iceberg too.

Alien they seemed to be:
No mortal eye could see
The intimate welding of their later history,

Or sign that they were bent
By paths coincident
On being anon twin halves of one august event,

Till the Spinner of the Years
Said 'Now!' And each one hears,
And consummation comes, and jars two hemispheres.

Thomas Hardy

The *Titanic* was the grandest ship ever built. On her maiden voyage she struck an iceberg and sank with a loss of 1,513 lives. She had been the supreme achievement of Victorian engineering, proof positive of man's triumph over nature, and her tragic fate had a suitably Victorian ring to it: women and children were allowed into the lifeboats first, the band struck up as she sank, and that great hymn 'Nearer, My God, to Thee' was sung. Her loss marked the end of an era.

1912

THE MARCONI SCANDAL

Gehazi

Whence comest thou, Gehazi,
    So reverend to behold,
In scarlet and in ermines
    And chain of England's gold?
'From following after Naaman
    To tell him all is well,
Whereby my zeal hath made me
    A Judge in Israel.'

Well done, well done, Gehazi!
  Stretch forth thy ready hand.
Thou barely 'scaped from judgment,
  Take oath to judge the land
Unswayed by gift of money
  Or privy bribe, more base,
Of knowledge which is profit
  In any market-place.

Search out and probe, Gehazi,
  As thou of all canst try.
The truthful, well-weighed answer
  That tells the blacker lie –
The loud, uneasy virtue,
  The answer feigned at will,
To overbear a witness
  And make the Court keep still.

Take order now, Gehazi,
  That no man talk aside
In secret with his judges
  The while his case is tried.
Lest he should show them – reason
  To keep a matter hid,
And subtly lead the questions
  Away from what he did.

Thou mirror of uprightness,
  What ails thee at thy vows?
What means the risen whiteness
  Of the skin between thy brows?
The boils that shine and burrow,
  The sores that slough and bleed –

The leprosy of Naaman
On thee and all thy seed?
Stand up, stand up, Gehazi,
Draw close thy robe and go,
Gehazi, Judge in Israel,
A leper white as snow!

Rudyard Kipling

Rumours had circulated that members of the Government, including
Sir Rufus Isaacs, the Attorney General – the Gehazi of this poem – and
Lloyd George, had bought shares in Marconi just before the issuing of a
large government contract. Although those accused denied it and went
to court to clear their names, they were obliged to confess that they had
bought shares in the American Marconi company, if not the British one
directly concerned. The Government was shaken, but not toppled. Yet
feelings ran high, and Kipling expressed the mood of the time, in which
a measure of anti-Semitism no doubt helped to fuel the general outrage,
when he used the Biblical story of Naaman and Gehazi in this vitu-
perative poem. As the servant of Elisha, Gehazi had dishonestly
obtained a reward from Naaman, whom Elisha had cured of leprosy,
and was punished by being cursed with the disease himself.

1914–18

THE GREAT WAR

Oh You Young Men

Awake, oh you young men of England,
For if, when your Country's in need,
You do not enlist in your thousands
You truly are cowards indeed.

Eric Blair (George Orwell), aged 11

MCMXIV

Those long uneven lines
Standing as patiently
As if they were stretched outside
The Oval or Villa Park,
The crowns of hats, the sun
On moustached archaic faces
Grinning as if it were all
An August Bank Holiday lark;

And the shut shops, the bleached
Established names on the sunblinds,
The farthings and sovereigns,
And dark-clothed children at play
Called after kings and queens,
The tin advertisements
For cocoa and twist, and the pubs
Wide open all day;

And the countryside not caring:
The place-names all hazed over
With flowering grasses, and fields
Shadowing Domesday lines;
Under wheat's restless silence;
The differently dressed servants
With tiny rooms in huge houses,
The dust behind limousines;

Never such innocence,
Never before or since,
As changed itself to past
Without a word – the men
Leaving the gardens tidy,
The thousands of marriages
Lasting a little while longer:
Never such innocence again.

Philip Larkin

1914

God heard the embattled nations shout
Gott strafe England and God save the King.
Good God, said God,
    I've got my work cut out.

J. C. Squire

In 1914 the major powers in Europe went to war to contain the military ambitions of Germany. The cause was popular, as the poem by the future George Orwell indicates, and men flocked to the colours encouraged by the famous poster showing the pointing Kitchener and bearing the slogan 'Your Country Needs You'. After the first few months of swift and traditional fighting, prolonged trench warfare took over. Generals on both sides sacrificed men and equipment on a scale unmatched before or since as they attempted to break through the ranks of the enemy, although this often meant gaining no more than a few hundred yards. The whole world was gradually embroiled, with troops pouring in from India, Australia, New Zealand, and eventually America. It was a war that changed global history: kingdoms and empires disappeared, the Bolsheviks assumed power in Russia, and Germany's defeat made the ground fertile for Nazism. If the leaders of Europe in 1914 could have foreseen the state of the continent twenty years later, every one of them would have done all that was possible to avoid war. The catastrophe, however, produced some of the finest poetry of the twentieth century, and the poems can be left to speak for themselves.

The Soldier

If I should die, think only this of me:
That there's some corner of a foreign field
That is for ever England. There shall be
In that rich earth a richer dust concealed;
A dust whom England bore, shaped, made aware,
Gave once her flowers to love, her ways to roam;
A body of England's, breathing English air,
Washed by the rivers, blest by suns of home.

And think, this heart, all evil shed away,
A pulse in the eternal mind, no less
Gives somewhere back the thoughts by England given;
Her sights and sounds; dreams happy as her day;
And laughter, learnt of friends; and gentleness
In hearts at peace, under an English heaven.

Rupert Brooke

Dulce Et Decorum Est

Bent double, like old beggars under sacks,
Knock-kneed, coughing like hags, we cursed through sludge,
Till on the haunting flares we turned our backs,
And towards our distant rest began to trudge.
Men marched asleep. Many had lost their boots,
But limped on, blood-shod. All went lame, all blind;
Drunk with fatigue; deaf even to the hoots
Of gas-shells dropping softly behind.

Gas! Gas! Quick, boys! – An ecstasy of fumbling,
Fitting the clumsy helmets just in time,
But someone still was yelling out and stumbling
And floundering like a man in fire or lime. –
Dim through the misty panes and thick green light,
As under a green sea, I saw him drowning.

In all my dreams, before my helpless sight,
He plunges at me, guttering, choking, drowning.

If in some smothering dreams, you too could pace
Behind the wagon that we flung him in,
And watch the white eyes writhing in his face,
His hanging face, like a devil's sick of sin;
If you could hear, at every jolt, the blood
Come gargling from the froth-corrupted lungs,
Obscene as cancer, bitter as the cud
Of vile, incurable sores on innocent tongues, –
My friend, you would not tell with such high zest
To children ardent for some desperate glory,
The old Lie: Dulce et decorum est
Pro patria mori.

Wilfred Owen

The General

'Good-morning, good-morning!' the General said
When we met him last week on our way to the line.
Now the soldiers he smiled at are most of 'em dead,
And we're cursing his staff for incompetent swine.
'He's a cheery old card,' grunted Harry to Jack
As they slogged up to Arras with rifle and pack.

But he did for them both by his plan of attack.

Siegfried Sassoon

For the Fallen

(*1917*)

With proud thanksgiving, a mother for her children,
England mourns for her dead across the sea.
Flesh of her flesh they were, spirit of her spirit,
Fallen in the cause of the free.

Solemn the drums thrill: Death august and royal
Sings sorrow up into immortal spheres.
There is music in the midst of desolation
And a glory that shines upon our tears.

They went with songs to the battle, they were young,
Straight of limb, true of eye, steady and aglow.
They were staunch to the end against odds uncounted,
They fell with their faces to the foe.

They shall grow not old, as we that are left grow old:
Age shall not weary them, nor the years condemn.
At the going down of the sun and in the morning
We will remember them.

They mingle not with their laughing comrades again;
They sit no more at familiar tables of home;
They have no lot in our labour of the day-time;
They sleep beyond England's foam.

Laurence Binyon

from **Hugh Selwyn Mauberley**

IV

These fought in any case,
and some believing,
                pro domo, in any case . . .

Some quick to arm,
some for adventure,
some from fear of weakness,
some from fear of censure,
some for love of slaughter, in imagination,
learning later . . .
some in fear, learning love of slaughter;

Died some, pro patria,
                    non 'dulce' non 'et decor' . . .
walked eye-deep in hell
believing in old men's lies, then unbelieving
came home, home to a lie,
home to many deceits,
home to old lies and new infamy;
usury age-old and age-thick
and liars in public places.

Daring as never before, wastage as never before.
Young blood and high blood,
fair cheeks, and fine bodies;

fortitude as never before

frankness as never before,
disillusions as never told in the old days,
hysterias, trench confessions,
laughter out of dead bellies.

V

There died a myriad,
And of the best, among them,
For an old bitch gone in the teeth,
For a botched civilization . . .

Ezra Pound

Elegy in a Country Churchyard

The men that worked for England
They have their graves at home:
And bees and birds of England
About the cross can roam.

But they that fought for England,
Following a falling star,
Alas, alas for England
They have their graves afar.

And they that rule in England,
In stately conclave met,
Alas, alas for England
They have no graves as yet.

G. K. Chesterton

Armistice Day, 1918

What's all this hubbub and yelling,
  Commotion and scamper of feet,
With ear-splitting clatter of kettles and cans,
  Wild laughter down Mafeking Street?

O, those are the kids whom we fought for
  (You might think they'd been scoffing our rum)
With flags that they waved when we marched off to war
  In the rapture of bugle and drum.

Now they'll hang Kaiser Bill from a lamp-post,
  Von Tirpitz they'll hang from a tree . . .
We've been promised a 'Land Fit for Heroes' –
  What heroes we heroes must be!

And the guns that we took from the Fritzes,
     That we paid for with rivers of blood,
Look, they're hauling them down to Old Battersea Bridge
     Where they'll topple them, souse, in the mud!

But there's old men and women in corners
     With tears falling fast on their cheeks,
There's the armless and legless and sightless –
     It's seldom that one of them speaks.

And there's flappers gone drunk and indecent
     Their skirts kilted up to the thigh,
The constables lifting no hand in reproof
     And the chaplain averting his eye . . .

When the days of rejoicing are over,
     When the flags are stowed safely away,
They will dream of another wild 'War to End Wars'
     And another wild Armistice day.

But the boys who were killed in the trenches,
     Who fought with no rage and no rant,
We left them stretched out on their pallets of mud
     Low down with the worm and the ant.

Robert Graves

Ode on the Death of Haig's Horse

I

Bury the Great Horse
With all clubdom's lamentation,
Let us bury the Great Horse
To the noise of the mourning of a horsey nation:
Mourning when their darlings fall,
Colonels carry the charger's pall,
And critics gather in smoke-room and stall.

II

Where shall we raise the statue they demand?
One in every home throughout the land.
Only thus shall all who saw him,
All who wrote long letters for him,
Recognize the work their fancy planned.

III

Set up the statue: dull and staid,
As fits an all too common jade,
Lo! our slow, slow decision's made,
And now the carping critics are dismayed
And now the public's piddling taste's displayed;
Another civic statue's made.

Douglas Garman

From the end of the First World War until his death in 1928, Field-Marshal Sir Douglas Haig, from 1915 Commander-in-Chief of British forces on the Western Front, was revered by the nation. Parliament voted him £100,000, he received the Order of Merit, and the ancestral home of the Haigs at Bemersyde was purchased by public subscription and presented to him as a gift. He refused a viscountcy in 1918 and the following year got an earldom. Haig's reputation was first questioned by Lloyd George in his memoirs of the war, and posterity has come to treat him harshly. But to a large extent he had only himself to blame, for, as Lord Beaverbrook said: 'With the publication of his Private Papers in 1952 he committed suicide twenty-five years after his death.' Garman's poem is a parody of Tennyson on Wellington.

SOME PRIME MINISTERS OF THE TWENTIETH CENTURY

David Lloyd George, PM 1916–22

Count not his broken pledges as a crime
He MEANT them, HOW he meant them – at the time.

Kensal Green

Andrew Bonar Law, PM 1922–3

Of all the politicians I ever saw
The least significant was Bonar Law.
Unless it was MacDonald, by the way:
Or Baldwin – it's impossible to say.

Hilaire Belloc

Stanley Baldwin, PM 1923–4, 1924–9, 1935–7

His fame endures; we shall not quite forget
The name of Baldwin till we're out of debt.

Kensal Green

Winston Churchill, PM 1940–5, 1951–4

A sad day this for Alexander
And many another dead commander.
Jealousy's rife in heroes' hall –
Winston Churchill has bluffed them all.

Kensal Green

The lines on Churchill were written in 1927.

the 1920s

A LAND FIT FOR HEROES

**Refutation of the Only Too Prevalent Slander that
Parliamentary Leaders are Indifferent to the Strict Fulfilment of
their Promises and the Preservation of their Reputation
for Veracity**

They said (when they had dined at Ciro's)
The land would soon be fit for heroes;
And now they've managed to ensure it,
For only heroes could endure it.

G. K. Chesterton

from **Cowardice**

Do you remember, in the Twenties,
the songs we used to sing,
reading our Westermans and Hentys,
before the days of Bing?
Gramophones were very sharp and tinny,
we could sit there and applaud
shows with stars like Laddie, Sonnie, Binnie,
Jack and Jessie, June and Claude.
We had no truck with opus numbers
or anything called Art –
and fox-trots (long before the rumbas)
gave us our happy start. . . .

This was our taste/ of the future,
we embraced/ that decade,
gleaming in glamour, with our hope not betrayed.
There lay Love – which our ten-year-old scoffing
felt above (girls with men!) – in the offing.

The sight of women set us giggling,
their bottoms broad and fat,
the Charleston and that sexy wriggling,
their bosoms not so flat,
as they jumped and bumped in that gay chorus –
though we watched the dance with scorn,
this was Life cavorting there before us,
and the reason we were born.
Of this we were just dimly conscious,
uneasily we'd sit
and judge, severe, like monks with tonsures –
soon to be part of it. . . .

It was all necks/ with arms round them,
grown-up sex/ on display –
a mystery coming our way.
We weren't too frightened,
we felt partly enlightened
in that faced-by-the-future far decade.

Gavin Ewart

The younger generation of the 1920s wanted to forget the Great War as soon as possible. The war had helped to accelerate social change. In fashion, frock coats were ousted by lounge suits, long skirts by short, and sometimes very short, ones. The radio supplanted the gramophone and the whole country went to the cinema – the first comprehensively popular art form. To be dashing and uninhibited was the thing: ladies smoked in public and contraception was no longer taboo. The chrome and sharp angles of Art Deco provided the blazonry of the times.

1926

THE GENERAL STRIKE

May 4th, 1926

May 4th, 1926 – morning,
East End classroom crowded
With youth and feeling unconfined,
Crimson ties proclaiming oneness
With workers – red flags fluttering
In the corridors of the mind.
To bull-like masters red rags,
Well-worn beyond those cockcrow years,
Beyond betrayals and disasters;
Remembrance that the battering shower
Of time, its storms can never nip.
Among her festivals and bitter tears
Comes home this memory
Like a well-laden, triumphant ship.

Bill Foot

On 1 May 1926, after a prolonged dispute over a miners' wage claim, to which colliery owners had responded by offering a reduction in wages, there was a lock-out. The General Council of the Trade Unions declared a national strike from 3 May, and this was widely supported. Stanley Baldwin, Prime Minister of the day, urged Winston Churchill to bring out a daily paper under the name of the *British Gazette*, in which he called for 'unconditional surrender'. Many people volunteered to keep basic services going. Throughout all this, George V played a moderating role and, when the strike was called off unconditionally, Baldwin resisted any vindictive inclination to turn the affair into a class-war victory.

THE MINERS ON STRIKE

What will you do with your shovel, Dai,
And your pick and your sledge and your spike,
And what will you do with your leisure, man,
Now that you're out on strike?

What will you do for your butter, Dai,
And your bread and your cheese and your fags,
And how will you pay for a dress for the wife,
And shall your children go in rags?

You have been, in your time, a hero, Dai,
And they wrote of your pluck in the press,
And now you have fallen on evil days,
And who will be there to bless?

And how will you stand with your honesty, Dai,
When the land is full of lies,
And how will you curb your anger, man,
When your natural patience dies?

O what will you dream on the mountains, Dai,
When you walk in the summer day,
And gaze on the derelict valleys below,
And the mountains farther away?

And how will the heart within you, Dai,
Respond to the distant sea,
And the dream that is born in the blaze of the sun,
And the vision of victory?

Idris Davies

1929

THE DEPRESSION

Unemployed

Moving through the silent crowd
Who stand behind dull cigarettes,
These men who idle in the road,
I have the sense of falling light.

They lounge at corners of the street
And greet friends with a shrug of shoulder
And turn their empty pockets out,
The cynical gestures of the poor.

Now they've no work, like better men
Who sit at desks and take much pay
They sleep long nights and rise at ten
To watch the hours that drain away.

I'm jealous of the weeping hours
They stare through with such hungry eyes
I'm haunted by these images,
I'm haunted by their emptiness.

Stephen Spender

The 1914–18 war effort had required a strict direction of resources and it proved difficult for many companies, particularly those in heavy engineering, to adapt to the needs of peacetime. The post-war boom soon petered out and unemployment rose to one million, 12 per cent of the British work force. In 1929, particularly as a result of the Wall Street Crash and the collapse of financial institutions in America, unemployment rose sharply to three million. Everyone was at a loss. The Coalition Government under the Labour leader, Ramsay MacDonald, wanted to cut benefits; the influential economist John Maynard Keynes advocated public works; others urged protection. Neville Chamberlain, as Chancellor of the Exchequer, nursed the economy back to health and by 1937 unemployment had been cut by half.

RAMSAY MACDONALD

Allelauder

Ramsay MacDonald to Sir Harry Lauder:
'For fifty years you have been making us happy, and the art you have employed
has not had a tinge of the degrading in it. You have dealt with the great
fundamental human simplicities, and have taught us to find joy and inspiration
in qualities and feelings which belong to the good things in human life.'

The curly nibby has put to flight
The legions of despair.
A flap of Sir Harry Lauder's kilt
And our woes are no longer there.
To God, our help in ages past,
There is no need to pray
When the softest of the family
Presents an easier way.
Most of us may lack the cash
To hear Lauder in person – yet
If we're too poor for the music halls,
Through gramophone disc or radio set,
The little man with the enlarged heart
Can make us wholly forget
All the horrors of war and peace
With which mankind's beset,
Every so-called crisis disappears
– 'He's made us happy for fifty years!'
Honour to Ramsay MacDonald who
Sees and proclaims this fact,
Knowing that pawky patter does more
Than an Ottawa or O-to-Hell pact.
Dire necessity and foul disease
Are vanquished by a variety act.
Unemployment, poverty, slums
Can be cured by a fatuous song
(If Lauder receives a suitable fee!) –
Then the Government policy's wrong.
Abolish all social services,

Hand Lauder the dough instead,
Give all other public men the sack
And put him alone at the head.
With a waggle here and a wiggle there
The world will soon be rid
Of all its troubles and doubts and fears
– *Happy for good as for fifty years!*
– But even his stupendous powers
May cure life's every loss and want
Save his or MacDonald's brainlessness,
Or stop their ghastly cant.
Oh, Lauder is bad enough, but we
Might have been happier still
If MacDonald every now and again
Hadn't figured too on the bill
– The cross-talk duo, it appears,
Toplining these fifty filthy years.

Hugh MacDiarmid

MacDiarmid kills two birds with one stone. It seems that there was nothing he hated more than the stage Scotsman, whether impersonated by Harry Lauder in the music-hall, or by Ramsay MacDonald at the despatch box of the House of Commons. MacDonald was Prime Minister in 1924, and again from 1929 to 1931. From 1931 to 1935, as leader of the minority party, he headed a coalition government – an act of apostasy for which the Labour Party has never forgiven him. There is no statue in the House of Commons to honour Labour's first PM.

1936

The Death of King George V

'New King arrives in his capital by air . . .'
Daily Newspaper

Spirits of well-shot woodcock, partridge, snipe
    Flutter and bear him up the Norfolk sky:
In that red house in a red mahogany book-case
    The stamp collection waits with mounts long dry.

The big blue eyes are shut which saw wrong clothing
    And favourite fields and coverts from a horse;
Old men in country houses hear clocks ticking
    Over thick carpets with a deadened force;

Old men who never cheated, never doubted,
    Communicated monthly, sit and stare
At the new suburb stretched beyond the run-way
    Where a young man lands hatless from the air.

John Betjeman

At Sandringham on the evening of 20 January 1936 the King's doctor, Lord Dawson of Penn, wrote this last bulletin on a menu card: 'The King's life is moving peacefully to its close.' Three hours later George V was dead. It was only in 1986 that the notes of Dawson were published to reveal that he had administered euthanasia. 'At about 11 o'clock', Dawson wrote, 'it was evident that the last stage might endure for many hours unknown to the patient, but little comporting with that dignity and serenity which he so richly merited and which demanded a brief final scene . . . I therefore decided myself to determine the end and injected myself morphia gr. ¾ and shortly afterwards cocaine gr. 1 into the distended jugular vein.' This meant that the King's death would first be announced 'in the morning papers rather than the less appropriate field of the evening journals'. Dawson had been the doctor of Edward VII and also of Lloyd George, who had insisted on his being made a peer in 1920. He had saved the King's life in 1928, but his treatment during the convalescence led to a good deal of professional jealousy and this piece of doggerel:

> Lord Dawson of Penn
> Has killed lots of men.
> So that's why we sing
> God save the King.

King Edward VIII, 1936

The hand that blew the sacred fire has failed,
Laid down the burden in the hour of need,
So brave begun but flinching in the deed.
Nor Mary's power nor Baldwin's word availed,
To curb the beating heart by love assailed.
Vainly did Delhi, Canberra, Capetown plead
The Empire's ruler flouts the Empire's creed
By princes, prelates, people sore bewailed
The triple pillars of the Empire shake
A shock of horror passes o'er the land.
The greatest throne in all the world forsake
To take a favour from a woman's hand?
The hallowed pleasures of a kingly life
Abandoned for a transatlantic wife.

Douglas Reed

This was the shortest reign in English history, if one overlooks that of Lady Jane Grey. Edward had fallen in love with Wallis Simpson, an American, who had been married twice before and was about to divorce her second husband. As head of the Church of England, Edward could not marry Mrs Simpson and remain on the throne. The country was divided. Beaverbook and Churchill supported the King, while Baldwin and Archbishop Lang forced him to the realization that he had to make a choice. He chose to abdicate.

My Lord Archbishop, what a scold you are,
And when a man is down, how bold you are,
Of Christian charity how scant you are
You auld Lang Swine, how full of cant you are!

Anonymous

King George VI, 1936–52

THE BLACKSHIRTS

October 1936

We stood at Gardiner's Corner,
We stood and watched the crowds,
We stood at Gardiner's Corner,
Firm, solid, voices loud.

Came the marching of the blackshirts,
Came the pounding of their feet,
Came the sound of ruffians marching
Where the five roads meet.

We thought of many refugees
Fleeing from the Fascist hordes,
The maimed, the sick,
The young, the old,
Those who had fought the Fascist lords.

So we stopped them there at Gardiner's,
We fought and won our way.
We fought the baton charges,
No Fascist passed that day!

Milly Harris

About 3,000 black-shirted Fascists, under the leadership of Oswald Mosley, were to have marched through the East End of London on 4 October 1936 – a calculated affront to its large Jewish population. The residents, however, blocked the roads at Gardiner's Corner and Cable Street, and Mosley was ignominiously forced to lead his men elsewhere. The following poem, written in the early years of the Second World War, shows the strength of Jewish identification with that part of London.

Whitechapel in Britain

Pumbedita, Cordova, Cracow, Amsterdam,
Vilna, Lublin, Berditchev and Volozhin,
Your names will always be sacred,
Places where Jews have been.

And sacred is Whitechapel,
It is numbered with our Jewish towns.
Holy, holy, holy
Are your bombed stones.

If we ever have to leave Whitechapel,
As other Jewish towns were left,
Its soul will remain a part of us,
Woven into us, woof and weft.

Avram Stencl

In 1938 the Conservative Prime Minister, Neville Chamberlain, came to terms with Adolf Hitler over the German leader's provocative seizing of the Sudetenland. Chamberlain flew back from Munich with the confident boast that he had secured 'peace in our time'. He was the hero of the hour, and all the press supported him, with the exception of the left-wing Sunday newspaper *Reynolds' News*. Duff Cooper was the only Cabinet minister to resign and only thirty Conservative MPs abstained from voting for the agreement. Six months before Munich, Hilaire Belloc had told Duff Cooper that Chamberlain had written this poem:

> Dear Czecho-Slovakia,
> I don't think they'll attack yer,
> But I'm not going to back yer.

1938

THE MUNICH AGREEMENT

from Autumn Journal

And the next day begins
 Again with alarm and anxious
Listening to bulletins
 From distant, measured voices
Arguing for peace
 While the zero hour approaches,
While the eagles gather and the petrol and oil and grease
 Have all been applied and the vultures back the eagles.
But once again
 The crisis is put off and things look better
And we feel negotiation is not vain –
 Save my skin and damn my conscience.
And negotiation wins,
 If you can call it winning,
And here we are – just as before – safe in our skins;
 Glory to God for Munich.
And stocks go up and wrecks
 Are salved and politicians' reputations
Go up like Jack-on-the-Beanstalk; only the Czechs
 Go down and without fighting.

Louis MacNeice

England, Autumn 1938

Plush bees above a bed of dahlias;
　Leisurely, timeless garden teas;
Brown bread and honey; scent of mowing;
　The still green light below tall trees.

The ancient custom of deception;
　A Press that seldom stoops to lies –
Merely suppresses truth and twists it,
　Blandly corrupt and slyly wise.

The Common Man; his mask of laughter;
　His back-chat while the roof falls in;
Minorities' long losing battles
　Fought that the sons of sons may win.

The politician's inward snigger
　(Big business on the private phone);
The knack of sitting snug on fences;
　The double face of flesh and stone.

Grape-bloom of distant woods at dusk;
　Storm-crown on Glaramara's head;
The fire-rose over London night;
　An old plough rusting autumn-red.

The 'incurruptible policeman'
　Gaoling the whore whose bribe's run out,
Guarding the rich against the poor man,
　Guarding the Settled Gods from doubt.

The generous smile of music-halls,
　Bars and bank-holidays and queues;
The private peace of public foes;
　The truce of pipe and football news.

The smile of privilege exultant;
  Smile at the 'bloody Red' defeated;
Smile at the striker starved and broken;
  Smile at the 'dirty nigger' cheated.

The old hereditary craftsman;
  The incommunicable skill;
The pride in long-loved tools, refusal
  To do the set job quick or ill.

The greater artist mocked, misflattered;
  The lesser forming clique and team,
Or crouching in his narrow corner,
  Narcissus with his secret dream.

England of rebels – Blake and Shelley;
  England where freedom's sometimes won,
Where Jew and Negro needn't fear yet
  Lynch-law and pogrom, whip and gun.

England of cant and smug discretion;
  England of wagecut-sweatshop-knight,
Of sportsman-churchman-slum-exploiter,
  Of puritan grown sour with spite.

England of clever fool, mad genius,
  Timorous lion and arrogant sheep,
Half-hearted snob and shamefaced bully,
  Of hands that wake and eyes that sleep . . .
England the snail that's shod with lightning . . .
  Shall we laugh or shall we weep?

                              A. S. J. Tessimond

A LOW DISHONEST DECADE

from **September 1, 1939**

I sit in one of the dives
On Fifty-Second Street
Uncertain and afraid
As the clever hopes expire
Of a low dishonest decade:
Waves of anger and fear
Circulate over the bright
And darkened lands of the earth,
Obsessing our private lives;
The unmentionable odour of death
Offends the September night.

Accurate scholarship can
Unearth the whole offence
From Luther until now
That has driven a culture mad,
Find what occurred at Linz,
What huge imago made
A psychopathic god:
I and the public know
What all schoolchildren learn,
Those to whom evil is done
Do evil in return.

Exiled Thucydides knew
All that a speech can say
About Democracy,
And what dictators do,
The elderly rubbish they talk,
To an apathetic grave;

Analysed all in his book,
The enlightenment driven away,
The habit-forming pain,
Mismanagement and grief:
We must suffer them all again.

*

All I have is a voice
To undo the folded lie,
The romantic lie in the brain
Of the sensual man-in-the-street
And the lie of Authority
Whose buildings grope the sky:
There is no such thing as the State
And no one exists alone;
Hunger allows no choice
To the citizen or the police;
We must love one another or die.

Defenceless under the night
Our world in stupor lies;
Yet, dotted everywhere,
Ironic points of light
Flash out wherever the Just
Exchange their messages:
May I, composed like them
Of Eros and of dust,
Beleaguered by the same
Negation and despair,
Show an affirming flame.

W. H. Auden

1939–45

THE SECOND WORLD WAR

By 1939, attempts to check Hitler's plans of expansion had led nowhere. In August of that year Russia and Germany signed a neutrality pact, both hoping to seize for themselves large parts of Poland; and on 1 September Germany invaded Poland itself. Reluctantly yielding to pressure from a hostile House of Commons – from the Labour Party under its acting leader Arthur Greenwood, and from his own Cabinet – Chamberlain issued an ultimatum demanding German withdrawal by midnight on 2 September. On the following day, when it was clear that this had been ignored, he declared that Britain was at war. It was a justified war, as the Nazi regime in Germany was one of the worst and most cruel tyrannies the world had ever seen.

After the fall of France in June 1940, Britain stood alone in opposing the German offensive. Churchill had by then succeeded Chamberlain as Prime Minister and, in prose as memorable as any poetry, choosing 18 June, the anniversary of the battle of Waterloo, as a suitable moment, he addressed the nation in a speech which included the sentence: 'Let us therefore brace ourselves to our duties, and so bear ourselves that, if the British Empire and its Commonwealth last for a thousand years, men will still say, "This was their finest hour".'

In 1941 Hitler made the decisive mistake of invading Russia, and when the Japanese destroyed an American fleet in Pearl Harbor it became a real world war. From it emerged two pre-eminent global powers, Russia and America. Germany itself was divided in two, and the states of Eastern Europe became Russian satellites. Britain had won a famous victory, but post-war adjustment to a less dominant position in the world was to prove painful.

1940

In Westminster Abbey

Let me take this other glove off
    As the *vox humana* swells,
And the beauteous fields of Eden
    Bask beneath the Abbey bells.
Here, where England's statesmen lie,
Listen to a lady's cry.

Gracious Lord, oh bomb the Germans.
    Spare their women for Thy Sake.
And if that is not too easy
    We will pardon Thy Mistake.
But, gracious Lord, whate'er shall be,
Don't let anyone bomb me.

Keep our Empire undismembered
    Guide our Forces by Thy Hand,
Gallant blacks from far Jamaica,
    Honduras and Togoland;
Protect them Lord in all their fights,
And, even more, protect the whites.

Think of what our Nation stands for,
    Books from Boots' and country lanes,
Free speech, free passes, class distinction,
    Democracy and proper drains.
Lord, put beneath Thy special care
One-eighty-nine Cadogan Square.

Although dear Lord I am a sinner,
    I have done no major crime;
Now I'll come to Evening Service
    Whensoever I have the time.
So, Lord, reserve for me a crown;
And do not let my shares go down.

I will labour for Thy Kingdom,
    Help our lads to win the war,
Send white feathers to the cowards
    Join the Women's Army Corps,
Then wash the Steps around Thy Throne
In the Eternal Safety Zone.

Now I feel a little better,
    What a treat to hear Thy Word,
Where the bones of leading statesmen,
    Have so often been interr'd.
And now, dear Lord, I cannot wait
Because I have a luncheon date.

John Betjeman

THE RETREAT FROM DUNKIRK

That night we blew our guns. We placed a shell
Fuze downwards in each muzzle. Then we put
Another in the breech, secured a wire
Fast to the firing lever, crouched, and pulled.
It sounded like a cry of agony,
The crash and clang of splitting, tempered steel.
Thus did our guns, our treasured colours, pass;
And we were left bewildered, weaponless,
And rose and marched, our faces to the sea.

We formed in line beside the water's edge.
The little waves made oddly home-like sounds,
Breaking in half-seen surf upon the strand.
The night was full of noise; the whistling thud
The shells made in the sand, and pattering stones;
The cries cut short, the shouts of units' names;
The crack of distant shots, and bren gun fire;
The sudden clattering crash of masonry.
Steadily, all the time, the marching tramp
Of feet passed by along the shell-torn road,
Under the growling thunder of the guns.

The major said 'The boats cannot get in,
'There is no depth of water. Follow me.'
And so we followed, wading in our ranks
Into the blackness of the sea. And there,
Lit by the burning oil across the swell,
We stood and waited for the unseen boats.

Oars in the darkness, rowlocks, shadowy shapes
Of boats that searched. We heard a seaman's hail.
Then we swam out, and struggled with our gear,
Clutching the looming gunwales. Strong hands pulled,
And we were in and heaving with the rest,
Until at last they turned. The dark oars dipped,
The laden craft crept slowly out to sea,
To where in silence lay the English ships.

> B. G. Bonallack

On 10 May 1940 the allied armies advanced into German-occupied Holland, but within five days the Dutch had surrendered and German troops swept through Northern France as far as the outskirts of Paris. The British army of ten divisions had been cut off by this advance and fell back to the coast. The Germans halted their attack on the British on 23 May, allowing an opportunity for evacuation from the port of Dunkirk. On 27 May the British fleet began to pick men up from the beaches, helped by an enormous flotilla of private boats – pleasure steamers, ferries, fishing vessels and so on. In all, 860 boats were able to rescue 338,226 men, 139,000 of them French. Most equipment had been sunk and 474 planes were lost. In immediate military terms, it was a great disaster, but it saved Britain from an even greater one. In his report to the House of Commons on 4 June, Churchill declared: 'We shall defend our Island whatever the cost may be. We shall fight on the beaches, we shall fight on the landing grounds, we shall fight in the fields and in the streets, we shall fight in the hills; we shall never surrender, and even if, which I do not for a moment believe, this Island or a large part of it were subjugated and starving, then our Empire beyond the seas, armed and guarded by the British fleet, would carry on the struggle, until, in God's good time, the New World, with all its power and might, steps forth to the rescue and liberation of the Old.'

THE BATTLE OF BRITAIN

For Johnny

Do not despair
For Johnny-head-in-air;
He sleeps as sound
As Johnny underground.

Fetch out no shroud
For Johnny-in-the-cloud;
And keep your tears
For him in after years.

Better by far
For Johnny-the-bright-star,
To keep your head,
And see his children fed.

John Pudney

After Dunkirk, Hitler prepared to invade Britain. He started by launching Goering's Luftwaffe on a campaign of bombing raids. British pilots, mostly flying Spitfires, took off from the small airfields of southern and eastern England and succeeded in destroying many of the German bombers. In August the Luftwaffe came close to wiping out the airfields of Kent, but on 7 September it switched its attack to London. Dowding's fighter-pilots brought down 1,733 German planes, while the RAF lost 915. In spite of such losses, by September it possessed as many planes as it had had in the previous spring, which says much for the work of Lord Beaverbrook as Minister of Aircraft Production. The bravery of these pilots saved Britain and on 17 September Hitler postponed his invasion. Churchill reported to the House of Commons: 'Never in the field of human conflict was so much owed by so many to so few.' The architect of the victory, Dowding, was removed from his command in November, Churchill having found him too cautious, but history has accorded him due honours.

THE BLITZ

London, 1940

After fourteen hours clearing they came to him
Under the twisted girders and the rubble.
They would not let me see his face.
Now I sit shiftlessly on the tube platforms
Or huddle, a little tipsy, in brick-built shelters.
I can see with an indifferent eye
The red glare over by the docks and hear
Impassively the bomb-thuds in the distance.

For me, a man with not many interests
And no pretensions to fame, that was my world,
My son of fifteen, my only concrete achievement,
Whom they could not protect. Stepping aside
From the Great Crusade, I will play the idiot's part.
You, if you like, may wave your fists and crash
On the wrong doorsteps brash retaliation.

Frank Thompson

On 7 September Goering assumed personal command of the German air offensive and directed his planes against London, which was bombed for fifty-seven consecutive nights. Each night 220 planes dropped incendiary as well as explosive bombs, causing widespread damage. The House of Commons was destroyed, Buckingham Palace was hit, and 30,000 civilians were killed. Londoners slept on the platforms of Underground stations, sandbags were piled around windows, and I remember spending the night under our stairs, which was considered the safest place in the house, and on some occasions being taken out to an air-raid shelter. Other cities besides London were also attacked: Coventry lost 1,236 civilians, Birmingham 2,162, Bristol 1,159, Sheffield 624, and Manchester 1,005. On 29 December the great onslaught on the City of London destroyed eight Wren churches and almost St Paul's Cathedral itself. George VI remained in London throughout the Blitz, as did Churchill, and their example helped stiffen the morale of the people.

Naming Of Parts

Today we have naming of parts. Yesterday,
We had daily cleaning. And tomorrow morning,
We shall have what to do after firing. But today,
Today we have naming of parts. Japonica
Glistens like coral in all of the neighbouring gardens,
    And today we have naming of parts.

This is the lower sling swivel. And this
Is the upper sling swivel, whose use you will see,
When you are given your slings. And this is the piling swivel,
Which in your case you have not got. The branches
Hold in the gardens their silent, eloquent gestures,
    Which in our case we have not got.

This is the safety-catch, which is always released
With an easy flick of the thumb. And please do not let me
See anyone using his finger. You can do it quite easy
If you have any strength in your thumb. The blossoms
Are fragile and motionless, never letting anyone see
    Any of them using their finger.

And this you can see is the bolt. The purpose of this
Is to open the breech, as you see. We can slide it
Rapidly backwards and forwards: we call this
Easing the spring. And rapidly backwards and forwards
The early bees are assaulting and fumbling the flowers:
    They call it easing the Spring.

They call it easing the Spring: it is perfectly easy
If you have any strength in your thumb: like the bolt,
And the breech, and the cocking-piece, and the point of balance,
Which in our case we have not got; and the almond-blossom
Silent in all of the gardens and the bees going backwards and
        forwards,
    For today we have naming of parts.

Henry Reed

1940–2

THE WAR IN THE WESTERN DESERT

Vergissmeinnicht

Three weeks gone and the combatants gone
returning over the nightmare ground
we found the place again, and found
the soldier sprawling in the sun.

The frowning barrel of his gun
overshadowing. As we came on
that day, he hit my tank with one
like the entry of a demon.

Look. Here in the gunpit spoil
the dishonoured picture of his girl
who has put: *Steffi. Vergissmeinnicht*
in a copybook gothic script.

We see him almost with content,
abased, and seeming to have paid
and mocked at by his own equipment
that's hard and good when he's decayed.

But she would weep to see today
how on his skin the swart flies move;
the dust upon the paper eye
and the burst stomach like a cave.

For here the lover and killer are mingled
who had one body and one heart.
And death who had the soldier singled
has done the lover mortal hurt.

Keith Douglas

Britain had a large army in Egypt and in 1940 won spectacular victories when it pushed Germany's Italian allies out of most of modern-day Libya. Germany came to Italy's help and their armies were brilliantly led by Rommel, the 'Desert Fox'. There were wide-ranging battles involving armoured tanks and infantry – just the sort of battles that soldiers of the time had been trained to fight. Rommel pushed the British troops back and in June 1942 Tobruk, on the borders of Egypt, fell to his advance. Montgomery was appointed to command the 8th Army, as Churchill had begun to despair of the defensive strategies of Wavell and Auchinleck. He proved a match for Rommel. He was a great field commander and a charismatic leader who soon won the devotion of his troops. Rommel was forced to evacuate North Africa and his retreat took him through Sicily and Italy.

The German title of Keith Douglas's poem means 'forget-me-not'.

1945

THE END OF THE WAR IN EUROPE

Mr Churchill

Five years of toil and blood and tears and sweat;
    Five years of faith and prophecy and plan!
He spoke our mind before our mind was set;
    He saw our deeds before our deeds began.
He rode the hurricane as none did yet;
    Our Finest Hour revealed our Finest Man.

A. P. Herbert

Germany's surrender on 8 May 1945 was celebrated with a thanksgiving service at St Margaret's, Westminster, and Churchill appeared on the balcony of Buckingham Palace to greet the crowds that had gathered outside. All the Conservative ministers in the coalition government agreed on an early election, so as to capitalize on their leader's great popularity. The result after polling was a huge Labour majority of 180 seats with 47.9 per cent of the popular vote. The nation preserved too many memories of how the Tories had acted in the thirties, and servicemen and their families wanted the assurance of homes, jobs and social security, for which Labour made the more convincing case.

VJ DAY

The Morning After

The fire left to itself might smoulder weeks.
Phone cables melt. Paint peels from off back gates.
Kitchen windows crack; the whole street reeks
of horsehair blazing. Still it celebrates.

Though people weep, their tears dry from the heat.
Faces flush with flame, beer, sheer relief
and such a sense of celebration in our street
for me it still means joy though banked with grief.

And that, now clouded, sense of public joy
with war-worn adults wild in their loud fling
has never come again since as a boy
I saw Leeds people dance and heard them sing.

There's still that dark, scorched circle on the road.
The morning after kids like me helped spray
hissing upholstery spring-wire that still glowed
and cobbles boiling with black gas-tar for VJ.

Tony Harrison

America dropped two atom bombs on Japan – one at Hiroshima on 8 August, and the other at Nagasaki on 29 August. Four days later Japan surrendered and that ended the war. There were parties and street celebrations all over Britain, and I can remember attending a huge bonfire party in Newport which local residents had quickly organized.

1945–51

THE PREMIERSHIP OF CLEMENT ATTLEE

Few thought he was even a starter;
There were many who thought themselves smarter;
But he ended PM,
CH and OM,
An Earl and a Knight of the Garter.

Clement Attlee

from **Lest Cowards Flinch**

1945

'Though cowards flinch,' the Labour Party trolled,
    'The people's scarlet standard we will raise!'
The Commons blushed beneath that sanguine fold,
    Flag of the revolutionary phase;
The Tories knew for whom the death-bell tolled,
    It tolled for them in Labour's *Marseillaise*,
And in the beat of that triumphant march
Heard tumbrils rumbling up to Marble Arch.

Grim was it in that dawn to be alive,
    Except to those who like their mornings bloody,
The ship of State headlong was seen to dive
    Engulfed in depths unutterly muddy,
As *Jacobins*, like swarms that leave the hive,
    Belched forth from foundry, factory and study,
A cut-throat crew of howling demagogues,
Leading hereditary underdogs.

1947

Two years of Parliamentary civility
    Abate the class, if not the Party, feud;
No Labour Member lacks respectability,
    Although his social background may be rude,
While several have a title to gentility
    Such as the Tory ranks might not exclude,
And manual labourers, if fairly prominent,
On the Front Bench at least are not predominant.

Both birth and intellect are there displayed;
    The Premier is impeccably Oxonian,
A younger son conducts the Board of Trade,
    The Chancellor's a perfect Old Etonian,
The Foreign Secretary, though self-made,
    Is quite magnificently Palmerstonian;
If such as these are Labour mediocrities,
Where is the Tory Cicero, or Socrates?

Sagittarius

In July 1945 the British electorate decisively snubbed its wartime leader, Churchill, by returning 393 Socialist MPs and only 213 Conservatives. Consoled by his wife, Clementine, that the defeat could be interpreted as a blessing disguise, Churchill retorted that the disguise was perfect. Under Attlee, the Socialist Government nationalized the Bank of England and several major industries, and it set up the National Health Service. Its achievements marked the high tide of Socialism in Britain. On the first day of the new Parliament, the Socialist MPs rose and sang 'The Red Flag'. Less than half of their number would have called themselves working-class, and forty-six had been educated at either Oxford or Cambridge.

Sagittarius was the *nom de plume* of the prolific topical poet, Olga Katzin Miller.

1947

THE END OF THE EMPIRE

Partition

Unbiased at least he was when he arrived on his mission.
Having never set eyes on this land he was called to partition
Between two peoples fanatically at odds,
With their different diets and incompatible gods.
'Time,' they had briefed him in London, 'is short. It's too late
For mutual reconciliation or rational debate;
The only solution now lies in separation.
The Viceroy thinks, as you see from his letter,
That the less you are seen in his company the better.
So we've arranged to provide you with other accommodation.
We can give you four judges, two Moslem and two Hindu,
To consult with, but the final decision must rest with you.'

Shut up in a lonely mansion, with police night and day
Patrolling the gardens to keep assassins away,
He got down to work, to the task of settling the fate
Of millions. The maps at his disposal were out of date
And the Census Returns almost certainly incorrect.
But there was no time to check them, no time to inspect
Contested areas. The weather was frightfully hot.
And a bout of dysentery kept him constantly on the trot.
But in seven weeks it was done, the frontiers decided,
A continent for better or worse divided.

The next day he sailed for England, where he quickly forged
The case, as a good lawyer must. Return he would not.
Afraid, as he told his Club, that he might get shot.

W. H. Auden

I Wonder What Happened to Him

The India that one read about
And may have been misled about
In one respect has kept itself intact.
Though 'Pukka Sahib' traditions may have cracked
And thinned
The good old Indian army's still a fact.
That famous monumental man
The Officer and Gentleman
Still lives and breathes and functions from Bombay to
   Kathmandu.
At any moment one can glimpse
Matured or embryonic 'Blimps'
Vivaciously speculating as to what became of who.
Though Eastern sounds may fascinate your ear
When West meets West you're always sure to hear –

What became of old Bagot?
I haven't seen him for a year.
Is it true that young Forbes had to marry that Faggot
He met in the Vale of Kashmir?
Have you had any news
Of that chap in the 'Blues',
Was it Prosser or Pyecroft or Pym?
He was stationed in Simla, or was it Bengal?
I know he got tight at a ball in Nepal
And wrote several four-letter words on the wall.
I wonder what happened to him!

Whatever became of old Shelley?
Is it true that young Briggs was cashiered
For riding quite nude on a push-bike through Delhi
The day the new Viceroy appeared?
Have you had any word
Of that bloke in the 'Third',
Was it Southerby, Sedgwick or Sim?
They had him thrown out of the club in Bombay
For, apart from his mess bills exceeding his pay,
He took to pig-sticking in *quite* the wrong way.
I wonder what happened to him!

Whatever became of old Tucker?
Have you heard any word of young Mills
Who ruptured himself at the end of a chukka
And had to be sent to the hills?
They say that young Lees
Had a go of 'DTs'
And his hopes of promotion are slim.
According to Stubbs, who's a bit of a louse,
The silly young blighter went out on a 'souse',
And took two old tarts into Government House.
I wonder what happened to him!

Noël Coward

Britain's rule in India came to an end at midnight on 14 August 1947. As the Indian leader Nehru put it: 'At the stroke of midnight when the world sleeps India will wake to life and freedom.' Mahatma Gandhi, a driving force behind the move towards independence, did not join in the celebrations as he was strongly opposed to the partition of India and Pakistan. The birth of these new states was not accomplished without pain, for hundreds of thousands of Muslims and Hindus were killed in communal violence and there were millions of refugees. Britain left behind a language which was to serve for communication in all parts of that vast sub-continent, an established bureaucracy, now lovingly embellished, and a democratic system of government. The legacy has stood up well. Many former colonial servants and old soldiers 'stayed on', but things were never to be the same for them.

Epilogue To An Empire 1600–1900

An Ode For Trafalgar Day

As I was crossing Trafalgar Square
whose but the Admiral's shadow hand
should tap my shoulder. At my ear:
'You Sir, stay-at-home citizen
poet, here's more use for your pen
than picking scabs. Tell them in England
this: when first I stuck my head in the air,

'winched from a cockpit's tar and blood
to my crow's nest over London, I
looked down on a singular crowd
moving with the confident swell
of the sea. As it rose and fell
every pulse in the estuary
carried them quayward, carried them seaward.

'Box-wallah, missionary, clerk,
lancer, planter, I saw them all
linked like the waves on the waves embark.
Their eyes looked out – as yours look in –
to harbour names on the cabin-
trunks carrying topees to Bengal,
maxims or gospels to lighten a dark

'continent. Blatant as the flag
they went out under were the bright
abstractions nailed to every mast.
Sharpshooters since have riddled most
and buried an empire in their rags –
scrivener, do you dare to write
a little 'e' in the epilogue

'to an empire that spread its wings
wider than Rome? They are folded,
you say, with the maps and flags; awnings
and verandahs overrun
by impis of the ant; sun-
downers sunk, and the planters' blood
turned tea or siphoned into rubber saplings.

'My one eye reports that their roads
remain, their laws, their language
seeding all winds. They were no gods
from harnessed clouds, as the islanders
thought them, nor were they monsters
but men, as you stooped over your page
and you and you and these wind-driven crowds

'are and are not. For you have lost
their rhythm, the pulse of the sea
in their salt blood. Your heart has missed
the beat of centuries, its channels
silted to their source. The muscles
of the will stricken by distrophy
dishonour those that bareback rode the crest

'of untamed seas. Acknowledge
their energy. If you condemn
their violence in a violent age
speak of their courage. Mock their pride
when, having built as well, in as wide
a compass, you have none. Tell them
in England this.'
                    And a pigeon sealed the page.

                              Jon Stallworthy

1950

THE GENERAL ELECTION

Parties drilled for the election,
All accoutred to perfection,
March for national inspection,
     Parties on parade!
Labour's serried ranks resplendent,
Tories with their aims transcendant,
Liberals , proudly independent,
     CP shock brigade.

Attlee in the saddle seated,
With his five year term completed,
Heads his cohorts undefeated,
     Near four hundred strong!
All the Party regimented,
Toryism circumvented,
All constituents contented
     Cheering loud and long.

Winston on his war-horse bounding,
With the Tory trumpets sounding,
After last election's pounding,
     His two hundred leads;
Eden, next in the succession,
Fighting forces of oppression,
With Young Tories, in procession,
     Also cheered, proceeds.

Bearers of the Liberal Charter!
Clement Davies is the starter,
Pressed by Lady Bonham Carter
     And McFadyean's men.
In the Liberal tradition
All condemn to demolition
Government and Opposition
     (Sitting Members, ten).

Gallacher with resolution,
Leads the ranks of revolution,
Hails the day of retribution
    With his faithful few;
Champion of the working classes,
Soon to free exploited masses,
When the present order passes
    (Sitting Members, two).

Voters, it's no time to dally!
None must shirk or shilly-shally!
To your chosen Party rally
    As for power they strive.
If too long you hesitate, or
If the ballot you are late for,
Voters, you will have to wait for
    1955.

Sagittarius

The Labour Government had weathered many storms: the devaluation of sterling, a fuel crisis in the severe winter of 1947, and a flourishing black market brought about by rationing. Yet since 1945 they had lost not a single by-election. At the general election of 1951, however, they took office again with a majority of only six over all other parties. Attlee soldiered on for a further eighteen months, until in 1951 he was defeated by Churchill, who was returned with a majority of seventeen. The people were tired of austerity and, under R. A. Butler's guidance, the Tory party presented a more attractive programme attuned to the requirements of post-war Britain.

1951

THE FESTIVAL OF BRITAIN

from **Don't Make Fun of the Fair**

Don't make fun of the festival,
Don't make fun of the fair,
We down-trodden British must learn to be skittish
And give an impression of devil-may-care
To the wide wide world,
We'll sing 'God for Harry',
And if it turns out all right
Knight Gerald Barry,
Clear the national decks, my lads,
Everyone of us counts,
Grab the traveller's cheques, my lads,
And pray that none of them bounce.
Boys and Girls come out to play,
Every day in every way
Help the tourist to defray
All that's underwritten.
Sell your rations and overcharge,
And don't let anyone sabotage
Our own dear Festival of Britain.

Don't make fun of the festival,
Don't make fun of the fair,
We must pull together in spite of the weather
That dampens our spirits and straightens our hair.
Let the people sing
Even though they shiver
Roses red and noses mauve
Over the river.

Though the area's fairly small,
Climb Discovery's Dome,
Take a snooze in the concert hall,
At least it's warmer than home.
March about in funny hats,
Show the foreign diplomats
That our proletariat's
Milder than a kitten.
We believe in the right to strike,
But now we've bloody well got to like
Our own dear festival of Britain.

Noël Coward

The Labour Party, largely at the instigation of Herbert Morrison, decided to try to cheer everyone up by holding a national festival on the South Bank of the Thames, where a brewery had to be pulled down and a tall chimney, once a shot tower, demolished to make room for the site. A celebratory exhibition was held in the Dome of Discovery, erected at the centre alongside a great cigar-shaped construction pointing into the sky and called the Skylon. The one permanent thing to come out of the Festival was the Festival Hall, which looks as if it may last a bit longer than the Crystal Palace. The stone lion which had adorned the brewery now stands at the southern end of Westminster Bridge.

It was typical of the austerity of the time that a huge sculpture of two naked females by one of Britain's leading sculptors, Frank Dobson – also a teacher of Henry Moore – could only be shown as a plaster model, being too expensive to cast in bronze. Later it was put away in a shed, only to be rediscovered in 1987, when £40,000 was found to have it cast in bronze and set up again on the South Bank.

the 1950s

Ancient and Modern

Back in 1950
when Mums did Palais Glides
and girls still got an earful
from dad's short back and sides

and creamy capuccino
overlaid the tongue
with sweet and sexy flavours
and pop was Jimmy Young

amd sweets came off the ration
and jazz sprang up in dives
and Comets screamed on newsreels
and Woodbines came in fives

and Tories ruled forever
and Empire meant Free Trade
and intellectuals took their stand
in corduroy and suede

and BBC announcers
said Churchill won applors
and Rank rebuffed Jane Russell
with young Diana Dors

and George gave way to Lizbet
and LPs offered gems
as the Festival of Britain
played sweetly by the Thames

and Compton creamed the bowlers
and Longhurst opened up
and Sunset fell at Beecher's
and Matthews won the Cup

and lady Docker's Daimler
glistened in the mews
and Beaverbrook lost Suez
and Dylan found his muse

and Humph blew infant solos
and Eden made it clear
that only a rich man ever earned
a thousand pounds a year

they brought *you* into being
yes, eyes and nose and chin
all set to smile and play, as if
the past had never been

and parents were for leaving
and history was bunk
and every kind of loving
was money in the bank!

William Scammell

Queen Elizabeth II, 1952–

1953

THE CORONATION OF ELIZABETH II

In a golden coach
There's a heart of gold
    That belongs to you and me.
And one day in June
When the flowers are in bloom
    That day will make history.

Donald Jamieson

The song from which this verse is taken was sung by Dickie Valentine and 200,000 copies of the record were sold. Another popular song of the time included the words:

Everybody's mad about ya
Where would Britain be without ya?
Sailing in the yacht Britannia
Nowhere in the world would ban ya.
Queenie Baby, I'm not foolin',
Only you could do the ruling,
In your own sweet royal way.

from Little Gidding, Four Quartets

V

What we call the beginning is often the end
And to make an end is to make a beginning.
The end is where we start from. And every phrase
And sentence that is right (where every word is at home,
Taking its place to support the others,
The word neither diffident nor ostentatious,
An easy commerce of the old and the new,
The common word exact without vulgarity,
The formal word precise but not pedantic,
The complete consort dancing together)
Every phrase and every sentence is an end and a beginning,
Every poem an epitaph. And any action
Is a step to the block, to the fire, down the sea's throat
Or to an illegible stone: and that is where we start.
We die with the dying:
See, they depart, and we go with them.
We are born with the dead:
See, they return, and bring us with them.
The moment of the rose and the moment of the yew-tree
Are of equal duration. A people without history
Is not redeemed from time, for history is a pattern
Of timeless moments. So, while the light fails
On a winter's afternoon, in a secluded chapel
History is now and England.

T. S. Eliot

Index of Titles

Index of First Lines

Acknowledgements

For permission to reprint copyright material the publishers gratefully acknowledge the following:

Faber and Faber Ltd for 'Alas! Poor Queen' from *The Turn of the Day* by Marion Angus; Earl Attlee for 'On Himself' by Clement Attlee; Faber and Faber Ltd for 'September 1, 1939' by W. H. Auden from *The English Auden: Poems, Essays and Dramatic Writings 1927–39* edited by Edward Mendelson (Faber, 1977), and 'Roman Wall Blues' and 'Partition' from *W. H. Auden: Collected Poems* edited by Edward Mendelson (Faber, 1976); Patricia Beer and the Carcanet Press for 'Mr Dombey' in 'Victorian Trains' from *Collected Poems* by Patricia Beer (Carcanet, 1988); A.D. Peters & Co. Ltd for 'On Edward VII' and 'On Bonar Law' by Hilaire Belloc; Oxford University Press for 'Rupert of the Rhine' and 'George III' by E.C. Bentley from *The Complete Clerihews of E. Clerihew Bentley* (Oxford University Press, 1981); John Murray (Publishers) for 'The Arrest of Oscar Wilde', 'Henley Regatta', 'Death of King George V' and 'In Westminster Abbey' from *Collected Poems* by John Betjeman (John Murray, 1958) and *Uncollected Poems* by John Betjeman (John Murray, 1982); Mrs Nicolete Gray and The Society of Authors on behalf of the Laurence Binyon Estate for 'For the Fallen (September 1914)' by Laurence Binyon; Oxford University Press for 'Briggflatts' from *Collected Poems* by Basil Bunting (Oxford University Press, 1978); Macmillan (Publishers) Ltd and David Higham Associates Ltd for 'At the Statue of William the Conqueror' from *Collected Poems* by Charles Causley (Macmillan, 1975); Carcanet Press for 'Kett's Rebellion' by Keith Chandler; Curtis Brown for 'Thus came enclosure – ruin was its guide' from 'The Fallen Elm' by John Clare; the author and Gerald Duckworth for 'After Edgehill, 1642' from *Leafburners: New and Selected Poems* by Gladys Mary Coles (Duckworth 1987); Methuen & Co Ltd for 'The Death of Queen Victoria' from '1901', 'I Wonder What Happened to Him and 'Don't Make Fun of the Fair' from *The Collected Verse of Noël Coward* edited by Martin Payne and Graham Tickner (Methuen, 1984); Kevin Crossley-Holland and Deborah Rogers Ltds for 'Cædmon's Hymn' and 'The Battle of Maldon' taken from *The Anglo-Saxon World: An Anthology* edited and translated by Kevin Crossley-Holland (Oxford University Press, 1984); Punch for 'George I – Star of Brunswick' from 'George Poems' by H. J. Daniel; Oxford University Press for 'Vergissmeinnicht' from *The Complete Poems of Keith Douglas* edited by Desmond Graham (Oxford University Press, 1978) Copyright © Marie J. Douglas; Faber and Faber Ltd. and Harcourt Brace Jovanovich, Inc. for lines from *Murder in the Cathedral* (Faber, 1935), copyright 1935 by Harcourt Brace Jovanovich, Inc., renewed by T. S. Eliot; and for 'Little Gidding' from

Four Quartets by T. S. Eliot (Harcourt Brace Jovanovich, Inc. 1935)/ *Collected Poems 1909–1962* (Faber, 1963) by T. S. Eliot, copyright 1943 by T. S. Eliot, renewed 1971 by Esme Valerie Eliot; Century Hutchinson for 'Cowardice' from *The New Ewart: Poems 1980–82* by Gavin Ewart (Century Hutchinson, 1983); Harry Chambers/Peterloo Poets for 'Portraits of Tudor Statesmen' from *Standing To* by U. A. Fanthorpe (Peterloo Poets 1982); Wishari Press for 'Ode on the Death of Haig's Horse' from *Whips and Scorpions* by Douglas Garman; A. P. Watt Ltd, the Estate of Robert Graves, and Oxford University Press, Inc. for '1805' and 'Armistice Day, 1918' from *The Collected Poems 1975* by Robert Graves, copyright © Robert Graves, 1975; Faber and Faber Ltd for 'The Site of the Crystal Palace' from *The Ice Factory* by Philip Gross (Faber, 1984); Centerprise Publications for 'October 1936' by Milly Harris; Rex Collings for 'The Morning After' by Tony Harrison; David Higham Associates for 'Great Black-Backed Gulls' from *A Parliament of Birds* by John Heath-Stubbs (Chatto, 1975); A.P. Watt Ltd on behalf of Lady Herbert for 'Mr Churchill' from *Light the Lights* by A. P. Herbert (Methuen, 1945); André Deutsch Ltd and Oxford University Press, Inc. for 'Requiem for the Plantagenet Kings' from *For the Unfallen: Poems 1952–1958* by Geoffrey Hill (Deutsch, 1959/*Collected Poems* by Geoffrey Hill (Oxford University Press, Inc., 1985), copyright © Geoffrey Hill, 1985; Faber and Faber Ltd and Harper & Row Publishers, Inc. for 'The Martyrdom of Bishop Farrar' from *The Hawk in the Rain* copyright © Ted Hughes, 1957; Faber and Faber Ltd for 'An Arundel Tomb' and 'MCMXIV' from *The Whitsun Weddings* by Philip Larkin (Faber, 1964); Clement (Publishers) Ltd for 'Elizabeth Reflects' from *God Save the Queen: Sonnets of Elizabeth I* by John Loveridge (Clement, 1981); Faber and Faber Ltd and Farrar Straus and Giroux, Inc. for 'Sir Thomas More' from *History* by Robert Lowell (Faber, 1973); Mrs Valda Grieve and Martin Brian and O'Keeffe Ltd for 'Allelauder' by Hugh MacDiarmid; Faber and Faber Ltd for lines from 'Autumn Journal' from *The Collected Poems of Louis MacNeice* (Faber, 1966); Peter Newbolt for 'Hawke', 'Drake's Drum' and 'Vitaï Lampada' by Sir Henry Newbolt; the Estate of the Late Sonia Brownell, Secker and Warburg Ltd and A. M. Heath & Co. Ltd for 'Oh You Young Men' by George Orwell; the Estate of William Plommer and Jonathan Cape Ltd for 'The Boer War' from *Collected Poems* by William Plommer (Cape, 1973); Faber and Faber Ltd and New Directions Publishing Corporation for lines from 'Hugh Selwyn Mauberley' from *Collected Shorter Poems* by Ezra Pound (Faber, 1949)/*Personae* by Ezra Pound (New Directions, 1926), copyright © 1926 by Ezra Pound; David Higham Associates Ltd for 'For Johnny' from *Collected Poems* by John Pudney (Putnam 1957); the Estate of Henry Reed and Jonathan Cape Ltd for 'Naming of Parts' from *A Map of Verona* by Henry Reed (Cape, 1946); Jonathan Cape Ltd and the Estate of Olga Katzin Miller for 'Lest Cowards Flinch' by 'Sagittarius'; George Sassoon and Viking Penguin, Inc. for 'The General' from *Collected Poems of Siegfried Sassoon 1908–1956* (Faber, 1947); Carcanet Press Ltd for 'Cranmer' from *Collected Poems* by C.H. Sisson (Carcanet, 1984); Random House, Inc. and Faber and Faber Ltd for 'Unemployed' from *Collected Poems 1928–85* by Stephen Spender

(Faber, 1985); Macmillan, London and Basingstoke, for 'God Heard the Embattled Nations' and 'It Did Not Last' from *Collected Poems* by J.C. Squire (Macmillan, 1959); the Director of the Whitechapel Art Gallery for 'Whitechapel in Britain' by Avram Stencl; Hubert Nicholson of Autolycus Publications and the Whiteknights Press for 'England (Autumn 1938)' from *Collected Poems of A.S.J. Tessimond* edited by Hubert Nicholson (1985); Carcanet Press for 'Mr Gradgrind's Country' from *The Collected Poems of Sylvia Townsend Warner* edited by Claire Hanman (Carcanet, 1982); Chatto & Windus Ltd for 'Gloriana Dying' from *12 Poems* by Sylvia Townsend Warner (Chatto, 1980).

Faber and Faber Ltd apologizes for any errors or omissions in the above list and would be grateful to be notified of any corrections that should be incorporated in the next edition of this volume.